Su~~...~~ **us-
tion, she** ~~closed her eyes and tried~~ **to remember even the smallest glimmer from her past.**

~~Bu~~t her memories were like a blackboard that had been ~~wip~~ed with a felt eraser. Faint white marks were still ~~pre~~sent, but none of them were clear enough to make ~~sense.~~

~~Th~~e only distinct image she possessed was that of ~~De~~tective Vincent Parcell. Even in her clouded confusion, ~~sh~~e'd noticed his thick brown hair and strong, tanned ~~fea~~tures. His warm brown eyes had studied her in a way ~~that ha~~d made her want to pull the sheet all the way up ~~ben~~eath her chin. He'd not said much, but when he had ~~spo~~ken to her, his voice had been a low, rich baritone that ~~h~~ad rumbled through her like a familiar melody.

~~The de~~tective with him had been an attractive man, and ~~nice t~~o boot. But meeting him hadn't affected her in the ~~sam~~e way as Vincent Parcell. Somehow, someway, she ~~felt c~~ertain their paths had crossed before tonight.

~~But~~ that was a ridiculous notion, she thought. He was ~~sim~~ply a man who was trying to help her get out of this ~~stran~~ge wonderland she'd fallen into. And no matter how ~~he~~ looked or sounded, she was going to have to trust ~~him~~ to lead her back to the real world.

* * *

Men of the West:
Whether ranchers or lawmen, these heartbreakers
can ride, shoot—and drive a woman crazy…

Suddenly overwhelmed with exhaustion, she closed her eyes and tried to remember even the smallest glimmer from her past.

HIS BADGE, HER BABY… THEIR FAMILY?

BY
STELLA BAGWELL

First Published in Great Britain 2016
By Mills & Boon, an imprint of HarperCollins*Publishers*
1 London Bridge Street, London, SE1 9GF

© 2016 Stella Bagwell

ISBN: 978-0-263-92010-9

23-0816

Our policy is to use papers that are natural, renewable and recyclable products and made from wood grown in sustainable forests. The logging and manufacturing processes conform to the legal environmental regulations of the country of origin.

Printed and bound in Spain
by CPI, Barcelona

Having written over eighty titles for Mills & Boon, *USA TODAY* bestselling author **Stella Bagwell** writes about families, the West, strong, silent men of honor and the women who love them. She appreciates her loyal readers and hopes her stories have brightened their lives in some small way. A cowgirl through and through, she recently learned how to rope a steer. Her days begin and end helping her husband on their south Texas ranch. In between she works on her next tale of love. Contact her at stellabagwell@gmail.com.

In loving memory of my late
mother-in-law, Dortha Bagwell.
Alzheimer's took you and your memory,
but you will forever live on in mine.

Prologue

Detective Vincent Parcell eyed the smoldering heap lying
at the bottom of the shallow ravine. Less than an hour
ago the ash and debris had been a small car driven by a
woman. Now the only thing resembling a vehicle was a
crumpled black frame.

"It's a miracle anyone survived that inferno," Vince remarked to his partner, Evan Calhoun. "Are you sure the
EMT reported her conscious when they left the scene?"

The two men stood together on the edge of the asphalt.
Behind them, a fire truck and lighted barricades blocked
all traffic from the eastbound side of the two-lane highway.
A few feet down the incline from where they stood, a pair
of firemen continued to douse a steady stream of water
over the charred object. Yet even with the flames dead,
puffs of smoke spiraled upward into the dark, desert sky
and the stench of burning rubber lingered on the night air.

"That's what the NHP officer reported," Evan answered.

Vince shook his head. "Let's hope she remains that way."

Fifteen minutes ago, the two detectives had been working a downtown robbery in Carson City when their captain had ordered them to wrap up and drive out here to the edge of the city to investigate a flaming car crash.

Vince was still irked by the interruption. The Nevada Highway Patrol had already investigated the accident. He didn't see much need for him and Evan to follow up. This wasn't a case of vehicular homicide. It was a simple case of identifying the injured driver. As far as he was concerned, the sheriff's office didn't need to get involved. But it was Vince's job to follow orders, not question them.

Vince said, "I'm trying to visualize how this scene played out. The first responding officer reported that when he arrived on the scene, the door on the driver's side of the car was open. So the woman must have been thrown clear of the car when it hit the ravine. Or she miraculously managed to open the door and crawl out on her own."

Evan pointed to a spot on the side of the highway, about ten feet from where the two of them were standing. "Supposedly she was discovered lying there. Between those clumps of sage and creosote bushes."

Images of how the first initial seconds of the crash might have occurred and the sequences that followed flashed through Vince's mind as he walked over to the area where the woman had been found. From the beam of his flashlight, he could see where her weight had flattened the dead vegetation. Blood from some type of wound was smeared at the base of a clump of buffalo grass, while a few drops had already dried to brown circles on the ground. Nearby a couple of fist-sized stones had been dislodged from the soil. Most likely from the movements of the paramedics when they'd loaded the victim onto a gurney, Vince figured.

Evan walked up behind him. "Not many skid marks on the asphalt," he commented. "Whatever caused the car to leave the highway must have happened fast. Maybe a deer or coyote."

"Maybe," Vince reasoned. "Or a drunk driver swerved over the middle line and didn't bother to stop when her car careened off the highway." He started to turn back to his partner when the beam of his flashlight crossed something shiny caught on a low branch of sage. Squatting on his heels, Vince carefully plucked the item from the brush and rose to his feet.

"Hmm. Guess no one noticed this." The murmured words were directed as much to himself as they were to Evan. He placed his find in the middle of his palm, and Evan centered the beam of his flashlight on a simple piece of jewelry.

"Looks like a fine silver chain with a small filigree cross," Evan said. "Probably hundreds like it around town."

Vince grimaced. "Other than her clothes, it might be the only thing we have to help identify her. And that is why we were called in on this case, isn't it?"

Evan let out a weary breath, reminding Vince that both of them had been at it since just before dawn this morning. The day had been long and was on its way to being even longer.

"That's what the captain said. All her ID went up in flames. Even the car tags are nothing but ash. Hopefully the VIN can be salvaged. But looks like it's going to be a while before that mess of scrap metal is cool enough to be hauled to the lab."

Vince glanced one more time at the silver cross in his palm before he slipped the item into his shirt pocket. Like Evan said, there were probably hundreds of women around here who owned the same necklace. In fact, he'd known someone in particular who'd worn one exactly like it. He'd given it to her as an Easter gift. But that had been years ago and a world away.

Vince rubbed a hand over his tired eyes. "There's nothing more we can do here," he said flatly. "Let's get over to the hospital and see if we can get some answers."

Evan reached over and slapped his shoulder. "Cheer up, buddy. This won't take long."

The two men returned to a black SUV with Carson City, Nevada, sheriff's emblems emblazoned on both front doors. Vince climbed beneath the wheel, while Evan buckled himself in the passenger seat.

As he made a sharp U-turn in the middle of the highway and headed toward the north side of town, Vince tried to shake off the strange premonition that had come over him the moment they'd walked up to the accident scene.

"I have a bad feeling about this, Evan. Maybe you ought to call the hospital before we make a trip over there. For all we know the driver might have already expired."

When Evan failed to reply, Vince glanced over to the see his partner glowering at him.

"What the hell is the matter with you?" Evan barked the question. "Even if she has expired, we'll still need to follow up. Especially if she dies as a Jane Doe. You know that."

What *was* the matter with him? Vince asked himself. At the age of thirty-three, he'd worked in law enforcement for twelve years, and during that time he'd never shunned any sort of assignment. No matter how trivial or important, he wanted to make sure the job was done and done right.

"Yeah, I know it. I'm just not keen on going to the hospital. Every time we walk through those doors, I get the urge to throw up."

Evan said, "Nothing strange about that. You nearly died

after the Christmas Eve shooting. And you spent weeks afterward in Tahoe General recuperating from your wounds. The place probably brings all that hell back to you. To be honest, it brings it all back to me, too. But the best way to deal with a bad memory is to face it head-on. At least, that's what Granddad Bart always says. And he ought to know. He's had plenty of bad memories to face," Evan added flatly.

Bart Calhoun just happened to be the patriarch of the wealthy ranching family that owned and operated the Silver Horn Ranch north of Carson City. Evan's other grandfather, Tuck Reeves, had been a sheriff in Storey County for more than twenty years.

As for Vince, his grandfathers had already passed on, along with his father, Parry Parcell. Vince had only been fourteen years old when his father had been shot and killed while serving on the Reno police force.

No, Vince thought, he and his partner had totally different backgrounds, but the moment the two of them had been paired together, they'd fit like hot coffee on a snowy morning. For several years now they'd been the best of friends on and off duty. And because they were, the two men didn't hold back on expressing their thoughts or opinions to each other.

"Sorry, Evan. I don't stop to think of the hell you went through that night. If you hadn't pulled me away from the gunfire, you'd have a different partner sitting here with you tonight."

"Shut up, Vince." Evan slid down in the seat and pulled the brim of his cowboy hat over his eyes. "We're not going to talk about that night anymore. Hear me?"

"Yeah, I hear you." They might keep quiet about that night, Vince thought, but that wasn't going to make either of them forget it.

* * *

Ten minutes later, Vince parked in a slot allotted for hospital visitors and reached for two denim jackets lying on the backseat. Although it was nearing the first of July, the night could still get cool in the high desert, and the inside of the hospital always felt like stepping into the Arctic Circle.

As the two men headed toward the emergency entrance, Evan said, "It'll be our luck they've filled her with pain meds and she won't be lucid enough to tell us anything."

Vince grunted. "From the looks of that wreck, she's going to need more than something for pain."

After a frustrating wait in the ER, a nurse finally supplied them with the room number of the unidentified crash victim. During the elevator ride up to the internal medicine floor, Vince tried to block out the memory of the searing pain from the bullets plowing into his side and abdomen.

By the time the EMTs had reached him that night and delivered him to this very hospital, Vince had lost consciousness. It wasn't until days later that he'd eventually woken to the reality of what had happened when he and Evan had gone to arrest a murder suspect.

"Vince? You look green around the gills. Why don't you go down to the cafeteria and have some coffee?" Evan suggested as the two of them stepped off the elevator. "I can handle this."

Casting him a droll look, Vince said, "That day-old sandwich I got off your desk for lunch is the reason my gills are green. Let's just get this job over with."

"All right, be a tough guy." Evan gestured to the room number guide posted on the wall in front of the elevator. "This way."

His partner took off in a long stride down the left wing and Vince followed. For early in the evening, the corridor was rather empty. They walked past a nurse carrying a tray of medicine and a janitor mopping a section of the tiled floor. Other than those two, the hallway was eerily quiet.

"You can hear a pin drop on this floor," Vince said in a hushed voice. "All the patients must have been shipped down to the morgue."

"Or they heard two detectives were coming and they all got the hell out of here," Evan joked, then pointed to a closed door on their right. "Here it is."

Evan rapped lightly on the door before the two of them stepped inside. Except for a strip of light over the head of the bed, the room was dark. As they moved farther into the room, Vince could see the slender shape of the patient beneath the light bedcover. She was lying on her side, facing the wall, making it impossible to see anything except a long curtain of honey-blond hair spilling over the white pillowcase.

When Evan's elbow suddenly dug into his rib cage, Vince glanced over to see his partner motioning for him to take the initiative.

After a glare that promised he'd deal with him later, Vince walked up to the head of the bed.

With his gaze fixed on the wavy blond tresses, he cleared his throat. "Ma'am? Sorry about the interruption. I'm Detective Parcell and this is my partner, Evan Calhoun. We're with the Carson City Sheriff's Department. Do you feel up to answering a few questions?"

Long moments passed before she finally stirred, then with a faint groan, she rolled in his direction.

Vince took one look at her face and the shock of what he was seeing propelled him backward, very nearly causing him to stumble smack into Evan.

Chapter One

She let out a groggy groan. "Detectives? Have I done something wrong?"

Dear God, it was Geena! His Geena!

His ex-wife was lying in bed, her lost gaze vacillating from one man to the other, making it plain to Vince that she didn't recognize him at all. How could that be?

"Uh—excuse us just a moment," he blurted, then grabbing Evan by the arm, he hustled the other man out of the room.

The moment they were standing on the other side of the door, Evan gripped him by the shoulder. "Vince! What in hell is going on with you? You've got to get a grip. The way you're behaving, she's not about to trust one word to us!"

Shaking his head, Vince wondered if his legs had turned into a pair of wet noodles. His insides were shaking. His mind whirling like a raging storm. "There's something you need to know, Evan. That woman in there—it's Geena! My ex-wife!"

Stunned confusion swept over Evan's face. "Your ex? That's crazy, Vince! She might resemble Geena, but it can't be her. You just spoke to the patient, and I didn't see a flicker of recognition on her face."

"Damn it, don't you think I saw the same thing! She looked as blank as that wall behind you! But it's Geena. I'm positive about that."

Evan glanced anxiously at the closed door. "We'd better go back in before she gets even more suspicious and rings for a nurse. No," he quickly corrected as he eyed Vince. "I'll go back in and question her. You're not in any shape to deal with this right now."

Annoyed that Evan considered him too weak to handle the situation, Vince scowled at him. "She's my ex. I'll do this job. You just back me up."

Evan studied him for a long moment, then nodded. "If that's the way you want it. I'll be right behind you."

Trying not to let himself think too much, Vince opened the door and walked back to the bed with Evan following close on his heels. By now Geena had elevated the head of the bed so that she was in a half-sitting position.

Vince's gaze was taking a furtive survey of her face when something else caught his attention. Although she was covered completely, it was very evident that her belly was far from normal size.

She was pregnant! And from the look of her, she couldn't be far from her delivery date.

His mind racing in a thousand directions, he pulled a leather holder from the side of his belt and held it up so that she could view his badge.

"Sorry about the interruption," he said. "Let me start this over. I'm Detective Vincent Parcell. And this is Detective Evan Calhoun. Do you feel like answering a few questions?"

Working as a detective for many years had taught Vince how to read the subtle expressions and reactions on a person's face. Now as he carefully watched a mix of doubt and confusion flicker in Geena's eyes, it was clear she didn't recognize his name or the sight of him. She had no clue she was looking at her ex-husband, and the reality of that cut him like a knife.

"My head hurts," she mumbled. "But I'll try. Why are you here, anyway? I wrecked my car. That isn't a crime, is it?"

The soft, raspy sound of her voice hadn't changed, Vince thought. Neither had her lovely features. Her smoky green eyes were still veiled by thick brown lashes and her plush pink lips bracketed by a pair of faint dimples. The proud thrust of her delicate chin was just as he remembered, along with a perfect little turned-up nose. Oh, yes, this was his Geena all right, he thought grimly. At least on the outside.

He answered her question, "No. It's not a crime. Not unless you were driving under the influence of alcohol or drugs. Or you were driving recklessly."

Her gaze focused on his face, and Vince could see confusion swimming in the green depths of her eyes. But to his immense relief, she didn't appear to be drunk.

"I told the highway patrolman I didn't remember what happened. I only recall crawling away from the car. There was a small explosion and then the flames started. They were small at first, but then the fire grew so big I couldn't see the car. By the time the firemen and paramedics got there, everything was burned. That's all I know."

Vince exchanged a grim look with Evan before turning his attention back to Geena. "So can you tell us your name and address?" he asked gently.

A deep frown furrowed her brow, and Vince could see she was struggling to think.

"I've been trying very hard to remember, but I don't know who I am or where I came from."

Fear and regret were laced through her words, and Vince could only imagine the terror that had to be consuming her thoughts. Right now she was in an unfamiliar place where every face was that of a stranger. Her baby was coming soon, and she clearly had no idea how to locate the father. At this point, the Geena he'd been married to would have been sobbing hysterically. Either she'd drastically changed, he decided, or the accident was playing havoc with her normal demeanor.

I can tell you exactly who you are. You were my wife for five years. You made love to me and slept in my arms.

Shaking away the voice in his head, Vince asked, "Has a doctor spoken to you about your injuries?"

Her eyes misted over, but she swallowed hard and quickly gathered her emotions. "Yes. He tells me I have a concussion and it's caused me to have amnesia. He couldn't find anything else wrong. My baby is okay. But I don't remember anything about my pregnancy—when I'm due, or even the father! It's maddening!"

The uneasy feeling that had come over Vince when he'd first walked up to the scene of Geena's accident had suddenly grown to a menacing cloud hovering over his head. What was he going to do? He couldn't simply blurt out that he knew who she was, or that she'd once been his wife. She'd gone through a traumatic accident. No telling what the shock might do to her. No, Vince decided, before he could even consider revealing that bit of truth to her, he needed to speak with her doctor.

"Do you have any idea why you were on the highway

leading into Carson City?" he continued. "Where you were going?"

With a miserable shake of her head, she said, "No. And now everything I had—my ID, my vehicle—they're gone!"

As her voice rose to a frantic note, Evan stepped up to Vince's side, as though to say he believed she'd had enough questions for one night. But Vince had already come to that conclusion.

Trying to sound as positive as possible, Vince said, "Don't worry. By tomorrow you'll probably start remembering. And if you don't, we have ways of figuring out all these things."

The expression on her face was the same imploring look she'd given him years ago when she'd begged him to give up being a lawman. The look in her eyes had torn at him then, just as it was tearing at him now.

"I hope you're right. Without my car or money I can't go anywhere," she said, then let out a miserable groan. "Dear God, what am I thinking? Money or transportation won't solve my problems. I wouldn't know where to go to find my home!"

Her home had once been with him, Vince thought. Now she was a lost little thing without a clue of her past or future. Nothing about this felt real.

Evan slanted her a reassuring smile, which was just what she needed at this very moment. But try as he might, Vince couldn't follow his partner's example. His face felt frozen.

Evan must have realized Vince had become dazed with it all, because he suddenly spoke up. "Don't worry. We'll figure out where you belong. Right now you need to rest. Vince and I will be back tomorrow."

The words didn't appear to give her much relief, as

she touched fingertips to the bandage on her temple and closed her eyes.

"Thank you," she said glumly.

"No thanks are needed, ma'am. We're just doing our job," Evan told her.

Vince couldn't bring himself to say another word. He was too busy fighting the urge to pull her into his arms. What in hell was coming over him? This woman had been completely out of his life for six years. He shouldn't be feeling anything except the need to find her family.

Turning on his heel, he strode out of the room and didn't stop until he was several feet down the corridor. He was leaning a shoulder against the wall and wiping a hand over his face when Evan came up behind him.

"That woman isn't putting on an act, Vince. She truly doesn't remember."

Vince squeezed his eyes shut and tried to shove away the raw emotions tearing through him. "Yeah. That much is obvious."

"You didn't know she was in the area?"

"Hell, no!" Vince muttered. "I would've already told you."

"Sorry I asked. I know we don't keep things from each other. But I thought—well, from everything you've told me about your marriage, I realize she's a bit of a sore spot and you might not have wanted to bring it up."

Vince let out a heavy breath before turning to face his partner. "I don't have a clue what reason she might have for coming to Carson City," he said, then let out a rueful groan. "Clearly she doesn't, either."

"So when are you going to tell her? I mean, who she is. That might be a start to easing her mind. And who knows, maybe she was on her way here to see you."

Evan's suggestion brought him up short. "That's crazy!

She couldn't have been coming here to see me. After we divorced, all ties between us were dropped. For all she knew I could've been living in Alaska."

"Hmm. You know as well as I that if she wanted to locate you, all she needed to do was make a quick computer search and she would've known exactly where you lived."

Shaking his head, Vince started walking in the direction of the elevator. "That's true. If she'd wanted to locate me. But I'd bet money she was driving into Carson City for some other reason. So let's go see what our data tells us about Geena."

Evan caught up to him. "You know she's Geena, but what is her last name now? Yours? Her maiden name? A new husband's name? This might not be simple."

Vince didn't expect anything about Geena's case to be simple. In fact, he figured being shot again would be easier to handle than dealing with his ex-wife. But he'd never shirked his duty or asked to be taken off a case just because he found it to be uncomfortable. And he wasn't about to start now.

"No. But let's hope it will be."

Without warning, Evan reached over and caught Vince by the arm.

Stopping in his tracks, Vince looked at him. "What now?"

A sheepish expression crossed Evan's face. "I hate to bring this up, Vince, but do you think Geena might have been drinking? Alcohol would explain the accident."

Vince let out a long breath. He'd told Evan more than once that Geena's drinking had been a huge part of the reason he'd called it quits on their marriage. Vince could easily understand why Evan was questioning her sobriety now.

"Believe me, Evan, when I saw that it was Geena lying in that bed, the thought of alcohol definitely ran through my mind. She was clearly confused. But that could've been a result of the concussion. Anyway, I certainly hate to think she'd be drinking in her pregnant condition. But we won't know for sure until a detailed toxicology report comes back."

"And that will probably take two weeks," Evan replied.

Not wanting to think what might happen between now and then, Vince nudged his partner toward the elevator. "Come on. We have work to do."

Inside the hospital room, the young woman waited until she was certain the two detectives weren't going to return, then slowly climbed out of bed. In spite of a swimmy head and a sore back, she managed to make it to a private bathroom located in one corner of the room.

To her relief there was a small mirror hanging over the lavatory. Clinging to the cold sink, she leaned forward and studied her image in the mirror.

Wavy blond hair touched a slender neck and shoulders. Slanted green eyes, full pink lips and pale ivory skin. This was the image she'd seen every day of her life for the past twenty-nine years. So why didn't she recognize herself? And if she didn't know her own name, how did she know her age? It was crazy!

Oh, God help her, she prayed. She was terrified to think what might happen to her and her baby. Did she have loved ones waiting for her, wondering why she hadn't arrived home? Or maybe she had no home and she'd been running from something or someone!

In spite of the slivers of cold fear racing down her spine, sweat popped out on her forehead and upper lip. A wave of dizziness prompted her to grip the edge of the sink even tighter.

She was clutching the cold porcelain, wondering how

she was going to make it back to the bed without falling, when she heard a soft gasp behind her.

"Young lady! What are you doing out of bed?"

From the corner of her eye, she could see a nurse hurrying toward her. The fact that help had suddenly arrived caused her to sigh with relief.

"I—I wanted to look in the mirror," she attempted to explain to the nurse. "To see what I looked like."

The nurse wrapped a supportive arm across her back and gently guided her away from the sink. "Now isn't the time to be concerned about your appearance! You're concussed. You're not to get out of bed without a nurse's assistance!"

"You don't understand," she tried to explain. "I didn't know what I looked like! I don't even know my name!"

"Don't get excited," she ordered. "It will only make everything worse for you and your baby."

After she'd helped her safely back into bed, the nurse spread a thin sheet and blanket back over her and pulled up the bed railing. From a pocket at the foot of the bed, she collected a clipboard and scanned the information on the top two sheets of paper.

"Hmm. I see. I was told you had a concussion, but I see here that you've also been diagnosed with amnesia." She looked up, her smile empathetic. "When you said you wanted to see what you looked like, you really meant it."

As the nurse walked up to the head of the bed, she noticed the woman appeared to be in her late twenties or early thirties. Thick auburn hair was twisted into a messy bun atop her head, while bright blue eyes peered compassionately back at her.

"Sounds crazy, doesn't it? Until I looked in the mirror, I didn't even know what color my hair was. But oddly enough, I think I remember my age. I believe I'm twenty-nine. I don't know why." She looked anxiously to the pretty nurse. The name *Marcella* was written on the name tag pinned to her breast. "Do you think that age is correct?"

The nurse's smile deepened. "Hard to tell. I'd estimate you a bit younger. But I wouldn't worry about any of that. You'll be remembering soon. I've seen these sorts of injuries before. Most of them fix themselves fairly quickly. In the meantime, what are you going to call yourself?"

"Oh. I'd not thought about that. I guess I'm what you'd call a Jane Doe." Feeling even more forlorn, she passed a protective hand over her belly. The baby continued to move with frequent vigor, so she had that much to be thankful for. "But I don't much like the idea of being tagged with that moniker."

"I wouldn't like it either. So let's call you something else. Like Alice," the nurse suggested.

"Alice? Why that name?"

Chuckling, she dropped the clipboard back into its holder at the foot of the bed. "Well, I have an idea that right about now you're feeling like you're in wonderland. Do you recall the story *Alice in Wonderland*?"

In spite of her anxious situation, she managed to chuckle along with the nurse. "Guess there are some things in my brain that haven't left. I do remember the childhood story," she said, then smiled. "Okay, Alice it will be."

With an encouraging pat on her shoulder, the nurse reached for the blood pressure cuff hanging behind the head of the bed. "All right, Alice, let's take your vitals and then I'll let you get some rest. But promise me one thing. Do not get out of bed unless you press your call button and ask for help. We don't want anything to happen to you or your baby."

"I may not know who I am or where I came from, but I

know I want my baby very much. I promise not to get out of bed again unless someone is here to help me."

"Good girl. Now you're making sense."

While Marcella took her vitals, Alice managed to keep her emotions together, but once the woman left the quiet room, tears began to stream from the corners of her eyes.

Naturally, the nurse was concerned about her and her baby's welfare. It was her job to see that her patient recovered. But why weren't any of her family or loved ones walking through the door? Was she that far from home? Had she been lost?

Suddenly overwhelmed with exhaustion, she closed her eyes and tried to remember even the smallest glimmer from her past. But her memories were like a blackboard that had been swiped with a felt eraser. Faint white marks were still evident, but none of them were clear enough to make sense.

The only distinct image she possessed was that of Detective Vincent Parcell. Even in her clouded confusion, she'd noticed his thick brown hair and strong, tanned features. His warm brown eyes had studied her in a way that had made her want to pull the sheet all the way up beneath her chin. He'd not said much, but when he had spoken to her, his voice had been a low, rich baritone that had rumbled through her like a familiar melody.

The detective with him had been an attractive man, and nice to boot. But meeting him hadn't affected her in the same way as Vincent Parcell. Somehow, someway she'd felt certain their paths had crossed before tonight.

But that was a ridiculous notion, she thought. He was merely a man who was trying to help her get out of this strange wonderland she'd fallen into. And no matter how he'd looked or sounded, she was going to have to trust him to lead her back to the real world.

Chapter Two

Early the next morning, Vince left Evan at the office diligently searching through a nationwide database for any type of link to Geena, while he headed to the hospital to attempt to have a word with her doctor.

Luckily, Vince spotted the middle-aged man striding toward the elevator doors located a few feet away from Geena's room.

"Dr. Merrick," he called to him. "Can you spare a minute?"

The red-bearded physician paused, and once Vince reached his side, he flashed his badge to identify himself. "Vince Parcell. Remember? You looked in on me a couple of times for Dr. Whitehorse. I had gunshot wounds."

Recognition flashed in the doctor's eyes, and he quickly thrust out his hand. "Yes, I remember now. Good to see you looking so well, Detective Parcell. Is there something I can help you with? I hope you're not having issues with your old injuries."

As a group of people approached the elevator door, the doctor stepped aside to clear the path and Vince followed him.

"Thanks, Doctor. I'm fine. I'm here regarding a patient of yours. She was involved in a car accident last evening. Blond. Expecting a baby."

"Oh, yes. I've already looked in on her this morning. She and the baby are coming along nicely. A miracle, considering the severity of the wreck."

"The car was incinerated. Along with her identification," Vince explained. "That's why I need to talk with you about her condition."

"Sorry, Detective, but I can't divulge details about her condition. That's reserved for family. And unfortunately it's impossible for her to locate them just now."

A spurt of hope rushed through Vince. "You mean she remembers her family?"

Frowning, the doctor slipped a pair of black-framed glasses from his nose and stuffed them in a pocket on his white lab coat. "You know about the amnesia?"

Nodding, Vince said, "My partner and I questioned her last night. We're trying to come up with her identity."

"Well, I hope you do, and soon. From what I can gauge, she's probably going to deliver her baby in the next two weeks or somewhere about. I don't have to tell you she needs to be in the care of her personal physician. Not to mention the support of her family."

Two weeks. That could feel like an eternity or the blink of an eye, Vince thought.

"Does that mean you don't expect her memory to return before then?"

The doctor considered his question for a moment before he finally answered, "That's impossible to predict.

Her memory could return at any moment. Or it could be weeks, even months from now."

It was all Vince could do to keep from cursing with frustration. "Then I need your medical advice."

"About Jane Doe?"

"Dr. Merrick, she isn't Jane Doe. Not exactly. Her name is Geena."

Relief passed over the doctor's face. "Oh, so you've found out that much already."

Vince grimaced. "I already knew that much. You see, Geena was my wife for five years."

"Was." The shocked doctor repeated the key word. "Obviously that was some time ago."

"Before last night I'd not seen her since we parted six years ago. When I questioned her, she looked at me like she'd never seen me before! Am I supposed to share this information with her? What will it do to her if I tell her she used to be Geena Parcell? Or should I not reveal anything about this until later?"

The other man thoughtfully stroked his beard, then glanced pointedly at his wristwatch. "Give me a few minutes to consult with Dr. Dunlevy and I'll get back to you."

"I'll wait down in the cafeteria," Vince told him.

A half hour later, Vince walked into Geena's hospital room and found her sitting up on the side of the bed, eating from a breakfast tray. Her gold-blond hair had been brushed loose around her shoulders and a soft pink color had returned to her cheeks. As he moved farther into the room, he realized the years had only added to her natural beauty.

Laying her fork aside, she looked at him hopefully. "Good morning, Detective. I hope you're here to tell me who I am."

The doctors had concurred that Geena was emotionally and physically sound enough to handle the revelation. As Dr. Merrick had reasoned, no matter the circumstances, she would have to confront her past at some point in her recovery. Yet the vulnerable look in her green eyes made him want to turn tail and run. It would be so much easier to let Evan, or someone else from the sheriff's department, deal with her.

But this woman had once been his wife. She'd loved him. Wanted him. And tried to give him everything he'd needed. She deserved to hear the truth from him and no one else.

"I don't want to interrupt your breakfast," he told her. "I can come back in a few minutes."

"I was nearly finished anyway." She pushed the mobile table to one side, then gestured to a plastic chair sitting near the head of the bed. "Please, have a seat."

"I'd rather stand." His heart was suddenly pounding so hard he felt sick. He'd often wondered how she might react if the two of them ever happened to cross paths again. But this was a different situation. As far as she was concerned, she was looking at a man she'd met less than twenty-four hours ago.

"I'll be honest, I didn't expect to see you or your partner today," she said. "My case must seem very petty compared to what you normally deal with."

He tried to smile, but his face felt stiff. "It's definitely a change from burglary or homicide."

She didn't reply. Instead, her green eyes remained fixed on his face as she waited for him to give her a glimmer of good news.

"The debris of your vehicle—what little was left of it—was hauled to the police lab last night. I'm sorry to say they were unable to recover the VIN. The tags were totally destroyed, too. So we'll have to use other means to find your identity."

Instead of appearing panicked by this news, she simply lifted her chin and gave him a brave smile. The Geena he'd known had been fragile and needy. This woman staring back at him was displaying strength in spite of her dire situation, and the courage on her face filled Vince with admiration.

"Well, I did remember one piece of information last night, Detective Parcell. I believe I'm twenty-nine years old. Why that fact came to me, I have no idea. And I'm not certain it's correct. But I wanted to pass it along just in case it might be helpful."

Swallowing at the tightness in his throat, he moved a step closer. "You're right."

Her delicate brows lifted in question. "Right?"

"About your age. You are twenty-nine."

Her eyes widened. "How could you know that? Even the doctor said he couldn't accurately determine my age."

Tell her, Vince. Just blurt it out and get it over with. Waiting isn't going to help either one of you.

As the taunting voice sounded in his head, he struggled to keep a professional rein on his emotions. This was more than his job, he thought, and Geena was far more than just a woman who'd lost her memory.

"I didn't come here just to give you the news about the tags and VIN," he said quietly. "There's something else— something very important, and you're going to be confused when you hear it. Probably even shocked. So maybe you should brace yourself."

Alarm flickered in her green eyes, and then she reached out to him. Instinctively, Vince clasped his hand around hers, and the feel of her soft fingers against his suddenly whirled him back to a time when she'd touched him with hot desire and tender love.

"What is it? You've discovered I'm a criminal?"

Her question made him realize she was living in a blank world. Without a past, she had no way of knowing where her future might lead. He couldn't imagine how terrifying that would be, and more than anything he wanted to make it all better for her. He wanted to take away her fears and doubts. Not add to them.

"No. Nothing like that." As he drew in a deep breath, his gaze drifted to the mound of baby. Somewhere out there a man was probably searching frantically for her. But so far, not one person had contacted the sheriff's department about a missing woman. Nor had anything that fit Geena's description popped up on the national database for missing persons. Vince wasn't sure what that might mean. He only knew that he felt responsible for her well-being. "I doubt you've ever committed a criminal act in your life."

A wry smile caused the corners of her lips to quiver. "You're a detective. I suppose you know what a criminal looks like. I'm glad I don't fit the description."

"Unfortunately, they look like me and you and everybody else on the street. I know you're not a criminal because I—" Pausing, he searched for the right words. Yet there were no right words, he realized. No way to buffer the shock. "I know who you are. Your name is Geena. It was Geena Parcell."

Her eyes grew wide, her lips parted. "Parcell? But that's your name! Am I related to you? Why didn't you tell me last night? I—"

"Wait. Slow down and let me explain," he interrupted. "I couldn't tell you about anything until I consulted with your doctor. I needed to make sure you could handle this news."

She lifted her chin to a challenging angle. "All right.

I'm not falling over in a dead faint or anything, so tell me. Are we relatives? You said my name was Parcell—does that mean I got married and it changed? If that's the case, why hasn't the rest of the family come forward?"

"Because I—we don't know about your family now. You see, we—you and I were once husband and wife. But we divorced six years ago. Since then I don't know what's happened in your life or have any idea what your last name might be."

Stunned couldn't begin to describe the look that swept over her face. Her cheeks were paper white and her eyes took on a wild, dazed light.

"You?" The one word came out as little more than a husky whisper. "You were my husband? That—that can't be!"

"I assure you that we were married. For five years to be exact. We lived in Reno during that time. I worked for the police department there and you were going to college."

"Reno? You and I—together? But I don't know you! If you were my husband I'd surely recognize you! I'd feel something—remember something!"

Her voice rose with each word while dark pink color spread across her white cheeks. He couldn't imagine what must be going through her mind, but the intimate thoughts racing through his only proved what he'd already known for years. He'd not forgotten one thing about Geena or their time together.

Clearing his throat, he said, "I understand this is disturbing to you. Frankly, it's not easy for me. If you're not up to dealing with this right now, we'll talk later. In fact, I'm beginning to think it might be best if I leave and give you time to digest everything."

A quiet calm suddenly came over her, and then she dropped her head in her hands and mumbled, "I'm sorry,

Mr. Parcell—" Lifting her head, she let out a hopeless groan. "That's great, isn't it? You were my husband and I'm calling you Mr. Parcell. Do you see how insane all of this is? I can't absorb it all."

Vince couldn't absorb it, either. He'd never expected that seeing Geena again, touching her hand, hearing her voice would be affecting him so deeply. It had to be her vulnerable situation that was making him feel so protective.

Turning away from her, he walked over to a window and gazed down on a small courtyard at the back of the building. A man was sitting on a concrete bench, smoking a cigarette and looking as lost as Vince felt at this moment.

"The doctor says your condition is temporary. Once your memory returns, you can put all this behind you. You'll be back with your present family and everything will return to normal."

"My present family," she said doubtfully. "What if I don't have one? What if I'm all alone and no one cares or knows that I'm missing?"

The desperation in her voice propelled him back to her bedside. "Your mind is running away with you. You have a mother. At least, she was still living while we were married. Before we divorced, she'd remarried for a third time and moved to Dallas, but apparently she's changed her name since then. I couldn't pick up any information on her."

A tortured frown twisted her features. "Third marriage! Was I close to my mother? Did we get along?"

"Not very well," he said, deciding it was best to leave it at that.

She let out a dismal groan. "I'm not sure I should even ask about my father."

Vince let out a long breath. In his line of work, he often

had to deliver bad news. But this wasn't the same. This was Geena. "I'm sorry, your father died when you were ten. And you don't have any siblings. Evan did manage to locate your stepfather—your mother's second husband—but he'd not been in contact with her or you in years. He couldn't help us."

Bewildered now, she cradled her belly with both hands. "There has to be someone out there who knows where I belong! I'm going to have some man's baby!"

As if she had to remind him of that fact. Ever since he'd walked into this room last night and realized she was pregnant, he'd been eaten up with the image of her carrying another man's child. "Believe me, I understand your frustration. But—"

"Do you?" she interrupted. "Unless all trace of memory has been knocked out of your brain at one time, then I don't expect you to understand anything about this situation I'm in!"

Vince was hardly surprised to see her growing angry, yet he was at a loss of how to deal with it. She was no longer his wife. He couldn't pull her into his arms, stroke her hair and murmur soothing words in her ear. And even if she did remember being his wife, he doubted she would want that sort of comfort from him now.

"Look, I think—"

His words halted as a slight knock sounded on the door. Glancing over his shoulder, he saw an auburn-haired nurse dressed in navy blue scrubs enter the room.

"Oh, so you have company this morning," she said to Geena, then turned a hopeful look on Vince. "Are you an acquaintance of Alice?"

From the corner of his eye, he could see Geena wiping a hand over her face and attempting to pull herself together.

"Alice? Where did that name come from?" Vince asked as his gaze vacillated from one woman to the other.

"I gave it to her last night," the nurse explained. "We needed to call our patient something more than Hey You or Jane Doe."

Geena quickly intervened. "This is Detective Parcell, Marcella. He's working my case."

The nurse extended her hand in greeting. "Nice to meet you, Detective."

Vince tilted his head as he studied the woman and her name tag. "Marcella. I think I remember seeing you somewhere before," he told her. "At some sort of party."

With a light laugh, the nurse dropped his hand and moved over to pick up the half-eaten breakfast tray. "You must be confusing me with someone who has time for a social life."

"No. I remember now," Vince said. "It was at a baby christening. Lilly and Rafe's youngest child. You had two little boys with you."

A surprised smile came over the nurse's face. "That was me. So you know the Calhouns?"

"Evan has been my partner for several years."

"I see. Well, Lilly Calhoun and I worked together in the ER for years. So I guess the two of us have something in common. We're both friends with the Calhouns. And we're both trying to help Alice."

The nurse turned a pointed look on Geena. "You didn't eat all of your breakfast. How are you feeling? Head still hurting?"

Geena glanced at him, as though to seek his advice about divulging her name. Her first name, at least. But the idea must not have appealed to her, because she answered the nurse's questions without expanding on the news.

"It's only a dull ache. I can bear it."

"Baby still moving about?"

Smiling faintly, Geena nodded. "I'm convinced he or she is going to be an athlete."

"Great," the nurse replied. "I'll take this tray out of here and let you finish your talk with Detective Parcell."

Vince watched the nurse leave the room before he turned back to Geena. "You didn't correct her about your name or say anything about us," he stated the obvious.

She looked away from him and swallowed. "No. I started to. But I need to think about all this before I say anything. Later today, I'll let her in on the news that I'm not Alice in a fairy-tale world anymore."

Too bad this wasn't a fairy tale they could both wake up from, Vince thought dismally. It would save them both a lot of awkward misery. But this wasn't a dream. It was reality. Something he dealt with every day.

"Well, it's time I leave and let you rest," he told her. "You've had enough excitement for one morning."

Her gaze jerked back to his face. "You're leaving? But I have so many questions! Can't you stay just a little longer?"

Her legs were dangling over the side of the bed and Vince's gaze followed the blue fabric of the hospital gown to the point where the hem stopped at the middle of her shins. Below it, he could see her calves were smooth and shapely, her toenails painted a bright neon pink.

There were so many things about her that had changed, he realized, yet so much that was still the same. And he suddenly wondered why he was noticing all these little things about her. Nothing about her gold-spun hair, creamy skin or pink toenails had anything to do with her current predicament. Yet he couldn't seem to keep his eyes off her.

"I can't give you answers now. My partner and I are pasting your photo on every form of social media. I'm certain there will be someone out there who will see it and give us the information we need. In the meantime just be thankful that you and your baby survived the car accident. Things could've certainly been worse."

"Believe me, I've very thankful for that. But I—can't you tell me a bit about us? Our marriage? You said we lived in Reno?"

Suddenly remembering the small photo he'd brought with him this morning, he fished it out of his shirt pocket.

"Just in case you still have doubts—here's a picture of the two of us on our wedding day." He handed her the snapshot. "We didn't have the money to have a professional photographer at the ceremony. A friend took this."

Vince watched her study the image of the smiling couple standing beneath an arch of flowers. He'd been dressed in a borrowed suit and a friend had made Geena's simple white dress. Everything about the wedding and small reception had been modest, but neither of them had cared. They'd been deliriously in love.

But she didn't remember that. She didn't remember the nights they'd made passionate love. And maybe he should thank God for that. Because he was doing enough remembering for the both of them.

"Did we have children?" she asked. "What happened?"

Lifting her head, she looked to him for answers. Vince couldn't give them to her. At least, not all of them.

Turning away from her, he walked back over to the window. The man with the cigarette was gone. And it was definitely past time for Vince to be gone, too.

"No. We didn't have children. And we simply decided that our lives were on different courses, that's all. We parted on friendly terms. After that, I moved down here to Carson City. I'd not seen or heard from you until last night when I walked into this room and saw that you were the accident victim."

"I see," she said quietly. "So everything ended between us long ago."

"Yeah. It ended."

Awkward silence stretched for long moments before she finally spoke again.

"Well, I must have had family other than you. Clearly my father is gone and my mother is questionable. I don't have siblings, but what about grandparents, aunts or uncles? Have you tried to contact them?"

"Your grandparents are no longer living," he informed her. "As for aunts and uncles, your father had a brother, Mort Cummings. He lives in Montana now. I've already spoken with him. He lost touch with you a few years ago. Other than him I don't recall any aunts or uncles you were well acquainted with."

"Cummings," she repeated thoughtfully. "So that was my maiden name?"

"That's right. Your mother's name is Rhonda. Your dad's was Gerome. I understand he had a heart condition. That's why he died when you were still so young."

She placed the wedding photo on the mattress next to her thigh, then pressed her palms to her cheeks. "I should be feeling grief or loss or something about my parents. But I can't feel anything! Not about people I don't know or remember. Oh, God, this is awful. So awful."

The fear and frustration in her voice pierced his heart. "You can't deal with everything at once. Don't worry about figuring out where your present family is or how you're going to find them. Leave that to me and Evan. All those feelings you're talking about—they'll come to you once your memory returns."

Dropping her hands, she stared at him. "I don't even know if I have other children or a husband!"

He tried to muster an encouraging smile. "No. But

you've learned your name is Geena and you're twenty-nine years old. And you once had a husband named Vince. That's a start. We'll figure out the rest."

Before she made any sort of reply, the phone holstered to the side of his belt vibrated. After quickly scanning the text message, he said, "I have to go. If we learn anything that progresses your case, I'll let you know."

In afterthought, he extracted a personal card from his wallet and handed it to her. "My number is on there. If you need me or if you remember anything, no matter how slight, call me. Okay?"

She nodded and then suddenly her lips began to quiver. "I'm sorry. I know I've been difficult and you're trying to help. Thank you for that. Really."

Lifting her hand, Vince gently patted the back of it. "Don't worry about anything. The best thing you can do is take care of yourself and your baby and let me do the rest."

She gave him a brave nod, and before Vince could get mushy over the lost look in her eyes, he dropped her hand and hurried out of the hospital room.

At the end of the long corridor, he spotted Marcella standing outside the door of a patient's room, writing intently on a clipboard balanced in the crook of her arm.

"Excuse me, Nurse. Do you have a moment?"

She glanced up, then smiled when she saw that it was him. "Of course, Detective. How can I help you?"

"It's about—" He'd started to say Geena, then decided against it. "The amnesia patient. When you have a bit of extra time, I think she might need a woman to talk to. She's feeling pretty lost."

Appreciation flashed in the nurse's eyes. "Sure. I'll check in on her in a few minutes. Thanks for being concerned, Detective."

Concerned. That was an understatement, Vince thought

as he hurried out of the hospital and across the parking lot to his department vehicle. Thoughts of his ex-wife were totally consuming him. How she looked, the scent of her skin, the sound of her voice and the touch of her hand were bombarding him with feelings he'd believed were long dead.

It had taken him years to reach a point where he could go to work each day without thoughts of Geena tormenting him, but he'd finally managed to move forward and away from the past they'd shared together. Now she'd shown up out of the blue, carrying more problems with her than one person should have to shoulder, and he could already feel himself falling under her spell.

It was useless to wonder why this had happened to her, or why she'd reentered his life after all these years. Why didn't matter anymore. The important thing was to find the father of her baby, and soon. Otherwise, she was going to go into labor without anyone to support her. Except Vince.

And he didn't want to be a temporary daddy or a stand-in husband. All he wanted to be was a good detective.

Chapter Three

Two days later on Friday afternoon, Vince was in a small break room, filling a stainless steel percolator with water and coffee grounds when Evan stuck his head around the door facing.

"Hey, Vince, telephone call for you. It's Dr. Merrick on line two."

With a sinking feeling in the pit of his stomach, Vince plopped the lid onto the antiquated coffeemaker and glanced around at his partner. "Did he say what he wanted?"

"No. I'm assuming he's calling about Geena and wanted to speak with you personally."

"You're working Geena's case, too," Vince bit back at him. "Why the hell can't he speak with you?"

Evan glared at him. "Probably because you're her ex-husband. There is a connection between you two. Whether you want to admit it or not."

"The definitive word here is *ex*, Evan. I'm not her husband anymore. Some other man holds that job now." With the percolator in hand, he walked past Evan and strode quickly back to the office the two men shared.

At the back of the room, he placed the coffeemaker on a small table and plugged it in before he sat down at his desk and punched the phone line to connect with the doctor.

"It's Vince Parcell, Doctor. Sorry for keeping you waiting."

"Thank you, Detective, for taking my call. This isn't something I normally do, but I think you'll agree that Geena's case is not the norm."

Releasing a long breath, Vince glanced across the small office to see Evan had returned to his desk and was studying a screen full of data on his computer. No doubt his partner was also keeping an ear on Vince's conversation.

"I've never encountered anything like it," Vince said, then had to stifle a mocking laugh. How had something that inane come out of his mouth? Bumping into his ex-wife, who just happened to be suffering from complete amnesia, along with being eight and a half months pregnant, was not something any man encountered. Not even in his wildest dreams.

"Have you made any headway in locating her family?" the doctor questioned.

Leaning forward, Vince propped his forearms on the edge of the desk and closed his burning eyes. For the past three days, he'd worked nearly nonstop, making calls and searching through countless media outlets in an effort to find a link to Geena's present life. With each day that passed, he was growing more exhausted and frustrated.

"Several people from Reno who knew her in the past have called to identify her. But none could give us any recent information that might help our cause. We're still trying to track her mother. But we're having no luck with that endeavor—yet."

There was a long pause, then the doctor said, "That's unfortunate. I don't like the idea of her going to a rescue shelter, but it looks like that's her only option. Unless you can come up with a better plan."

Vince sat straights up. "Shelter? What do you mean? Aren't you going to keep her in the hospital? She's messed up—I mean, her head—she needs medical care, doesn't she?"

"Physically, she's well enough to leave the hospital. As for her amnesia, she'll be checking in with Dr. Dunlevy once a week until her memory returns. Or at least until she's able to mentally deal with the situation. In the meantime, she needs somewhere to live. And I thought you might know of someone who might take her in for a few days. Maybe someone you were both friends with while you were still married?"

Even though his brain was half-dead with fatigue, it began to spin wildly. "We lived in Reno then. There's no one here in Carson City who's acquainted with Geena."

"Except you."

Vince's eyes popped open. "Me? Surely you're not suggesting—"

"I realize I'm asking a lot from you. But I don't have to tell you that this woman is in a fragile state right now. She needs to be with someone she can trust. Someone she feels safe with. Right now, you're the only person she feels any sort of connection to."

"I'm a bachelor, Dr. Merrick. I wouldn't know what to do with a woman in the house!"

"If I remember correctly, you told me the two of you were married for five years. Surely you remember how to share your living space with a woman."

Oh, yeah, he remembered way too much, Vince thought

grimly. These past few days he'd been in a constant fight to push and shove memories of Geena out of his mind.

"You're putting me on the spot, Doctor. It—"

"I realize that. And I apologize for doing so. But I got the impression that you cared about Geena. I didn't think you'd feel comfortable with her going to a public shelter—especially with her being pregnant. There's not much privacy there. And as a lawman, I hardly have to tell you that unsavory characters go in and out of those places on a regular basis." He paused for a moment, then said, "I'm sorry I bothered you with this problem, Detective. I'm going to make a few calls to some of the local churches. Most of them have members who are willing to take in a homeless person. Thanks anyway."

Realizing the doctor was about to end the call, Vince practically shouted, "Doctor, wait! Uh—when did you say Geena was going to be released from the hospital?"

"The paperwork is being done as we speak. She'll be ready to go as soon as you can pick her up. If that's something you can't deal with, then I'll call social services and let them make other arrangements for her."

Biting back a curse, Vince raked a hand through his tumbled hair. The doctor had missed his calling, he thought. A lawyer couldn't have argued a more perfect case for Vince to give Geena a temporary home.

"Okay. I'll take her in," Vince told him. "But only until other, more suitable, arrangements can be made. I can pick her up in the next hour."

"You're doing the right thing, Detective. For the both of you."

Vince was hardly convinced. The doctor couldn't know the pain and heartache each of them had endured while trying to patch together a crumbling marriage. He supposed the only good thing about the situation was that Geena couldn't remember those bad times. Or the good ones.

"Yes, well, let's hope Dr. Dunlevy can make a break-through. Having her memory return would fix things for all of us."

The doctor agreed and ended the call. Vince tossed the phone back onto its cradle, then glanced across the room to see Evan watching him keenly.

"I suppose you heard enough to know what I'm going to do," Vince said grimly.

Evan swiveled his chair so that he was facing Vince's desk. "Sounds like you're going to let Geena live with you for a while. You think that's wise?"

"Wise, hell! Is jumping into a den of rattlesnakes wise?"

Evan shook his head. "Your ex-wife isn't poisonous. Besides, in her state of mind, it will be like a stranger living in your house."

"She won't be a stranger to me," he muttered.

Evan got to his feet and walked over to the small table that held the coffeepot, a few chipped cups and an odd assortment of snacks.

After he filled one of the cups with the freshly brewed coffee, he moved over to Vince's desk and set the steaming cup in front of him. "Here, drink up. You look like you need it."

Vince glanced gratefully up at him. "Thanks."

Evan lowered a hip onto the edge of the desk. "Look, Vince, if having Geena in the house is going to tear you up, then you shouldn't do it. She's not your responsibility. Anyway, she's welcome to come stay with me and Noelle for a while."

Frowning, Vince took a long sip of coffee, then said, "Don't be crazy. Noelle already has her hands full taking care of little Joanna and keeping up with the ranching chores. She doesn't need a pregnant woman added to that."

"Noelle is a tough cookie, and she'd be gentle with Geena."

Vince cut him a dry look. "Noelle is only tough when she needs to be. Except when it comes to you, then she's not nearly as firm as she ought to be. As for Geena, I have no doubt she'd treat her like a princess. But, no. It's not your place to take my ex-wife into your home."

Evan shrugged while Vince continued to sip his coffee. "Like you said, the crucial word is *ex*. And a shelter isn't that bad. At least she'll have a roof over her head and a bed to sleep in. I imagine they'll find her something to wear. If not, Noelle can take her some of her old maternity things. She won't be needing them for a while."

"For a while? Is Noelle expecting again?"

A sly grin put a twinkle in Evan's eyes. "We're hoping. And trying."

His partner had a loving wife and an adorable two-year-old daughter. The couple managed to juggle his career with her desire to work the ranch. Together, they were able to keep their love healthy and strong in spite of their busy schedules. Vince often envied the other man for having the things he'd tried so hard to have with Geena.

"So that's why you've been looking so tired here lately. I thought it was because we've been working overtime."

"Ha! I don't look any more exhausted than you do," Evan argued. "Who have you been spending your nights with?"

A sardonic twist slanted Vince's lips. "Oh, just half the female population of Carson City."

"Sure," Evan muttered. "You haven't had a date in months. No, make that years!"

"I have better things to do with my time." Vince drained

the last of his coffee and stood up. "If you can handle things here, I need to get over to the hospital."

"I'll hold down the fort," Evan assured him. "You go do what you have to do."

"Thanks. I'll be back as quick as I can."

Vince was almost to the door when Evan called to him.

"Uh, Vince, it's none of my business, but it might be nice if you'd pick up some flowers for Geena. You know, just to tell her you're glad she's feeling well enough to leave the hospital."

Vince rolled his eyes with exasperation. "You're not only a hopeless romantic, you're clueless. To her I'm a stranger. She doesn't need or want flowers from a stranger."

"Wanna bet?"

Vince didn't bother with a retort. Anyone could take one look at Geena's expanded waist and see that she had a man in her life. And it damned sure wasn't Vince.

Across town at Tahoe General Hospital, Geena stood at the window in her room and stared at the mountain range in the far distance. When she'd first arrived at the emergency room the night of the accident, the nurses had informed her that she was in Carson City, Nevada. Nothing about the revelation had made sense. And in her mental state, she could only guess as to whether she'd ever been here before.

Now as she studied the ridge of mountains, she could only wonder why she'd been traveling on the highway between here and Lake Tahoe. Had this town been her destination? Or had she merely been passing through? Apparently she didn't live in this area or someone would have already identified her. At least, someone other than Detective Vince Parcell.

Thoughts of the man brought a sigh to her lips. Learning

that she'd once been married to him continued to amaze her. How could he have been her husband? He was a tall, sexy hunk of man. Just looking at him stirred every female cell in her body. There was no way she could have forgotten sharing a bed with him. And yet she had the photo of their wedding proving that the two of them had exchanged vows.

Yesterday he'd stopped by her room for a few brief minutes to check on her health and give her an update on the investigation, but she'd hardly taken note of anything he'd been saying. All she could do was look at him and wonder what it must have been like to be his wife and speculate as to why their marriage ended.

He'd said their lives had taken different courses and they'd parted on friendly terms. Yet she couldn't imagine letting this man go without fighting tooth and nail. Unless there was something else that had gone on that he'd purposely avoided telling her. Like infidelity or something she'd considered unforgivable. If that had been the case, then she didn't want to know the true cause of their divorce. It would be too embarrassing.

Stop it, Geena! Quit thinking about Vince Parcell. The man is not your husband anymore! Somewhere out there is a man who you must be in love with. You're about to have his child. Finding him is what you need to be thinking about. Not mooning over a lost marriage you don't even remember.

A light tap on the door had Geena turning away from the window just in time to see the object of her troubled thoughts walking through the door. The sight of him caused her heart to leap with hope and a strange sort of excitement. Perhaps he'd brought good news.

"Hello, Detective Parcell."

"It's Vince. Remember?"

A blush stung her cheeks. "Okay—Vince. If you've come by to give me news, you timed it just right. A few more minutes and I'll be leaving."

She noticed his gaze passing over her black slacks and thin white blouse, then on to the strappy black sandals covering her feet. The clothes and shoes were the things she'd been wearing when the accident had occurred. Since then, a nurse had taken the garments home and washed them for her.

"Looks like you're ready to go."

She smiled and shrugged. "I guess Dr. Merrick told you he's made arrangements with social services to find a place where I can stay until—well, until you and Detective Calhoun figure out where I really belong."

He moved farther into the room and Geena noticed he was dressed the same way he'd been on the other occasions he'd visited her room. A pale blue dress shirt was tucked into a pair of dark blue jeans. Brown cowboy boots that appeared to be made of lizard or some other exotic skin matched the wide belt fastened around his lean waist. She supposed being a detective allowed him to wear street clothes on the job, but he certainly wouldn't have any trouble filling out a uniform if one was required, she thought.

"I've spoken with Dr. Merrick. He's says you're ready to leave the hospital. I wish I could tell you that we've located your family and they're coming to pick you up. Unfortunately, that hasn't happened yet."

Suddenly the isolation and uncertainty she'd been feeling swamped her, and not wanting him to see the desperation on her face, she quickly turned toward the bed and the small bag of items Marcella had kindly given her.

"Oh. I was hoping you had good news. But it will come. I'm not giving up. And staying in a shelter won't be so bad. Until I have the baby and then—well, I hope by then I'll be able to take him or her home—to my real home."

"I'm going to do my best to see that happens," he said. "Besides, you might get your memory back long before the baby comes."

Bending her head, she trailed fingertips over the cloth tote bag. Inside it was everything she possessed, and she only had those things because a nurse was kind enough to give them to her. At the moment the reality of the future facing her was overwhelming.

"Believe me," she said quietly, "I'm praying for that."

She heard his footsteps approach her from behind her, but she didn't turn to face him. Tears were burning her eyes and she didn't want him to think she was breaking apart.

"If you're ready to go, you should probably ring for the nurse. I'm sure you'll have to leave the building in a wheelchair."

Blinking her misty eyes, she turned to him. "I can't go until someone from social services comes to collect me."

He shook his head. "Dr. Merrick must have gotten busy. Otherwise, he would've told you that your plans have been changed. You're not going to a shelter. You're coming home with me."

Her mouth fell open. "You! I don't understand. If this is some sort of crude joke, it's not funny."

His nostrils flared, and Geena found her gaze slipping to the hard line of his lips. No doubt she'd kissed those lips many times, and she imagined they'd transported her to heaven and back. But that was years ago, and for some reason the kissing between them had stopped. Along with everything else. Now she was supposed to move into his home as though he was nothing more than a Good Samaritan? It was ludicrous!

"This is hardly a time to be joking," he said flatly. "You need a place to stay, and I have an extra room at my house."

"But I don't know you!"

"You don't know the people at the shelter, either. Or anyone else, for that matter. Don't you think you'd feel safer staying in the home of a law officer rather than a public shelter?"

Put like that, she could hardly argue. And why would she want to? At least he was a familiar face. The fact that he'd once been her husband had nothing to do with the situation now, she reasoned with herself.

"Yes, I would feel safer. And it would be nice to have a bit of privacy. Uh—what about your family? Will they mind sharing their home for a few days?"

Stepping away from her, he picked up the call button lying on the pillow and pressed it.

"I don't have a family. It's just me. And since I don't have much down time, you'll have the house mostly to yourself."

Totally surprised by this information, her thoughts began to dart in all directions. If he had no family that meant the two of them would be alone! That was definitely going to be awkward. But given her predicament, she could hardly make a fuss about anything.

"You don't have a wife?"

He slanted her a wry smile. "You're the only wife I've ever had."

"Oh." She didn't know why, but his revelation jolted her. "I—uh—I'll go finish getting ready," she told him, then made a desperate rush toward the bathroom.

After she shut the door on the small, utilitarian room, Geena splashed cold water on her hot face, then reached for a comb she'd left lying on the edge of the sink. As she mindlessly tugged it through the waves of her blond hair, she ordered herself to compose her rattled emotions.

This fix you're in isn't going to be resolved overnight, Geena. Vince Parcell is merely trying to help you. The fact that you were his wife means nothing to him now. So get over this silly notion that he'd like to rekindle your romance. He doesn't want anything from you. The only thing he wants is to find the man you belong to and hand you over.

Gripping the comb, she stepped back from the sink and stared at her image. Was there a man out there somewhere who loved her, who was searching for her and praying for her safe return? When the paramedics had found her near the burning car, she'd not been wearing a wedding ring. And from the looks of her finger, it had been bare even before the accident.

But the lack of a ring wasn't the reason she had doubts about a man. There was something deep within her that kept saying she was a woman alone. And that she'd been on her own for a long time. So how did the baby happen? A one-night stand? A visit to a fertility clinic?

The questions were pounding at her temples when she suddenly heard the sound of Vince and a nurse talking outside the bathroom door.

It was time to go. With Vince.

Resting a hand on her belly, she whispered, "Don't worry, my baby. Even though Vince isn't your daddy, I believe he'll step up to the plate until we can find your real daddy."

Ten minutes later, Vince stowed Geena's one simple bag in the backseat of the SUV and helped her into the passenger seat. As she strapped herself in, he noticed her attention go to the police radio fastened to the dash and the low, intermittent crackle of a dispatcher's voice. This was his job, his life. And something she'd never wanted to be a part of.

Trying to push the dark memories from his thoughts, Vince took his place behind the wheel, and after the nurse bid them farewell, he reached to the backseat for the bouquet of mixed flowers he'd picked up on the way to the hospital.

"Maybe these flowers will help take the forlorn look off your face," Vince told her.

Her eyes wide, she stared at the bouquet.

"Flowers! For me?"

"For you. I'm glad you're well enough to leave the hospital, Geena."

A smile started in her eyes, then quickly spread to her lips. The happy expression lit up her face, and Vince was shocked at how good it made him feel to think he'd pleased her. That he'd given her even a tiny spark of pleasure.

Accepting the flowers, she bent her nose to the colorful blossoms. "How beautiful. Thank you, Vince. I—"

Her voice abruptly ended on a choked note and Vince realized she was crying. And though he knew her emotionally wrought state was no fault of his, her tears tortured him in a way he didn't understand.

"Geena, it's going to be okay."

She sniffed, then gave him a wobbly smile. "I'm sorry about the waterworks. It's just that I—I have the feeling that it's been a long time since anyone gave me flowers. Thank you, Vince."

The need to assure her, to comfort and protect her hit him all at once, leaving a strange, hollow ache in the middle of his chest. Damn Evan and his idea for the flowers! He should've had better sense than to follow his partner's advice. Now Geena was in tears and he was feeling like a helpless sap.

But she was clutching the bouquet like it was a precious possession. Which was understandable, he thought bleakly. At this moment, the only things that belonged to her were the baby she was carrying, the items in her tote bag and the flowers.

Clearing his throat, he put the vehicle in gear and pulled away from the curb. "I'd better get you on home. I have work waiting on me back at the office."

He pulled onto the nearest street and mixed in with the traffic. When they finally reached the main thoroughfare, he noticed Geena was looking around her with interest.

"Does any of this look familiar?" he asked.

"No. Everything looks new to me." She glanced over at him. "You said we used to live in Reno. Did we ever drive down here for any reason?"

"Not here. We drove over to Virginia City a couple of times, but that's the closest we got to Carson City."

"Hmm. Maybe this town looks new to me because I've never seen it before. That's possible, isn't it?"

"Very possible," he agreed, then suddenly remembered the piece of jewelry he'd found at the accident site. While keeping his eye on the traffic, he fished the dainty necklace from his shirt pocket and handed it over to her. "Here. I found this dangling from a limb of sagebrush."

"That's mine! That's my cross!"

Her unexpected reaction had him glancing across the console to see her gripping the piece of silver.

"You recognize it?"

"Of course I do! I've had it for years!"

Nearly eleven, Vince could have told her. Ever since he'd given it to her for their first Easter together. But he held that information back. He didn't want her to think there was some special reason she'd been wearing the necklace or why it was the only single thing she remembered, other than her age. He didn't want to think it himself.

"That's good. That means your concussion is healing. Are you still having headaches?"

She lifted a hand to her left temple. "There's still a bump and a cut, but the headaches seem to be gone."

From the corner of his eye, he could see her studying the necklace dangling from her fingers. A confused frown marred her forehead, and he realized she was straining to remember the significance of the little cross.

In a soft, thoughtful voice, she asked, "I wonder why I remember this necklace being mine. What does it mean?"

He stared straight ahead, and a feeling of tremendous loss washed over him.

"Probably that you like silver. And that you have a deep faith."

"Hmm. Maybe so." She fastened the chain at the back of her neck, then adjusted the cross in the hollow of her throat. "There. I have a piece of my old life back. And it tells me everything is going to get better."

Better for her. Yes, Vince wanted that very much. As for himself, nothing could get better. He was stuck in a past that she'd totally forgotten.

Chapter Four

The next day Geena was sitting on the couch, staring at a credit card and set of truck keys lying on the coffee table. Before he'd gone to work this morning, Vince had left the items there with the suggestion she drive downtown and do some shopping for herself. When he'd asked if she remembered how to drive, she'd assured him she'd not forgotten. She'd even promised to be extra safe while driving his truck.

Yet, two hours later, she'd not made a move to pick up the card or the keys. Instead, she'd turned the television on and off, gone outside and walked around the house three times, then tried to read a magazine she'd found lying on the bar in the kitchen. But the subject of lawmen and the tactical gear they used on the job was hardly her taste of entertainment.

No doubt when Vince returned home, he'd want to know why she hadn't accepted his offer to replenish some of her lost things. Especially when she desperately needed a change of clothes and some toiletries. But something about spending his money made her feel like a leech.

With a mental groan, she started to reach for the television remote when the sound of the doorbell caused her to pause.

Since Vince worked during the day, she didn't expect he had people stopping by just to say hello. More than likely someone was going door to door trying to sell or promote something.

Leaving the couch, she walked out to the foyer and, for the sake of caution, peered into the peephole on the door.

"Marcella!" She practically yelled the nurse's name as she quickly jerked open the door. "Oh, I'm so happy to see you! Please, come in. What in the world are you doing here? I'm not supposed to need a nurse's care!"

Laughing, the red-haired nurse stepped into the foyer. She was carrying a large denim tote in one hand and a smaller canvas bag in the other. "I'm not here as a nurse. I'm here as a friend."

Geena gave the woman a grateful hug. "This is so nice of you. But how did you know where to find me? When I was discharged from the hospital yesterday, you'd already gone home."

Marcella smiled coyly. "I called Detective Parcell. He explained that you were here and gave me the address."

Geena didn't know why she was suddenly blushing. The only reason she was at her ex-husband's house was to avoid going to a public shelter.

"Well, I hope you can stay for a bit. Please, come into the living room and make yourself comfortable," she invited.

Marcella walked ahead of her and once they reached the living area, she placed the bags on the floor next to a green suede couch, then took a seat at one end. Geena eased down on the opposite end and squared around so that she was facing her new found friend.

"What a nice place. Very homey for a bachelor," the nurse commented as she glanced around at the comfortable furnishings. "Art on the wall, colorful throw rugs exactly where they should be and no half-eaten food or beer bottles lying about. Detective Parcell must be special."

"Well, I'd say so. But not because his house is clean and nice, but because he offered to share it with me. At least, until I can get everything with my identity straightened out."

"Hmm. You're right. Not many men would be so generous with their ex-wives."

Shortly after Vince had explained her name was Geena and they'd once been married, she'd shared the information with Marcella. Mainly because she felt like the special nurse deserved to know what was going on.

"I think he feels obligated," Geena said glumly. "Because I have no one else."

"Could be. But I'd like to think he's doing it because he wants to help you."

Sighing, Geena motioned to the credit card and keys lying on the coffee table. "He left those this morning and told me to go shopping for whatever I needed."

Marcella regarded her with a meaningful glance. "That is generous. So what did you buy?"

"Nothing! And I'm not going to. Just giving me a roof over my head is more than enough. I don't want to take advantage of his generosity. Especially when it might be a while before I can pay him back."

Smiling drily, Marcella shook her head, and Geena couldn't help but notice how pretty the woman looked with her long red hair hanging against her back and a touch of makeup brightening her face. Her slender figure was perfect, which only made Geena feel even more like a walrus.

"Why are you smiling like that?" Geena asked.

"I was just thinking about my ex-husband. We've been divorced for several years now, but it still doesn't bother him to ask me for money. Among other things he shouldn't be asking for. I'd fall over in a dead faint if he ever offered to give me or the boys anything."

"Doesn't he give you child support?"

"Only to our son, Harry. I adopted my youngest son, Peter, after we divorced."

"Wow. You must be a brave, confident woman to take on another child on your own," Geena said with renewed admiration for her friend. "My child isn't even born yet and I'm wondering how I'm going to take care of him or her."

A humble smile touched Marcella's face. "I first saw Peter when he was brought to the ER. At that time he was in a bad situation of neglect. I took one look at him and fell in love. It took some legal doings to adopt him. But I managed. Now it's a privilege to be his mother. When your little one comes, you'll feel that way, too."

She rested a hand on the top of her extended stomach. "I already love my baby fiercely. But Marcella, I'm not even sure I have a home. I could've been living out of my car!"

The other woman suddenly chuckled. "Well, it's a cinch you can't do that anymore. It's a pile of ashes now!"

The absurdity of it all had Geena chuckling along with her friend. "I might as well laugh, hadn't I? Because crying won't do a darned bit of good. Except make my face puffier than it already is."

"You shouldn't worry about whether you have a home, your torched car, or even having puffy cheeks. Everything will work out. Especially with Detective Parcell helping you."

Restless now, Geena rose to her feet and walked over to a wooden console table situated in front of a picture window. Several framed photos, along with various ribbons and medals pertaining to school and work were on display. Except for one blown-up snapshot of Vince and his partner, Evan Calhoun, Geena didn't recognize any of the people in the pictures, and she could only wonder if some of them might have been her relatives back when she and Vince had been married.

"Marcella, from what you've told me, you've lived here all your life. Do you know much about Vince?"

"Not really. Just from what I read in crime articles in the newspaper. I do know he and his partner have solved quite a few important cases. One involved a murder connected to a cattle-rustling ring."

"Hmm. Sounds like he's very good at his job." She picked up a photo of a man dressed in some sort of uniform and closely studied his smiling face. Although she didn't recognize the dark-haired man, she felt some sort of connection, as though something about him had once been important to her. But what? And why it should matter now didn't make sense.

"I'd say very good is probably understating it," Marcella said. "My best friend, Lilly, is married to Rafe Calhoun. He's Detective Calhoun's brother. They're very rich, the Calhouns. They own one of the largest ranches in Nevada. Plus they own a lot of other holdings in the mining and oil business. As for Vince, I've not heard Lilly say much about him. Other than the incident that occurred eighteen months ago on Christmas Eve. That's when Vince was critically wounded on the job. Everyone in the family was devastated. You see, it was touch and go as to whether Vince was going to live or die. And the two men are like brothers."

Geena's fingers tightened around the photo. Just hearing Vince had been critically wounded on the job was a jolt to her senses. He was so strong and fit and confident. But that was on the outside, she thought. Beneath all that masculine swagger he must be wearing scars. It was very hard for her to imagine.

"Oh, my, that's like something you hear about on the news or see in the movies. It's not something you imagine happening to someone close to you. And on Christmas Eve—how awful for Vince and his loved ones."

"Actually, it makes me wonder why he's still on the force," Marcella commented. "After nearly being killed, you'd think he'd want to choose a safer job."

Geena moved back to the couch. "What little I've been around Vince, I can see he wouldn't be a man to quit on anything. Except our marriage, I suppose." As soon as the words were out, she sighed and rolled her eyes. "Now why did I say that? I have no idea what happened with us. And it hardly matters now. I have a life somewhere else, with someone else."

Marcella gave her a gentle smile. "Sure you do. The coming baby proves that much." She reached for the totes she'd propped against the end of the couch. "Speaking of your baby, I gathered up a few things I thought you could probably use. Actually, most of it was sent to you by Lilly. She dug out some things she wore when she was carrying her last baby. And we both put in some girly items you might enjoy. Come sit and look."

A few minutes ago Geena had been so happy to see Marcella at the door, she'd not taken much notice of what the woman carried into the house with her. Now as she eased down on the couch, she stared in amazement at the bulging totes.

"All of that is for me?"

Marcella laughed softly. "If you're not going to use Detective Parcell's credit card, then you're certainly going to need them."

Feeling like Christmas had come early, Geena reached for the totes. "Come on. Let's take them in the kitchen and I'll look at everything while we have coffee."

"Sounds like a nice trade," Marcella happily agreed.

Much later that evening, well after dark, Vince let himself into the house and was instantly struck by light and the smells of cooking food coming from the direction of the kitchen. For the six years he'd lived here, he'd always come home to an empty house. The reality of having Geena back in his life filled him with a strange, warm emotion he wanted to ignore. Yet as he strode toward the light and the delicious smell, the silly urge to smile kept tugging at the corners of his lips.

When he stepped into the kitchen, Geena was sitting at the glass-topped table reading a hardback book. The moment she heard his footsteps on the tile, she looked up and smiled.

"Well, hello," she greeted. "I didn't hear you come in."

"Looks like you were distracted."

She closed the book and rose to her feet. "I went to the library this afternoon," she explained. "And checked out several books that looked interesting. Hopefully I can get them read before the baby gets here. Or before I leave to go home."

Home. Where was her home? And what was waiting for her there? Vince wondered. A few days ago, he'd felt a desperate urge to find her family and quickly send her on her way. But now he was reluctant to think of her leaving. At least, not until he was certain she was going back to a home where she was loved and wanted. If that made him a sap, then so be it.

"I'm glad you ventured out of the house. Did you have any trouble finding where to go around town?"

She walked over and placed the book at the far end of the cabinet countertop. "No. I had company this morning, and she gave me general directions on where to find things."

He moved over to where she stood. "Company? Did someone from social services come by?"

She frowned at him. "Why, no. Did you contact them?"

He shook his head. "No. Then your visitor must have been Noelle, Evan's wife," he surmised.

"I'd like to meet Noelle. But it wasn't her. It was Marcella, the nurse." She gestured downward to the magenta sweater and blue jeans she was wearing. "See, she brought me a whole pile of things to wear. She said they belonged to her friend Lilly Calhoun."

"Oh, yes, I forgot about Marcella calling and inquiring as to your whereabouts. I didn't realize she was coming by to see you today."

A wide smile spread across Geena's face, and Vince was glad to see her spirits were so high. The last year of their marriage, she'd mostly been depressed and constantly crying over things he couldn't understand. This was definitely a different Geena, and he wondered if the passing years had changed her that much. Or had the concussion and resulting amnesia done something to her personality?

"I'll say one thing, the woman must be very generous. And all the clothes are practically like new. She even sent a couple of outfits for me to wear after the baby is born."

"So Lilly sent you some things," Vince replied. "That was nice of her."

"She and Marcella have been so kind and thoughtful. And so have you, Vince. I only hope that someday I can repay all of you for everything you're doing for me."

Feeling a bit uncomfortable with her gratitude, he cleared his throat and stepped around her. At the stove, he lifted the lid on a large stainless steel pot and discovered it was full of spaghetti. Next to it, in a smaller pot, a meaty sauce was gently simmering.

"None of us expect to be repaid, Geena."

She followed him over to the stove. "I understand that. But it would make me feel good to give back."

He dropped the lid back onto the spaghetti, then looked at her. She'd pinned her hair atop her head and fastened it with a glittery clip. The silver cross he'd given her oh so many years ago was resting in the gentle hollow of her throat. Would she be wearing it, he wondered, if she knew exactly what it signified?

Why wouldn't she, Vince? She had the necklace with her when she'd wrecked her car. Apparently the fact that you gave it to her as a gift hasn't stopped her from wearing it.

Ignoring the voice in his head, he asked, "So did you use my credit card and get whatever you needed?"

"No. After Marcella brought all this stuff, there wasn't any need. Besides, I don't want to spend your money. It wouldn't be right."

"Why? You used to spend it."

Her lips parted, and as Vince looked at them, vivid memories of their taste and texture assaulted him. Kissing her had always sent his senses reeling, and he had the frightening feeling that if, for some crazy reason, his lips were to come in contact with hers, the magic would start all over again.

"Oh. You say that like—was that a problem with us? I spent too much money?"

He groaned. "No! On the contrary. You were always a frugal person. Why the hell would you ask that, anyway?"

The dainty flare of her nostrils told him she was irked

by his short response, but at the moment, he didn't care. Her accidental appearance in Carson City had upset his whole life, and for the past few days he'd been living on little more than raw nerves.

"Sorry," she said in a clipped voice. "But my memory is blank. I'm desperate to know anything about myself—my past. That's probably hard for you to understand, though."

A pent-up breath eased out of him. "Some things are best forgotten, Geena. You're smart enough to understand that."

Her gaze made one slow search of his face before she walked to the end of the counter where she'd left her book. Deciding it was time to make a quick exit, Vince started out of the room, only to have her intercept him at the doorway.

"Here," she said as she thrust his credit card at him, "you'd better put this away where it belongs. Thanks for the offer. But it wasn't needed."

The stilted tone of her voice cut him, and as he took the piece of plastic, he wondered why she was the one person in the world who could make him feel useless.

"If you do need it, all you have to do is ask," he told her.

She nodded, and he quickly slipped past her and out the door.

In his bedroom, he switched on a lamp on the night-stand, then pulled off his jean jacket and tossed it onto the bed. He was about to unbuckle the shoulder holster carrying his weapon when a light tap on the door facing had him turning to see Geena standing just inside the room. The fact that she'd followed him caught him completely off guard, and for a moment he couldn't get a word out.

"Was there something else?" he finally asked.

Linking her hands beneath the swell of her belly, she took several steps toward him. And suddenly the stilted conversation they'd had in the kitchen was forgotten. All he could think about was the plans they'd once made to have children together. After their sessions of lovemaking, he'd often rested his hand on her flat belly and imagined his child growing there. But that had been before she'd grown disenchanted with his job. Before she'd become weary of his long hours away from home.

"I wanted to apologize," she said.

"There's no reason for you to apologize."

She stepped closer, and Vince was certain the walls of the bedroom were narrowing down to the size of a tiny closet.

"Yes, there is. I've been so busy thinking of myself and my situation that I've not stopped to consider what all of this is doing to you. My problems are disrupting your life. And I shouldn't be adding to them with a bunch of questions that have no bearing on the present."

Feeling like a heel, though he wasn't sure why, he removed the holster and weapon. After placing it safely in the top drawer of the nightstand, he pulled off the detective's badge clipped to his belt and tossed it next to the base of the lamp.

"Don't worry about what this is doing to me. I have a tough hide. I'll survive."

A wry smile slanted her lips. "Compared to being shot, I imagine fielding my questions is nothing but an annoyance."

A chill crept over him. "Who told you I was wounded?"

"Marcella. She was telling me about the Calhoun family and somehow it just came up. Why? It's not something you've tried to keep secret, is it?"

"Not hardly. Details of the shootout were plastered in all the papers. Anyone who could read was aware that I'd been wounded." Sighing, he turned his back to her and began to unbutton his shirt. "But I wish people would forget it. I'd certainly like to."

"Marcella said you very nearly died," she said softly. "The memory must be terrifying."

"Most of that night is just a blur to me. Thinking about it doesn't scare me. It makes me angry, because I should've used more protection when we approached the suspect's house. I failed to see movement at the window. So I got shot up and my partner had to risk his life to pull me to safety. That's not something I like to remember," he said flatly.

"I don't know anything about the circumstances of that night, but I am certain of one thing, Vince. If the situation had been reversed, you wouldn't have hesitated to risk your life to save your partner."

Bending his head, he wearily pinched the bridge of his nose. He couldn't expect her to understand the guilt he'd lived with for the past year and a half or how the tragic incident had shaken his confidence as a lawman. Yet even with a broken memory, she was seeing him as a brave man, and the notion was like a soothing balm to the jagged scars in his soul.

"You're right about that," he murmured, then turned to face her. "Thank you, Geena."

For some reason, she moved even closer, and suddenly Vince could smell the sweet scent of her skin and hair, feel the warmth emanating from her body.

"Thank me for what?" she asked softly.

"For saying exactly what I needed to hear."

Confusion flickered in her eyes, and then with a slight shake of her head, she reached out and rested her palms against his chest. The contact stunned him, along with the searing heat that flowed from her fingers to his skin.

"Something is happening to me, Vince."

The plaintive note in her voice, coupled with the beseeching look in her eyes, very nearly took his breath away. "What do you mean?"

"I don't remember being your wife or anything about our marriage. Yet I feel a connection to you. I have a sense that I loved you very much. Tell me, Vince, is that right? Did we love each other?"

"Oh, Geena, don't—"

His words halted as her hands moved outward until they were clutching each arm. "Please, Vince, I need to know. This confusion that's going on inside me is torture."

"And you think having you this close to me isn't tearing me to shreds?" Without waiting for her response or weighing the consequences of his actions, he pulled her into his arms and tucked the top of her head beneath his chin. "Yes! You loved me very much. And I loved you."

With a sound that was something between a sob and a groan, she tilted her head in order to look up at him. Vince's gaze instantly fell to her lips, and that was all it took for his common sense to fly out the door.

Before he realized what he was about to do, his lips were settling over hers while his arms were drawing her forward until the fullness of her breasts crushed against his chest and the roundness of her belly bumped against his navel.

Kissing Geena was everything it used to be and a whole lot more. He couldn't remember her lips being this soft or plush, or the taste of her reminding him of wild honey. Sweet sensations darted through him until his mind was on a wild downhill tumble that was gaining speed with each passing second.

It wasn't until he heard the tiny groan in her throat and felt her hands curling over the tops of his shoulders that reality managed to creep into his brain, enabling him to break the contact of their lips and twist his head aside.

While he sucked in ragged breaths, Geena pressed her cheek against his chest.

"Oh, my—" she sputtered. "What—just—happened?"

Vince didn't have to wonder if the kiss had affected her. She was gulping for air and gripping his arms as though she needed a lifeline.

His jaw tight with sudden resolve, he gently eased her away from him. Yet even with a respectable distance between them, tremors continued to rattle him. "I think we both momentarily lost our minds."

When she failed to respond, he glanced down to see she was pressing fingertips against her lips. For one wild second, Vince wanted to push her hand away and kiss her all over again.

"You're right," she finally said. "My accident has put us in an unusual situation. It's made both of us a little crazy. That's understandable. Right?"

She was looking to him for a reasonable excuse for the passion they'd just exchanged, but Vince realized there wasn't one. At least, not in his mind. The truth of the matter was simple. He'd kissed Geena like that because he'd wanted to. Because he'd wanted *her*. As to why she'd kissed him back, he couldn't let himself wonder about her motives.

"Sure," he said gruffly. "You feel lost and I—want to help you. We just got off track for a moment. It won't happen again."

"No. It can't happen again." She swiped a hand through her tumbled hair, then turned and started out of the room. "I'll go put supper on the table. I hope you're hungry."

He was hungry all right, Vince thought sadly. For all the things he'd once let go. And for a woman he could never have again.

Chapter Five

A week later Vince was no closer to finding a link to Geena's life before she'd crashed her car on the edge of Carson City. And she had yet to recall a glimmer of anything about her recent home and family. To make matters worse, in the past few days several crimes had been committed around the county, forcing Vince and Evan to direct their time and energy away from Geena's case.

Uncovering a person's identity wasn't nearly as important as figuring out who was responsible for an assault or robbery. Yet in any case, time played a major factor and no one had to tell Vince that the quicker Geena's problem could be solved, the sooner his life could get back to normal. Maybe then he'd be able to focus on his work instead of constantly fighting to keep Geena out of his thoughts.

"I'm not so sure I believe Collier's story of how the horse went missing. It all sounded ridiculous to me. He's the barn manager. How could someone have gotten that stallion out of his stall and loaded him into a trailer without him knowing it? In broad daylight?"

"Hmm."

"Yeah, I think Santa Claus probably hooked him up with his reindeer and they all flew away into the night."

"Sounds plausible," Vince mumbled absently.

"Damn, Vince! Would you come back to earth? I could use a little assistance with this case."

The SUV came to a jarring halt, and Vince looked around to see Evan had stopped the vehicle at an intersection of dirt roads. For the past hour and a half, they'd been interviewing a number of ranch hands, inspecting horse barns and traipsing through dusty paddocks in an effort to solve the mystery of how someone had made off with a cutting horse worth a whopping six figures.

To complicate matters, the ranch where the crime had occurred lay adjacent to Storey County. If the horse had been taken across the county line, then Storey law officials would have to get involved with the investigation.

Normally a case like this would get Vince's blood pumping. Instead, he was spending all his energy trying to push Geena from his mind, and the distraction was making him crazy.

Closing his eyes, Vince wearily rubbed the burning lids. "Sorry, Evan. I was thinking about something else."

"Duh. About Geena, right?"

Vince cut his partner an annoyed glance. "What else? The woman is living in my house! I—we need to get this thing with her figured out so that she can go home, where she belongs!"

Evan turned the vehicle onto a road that would eventually connect them with the highway leading back to Carson City. "You look like you haven't slept in days. What's wrong? You two been sniping at each other?"

Sniping? Far from it, Vince thought. Since that night they'd kissed in his bedroom, everything between them had remained nice and polite. Vince had carefully kept a proper distance from her and Geena had come no closer than arm's length to him. Each night he came home to find she'd cooked something for dinner. Not only that, she waited to eat her meals with him. He should be pleased that everything was going smoothly. Instead he was growing edgier with each day that passed.

"No. She's been pleasant and I—I've tried my best to be polite with her. There've been no arguments. It's just that I—need my house back. My life back. I'm not used to sharing it with a woman. And I don't want to get used to it—again!"

He wanted to be able to go to bed at night and fall asleep, Vince thought. Instead of thinking about his ex-wife lying in the bedroom next to his.

"Hmm. You and Geena used to share a house and a life together," Evan said thoughtfully. "Maybe that's the thing that's bothering you. It's too much like it used to be—before things went south and she started drinking."

Vince started to tell his partner he was way off track. But quickly decided he'd be wasting his breath trying to hide the truth from Evan. The other man knew him too well.

"None of this should be happening, Evan. But I'm getting used to going home and finding her in the kitchen, stirring up something good to eat, to seeing her curled up on the couch reading a book or watching TV—it's almost like she's supposed to be there. But then I take one look at that mound of baby she's carrying and the cold facts hit me. She belongs to another man. She doesn't belong in my house. Or my heart."

Frowning, Evan glanced his way. "You sound like you wish she was still your wife. Do you?"

Vince sighed. "I didn't give Geena up all those years ago because I stopped loving her. I got the divorce because I realized I was making her unhappy."

"Well, what the hell was she doing to you?" Evan suddenly snapped at him. "Maybe you ought to remember she was spending her days throwing back scotch or vodka, or whatever the hell she was drinking, and crying for you to quit the police force. She should have been doing everything to support you. Instead, she was ruining herself and you! Surely you don't want that kind of heartache back in your life."

Evan's vehement reaction had Vince squaring around in the seat to look at him. "There's no reason for you to be concerned. I have no intentions of getting Geena back in my life! Hellfire, the woman is married, along with being pregnant. She's off-limits."

Sarcasm twisted Evan's features. "You can verify that she's married? You need to wake up, Vince. Just because she's going to have a baby doesn't mean she's married or even engaged."

Damn it, that possibility had been going around in Vince's head for days now. Practically since the first night he saw her lying in the hospital bed.

"I'm not stupid, Evan. That notion has already crossed my mind."

Evan tugged at the brim of his cowboy hat. "I don't have to tell you that you're a brother to me, Vince. It bothers me to think of you pining for a wife who broke your heart a few years ago. I want you to find a woman who will appreciate you for the man you are."

"I'm not pining for Geena," Vince said crossly, then let out a heavy sigh. "It's just that being around her again is bringing up too many old memories. And the hell of it is, she doesn't remember any of them."

"Maybe that's a good thing. In her situation, she doesn't need to be distracted. She needs to be focused on the future and finding her home and family. Wherever that might be."

"Yeah, but we don't seem to be making any headway in that department," Vince said glumly. "It's driving me crazy that we can't come up with anything on her mother, Rhonda."

By now they'd reached the paved highway, and while Evan waited at the stop sign for the oncoming traffic to pass, he said, "From what you've told me, Geena was never that close to her mother. Even if we did locate this Rhonda, she might not have kept in touch with her daughter."

"You could be right about that. Geena loved her mother, but after her father died, Rhonda made the front door to their home a revolving door for men. By the time Geena and I divorced, she was on her third husband, and he was a real jerk. I wouldn't be surprised if the woman has gone through two or three more husbands since then."

"Sounds like she had some serious issues," Evan commented.

"She did. But if she could give us some clues about Geena, I'd be willing to talk with her."

"I'm hopeful it won't come to that," Evan said. "We've been getting a lot of hits on the pic we posted on our missing persons site. I think someone will eventually contact us with the information we need."

And then he could say goodbye to her once and for all, Vince thought. Although it shouldn't, the idea left him feeling strangely hollow. "She could go into labor any day now, Evan. How am I going to deal with a baby in the house?"

Evan shrugged. "You'll be a temporary daddy. It'll be

good training for when you have kids of your own. With the right woman, that is."

It was clear his partner didn't believe Geena was the right one. Well, he could understand Evan's thinking. The man only knew of Geena's faults. He had no way of knowing she'd been gentle and loving and completely devoted to him. But all of that was irrelevant now.

"Sometimes you can be a very funny guy without even trying," Vince muttered. "Being a detective is the only job I want."

"There's more to life than being a detective."

Geena had told him those very words an endless number of times, he thought. But he'd not listened. Not completely, anyway. In the end his job had torn them apart. And now, ironically, it had thrown them back together.

"Just because you and Noelle want a passel of kids doesn't mean I do."

Evan made a scoffing noise. "Sometimes I wonder how you and I ever became friends. You have a weird sense of humor, you watch too much damned basketball and you eat way too much junk food. You don't know the back end of the horse from the front and you think a tapadero is some kind of dance. But somehow you've managed to become my brother."

"Gee, what an honor," Vince joked.

Evan scowled at him. "Brother or not, though, I'm giving you two weeks to get rid of that blasted relic in the office. And if you don't I'm going to throw it in the Dumpster!"

Feigning ignorance, Vince asked, "Relic? What are you talking about?"

"You know damned well what I'm talking about. That antiquated percolator of yours that I've had to put up with ever since I got promoted to detective. When I want coffee, I don't like being forced to wait thirty minutes until I can pour myself a cup."

"Instant gratification," Vince grumbled. "That's what's wrong with people like you. You don't understand that getting the best is worth the wait."

Evan glanced over at him and slowly began to chuckle. After a moment Vince found himself laughing along with him. Through the years, whenever things got too serious, Evan never failed to bring up the issue of the percolator. And every time the two men ended up with the chuckles.

"One of these days I'm going to surprise you and get a new coffeemaker," Vince taunted.

"You do and I'll kick your butt."

Back in Carson City, at Tahoe General Hospital, Geena had just finished her checkup with Dr. Dunlevy and gone down to the cafeteria to meet Marcella for lunch. The nurse was fast becoming a good friend, and Geena didn't want to think of the time she'd have to say goodbye to the woman.

Now, as they sat a table positioned near a wall of plate glass with a view of a small landscaped courtyard, Marcella plied her with questions.

"So what does the doctor think? Is he concerned that you've not remembered anything yet?"

Geena swallowed a bite of chicken sandwich before she answered. "He says amnesia is unpredictable. From what he says, my concussion is healed and I might be unconsciously blocking out thoughts of my past because I'm comfortable with things as they are now. Honestly, I'm beginning to think he's a quack. Why would I be comfortable with this hellish limbo I'm stuck in? I want to go home. I want to be with my baby's father."

Marcella forked a French fry to her mouth. "Is it really that hellish? You have a nice home to live in and a strong, handsome detective to look after you. Most women would consider that heavenly."

Frowning, Geena reached for her glass of milk. "That's just it, Marcella. So I guess in a way Dr. Dunlevy is right. Living with Vince has gotten to be—well, pleasant. And I—this is going to sound awful—but I've been having strange feelings about the man. They're soft and sexy and—I should be ashamed of myself." She groaned as a blush stung her cheeks. "I only hope that once I get back with the baby's father, I'll forget all about Vince."

An empathetic smile crossed Marcella's face. "Don't worry about it. Right now your body is on hormone overload. It's only normal for you to look at Vince and feel a little hot and bothered."

Normal? There was nothing natural about the way her heart pounded every time she got within ten feet of the man. And there was nothing ordinary about the way she'd kissed him or the way she'd been dreaming about doing it again. But she couldn't make that confession to Marcella. It was far too embarrassing.

"So Vince and Evan haven't unearthed any new information concerning your situation?" Marcella asked after a moment.

Geena let out a hopeless sigh. "No. And you want to know what I'm beginning to think?"

A vague smile crossed Marcella's face. "You mean besides having erotic daydreams about your ex and deciding your neurologist is a quack?"

Grimacing, Geena used her fingers to tear off a bite of the sandwich. "Yes, besides those things. It's becoming fairly obvious to me that I don't have a family."

"Oh, Geena, that can't be right. I mean, look at you. You had a serious connection to a man."

"Obviously. But think about it, Marcella, several days

have passed since my accident, and no one has bothered to look for me. No one has reported me missing. No one has called the sheriff's department asking about a pregnant woman. If I had a family, some of them would've been aware that I was traveling and where I was headed. A man, whether it be a boyfriend, fiancé or husband, wouldn't need to be some sort of Sherlock Holmes to track me here."

Regarding her thoughtfully, Marcella leaned back in her chair. "You are making sense, Geena. Except that everyone has relatives of some sort."

"According to Vince my father died when I was child. And I wasn't very close to my mother. I had no siblings. So that only leaves distant relatives that I didn't associate with."

"I see. So you've talked to Vince about this?"

"I've told him I believe there's no one out there looking for me. But he—well, I honestly don't think he wants to accept the idea. After all, he doesn't want to feed and house me forever."

Leaning forward, Marcella gave her an encouraging smile. "Well, you shouldn't worry about any of that now. The most important thing is the baby. Have you seen the OB that Dr. Merrick referred you to?"

Geena nodded. "I went to his office yesterday. He said everything seems normal and in his opinion I could go into labor any time now."

"That's so exciting! I'm keeping my fingers crossed that you'll have the baby before something or someone pulls you away from here. I want to be able to spend some time with the little guy before you go."

Geena smiled. "It might be a little girl."

The nurse's eyes widened with curiosity. "Oh, did the doctor do an ultrasound and tell you the gender?"

"He did an ultrasound, but I told him I didn't want to know the sex. I want it to be a surprise."

"Hmm. So you're an old-fashioned girl." She grinned. "Have you picked out names?"

Geena turned her gaze away from the partially eaten sandwich on her plate, to the courtyard outside the glass wall. Presently summer was in full swing, but where would she be by the time autumn began to tinge the leaves with bright reds and golds? Cold weather was a few months away yet, but the uncertainty of her and her baby's future was already leaving a chill in her heart.

"If I had picked out names before the accident, I don't remember them. I have no idea if I'd planned to name the baby after a relative or some other person I was close to. Dear God, I didn't realize a person's past had so much influence on the future."

Marcella reached across the small round table and touched her hand to the back of Geena's. "Don't let it get you down. Heck, what's in a name anyway? I'd just be thrilled to have the baby."

She turned her attention back to the nurse's kind face. "You say that like you want more children. Would you like to have siblings for Harry and Peter?"

Marcella's blue eyes grew soft and misty, and in that moment Geena was reminded that she wasn't the only woman to encounter a troubled spot in the road. The nurse's life hadn't exactly gone down a path of roses.

"I couldn't imagine anything more wonderful. But I seriously doubt that will ever happen. There's not many men around who'd be willing to saddle himself with a woman who already has two kids and wants more." She shook her head with certainty. "No, I expect the dream of me having more babies is probably over. But at least I have my two sons."

"Never say never, Marcella. You might meet the perfect guy for you and the boys."

Marcella chuckled. "Believe me, I'm not holding my breath."

For the next few minutes the two women turned their attention to the food on their plates until Marcella broke the companionable silence.

"Geena, I notice you're often touching the silver cross you're wearing. Is that something you bought for yourself? I don't remember it being in the few pieces of jewelry Lilly sent to you."

Unaware that she'd been fingering the cross, Geena dropped her hand. "Actually, other than the clothes I had on, this is the only thing I have from my other life. Vince found it at the accident scene. It was caught on a piece of sagebrush. Funny thing, when he first showed it to me, I recognized it."

"It must have held a very special meaning for you," Marcella remarked.

"I think so, too," she murmured. "But right now I don't have any idea who gave it to me or why."

"Maybe the answers to those questions will get you on the path to your real home."

Her real home. Yes, she had to keep reminding herself that Vince's place was only her temporary home. And sooner rather than later she was going to have to move on.

It was very late that night before Vince finally let himself into the house. When he walked into the living room, he discovered the TV was playing with the volume on low and Geena was lying on the couch sound asleep.

For long moments, he stood staring down at her and thinking back to the times he'd come home late from work and found her asleep. In those instances an empty cocktail glass had always been sitting close by. Tonight there was nothing but a milk glass resting on the coffee table.

No doubt the years they'd been apart had changed her for the better. Which only proved to Vince that he'd done the right thing by letting her go. Still, there were moments like this when he looked at her quiet, lovely face and the ache of losing her very nearly choked him with pain.

Determined to shove the dismal thoughts away, he switched off the TV and then picked up a small blanket off the back of the couch and carefully spread it over her. She didn't stir, and after one last glance at her sleeping face, he walked out of the room.

A few minutes later, after changing into a pair of jeans and a plain white T-shirt, he was sitting at the kitchen table, eating a plateful of chicken and rice, when he heard her footsteps.

Looking up, he saw her yawning and wiping her eyes as she entered the kitchen.

"Hello," she said.

"Hello. Sorry I woke you."

She came over to the table and pulled out the chair next to his. "You didn't wake me," she said as she took a seat. "My back did. It feels like I've been mopping floors all day."

"It's almost midnight. You should go to bed and get some rest," he told her.

"I will—in a few minutes." She gestured to his plate. "I see you found the chicken and rice. There was tossed salad in the fridge."

"Thanks, but this is plenty."

She glanced at a small digital clock sitting on the cabinet counter. "It's after midnight. You must've had a busy day."

"Very. A cutting horse was stolen off a ranch near Storey County. Evan and I had to make a trip out there to investigate. That took most of the afternoon. Tonight we were going over evidence."

"You spent that much time over a horse?" she asked with surprise.

"The stallion is worth six figures. Not counting the money the ranch makes in stud fees. Our initial thoughts are that the theft is an inside job. But Evan and I will have to come up with the evidence to prove it."

"I have every confidence that you will. From what Marcella tells me, you two guys have solved some high-profile crimes around here."

Vince made a scoffing noise. "She's exaggerating. Probably to make you feel like your case is in competent hands."

She shook her head. "I understand that my sort of problem can take time. No one called into the department today about me, did they?"

"That's why I was late coming home. I wanted to check all the media postings and phone calls. Sorry to tell you, but nothing today."

She left the chair and collected a small glass from the cabinet. After she filled it with orange juice, she returned to her seat and slowly sipped the drink.

Vince tried to keep his eyes off her, but there was something about her tonight that made her look even lovelier than usual. Although her face was bare of makeup, there was a glow about her skin and a soft light in her eyes that made her look almost ethereal.

You're losing it, Vince. Geena isn't an angel. And she damned sure isn't yours. So snap out of it and get your mind back to the real world.

"Vince, there's something I've been wanting to ask you."

He glanced at her while the pestering voice in his head continued to nag at him. "What's that?"

She placed her glass on the table. "I understand you don't like to talk about the past—I mean, our past. But there's a picture of a man wearing a uniform—it's sitting on the console table in the living room. Did I ever meet him or know him at one time?"

He quickly glanced down to his plate. "Why? Do you think you should recognize him?"

"Well, yes, I believe I have some sort of connection to the man, but I can't figure it out. It's mainly just a feeling I get whenever I look at the photo."

Whether her amnesia was physical or psychological, it was clear the injury was beginning to heal itself, and Vince didn't know whether to feel relieved or sad that their days together would soon end.

"You must be getting well, Geena, because you did have a connection to him. Even though you never met him, Parry Parcell was your father-in-law. My father."

Confusion puckered her brow. "Oh. Then why did I never meet him? He didn't approve of me? You two were estranged or something?"

Shaking his head, Vince pushed the plate aside. "You never met my father because he was killed when I was fourteen years old. He was a police officer in Reno. He got shot answering a domestic violence call."

Her lips parted as she stared at him in disbelief. "I'm so sorry, Vince. Losing your dad like that—I can't imagine how awful it was for you. Especially at that young age."

"It wasn't easy. Understandably, my mother fell apart. She blamed the police force for taking her husband. After that she wasn't too much help in raising me and my older sister. By the time I entered the police academy, she'd re-married and moved away."

"Did I get along with her? Do you communicate with her now?"

Vince could understand that Geena was desperate to fill in the gaps of her life, and right now he was the only one who could help her do that. But there were parts of his life that he didn't like to revisit.

"You didn't have much chance to get along with her. I think we only saw her two times during the five years we were married. She lives back east now. Somewhere in Virginia. We don't talk much. You see, she's never forgiven me for becoming a lawman."

"That's awful. I mean, she should be proud of you for choosing such an admirable job."

If Vince had still been eating he probably would have choked on Geena's comment. He couldn't count the times that she'd accused him of loving his job more than her. But there was no point in telling her any of that. The problems the two of them had then held no significance now.

"It killed her husband and she swore it will kill me. She says doesn't want to be around to see it. And who knows, maybe she's right. Maybe someday a fatal bullet or something else will take my life. But until then, I'm going to be a detective. Not just because it makes me a living, but because it's my calling."

Picking up his plate, he carried it over to the sink and scraped the leftovers into the garbage disposal.

Geena followed and stood watching as he washed the plate and dried it.

"What about your sister? Does she live close by?" she asked.

"No. She lives in California. She's divorced. No kids. And before you ask, yes, you two liked each other. Her name is Nicki." He moved past her and opened the cabinets. "Is there still some of that decaffeinated coffee? It's late, but I'd like a cup before I go to bed. What about you?"

"I don't want a cup, but I'll make it for you," she offered. "You've had a long day. Go have a seat in the living room and I'll bring it to you."

He hardly needed a pregnant woman to be serving him coffee, but rather than argue with her, he simply thanked her and left for the living room.

Five minutes later, he was sitting in an armchair, his head resting against the back, his eyes closed, when Geena appeared with his coffee.

"I put cream in it. That is the way you like it, isn't it?" she asked as she leaned over and set the cup and saucer on a table near the arm of his chair.

"Yes, thanks."

She straightened, then immediately began to rub her lower back. "I forgot to ask if you wanted something for dessert. Cookies? Fruit?"

"I'm fine. But I'm not sure you are. Maybe you should take some over-the-counter pain relief."

She shook her head. "No. I don't want to take anything that might harm the baby. I think I'll go have a nice warm bath and go to bed."

For the past few days it had become evident to Vince that the extra weight she was carrying was beginning to put even more of a strain on her body. She was moving more slowly, and when she took off her shoes he could see her ankles were slightly swollen. The idea that she was going through such discomfort to give some other man a child was not something he wanted to think about.

"Sounds like a good idea," he told her.

After telling him good-night, she started out of the room, and Vince reached for his coffee. But he'd barely taken two sips when, from somewhere behind him, he heard her let out a loud gasp.

"Geena?"

The cup clattered and nearly tipped over as he hurriedly slammed it onto the saucer and leaped from the chair.

In the hallway, leading to the bedrooms, he found Geena doubled over, her arms clutching the weight of her belly. Fear raced through him as he sprinted to her side.

"Geena, what's wrong? Is it the baby?"

She reached out to him, and Vince wrapped a supporting arm around her shoulders.

Her head bent, she said in a strained voice, "I think so. I think my labor is starting."

Even though Vince had known this moment was drawing near, he still wasn't prepared for the reality that Geena was going to give birth.

He leaned his head down in order to look at her face. "Are you sure?" he asked anxiously. "Maybe this is some of those false pains."

Her lips stretched to a taut, thin line. "There's nothing false about this! The pain is—awful!"

"Okay. Okay. We need to get you to the hospital. Do you think you can walk to the car, or do I need to carry you?"

"I'll walk. You need to collect my bag from the bedroom. I packed it today. So it has everything I—"

The remainder of her words ended abruptly as another violent pain struck her. Cradling her belly, she bent forward and groaned loudly.

Vince had never felt so helpless in his life.

"You can't walk like this," he told her. "I'll carry you."

"No, I—"

Her protest was halted by a sudden gush of amniotic fluid that rushed down both legs and splattered in puddles on the hardwood floor.

"Oh! Vince, I—I'm so sorry! My water—"

"Don't be crazy! It's just a floor!" Bending, he carefully picked her up and started to the front of the house. "The hospital is only a few blocks away. I can drive you there quicker than waiting on an ambulance."

She wrapped her arms tightly around him and buried her face in the side of his neck. "Just promise you won't leave me, Vince. That's all I ask. That you stay with me."

"I promise."

He'd stay, he thought grimly, until the baby arrived. Until she finally remembered the man she really loved.

Chapter Six

Outside, Vince carried her to his personal truck and carefully laid her on the backseat, then raced back into the house to collect the things she needed.

On the short drive to the hospital, he drove as fast as safety would allow, while Geena grew unexpectedly quiet and still.

Glancing over his shoulder for the umpteenth time, he asked, "Have the pains stopped? Do you think the baby is about to arrive?"

Her head moved back and forth against the seat. "I can't tell you that, Vince. I've never done this before! Right now everything feels—numb with pain."

Not feeling a bit reassured by her response, Vince steered the truck into an open lane of the thoroughfare and pressed down on the accelerator. "Just hang on," he told her. "We're almost there."

At the hospital, Vince drove straight to the emergency

entrance, where a pair of nurses quickly helped Geena out of the truck and into a wheelchair.

As they wheeled her through a set of double glass doors, Vince was left to follow with her bag and a robe he'd found hanging on a hook in the bathroom.

Inside the ER waiting room, one of the nurses, a tall woman with gray hair and a no-nonsense expression, snatched hold of Vince's sleeve and pointed to the admitting office.

"You go there, Daddy, and take care of the admission papers. We'll take care of her and the baby. When you finish in admitting, go to the second floor. The nurses at the desk there will give you any further information about your wife," she instructed. "Give me her things. I'll put them away until she's assigned a room."

While handing her the bag and robe, Vince started to explain to the nurse that he wasn't the daddy or the husband, but just as quickly he decided there was no point. Geena was in too much pain to deal with a bunch of paperwork. Someone had to do it for her, and he was the only one available.

He thanked the nurse, then turned around to see that Geena had already been wheeled away. So much for giving her a parting word of encouragement, Vince thought.

What could you have said to her anyway, Vince? It isn't your baby she's having. Your job isn't to be a daddy. Your job is to find the real one.

Disgusted with the sarcastic voice in his head, Vince hurried over to the admissions office and sat down in a hard plastic chair to wait his turn.

Several minutes later, as his anxious nerves continued to build to the breaking point, he finally moved to another plastic chair, where he was facing a woman with curly brown hair and a wide, stern face. And naturally, she had to start out with the hardest question of all.

"Patient's name, please."

"Her first name is Geena. I can't tell you her last name."

"What do you mean, you can't tell me? Are you saying you brought a stranger to the emergency unit?"

Vince bit back a weary sigh. He'd been going for the past nineteen hours and he was worried sick about Geena. He wasn't in the mood to go around in silly circles with this woman. "No. She isn't a stranger. She's my ex-wife."

"Then you should certainly know her last name."

"I should, but I don't. You see, she has amnesia," Vince explained.

"Oh, so that's why she's entering the hospital? For a head injury?"

"No, she's having a baby."

Clearly annoyed now, the woman lifted her hands from the keyboard and leveled a scathing look at him. "Yours, I presume?"

Vince was shocked at how much he wanted to give the woman a loud, resounding yes to her question. "No, I'm not the father."

She let out a frustrated sigh. "Do you know the biological father's name?"

"If I did, he'd be sitting here now instead of me."

She flattened both her hands on the desktop as though she was about to rise to her feet. "Is this some sort of joke? Sir, this is a hospital where people are dealing with serious issues. And a few of them are behind you, waiting for you to finish this farcical exchange!"

Vince pulled his badge from the back pocket of his jeans and laid it on the counter for the woman to see.

"I'm sorry, ma'am, but there's nothing amusing about

Geena's situation. The sheriff's department is presently trying to resolve the issue of her identification."

She cast him a sheepish look. "I'm sorry, too, Detective. Perhaps it would be best, under the circumstances, to admit her as a Jane Doe."

The suggestion caused something in Vince to snap, and before he could stop himself, he burst out, "No! Damn it! She's isn't a Jane Doe! She's Geena!"

"I understand—I think. And I'm sorry," the woman said gently. "But the hospital requires a patient to have a last name. For insurance and billing purposes. I suppose it would be pointless of me to ask for a Social Security number?"

Feeling utterly drained, he wiped a hand over his face. This woman couldn't possibly know all the barriers and roadblocks he'd encountered since he'd started the search for Geena's current identification. A Social Security number would have answered plenty of questions, but he could barely remember his own, much less his ex-wife's. And since she'd always filed her income tax separately, he didn't have any old returns stored away with that information. In the past few days, he'd contacted two federal agencies for help, but so far he'd only gotten red tape deferrals and holdups.

"Trust me, once I do get the number I'll pass it on to you. For now, just list her as Geena Parcell. That was her name for a while."

"Very well." She typed in the name. "Now let's move on to her address."

By now Vince was past wasting time with explanations, so he simply gave her his home address. Even if it was only temporary, it was actually Geena's present place of residence.

By the time the office worker had completed the list

of endless questions and Vince had signed his name to the necessary documents, he was so frustrated and worried, he practically ran to the nearest set of elevators. On his way up to the second floor, he hurriedly sent a text to Evan to inform his partner that Geena's baby was on its way. If by some chance Evan was still working late at their office, Vince believed his partner would probably stop by the hospital before he headed home.

Twenty minutes later, after several sessions of sitting and standing and pacing as he waited for some sort of word on Geena's condition, he was back in one of the cushioned chairs, flipping blindly through a magazine when he spotted a pair of familiar cowboy boots standing in front of him.

Relieved to see his friend, Vince tossed down the magazine and jumped to his feet. "You never returned my text, so I decided you were already home in bed."

"I got busy after you left the office, so I've not gone home yet. And I didn't want to text you. I wanted to talk with you in person. How's Geena?" he asked.

"I was told a doctor was examining her. But that was fifteen minutes ago!"

"They won't let you see her?"

Vince shook his head. "Not yet. The nurse said they had to get her settled first. Settled, hell! The baby is probably being born this very minute!"

Evan patted his shoulder. "Calm down. These things usually take a while. Besides, I'm glad I caught you here in the waiting room." He pointed to the chair Vince had just vacated. "Maybe you'd better sit down."

Alarm raced through Vince, jangling his already frayed nerves. "I don't want to sit. What's happened? We've been called to a homicide scene or something?"

"Nothing like that."

Evan pushed back the brim of his cowboy hat and passed a hand over her forehead. Vince could see his partner was bleary-eyed with exhaustion, which made him feel doubly guilty. As a favor to him, Evan had been working above and beyond on Geena's case.

"Then why do I need to sit? Is this something about Noelle or Joanna?"

"No. It's Geena's case. Shortly after you left the office, I was closing things down for the night when a call came in. A credible call."

Stunned, Vince stared at him. "Credible? How can you be sure?"

"Believe me, everything fits. This person is well acquainted with Geena—she's a friend. She hasn't called before tonight because she just now spotted Geena's picture on a missing-persons website."

Vince's head was spinning. Geena was about to deliver the baby. Until this very moment, he'd not realized how much he'd been looking forward to having a child in the house. Now he was faced with the news that she and the baby would be leaving the hospital with someone else.

You should be dancing a jig, Vince. Your troubles are over. You'll have your house back. Your life back. No crying baby. No woman with an endearing smile and soft, tempting lips.

He let out a heavy sigh. "So when will her husband or boyfriend be coming to collect her and the baby?"

Taking him by the shoulder, Evan guided him over to a more private area of the room. "Hold your horses, Vince. You're going way too fast. First of all, according to what this friend, Megan O'Dell, tells me, there is no man in Geena's life. There was a husband for about four weeks, but the marriage was annulled and he skedaddled out of the picture. As for the rest, Geena was living in Pendleton, Oregon, and teaching art at a private school there. But in recent months she decided to make a move here to Carson City."

Because he was living here? Because she was pregnant and alone and seeking his help? No, that was inconceivable, Vince thought. Geena hadn't known where he lived. Or had she?

The questions were rolling through his mind like a giant windstorm. "So that's why she was driving into Carson City the night she had the accident? She was moving here?"

Evan nodded. "From what this Megan explained to me, the day before the accident, Geena left Pendleton with her car loaded to the brim with her belongings. So that explains why the car burned so quickly. The packed boxes must have acted as an accelerant."

Wiping a hand over his face, Vince tried to digest all of Evan's news, but it was more than his weary brain could absorb. "What am I going to do, Evan, when I see her? She's having a baby! Am I supposed to throw all this stuff at her?"

Evan sighed. "I'm not a doctor. But from my experience a woman doesn't need that sort of distraction when she's trying to deliver a baby."

Vince felt sick and sad and scared all at once. "Evan, I—"

The remainder of his words were cut short as a tall young nurse with a thick messy bun on top of her head approached the two men.

"Which one of you is Mr. Parcell?" she asked.

Vince quickly answered, "I am. Has Geena had the baby?"

The nurse gave him a patient smile. "Not yet. We have her settled in a room now and she's asking for you. If you'll come with me, I'll help you get dressed."

"Dressed?" Vince looked down at his T-shirt and jeans,

then helplessly over to Evan, who'd started to chuckle. "What's wrong with my clothes?"

Evan said, "The nurse will explain. You go. I've got to head home before Noelle puts an APB out for me. I'll check back with you in the morning. Uh—I forgot, it's already morning. In a few hours." Grinning, he made a shooing gesture at Vince. "Go! Hop to it, Daddy!"

Not bothering to make a parting shot at his partner, Vince left with the nurse, and after she'd helped him cover his clothing, head and feet with protective gear, she guided him into a private room that felt even cooler than the waiting area, which had been downright chilly.

Geena was lying in a narrow bed with rails on both sides. Her head was propped on a single pillow, while the lower half of her body was covered with a thin sheet. Her face was incredibly pale and drawn, and as he drew closer, he was pierced with unreasonable fear. Women had babies every day, he mentally argued. It was a natural thing. There wasn't anything for him to worry about. Yet if anything were to happen to Geena or the baby, he didn't think he could bear it.

"Vince," she said, her voice strained and thin. "I wasn't sure you'd be out there waiting."

He gave her a lopsided smile. "Where else would I be?"

She reached for his hand and as he wrapped his fingers tightly around hers, he noticed something different in her eyes, a sadness he'd not seen until this very moment.

"I'm not sure. I guess—" Pain suddenly twisted her features, and she squeezed his fingers tightly until it eased. "Frankly, I'm a bit surprised that you're here at all."

"What? Geena, they must have given you some sort of drug that's clouded your thinking. You're not making sense."

Her gaze fell warily to the sheet lying across her breasts.

"I've not been given any sort of drug. In fact, my thinking hasn't been this clear since I had the accident."

As soon as Vince had walked into the room and spotted Geena, he'd forgotten all about the news Evan had given him. Now it all hit him like a brick. But he couldn't slap her with such news. She was still holding out a thread of hope that somewhere she had a family. He didn't want to take that hope away from her until the baby was safely here and the time was right.

His expression guarded, he said, "Maybe you should explain what you mean by that."

Geena lifted her gaze to his face and was once again amazed that she could have forgotten this man. How could the memories of her love for him have been locked out of her mind for all these days?

"My memory has returned, Vince. All of it."

His brown eyes widened with disbelief. "Your amnesia is gone! When—how did this happen?"

No doubt he was shocked, Geena thought. She was still reeling from the sudden jolt of reality. There was no loving family searching for her. No husband or boyfriend. Even her mother had disappeared from her life. Somehow the deepest part of her had always known that. But her memory hadn't wanted to face that lonely reality.

She said, "After you'd gone to admissions, the nurses were helping me get undressed and into bed. All of a sudden I started feeling strange and then it was like something tilted in my head and everything about my life came rushing in. The doctor tending me believes something about the labor pains must have triggered my memory. Anyway, the amnesia is gone, and now I feel worse than a fool. I don't know what to say."

Bending over the rail of the bed, he touched a hand to

her forehead, and Geena's heart squeezed with longing and regret. If only she'd not ruined her chances with this man all those years ago. If only she'd been mature and wise enough to realize what she'd been doing to herself and to Vince. But that was the past. She had to concentrate on her baby now.

"You don't have to say anything. I already know. Evan has been talking with Megan, your friend in Pendleton."

"Oh! You mean—you—" Another racking pain prevented her from finishing the rest of her sentence, and she bit down on her bottom lip as she waited for it to abate.

Vince said, "She told Evan that your marriage had been annulled and that you were moving here to Carson City."

She panted in an attempt to regain her breath enough to speak. "That's right. I'll be starting a job this fall. Teaching art—at a private school." Shaking her head, she looked at him and silently prayed he'd understand. "Vince, I had no idea you lived in this town. I didn't come here with plans to intrude on your life. I hope you'll believe that— because it's true."

Frowning, he smoothed her hair back from her forehead. The gentle touch of his hand was everything she needed at this moment.

"Hush, Geena. None of that is important now. The baby is coming. That's all that matters."

As if on cue, a pair of nurses entered the room. Vince was forced to move out of the way while they took Geena's vitals and made sure she was as comfortable as possible. Once they left the room, he moved back to the bedside and took her hand. The caring gesture brought stinging tears to the backs of Geena's eyes.

"How much longer do they think it will be before the baby arrives?" he asked.

She tried to smile, but another giant pain was gathering in the middle of her back and radiating like a crushing band to the front of her belly. "The doctor says I'm progressing quickly—especially for a first baby. From what the nurses told me, I'll be moved to the delivery room pretty soon."

His hand was still in her hair, and she had the crazy urge to turn her head and press her lips to his palm. What would he think? That the labor pains were making her delirious? Oh, God, she couldn't let him know that she'd never quit loving him. She'd already caused the man enough misery in his life to put him through more.

"That's good," he said, then gave her a gentle smile that lit his brown eyes. "I don't know about you, but I'm pretty excited to see him or her."

"I'm pretty excited, too," she said, then, biting back a groan, she turned her face away. "I guess Megan explained about the father."

"Only that the marriage was annulled."

She swallowed hard. "It only lasted a month. When I unexpectedly turned up pregnant, he got cold feet and decided he didn't want any part of me or the baby. An annulment was granted on grounds of desertion."

"You mean he just took off and never came back?"

The incredulous tone of his voice had her turning to look at him. "That's right. But not before I made sure he signed away all his parental rights to the child."

His expression grim, he straightened to his full height, then stared at a spot on the opposite side of the room. "I'm sorry, Geena. Sorry things didn't work out for you."

"I'm not. Brad was a jerk. I misjudged him badly, and marrying him was a mistake. But I'm not sorry about the baby. I'll never be sorry for having my child."

He turned back to her, and she was surprised to see

his features had suddenly softened. "I'm glad to hear you say that."

"Vince, I—" Her jaw clamped tight as she fought back another wave of excruciating pain. "I remember everything about us—our marriage. And I remember why you ended it. That's the thing I'm truly sorry about."

Bending over her once again, he touched a hand to her cheek. "Don't think about any of that, Geena. It's over and done with. You're a different person now and you're starting a new life with a new baby."

Yes, she thought, a new life with a new baby. That had to be enough.

A half hour later, Vince was wondering if he was crazy or the biggest coward that ever walked the earth. When the nurses had finally wheeled Geena into the delivery room, he'd willingly gone along, believing that she needed his support and believing that seeing a child enter the world wouldn't be that difficult. After all, he was a strong man. And being a detective, he'd dealt with all sorts of horrific sights, many of which he would carry in his mind for the rest of his life.

But seeing the agony twisting Geena's slight body, hearing the suffering in her groans was almost too much for him to bear. He wanted to run from the room and away from the torturous sight. Still, Geena had once been his wife and the woman he'd loved. That fact was enough to keep his feet planted to the floor and his hand wrapped tightly around hers.

"You're doing great, Geena. The baby is almost here. Give me one more big push."

The doctor's instructions prompted Vince to glance down just in time to see the baby's head emerging. The sight left him light-headed, and for a moment he thought he was going to hit the floor in a dead faint.

Swallowing hard, he drew in several bracing breaths and fixed his gaze on Geena's face. Sweat drenched her forehead and upper lip while dark pink color stained her cheeks and throat.

Gripping her hand, he urged in a hoarse voice, "Hold on, Geena. It's nearly over."

Vince had barely finished speaking the words when the baby slipped into the doctor's waiting hands. A huge breath rushed out of Geena and her head fell limply back on the pillow.

"It's a girl," the doctor announced.

The infant made a small mewing noise that quickly turned into a loud, healthy cry.

"Sounds like she has a strong set of lungs," one of the attending nurses spoke up.

"But not much hair," another nurse joked.

The doctor gently placed the baby on Geena's chest and she lifted her hand to cradle the tiny head against her breast.

"A girl," she murmured weakly. "My girl."

It took Vince a moment to realize the stinging at the backs of his eyes was tears. Blinking back the foolish display of emotion, he touched fingertips to the baby's back, then bent and placed a kiss in the middle of Geena's forehead.

"Congratulations," he whispered. "You have a daughter."

The midmorning sun was streaming through the window of the hospital room, bathing Geena and the baby in warm, golden light. Several hours had passed since she'd given birth to her daughter, yet the wondrous glow of being a mother was still putting a wide smile on her face.

"Up to some company?"

The question had her glancing around to see Marcella's face peeping around the edge of the door.

"I'd love some. Come in!"

The nurse, wearing hunter green scrubs and her hair in a single long braid, hurried over to the bed. "I'm on break so I only have a few minutes. I always check the nursery, so when I saw your name I knew the little one had arrived. How does it feel to be a mommy?"

Geena laughed softly as she cuddled the nursing baby closer to her breast. "I feel like I'm dreaming." She motioned for Marcella to come closer. "Look at her. She's beautiful. Of course."

"Of course," Marcella said with a knowing grin. She leaned close enough to inspect the baby's face. "I wouldn't expect her to be anything but beautiful. And she definitely is."

"What little hair she has is light like mine," Geena said. "Do you think it will stay that way?"

Marcella touched her finger to the girl's fine golden hair. "She's going to be a knockout no matter what color her hair turns out to be. She looks like you, Geena. You must be in heaven."

"I never dreamed it was possible to instantly fall in love, but it happened the moment the doctor laid her in my arms."

"Looks like you both came out of the delivery just fine. Was the labor tough?"

"It wasn't easy. Thankfully, Vince stayed with me the whole time so I didn't have to go through it alone."

Straightening away from the bed, Marcella slanted her a curious look. "The detective must be one in a million. I suppose having a past husband with you is better than giving birth alone. It's just too bad your present husband couldn't have been located in time for your daughter's arrival."

By now the baby had fallen asleep. Geena straightened her gown, then shifted the weight of the baby to a more comfortable position. "That isn't going to happen," she said flatly. "I don't have a husband."

"You sound pretty certain of that. Has—"

"My amnesia is gone," Geena interrupted, then quickly went on to explain how her memory had suddenly returned and she'd been faced with the reality of her present circumstances. "Silly of me, wasn't it? To believe I had a family somewhere that was looking for me."

"Geena," the nurse gently scolded. "There's nothing silly about wanting to feel connected—of wanting to belong to someone."

"Well, even before I remembered everything, logic was beginning to tell me that I was a single mom-to-be."

"So how did Vince react when you told him?"

She shrugged and tried not to think about how embarrassed she'd felt when she'd had to face him with the truth of the past.

"Incredibly, a call had come through to the sheriff's office last night from one of my friends back in Oregon. Vince learned the details about my life about the same time my memory returned, so it didn't surprise him."

"That's not what I was talking about," Marcella said with a shake of her head. "How did he react to you being single?"

A sigh of resignation slipped out of her. "He felt sorry for me. That's all. I didn't want his sympathy. But he's been kind about everything and that's more than I would've expected him to be."

Marcella smiled cleverly. "Kind. That's a mild way of putting it."

Geena frowned. "What do you mean by that?"

"Nothing." She glanced at her watch. "Oh! I've been here longer than I thought. I've got to get back to work. But before I go, what have you named your new daughter?"

Geena's gaze fell lovingly to the baby in her arms. "I haven't decided yet. I'm still trying to decide what suits her."

Grinning, Marcella waggled her fingers and started toward the door. "I'll check back in this evening. Maybe you'll have a name by then."

The nurse had barely disappeared through the door when it opened again. Geena's heart thumped with reckless joy as Vince stepped into the room carrying a bottle green vase filled with pale pink roses.

Smiling, she said, "I thought you were Marcella coming back."

"I practically bumped into her. She appeared to be in a rush."

"She was in a hurry to get back to work."

As he walked over to the bed, Geena noticed he'd changed out of the clothing he'd been wearing last night when she'd suddenly gone into labor. A pair of Levi's covered his long muscled legs while a burgundy-colored shirt was tucked in at his lean waist. The man was just as fit now, she thought, as he'd been when they'd married eleven years ago.

"Is she working this floor today?" he inquired.

"No. She came by to see the baby."

He placed the roses on the metal nightstand near the head of her bed. "She's become quite a friend to you."

"Yes. And I'm very grateful. For all she knew, I could've been an unscrupulous person. But she trusted me enough to be my friend. She's a special woman." She looked at the huge bouquet. The roses were the second bunch of flowers he'd given her since she'd arrived in Carson City, and though she would've liked to place some romantic importance on that fact, she didn't. Vince was simply a thoughtful guy who wanted to show her a measure of kindness. "The roses are gorgeous, Vince. Thank you."

Smiling faintly, he shrugged. "A woman deserves flowers after she gives birth."

Flowers from the father, at least, she thought bitterly. But that would never happen. Clearing her throat, she said, "I hope you got some rest after you left the hospital this morning."

"I slept a few hours. I'm fine. Evan is holding down the fort at the office. I'm heading to work as soon as I leave here."

So that meant his visit would be short. She shouldn't have felt disappointed at the news, but she did. Throughout their marriage, Vince's job had come first with him. She'd always been second.

You're being stupid, Geena. Sure, you just gave birth to a beautiful little girl. But Vince isn't the father. This isn't a special event for him. Besides, clinging and whining were the reasons you lost the man in the first place. Do you want to fall back to being that pitiful person again?

The accusing voice in her head made her even more determined to show Vince she was a different woman than the one who'd been his wife.

Giving him her brightest smile, she said, "I'm glad you stopped by. Would you like to hold the baby?"

Vince's gaze dropped from Geena's sweet smile to the pink bundle resting in the crook of her arm. Shortly after the doctor had cut the umbilical cord and the nurses had dried and wrapped the baby, he'd been allowed to hold her.

For as long as he lived, he'd never forget those few precious moments with the warm weight of the baby cradled against his chest. All at once, he'd felt like a mountain of a man, capable of slaying dragons for the tiny girl in his arms. Yet at the same time he'd felt incredibly humble. He still didn't know what any of it meant.

"Sure. If you think it would be okay."

She chuckled. "Why wouldn't it be okay? You're not going to drop her."

"Not on your life. But I might wake her and start her crying."

"I doubt that. Her tummy is full."

Vince reached for the baby, and Geena carefully eased her over to him. With a hand carefully cradling the back of her head, he positioned the girl snugly in the crook of his left arm, then eased down in a plastic chair angled close to the bedside.

"Aw. She's even prettier now." He tucked the thin pink blanket beneath the baby's dimpled chin. "She doesn't look nearly as red as when she was first born."

"Marcella says she looks like me."

"The nurse is right. I can see the resemblance, too."

Geena rolled onto her side so that she was facing Vince and the baby. "I guess that's a good thing. Not because I'm pretty or anything. But after the way things turned out with Brad, well—you understand."

Just the mention of the unknown man stuck in Vince's craw. Not because he was jealous, he argued with himself. But because the man was a worthless jerk who'd taken advantage of Geena's soft heart.

"You're not sad, are you? That he's not around?"

She let out a long sigh, and his gaze left the baby to look at her solemn face.

"The only thing that makes me sad is the fact that Emma's biological father didn't want her."

"She doesn't need a man like him in her life," Vince said gruffly.

A wash of pale pink crossed her cheeks. "You're so right. But she's going to need a father. Every little girl deserves to have a father. At least for part of their life."

For reasons he didn't quite understand, Geena's remarks left him feeling hopelessly empty. "I'm sure you'll eventually find a man who will be a wonderful father to your daughter."

A vague smile tilted her lips, and suddenly Vince was remembering the night he'd kissed her, when she hadn't yet remembered him or their failed marriage. Her mouth had been warm and eager and giving, and for those few moments he'd had her in his arms, he'd forgotten all the tears she'd spilled while being his wife.

"Maybe. But after two strikes at marriage, I honestly don't know if I can find the courage to try for a third time."

Not liking the uncomfortable feeling coming over him, Vince rose from the chair and walked over to a window with a wide view of the west side of the city. In the far distance, he could see the jagged outline of the mountains surrounding Lake Tahoe. While he and Geena had been married, he'd often promised to take her to one of the ski resorts for a Christmas gift. But his job had never allowed him enough money or time to make good on his promise. It was no wonder that Geena had finally given up on him, Vince thought crossly. Over the five years of their marriage, he'd continually disappointed her with canceled plans and endless excuses.

"It's a scorcher today," he said, changing the subject completely. "All the ranchers are praying this winter will bring tons of snow. Before you know it this little girl will be big enough to build a snowman."

Geena chuckled. "At the moment I'm still trying to decide on a name for her."

Vince returned to Geena's bedside but continued to keep the infant gathered close to his chest. He'd never imagined that holding a baby would make him feel so protective, even possessive.

"Guess naming her after your mother is probably out of the question," he stated.

Grimacing, she said, "After Dad died, finding a rich husband became more important to her than maintaining a relationship with her daughter. She doesn't keep in touch, and frankly, I prefer it that way."

"Well, the woman did give you a lesson on things you shouldn't do as a mother."

A faint smile crossed her face. "I expect I'll make mistakes raising my daughter, but I'm going to try my best to be a good mother. Hopefully I'll be better at being a mom than I was a wife to you."

Groaning, Vince moved away from the bed and ambled back to the window. "Geena, we both made mistakes. And we made each other miserable. That's why we're better off as we are now—as friends."

Several seconds of awkward silence passed before she finally said, "Friends. I suppose that's more than most exes can be."

Friends? Who the hell are you kidding, Vince? Each time you look at Geena all you can think about is making love to her. That's hardly a friendly connection to your ex.

Shutting his ears to the mocking voice in his head, he walked back over to Geena's bedside. "That's right. So let's forget and move on. We were discussing your daughter's name. Do you have any more ideas?"

"Well, I was particularly close to my paternal grandmother before she passed on. I'm thinking I'd like to name the baby after her."

Vince looked down at the infant's sleeping face, and his heart swelled with bittersweet emotions. "Emma Pearl. It suits her," he said huskily.

"You remembered?"

The softly spoken question lifted his gaze to Geena. A look of vague surprise parted her lips, and it was all he could do to keep from bending his head and kissing her.

"I remember your grandmother."

Along with everything else about their life together, he thought sadly. The love and laughter. And especially the tears.

Chapter Seven

The next afternoon the sky was crystal blue and the breeze little more than a warm whisper as Vince drove Geena and baby Emma home from the hospital. But the perfect weather was hardly on his mind. Since Emma had been born and Geena's memory had returned, his thoughts and emotions had been in a perpetual tug-of-war.

There would be no husband coming to claim Geena. There would be no father to welcome his new daughter home. So that only left Vince to see to their needs.

This morning at the office, Evan had kindly pointed out that Geena and the child were not Vince's responsibility. That it wasn't his place to give them a temporary home. But Vince couldn't be that callous or indifferent. Geena had just given birth. She wasn't yet up to physically going out to search for an apartment.

Yeah, Vince, keep on making excuses. Why can't you simply admit that you've already fallen in love with little

*Emma? Why can't you admit that where Geena is con-
cerned you're just as big a sucker as you were the day
you married her?*

Trying to ignore the censuring voice in his head, Vince
steered the truck onto his driveway and killed the engine.
Across from him, Geena looked around in dismay. "I can't
believe only two nights ago you were rushing me to the
hospital. It feels more like a whole week."

"A lot has happened since then. You've gained a baby
and your memory," Vince told her.

"And thank God for both," she replied.

"I couldn't agree more." He left the vehicle and went
around to the passenger door to help Geena to the ground.
Once she was standing next to the truck, he opened the
back door and unbuckled the infant from a safety seat.

"It was very nice of Evan to let us borrow the car carrier," Geena said. "As soon as I'm able to go shopping, I'll
get one and you can return this one to him."

"Evan said for us—er, for you to keep the car seat,"
Vince told her. "Their daughter, Joanna, has already grown
out of this one."

"That's very generous. I'll be sure and send him and
his wife a thank-you card." Geena stepped up beside him
and peered around his sleeve at the baby. "Would you
mind carrying Emma into the house? I'm still moving a
little stiffly."

"Are you sure? This is your special time. I wouldn't
want to take it away from you. If you like, I can keep a
steadying arm at the back of your waist while you carry
the baby."

She smiled. "No. I'd rather you do it. I'll have plenty
more special times with my daughter."

And he wouldn't.

The unspoken words sliced him deep, but they were a

fact he couldn't deny. And the sooner he faced the reality of the future, the sooner he could get back to being a detective instead of a stand-in daddy.

His throat tight, he didn't say anything. Instead, he carefully extricated the baby from the car seat and positioned her safely against his chest.

Once the three of them were inside the house, he said, "I'll take Emma to your bedroom. Or would you rather sit here in the living room and hold her?"

"Since she's asleep, let's put her on the bed. Thank goodness it will take some time before she starts rolling. As soon as I get an apartment, I'll buy a crib for her. There's no sense in putting one up here. I'd have to take it down in a few days when I move."

A few days. So she was already making plans to move out soon. Well, that was only natural, he told himself. She had her own life to lead. And it didn't include hanging out with an ex-husband.

Geena followed him down the hallway and into the bedroom she'd been using since her accident. As soon as she spotted the bassinet with its white lace skirting, she let out a loud gasp and rushed over to the mobile baby bed.

"A bassinet!" she exclaimed. "Vince, where did this come from?"

With the baby still cradled in his arms, he walked over to where she was sliding her hand over the arched hood covering one end of the bed.

"I bought it this morning," he confessed. "I figured little Emma would need a bed that was more her size."

"Oh, Vince, it's just beautiful! It's fit for a princess! Thank you. Thank you so much!"

"You're making too big of a fuss about a little baby bed."

She looked up at him, and Vince couldn't ignore the

tears in her green eyes. The sight of them tore at his scarred heart.

"You don't understand, Vince. She'll never get anything from her father. Not even simple basic needs like blankets, clothing or diapers." She used her hand to dash away the tears rolling down her cheeks. "I realize you aren't her father, but that doesn't matter. When Emma gets old enough to understand, I'll explain how you thought of her."

Not trusting his voice, he took his time placing Emma in the bassinet and covering her with a lacy pink blanket. After touching a fingertip to her soft cheek, he straightened to his full height and cleared his throat.

"I'll go get the rest of your things from the truck before I head back to work," he said thickly.

"Vince, wait."

She caught his arm and he was forced to meet her searching gaze.

"I don't know why you're being so kind to me and Emma. You and I haven't seen or spoken to each other in six years. But whatever the reason, I'm grateful to you."

He didn't want her gratitude. He wanted her love.

Like hell! He didn't want her love, he quickly scolded himself. No more than he wanted her body. Everything he'd done so far was for the baby and no other reason.

"I like to think I'm a decent kind of guy, Geena."

"You are decent and fine. And I—" Her words trailed away as her hand slid slowly up his arm and then suddenly she was stepping forward and resting her cheek against his chest. "Oh, Vince, forgive me. Having a baby—I didn't expect it to make me feel this emotional. A few minutes ago, when we walked into the house together with Emma—I was filled with regret."

Confused, he tilted her chin up so that he could look

into her face. "Regret? What are you talking about? You adore your new daughter."

She gave him a wobbly smile. "I love Emma so much my heart is nearly bursting with it. I just regret that we... didn't have a child while we were married."

She couldn't know how much he'd been thinking that very thing. Ever since he'd recognized she was pregnant on the night of her accident, he'd been reminded of their hopes and plans to have a family. Hearing her admit she was having the same sort of feelings was bittersweet for Vince.

"Geena, you weren't ready for a child then," he said huskily. "And neither was I."

Dark shadows flickered in her eyes, and then with a heavy sigh, she turned away from him. "Forgive me, Vince. In a few days I'll be over this silly, sentimental stuff. I promise."

He probably should have made some sort of effort to comfort her, to reassure her that he understood the emotional upheaval she was going through. But he couldn't bring himself to utter a word. And he certainly couldn't allow himself to wrap his arms around her. If he did, he was afraid he might never let her go.

Without a backward glance, he squared his shoulders with resolve and walked out of the bedroom.

Over the next several days Vince's workload grew so heavy he didn't have to worry about spending too much time with Geena and the baby. A few words exchanged at the breakfast table and some quick glances at sleeping Emma were all he'd managed to fit into his busy schedule. Which only gave Vince further proof that he had no business entertaining the idea that he could ever be a husband or father.

So how did Evan do it? The man spent just as many

hours as Vince on the job, yet he managed to have a happy marriage with Noelle.

But Noelle was different, Vince reasoned. She was a very strong woman with interests and a job of her own. She didn't need Evan around to hold her hand and remind her she was loved. Geena was fragile. She'd not been able to deal with the demands of his job six years ago. He'd be a chump to believe she could handle it now.

Geena has become a different woman. Since you divorced her, she's been taking care of herself. She's finished her college education and become a teacher. She's a mother now, and she's not crying or whining for help. In fact, she's planning on moving into her own place soon. You're a fool, all right. A fool for thinking she needs you.

"Where would a person hide a high-profile stallion? It's a cinch he can't be taken to a sale barn." Evan spoke as the two men paused their search next to an empty horse stall. "He can't even be used for stud services. Most any rancher in this area would recognize the horse. The only scenario I can think of is that someone wanted the horse to breed a band of mares without paying the exorbitant fees. So they've hidden the stallion in the mountains somewhere with plans to use him. Sound logical?"

Thankfully, Evan's question was enough to push the tormenting voice from Vince's head, and he looked thoughtfully over at his partner. During the past week the two men had devoted most of their waking hours to the theft of the horse, but so far the stallion hadn't been located or the thieves apprehended.

"It's logical, but I'd rather think the bandits have plans to ship the animal to Mexico, where it would be practically impossible to find. There are plenty of barren stretches in Arizona or Texas where the horse could've been led or ridden across the border," Vince said as he rested a shoulder against the wooden gate of the stall. "That is, if they managed to miss all the livestock checks between here and there."

This was the third visit he and Evan had made to the Rinehart ranch in as just as many days. So far none of the trips had turned up new clues, but both men were convinced if they continued to look, something would show up to propel the case forward.

"I hope to hell you're wrong and the horse is still somewhere close." Evan discreetly caught Vince by the sleeve, then spoke close to his ear. "Don't look behind you, but we have an audience at the end of the barn. The young blond-headed wrangler, Skip, and his buddy Ted seem to find us interesting for some reason."

Lowering his voice, Vince replied, "Well, when two detectives keep showing up for three days in a row, it tends to make people nervous. Guilty people, that is. We could confront them with a few more questions, but I think it might be better to let them stew and worry for a while."

"Hmm. Well, it could be they're completely ignorant about the horse's disappearance," Evan remarked.

"Somebody around here sure as heck knows what happened," Vince muttered, then inclined his head toward a side door that led outside to the open ranch yard. "Come on. Let's go. We've done enough here for today."

The two detectives exited the building and climbed into the SUV they'd left parked in the shade of a cottonwood tree near the far end of the barn.

Evan was on the verge of starting the motor when Vince quickly reached over and jerked his hand away from the ignition.

"Wait," Vince ordered. "Let's see where she's going first."

"She?" Evan looked up to see a woman striding purposely across the ranch yard toward the barn the two men had just exited. "That's Rinehart's daughter, Liv. She's probably going riding or something."

"Damn, Evan, your brain must be on vacation. She's wearing a skirt. I don't think she has intentions of going riding."

"Well, she could be planning to change clothes in the barn," he reasoned.

"I seriously doubt it. She's the sort that needs a mirror to change outfits."

Without so much as a glance in their direction, the woman entered the barn at the opposite end of the building and disappeared from the men's view.

"Ready to go now?" Evan asked.

"No. Let's just sit here and see how long she remains in there. I have a feeling Miss Liv is not the little princess old Rinehart paints his daughter to be."

Evan grunted. "She's his only daughter. And from what I gathered when we talked to the old man, he dotes on her. But that's nothing strange. I dote on little Joanna, too."

With baby Emma in the house, Vince was quickly learning how easy it would be to fall under her spell, to have his heart all wrapped up in her blue eyes and dimpled cheeks. But he wasn't going to let himself be wound around her tiny finger. Because her place in his life was only temporary.

"Joanna is still a baby," Vince reasoned. "Liv Rinehart is a grown woman and as spoiled as the jug of milk Geena found in the back of my refrigerator. The old man is blind to her."

"Being spoiled doesn't mean she's a criminal or anything close to it," Evan reasoned, then grinned. "Noelle is always telling me how spoiled I am. And she's right."

"I hope you're right about Liv, too. I've come to like

Mr. Rinehart. It would be a shame for him to learn his daughter has betrayed him."

"Okay, we both agree that someone here on the ranch committed the crime. But I can't see how Liv might fit in. She appears to have everything she wants."

"Maybe she wants more than money," Vince reasoned.

Evan rolled his eyes. "And I want to get the heck out of here. We have all kinds of work waiting on us back at the office."

Vince lowered himself until his head was resting against the back of the seat. "Can you see the front entrance of the barn from where you're sitting?"

"Yes."

"Then keep your eyes on it and let me know when she comes out."

"What are you going to do in the meantime?" Evan asked wryly.

"Sleep. That is, if I haven't forgotten how."

Evan made an amused snort. "Emma's crying keeping you awake at night?"

Vince closed his eyes. "No. Geena is breast-feeding. Emma doesn't have to wait for a bottle to be heated. I guess I've been taking my work home with me. Once I climb in bed I can't turn off my brain."

"Might be you're just not used to having a woman and a baby in the house," Evan commented. "I think Joanna was three months old before I slept through the night. Remember, you said I looked like I had some sort of chronic disease. Well, I did. It's called babyitis."

Evan was wrong, Vince thought ruefully. He was getting far too accustomed to having Geena and the baby filling up the lonely quietness of his house.

"You still have a chronic disease," Vince mumbled. "It's called idiocy."

"Thanks, buddy. Good to learn you haven't lost your sense of humor. I—"

The abrupt halting of Evan's words had Vince glancing over to see his partner shoving a pair of aviator sunglasses onto his nose, then peering through the windshield.

"She's come out of the barn, Vince. And Skip, the blond, is with her."

Vince leaned toward Evan until he could pick up the view of Liv and the wrangler. "Yeah. They look pretty chummy, don't you think?"

"Well, you'd have to do some prying to wedge a piece of paper between them. And the way she's laughing up at him, he seems to be making her happy. But that doesn't mean anything. So what if she's rolling in the hay with the guy? That doesn't spell horse thieves."

"No. It spells partners in crime."

"Oh brother, you need to press the control button on your imagination. It's definitely gone haywire."

"Just be patient, partner. He thinks we've left the premises. Let's see how he reacts when he realizes we're watching him."

Vince had no sooner gotten the words out when Skip suddenly looked in their direction. As soon as he spotted the two detectives sitting in the SUV, he set Liv away from him and took off in long, angry stride.

"Uh-oh," Evan said as they watched the tall cowboy approach their vehicle. "He hardly looks like a happy camper."

"Good. If we can make him lose his cool, we might get this case on a roll."

When the young man reached the SUV, he bent his head and glared through the open window at Evan and Vince.

"What are you two looking at?" he demanded.

"I'd say I'm looking at a jerk," Vince answered calmly.

Evan let out a meaningful groan while the cowboy's face turned as red as the bandanna tied around his neck.

With the sneer on his face deepening, Skip goaded, "Bet you won't come out of that vehicle and say that to me again, big detective."

"You stay here," Vince muttered under his breath to Evan. "I'll handle this."

Evan gave Vince a cheery smile. "I'll be happy to sit and watch."

Vince climbed out of the vehicle and skirted the hood until he was standing directly in front of the wrangler. "I said I was looking at a jerk."

"You two are the jerks," Skip jeered. "Nobody asked you to come around here snooping day after day, trying to cause even more trouble for the Rineharts. The both of you need to get lost and stay lost!"

Vince shot the young man a sardonic smile. "No doubt you and Liv would like to see the last of us. But you're out of luck. You're about to get well acquainted with the Carson City Sheriff's Department."

"What are you talking about?"

"My partner and I have had second thoughts about you. We've decided to haul your ass downtown for further questioning."

"Like hell!"

All of a sudden, the cowboy decided to take a swing at Vince, but he swiftly caught the combative man's wrist in midair and twisted his arm against his back.

"Okay. You can either go with us peaceably or go in cuffs," Vince said roughly. "Either way is fine with me."

At that moment Liv came trotting up, her anxious gaze darting between the two men. "What's going on?" she asked anxiously. "Skip? Are you being arrested?"

Vince looked at the woman. "That depends on what comes out of his mouth."

The young woman started to speak, but at the last moment decided her best course of action would be to flee the scene altogether.

As she hurried off in the direction of the house, Vince said, "Guess she doesn't want to wait around and hear what you have to say."

"She'll tell her daddy about this," Skip warned. "You can bet on that."

Chuckling, Vince opened the back door of the patrol vehicle and nudged the cowboy onto the seat. "That's exactly what I am betting on."

A half hour later, after Vince and Evan had deposited Skip in an interrogation room, they stepped out in the hallway to give the suspect time to cool his heels.

"You've been a detective a lot longer than I have," Evan said to Vince, "but I'm wondering if you're on the right track here. Yeah, Skip is an arrogant punk, but I'd rather think he's got his sights on becoming the old man's son-in-law. He probably figures it would be easier to leech off the family than to steal."

Vince thoughtfully stroked his chin. "You make a good point. But either way, I have a feeling that shaking up Skip might prove fruitful. In any case, we had a right to bring him in. He attempted to assault a law officer."

Evan's grin was full of mischief. "Right. So you begin questioning him and I'll go make us some coffee. This might take a while."

Later that night, Geena was sitting at the kitchen table going through the classified ads in the newspaper when Vince walked tiredly into the room. At a few minutes past nine, it was the earliest he'd come home in the past several nights and the first time she'd actually seen him in the last two days.

She dropped the paper to the tabletop and smiled at him. "Hello, stranger. Another busy day?"

"Always."

He pulled off his jean jacket and tossed it on the back of the chair, then quickly removed his holstered weapon and placed it in a cabinet drawer. As he moved around the kitchen, Geena couldn't help but notice the weary slump of his shoulders and the dark crescents beneath his eyes.

She knew from experience it would do no good to tell him he needed to rest or slack off at work. At the age of fourteen, after losing his father to a criminal's bullet, Vince had been driven to become a lawman, to work his way up to being a detective. Along the way his mother had forsaken him and his wife had crumbled beneath the strain of his job. But none of that had deterred him from the purpose he'd given himself. Now Geena could only wonder if he believed the sacrifices had been worth it.

"I left a plate for you on the stove. Just in case you haven't eaten," she said. "Why don't you sit and I'll heat it in the microwave for you."

"I can do it."

She rose from the chair and plucked up the covered plate before he could reach it. "Nonsense," she told him. "I need the exercise. Emma has been so good today I've hardly had to do anything."

"So she's asleep?"

Geena gestured toward the breakfast bar. "She's over there in her bassinet. I rolled it in here so I could keep an eye on her while I cooked."

Spotting the baby bed, he crossed the room to where Emma lay sleeping. Geena watched for a moment as he leaned over the baby, then turned away as her throat grew thick with emotion. Vince was so incredibly gentle and loving with Emma that Geena had no doubt he would be a wonderful father. But the attention he could give a child would be limited by the hours he devoted to the sheriff's department. Perhaps that was the reason he'd never remarried or had a child of his own, she thought sadly. Maybe he'd already decided he couldn't be a detective and have a family, too.

"She already looks like she's grown since we brought her home from the hospital," he said as he returned to the table and took a seat.

"So far she seems as healthy as a horse. She hardly ever spits up and she only fusses when she's wet or hungry. Sometimes I worry that she's too good."

"Hmm. That might change soon enough. I've heard Evan speak of the hell they went through when Joanna started teething."

She set the plate in front of him along with a set of silverware, then crossed to the refrigerator to fill a glass with ice and tea.

After she'd served him the drink, she took the seat kitty-corner to him.

He inclined his head toward the paper. "Looking to buy something in the classifieds?"

She picked up the paper, and after folding it into a small rectangle, placed it out of the way. "Not buy. To rent. When I left Pendleton I'd thought I'd have a few days before the baby arrived to look around for an apartment. I didn't know I was going to be waylaid with amnesia. Before you walked in the kitchen I was going through the listings to see if there was anything I might like or could afford."

"Find anything?"

She was glad he was looking down at his food instead of her. She didn't want him to guess how desperately she was going to miss him once she and the baby moved to a place of their own.

"Actually, there's a house on the northwest side of town that sounds interesting. It has a small fenced-in yard and it's not far from the school where I'll be teaching. And the price is right. The owner has promised to show it to me tomorrow. So I wanted to ask you about driving your truck. I could take a taxi, but I need to go by the mall and pick up a cell phone, too."

"You're welcome to use the truck whenever you want."

She folded her hands on the tabletop. "That's another thing I need to do. Start looking for a car. Thankfully I had complete coverage on the one that burned. The insurance agent said I should be getting the check for it next week."

He looked up. "Are you sure you can afford a new vehicle?"

She supposed it was logical for him to think she'd be short on money. Up until her memory had returned, she'd not possessed a dime. But now that she had access to her bank accounts, she had enough to see to her needs.

"A nice used one will work fine for me. And the insurance refund will cover most of the cost. The rest I can manage." She gave him a reassuring smile. "You know me, Vince—I always did save my money. And I got a nice signing bonus from the school here in Carson City. I have enough to take care of myself and Emma."

His head bent over his plate, but not before she'd spotted the tight, thin line of his lips.

"What's the matter?" she asked. "Don't you believe me?"

"Sure. I believe you." He took a few more bites of food, then looked up at her. "What about Emma? Surely you're not going to drag her out and about while you do all this running around?"

Geena stiffened. Where did he come off questioning her financial situation or her mothering decisions? He gave up that right when he divorced her.

"Actually, Marcella has volunteered to watch her tomorrow while I look at the house and pick up the phone. But I'll soon be taking her on short outings."

"Well, she certainly doesn't need to be out in public, where she could pick up all sorts of germs," he said crossly.

Unable to hide her irritation, she scowled at him. "Do you honestly think I would needlessly put my daughter's health in danger? Emma isn't a preemie! She was born a hefty seven and a half pounds, and the pediatrician pronounced her very healthy. I have enough sense to keep her safely dressed and covered, and I know to keep her away from crowded places. She can't stay in the house forever, Vince, and neither can I, for that matter!"

Her outburst seemed to catch his attention, and he studied her for long moments. "Sorry," he said finally. "What you do with your daughter is none of my business."

He got up from the table and carried his plate over to the sink. Geena shoved a hand through her tumbled hair and wondered why she suddenly felt like an ungrateful heel.

Rising from her chair, she joined him at the sink. "I didn't mean to sound so cross, Vince. It's just that I—with the car burning all my belongings, I'm having to virtually start over. There's so many pieces of business I need to take care of and things I need to get that it's getting to be overwhelming."

He rinsed the plate beneath the faucet, then placed it in a wire drainer. "There's no urgency for you to try to get everything done at once. Seems to me you're in a big hurry to move out of here."

She drew in a bracing breath and blew it out. "I am in a hurry, Vince. I can't keep living here with you."

That brought his head around, and Geena swallowed as his piercing gaze slipped over her face.

"Why? I couldn't be getting on your nerves. I'm not here that much."

Heat flowed into her cheeks, and she didn't need a mirror in front of her to know her face had turned pink. "No. It's not that. You—you've been more than generous letting me have the run of the house."

He moved closer, and Geena was amazed at how six years apart had done nothing to dim the rush of awareness she got whenever he grew near. "Surely you're not worried what people are thinking about you living with your ex-husband."

Her short laugh came out more like a strangled cough. "Not hardly, Vince. Other than Marcella, I haven't made many acquaintances around here yet. It hardly bothers me if your friends have wagging tongues."

"Then what's your hurry? Emma isn't quite two weeks old yet. You need to give yourself time before you take on a move."

"I don't have time. School starts in a little over two weeks' time. It would be much easier for me to move now than after I start work."

"You can drive to work from this house as easily as you can another," he pointed out.

He didn't understand. But then, how could she expect him to? He'd gotten over her years ago. Being near her didn't make him all shaky and weak the way it did whenever she got within ten feet of him. He didn't ache with longing to touch her, kiss her. He didn't wish he could go back and erase their divorce.

Suddenly she wanted to touch him so badly that she linked her hands together and squeezed so tightly the tips of her fingers turned red. "Yes, I could. But—oh, Vince, do I have to spell it out to you? I can't—well, being around you like this isn't a good thing."

"Why?"

The fact that he was so blind to her feelings caused desperate frustration to take hold of her. "Why? Because every time you walk into the house I want to do this!"

Before he could guess her intentions, she wrapped her arms around his neck and planted her lips on his.

For a brief second, her action must have stunned him. He stood motionless, his lips a stiff line beneath hers. Then just as suddenly his arms were around her, crushing her against his chest. His lips opened to begin a wild, hungry search of her mouth.

The feel of his hard body next to hers, the subtle male scent of his skin and the taste of his lips rapidly filled her senses until she was floundering to stay afloat, to remind herself to keep breathing.

Behind her closed eyes, her head was spinning, while the rest of her body was on fire with the need to get closer to the pleasure only he could give her.

Somehow the kiss grew from a hungry search to raging hot passion, and before Geena knew what was happening, her back was pressed against the counter and Vince's hands were cupped around her breasts.

The tight ache building deep within her caused her body to instinctively arch into his. The shift brought her hips in perfect alignment with his and suddenly his hard arousal was pressing against her, telling her exactly how much he wanted her.

The sensation was so heady it was almost painful, making the tiny moan in her throat turn into a deep, urgent groan. Her arms slipped from his neck to wrap tightly around his waist and draw him even closer.

One second his tongue was inside her mouth, tasting

and tempting, his hands cupping her rounded bottom. And then a few seconds later, he was stepping away, drawing in ragged breaths and staring at her as though he'd been kissing a stranger.

"Geena! I—"

The remainder of his words never came as he suddenly turned on his heel and hurried out of the room.

Pressing a hand over her hot lips, she stared at his retreating back. Had she lost her mind? She'd grabbed and kissed him like some sort of wanton hussy inviting him to make love to her! Now she'd probably ruined their tenuous friendship!

But she couldn't worry about that now. Vince was more than a friend. More than an ex-husband. He was the man she'd never stopped loving. Maybe it was time she quit trying to hide that fact from him and herself.

Chapter Eight

"May I come in?"

Vince paused in the process of unbuttoning his shirt and turned to see Geena standing in the open doorway to his bedroom. The sight of her shapely figure silhouetted against the dim light in the hallway caused his gut to clench with longing, his lips ache to kiss hers all over again.

"Would it stop you if I said no?" he asked gruffly, then shook his head. "Come in. We might as well clear the air right now."

She quickly crossed the few steps between them, and Vince had the ridiculous urge to jerk the front of his shirt back together. As though covering his naked chest could hide the desire that was still flooding his body with heat.

"Vince, I want to explain."

Grunting, he jerked off the shirt and tossed it on the bed. "Can you?" He tugged on a T-shirt, then glanced at her. "Because I sure as hell can't. Other than the fact that we both just behaved like a couple of fools."

She blew out a long breath and raked her tangled hair back from her face. Vince told himself to look across the room, anywhere but at her smoky green eyes and tempting soft lips. But his eyes refused to give up the pleasure.

After six long years, how could kissing her, holding her, still feel as familiar as breathing, he wondered. Why couldn't he look at her and forget how incredible it had been to make love to her?

"Apparently I've made you angry. I'm sorry about that. But if you think I'm going to apologize for kissing you, I'm not."

Her husky voice was like fingertips brushing over his skin. "I don't want an apology for the kiss—or anything else! I just want to be...left alone."

"Really? Five minutes ago it didn't feel like you wanted to be alone."

He certainly couldn't argue that point. After the way he'd behaved, she was probably thinking he was sex starved or desperately hungry for her. Either image painted him guilty.

"Geena, I don't know what you expect me to say. I—"

Suddenly she moved close enough to wrap her hand around his forearm, and the touch of her fingers made Vince want to groan out loud. Even worse, it made him want to slip his arms around her slender waist and draw her against him.

She licked her lips. "I don't want you to say anything, Vince. I came in here to finish explaining what I was trying to tell you before I—well, before that kiss happened. I'm still very attracted to you. And it's pretty clear you don't want to be that close to me. That's why I have to move out. As soon as possible."

He understood what she was saying. He even agreed with her. Yet there was something deep within him that was reluctant to give in to the inevitable. Maybe because giving her up the first time had proved to be the most painful thing he'd ever gone through.

"Are you blind, Geena? A few minutes ago, I could've easily carried you in here to my bed and made love to you. That's how close I'd like to be to you! But we both know that sex wasn't enough to fix the problems of our marriage six years ago. And it won't fix anything now."

Turning her back to him, she bent her head and let out a woeful sigh. "I'm not trying to *fix* anything, Vince. I'll admit my memory went haywire for a few days after the accident. But it's working perfectly now. And I've not forgotten that you divorced me. I clearly remember you were the one who wanted our marriage to end. So I hardly expect you to forgive me. Much less want me."

Frustration hijacked his common sense, and before he could stop himself, he snatched her body next to his and buried his face in the side of her neck.

"You don't know anything about what I want!" he said, his voice muffled by her soft skin. "Do you think I've forgotten how it feels to make love to you? Do you think I don't remember how it was when we were together? Like this?"

He didn't give her time to answer. The need to taste her lips was far greater than hearing any words she might have said. Instead, he caught her lips beneath his, and she instantly responded by welcoming the thrust of his tongue and wrapping her arms in a tight circle around his waist.

Years of loneliness and regret suddenly pushed everything from his mind. Having Geena back in his arms and in his bed was all that mattered. Making love to her was the only way he could ease the awful, empty aching inside him.

Without breaking the contact of their lips, he lowered

them over and onto the side of the mattress. Lying face-to-face, he continued to feast on her mouth while his hands began a wild, urgent foray of her body. The soft curves of her breasts and hips, the smooth heat of her skin felt like heaven beneath his fingers. But he wanted more, and the barrier of her clothing was preventing him from getting it.

He'd unbuttoned her shirt and was about to push the fabric off her shoulder, when she suddenly tore her mouth from his and jumped off the bed.

"I—I'm sorry, Vince," she said in a strained voice. "But I can't let things go any farther."

With the warmth of her body more than an arm's length away, cool sanity managed to rush to Vince's brain and he sat up and watched in stunned silence as she hastily buttoned her shirt back over her breasts.

"Well, at least one of us has come to our senses," he said with bitter resignation.

Her cheeks were pink, her expression full of regret as she glanced at him. "You don't understand, Vince. I didn't have a change of heart about wanting you, if that's what you're thinking. I had to stop because my body is still recovering from childbirth. It's not ready for intimate relations. It will be soon, but not yet."

Vince felt worse than an idiot. "I should've already known you weren't physically ready for sex," he muttered. "And I damned sure shouldn't have been asking you for it."

Wiping a hand over her face, she turned her back to him, and he could see she was still trying to gather her composure. The idea that their embrace had affected her as much as it had him shook Vince even more.

"This is all my fault," she said tightly. "I started something I couldn't finish. Sort of like our marriage."

The sour note in her voice bothered him far more than it should have. It was one thing for him to be bitter and accusing, but Geena had never been a caustic person. In fact, she'd almost been too accepting of his faults, and quick to blame herself for not being able to deal with his job.

"Let's not talk about our marriage."

She turned to face him. "That's over and done with. The only thing I want you to know now is that I'm not the same Geena I was back then. I might look the same and my kiss might taste the same, but I'm different in here." She tapped a finger against her chest. "I'm grown up, Vince. I'm strong enough to stand on my own—to take care of myself and my child. And I'm not about to let anyone or anything cause me to crumble again."

She didn't give him time to fully digest her words, much less make a reply. She hurried out of the bedroom and carefully shut the door behind her.

The next afternoon, Geena made a hurried inspection of the rental house, then stopped by the cell phone carrier to replace the one that had burned in the wreck. When she finally finished her chores and returned to Vince's house, she found Marcella on the back patio in a wooden rocker with Emma sound asleep in her arms.

"Oh, you're back so soon!" Marcella exclaimed the moment Geena stepped onto the shaded patio. "Just when Emma and I have been having such fun!"

Geena sank into a lawn chair angled to the rocker. "Has she been a good girl? I tried to get everything done as quickly as I could."

Smiling, Marcella gently rubbed the baby's back. "She's been wonderful. You wouldn't consider letting me take her home with me, would you?"

Geena chuckled. "Sorry. I think I'd miss her too much."

Marcella sighed. "I'm not going to give up on having

a little girl of my own someday. I still have a few fertile years left."

Chuckling again, Geena said, "I'd say you have plenty of fertile years left. All you need to do is find a good man."

"Finding a man is easy. Finding a good one is nearly impossible," she joked, then glanced over at Geena. "So tell me about the house."

"I've already signed the lease."

Surprised, Marcella asked, "Already? It's the first place you looked at!"

Geena shrugged. "It was just the type of place I had in mind, so I didn't see any need to look farther. It's nice and cozy with a cute backyard, and with school about six blocks away, it will take me only a few minutes to zip to work from there. Plus the rent fit my budget."

"Well, sounds nice," Marcella replied. "So when are you planning to move? I'll try to get a day off work to help you."

Geena shook her head. "No. I couldn't ask you to do that. You've already done so much for me."

"That's what friends are for. Besides, once you get settled I might ask you to watch the boys for me from time to time. That is, if you can bear putting up with two rowdies."

Geena smiled. "I'm a teacher, Marcella. I'm used to rowdies. I'd love to keep the boys."

"School starts in less than three weeks. Have you started thinking about child care for Emma?"

Sighing, Geena leaned back in the lawn chair. "It's something I don't want to think about. I'm not sure I can go to work and leave her. But unfortunately, I'm going to have to force myself. Since I've just now become employed by this school I'm not eligible for maternity leave. And I can't afford to take off any unpaid days."

Marcella reached over and gave her arm a reassuring

pat. "You're not alone, Geena. It's just a part of being a working mother. Once you find a babysitter you really trust, you'll feel better about it."

"I had hopes you might be able to help me in that department. I have no idea where to start looking for a dependable babysitter."

A clever smile crossed Marcella's face. "I know someone who'd be perfect for baby Emma. Annie lives two doors down from me and I've known her for years. She's a widow in her fifties. Sweet and gentle and knows all about babies. She should—she's raised four of her own."

"So how many children does she care for?"

"Usually just one or two. And she's very picky about the families she allows into her home," Marcella answered. "At the moment she doesn't have any kids. She was keeping a boy, a toddler, but the family moved away. Broke her heart. She'd become pretty attached to the little guy. Would you like to meet her?"

"She sounds like just the sort of person I'm looking for," Geena agreed.

"Great," Marcella said happily. "I'll call her tonight and set up a meeting."

Geena looked around Vince's backyard. Since she'd been living here, she'd grown accustomed to sitting on the patio and watching the birds flit around the branches of a piñon tree and squirrels race around the top of the privacy fence and up the fat trunk of a hackberry tree. A charcoal cooker was pushed along one side of the house and a wooden picnic table sat in the flimsy shade of a honey locust.

The large yard was a relaxing piece of outdoors, a space perfectly made for a family. In fact, she could easily picture a swing set sitting in one corner with a sand pile nearby. She could imagine a dog with long hair, floppy ears and a happy yip chasing a tennis ball and a pair of squealing kids.

"You have something else on your mind."

Yes, Geena thought, she had an impossible fairy tale on her mind. But she didn't want to admit to her friend, or even herself, that she'd never quit dreaming of a life with Vince.

A hopeless sigh escaped her. "I've been thinking how ironic it is that I ended up here in Vince's home. I never expected to see him again in my lifetime."

One of Marcella's brows lifted with speculation. "You mean you really didn't plan to come here because of him?"

Geena shook her head. "I realize it looks that way," she said ruefully. "But I honestly didn't know Vince was living in Carson City. After my marriage to Brad was dissolved, I felt a little lost and homesick. I decided to come back to Nevada, start over and put the mistake behind me. But I didn't want to settle in Reno. Not with all the memories of Vince and our marriage there. So I decided Carson City would be nice. Especially with it being close to Lake Tahoe."

"It would have been easy to search Vince's name before you made the decision to move here," Marcella gently pointed out.

Geena stared down at her lap. "Easy, yes. But too painful. It was better for my peace of mind not to know where he lived or what he was doing. But in this case, I guess I should've made that search. Then I could've changed my plans and moved to Ely or Las Vegas—anywhere but Carson City."

She looked up to see Marcella's head swinging back and forth.

"Things happen for a reason, Geena," she said. "You were meant to see Vince again. And I'm just wondering if moving out of this house and getting away from the man is really going to make you happy."

A tiny pain stabbed Geena in the chest, then quickly filled her heart with a heavy ache. "I have to move on, Marcella. It's not healthy to be in a place where you're unwanted," she said glumly. "No matter how much you like it there."

"Hmm. I didn't see anyone twisting Vince's arm when I spotted him going into your hospital room with a bouquet of roses."

The pain in her chest grew worse. "Vince is a decent guy and he does the decent thing when he's needed."

"Obviously."

Geena looked at her friend. "Look, Marcella, there's a lot you don't know. Vince is the one who divorced me. I couldn't deal with seeing my husband for just a few hours every week. And he loved his job too much to change."

"Did you ask him to quit?"

Closing her eyes, Geena pinched the bridge of her nose. "Not outright. But I suppose I asked him in a thousand other ways. Finally, I got so miserable I began drinking wine in the evenings to numb myself. After a while I became more dependent on it—until I ruined everything good between us."

She opened her eyes and was surprised to see Marcella studying her with empathy rather than disdain.

"Geena, you're obviously not that person now. I'm sure Vince can see that."

"Yes. I've grown up since then, and I learned from my mistakes. I'm not that Geena anymore. But Vince hasn't changed. He's the same detective living out the same long hours on the job. It would never work between us again. At least, he believes it wouldn't."

"Hmm. What do you think?"

Geena sighed. "What I think doesn't matter. He'll never give me a second chance."

* * *

"Remember, Noelle wants this baby shower to be a sur-prise for Geena. So you'll have to act like you're taking her to our place just to have dinner and get acquainted. Think you can handle it?"

Vince forced a bite of cold sandwich down his throat as he glanced over his shoulder to see Evan leaned back in his office chair and his cowboy boots resting on the edge of his desk.

"Evan, you should have told Noelle not to go to all this trouble. I can easily buy everything Emma needs. That is, if Geena will let me," he added dourly.

With an impatient shake of his head, Evan said, "You don't get it, partner. This kind of stuff is important to women. Geena needs to make new friends. She needs to see that people care about her and the baby. Besides, No-elle is thrilled about this party—she's been planning it ever since Emma was born. I know you don't want to disappoint her. And I'd break your neck if you tried."

Seeing there was no way out, Vince said in the most casual voice he could muster, "Okay, okay. I'll have her there. What time?"

"No later than seven. Tonight—you do remember that, don't you?"

"Tonight! I thought you said it was tomorrow night."

"Hell, Vince, are you in a daze or something? I talked with you about this three days ago!"

Vince's mental condition went far beyond dazed. Ever since he and Geena had ended up on his bed two nights ago, the woman had been like a thick fog, clouding every cell in his brain.

It was still difficult for him to believe how much he'd wanted to make love to her that night. Just thinking about the way her soft body had felt against his was enough to make his toes curl.

Damn it! He didn't know why she'd ever touched him in the first place. To find out for herself if he still had the hots for her body? Well, he'd certainly given her a clear answer to that question.

I'm strong enough to stand on my own—to take care of myself and my child. And I'm not about to let anyone or anything cause me to crumble again.

Geena's words that night were still lurking around to haunt him. Yes, he could see that Geena had changed into a better, stronger person. But that hardly meant the two of them could make a go of marriage again. Dear God, he'd gone through hell trying to deal with her unhappiness. Since then, his job had become even more important to him. He'd become a detective and a damned good one. If his father could see him now, he'd be smiling.

Or would he? Parry Parcell had been a family man. He'd adored his wife and two children. And while he'd been alive, they'd been one happy family. What would his father think of Vince's crumbled marriage? Would he have praised Vince for standing up for himself and his job? Or would he have been disappointed that his son hadn't figured out a way to juggle his job and a wife?

Shaking himself back to the present, he looked over at Evan. "I'm just dealing with a lot of things right now. Geena's planning on moving out soon. She's already rented a house and put down her deposits on the utilities."

"That ought to be making you happy. You can go back to being a bachelor with no one to interfere or answer to."

"Yeah," he said gruffly. "That's just the way I want it, too."

Frowning, Evan gestured to the sandwich lying on Vince's desk. "Finish that damned thing. If we're going out to the Rinehart ranch this afternoon, we've got to get going or we won't be finished by quitting time."

Even though his appetite had disappeared, Vince picked up the sandwich. "I'm beginning to think we're wasting our time. Skip wouldn't break under questioning. Where he and Liv are concerned, I could be barking up the wrong tree."

Evan got up from his desk and began to fill an insulated mug with coffee from the percolator. "From my experience your hunches have always been right. We need to apply more pressure. The more we push, the more likely something will break."

The same scenario was happening to him, he thought, as he tossed the last of his sandwich into a wastebasket. The more Geena talked about moving out, the more he felt as though he was breaking into helpless pieces.

"What we need to do is put pressure on Liv," Vince reasoned. "But that could cause major problems. Stallion or no stallion. If it meant keeping his daughter out of jail, Rinehart wouldn't hesitate to get her lawyered up. We'd have hell getting any information from her then."

"Yeah. Well, just showing up on the ranch will tell her we're not going to close this case or forget it," Evan reasoned, then made a rolling motion with his finger for Vince to get to his feet and get going.

"All right. Let's go."

The two men were on the verge of walking out of the office when a long-legged young deputy with a shock of blond hair appeared in the doorway.

"Are you two going somewhere?" he asked.

"That's right," Vince said. "The Rinehart ranch. Why? What's up?"

"You might not need to make the trip. Liv Rinehart

walked in the building a few minutes ago. Said she needs to talk with you two."

Vince and Evan exchanged smug looks.

"Where is she now?" Evan asked.

"In one of the interrogation rooms. I gave her some coffee and a magazine, but she seems pretty restless."

Vince said, "Thanks, Randy. We'll take over."

Nodding, the deputy left, and Evan immediately began to chuckle and do a jig that had Vince grinning in spite of himself.

"Stop that silly dancing! It's bad luck to celebrate before the egg is laid."

Laughing, Evan crossed the office and slapped a hand on Vince's shoulder. "The egg might not be laid yet, partner, but the hen is about to cackle."

Later that afternoon, Geena was shocked when Vince showed up early from work and announced he was taking her to Evan Calhoun's ranch for dinner.

"Dinner! But I've not even met Noelle!" she exclaimed. "And how am I supposed to get myself and the baby ready in thirty minutes?"

"I'm sorry. I was supposed to have told you about this outing last night. I got the days mixed up. But don't worry. This is just a casual thing. You look great as you are."

She glanced down at her denim capris and black tank top, then back to him. "You've got to be kidding! I can't go like this. Will you change Emma while I take a quick shower?"

He glanced anxiously at the baby lying in the middle of Geena's bed. "Dress Emma? I've only held her a few times. I don't know anything about dressing a baby."

Geena hurried over to a chest of drawers and pulled out a diaper and a tiny mint-green dress with pink trim around

the collar and puffed sleeves. The dress was only one of
two that she'd purchased for the baby.

"Here. It's time you learned," she told Vince as she
placed the garments on the bed. "While you put this on
her I'll hurry with the shower."

He looked helplessly from her to the baby, and just for
an instant Geena nearly burst out laughing. How could
such a big, tough lawman be so frightened of one tiny
infant?

"What if she starts crying?" he asked.

Smiling, Geena started out the room. "It won't hurt
her or you."

Twenty minutes later, the three of them were in Vince's
personal truck, traveling on the far south side of the city.
Geena was still trying to relax and catch her breath after
the mad dash of trying to dress and do her hair and makeup
in a handful of minutes.

She glanced down at her simple red flowered sundress.
The garment was one of the things Lilly Calhoun had sent
to her before Emma was born. Geena had tied a scarf
around the loose waist to make it more fitted and thrown
a lacy shawl over her shoulders. She looked neat and clean,
but hardly dressed for a dinner party.

"I hope you're right about this gathering being casual,"
she said. "I look like I'm ready to clean house instead of
eat dinner with your friends."

He glanced over at her, and Geena's cheeks grew warm
under the scrutiny of his brown eyes.

"I've never had a cleaning woman in my house that
looked like you."

Determined to take his compliment in a light way, she
let out a short laugh. "I doubt you ever looked that closely
at your cleaning ladies."

A faint grin slanted his lips, and the expression lifted

Geena's spirits. For the first time in a long time, he resembled the happy guy she'd first married, the man she'd laughed with and loved with all her heart. She so wanted to see that man again.

"Not unless they were dressed like a little French maid."

Laughing, she looked out the window at the landscape, which was growing more like desert with each passing mile. "It feels good to laugh. These past few months haven't been easy."

"No. I don't expect they have."

She glanced over her shoulder to see Emma sound asleep in the safety seat. Vince had managed to change the baby's diaper and put the little green dress on her. He'd even tied on a pair of white booties and brushed her fair hair to one side. The fact that he'd tended the baby just as if she was his own swelled her heart with emotion.

No, Vince could understand and forgive her for giving birth to another man's child, she decided. But he couldn't look past the mistakes she'd made as his wife.

It was just as well, she told herself. She didn't want another part-time husband. No matter how much she still loved him.

Determined not to let herself slip into a melancholy mood, she tried to concentrate on the evening ahead. "Do Evan and Noelle live very far out of town?"

"Several miles. It'll take about twenty more minutes to get there."

"The land is more stark and open out here," she observed. "It must take a lot of acres just to graze one cow."

"Evan and Noelle's ranch covers a fair amount of land, but they have to supplement the herd with feed and hay. Especially since the drought has worsened."

"Marcella explained that Evan's family owns one of the largest ranches in the state of Nevada. Is that true?"

He nodded. "Probably the largest. The Silver Horn stretches for miles and miles and extends west nearly to the California state line. The old man, Bart Calhoun, had one son and two daughters, but Orin, the son, was the only one who stuck around and helped him build the empire. He had five sons and two daughters. One of the daughters— she was younger than Evan—died when she was only two of a heart defect. The other daughter, Sassy, was born out of wedlock. She and Jett have a ranch of their own northwest of Carson City, and he's also the Silver Horn lawyer."

"Hmm. With a family that big, I'm sure there's plenty of family history. I've been wondering why Evan has a ranch of his own and why he became a detective. It certainly doesn't sound like he's doing it for the salary."

Vince grunted. "Not hardly. The Calhouns are incredibly rich. But they're a responsible, hardworking family. It's not in any of them to just laze around and live off their wealth."

She slanted a thoughtful glance at him. "I guess it's true that every person needs a purpose to be happy. Without one you just sort of drift."

"I remember when you started college right after we were first married," he said. "You were determined to become a teacher. After we divorced I figured you'd given up on that goal. I'm glad I was wrong. I'm very proud of you for going after what you wanted."

Yes, after the divorce she'd somehow found the strength and the determination to acquire her teaching degree. But she'd not had the courage to go after Vince and fight to get him back into her life. A woman had to know her limitations to survive in this world, she thought grimly.

"Thank you," she murmured. "I'm proud you achieved your dream of becoming a detective, too."

That pulled his gaze off the highway and around to her face. "Are you?"

His simple question put a resigned smile on her face. "Whatever you might think, Vince, I've always wanted you to be happy. And becoming a detective always was your main objective in life."

Frowning at the empty highway in front of them, he said, "Yeah. I got what I wanted."

At that moment Emma began to fuss, and as Geena looked over the seat at her beautiful little daughter, she wondered if Vince would ever wake up some day and realize he needed more than a gun and a badge to make his life complete.

Chapter Nine

A few minutes later, when Vince pulled down the short drive to Evan and Noelle's ranch house, he tried not to express his surprise. There were only two trucks parked near the yard fence. One belonged to Noelle and the other to Evan. If there was going to be a party tonight, the guests must have walked to get here, he decided. Or more likely they'd parked behind the barn.

"Oh! You said the Calhouns were wealthy, so I was expecting this place to be—extravagant. But it doesn't look anything like that," Geena exclaimed with a smile of relief. "It looks like regular folks live here!"

"The Calhouns are regular folks. Trust me, this house used to be tiny and pretty run-down. After they married, Evan wanted to build Noelle a grand two-story house with all the conveniences, but she wouldn't hear of it. She's a simple cowgirl. And a beloved aunt and uncle left her this place. She refuses to change it. Evan was able to persuade her to get a few rooms built on and cover it all with new cedar siding."

"From what you say, I already know I'm going to like her," Geena said.

Vince smiled to himself. "I'm sure you will."

He parked the truck next to Evan's, and after helping Geena to the ground, he went to the back door to retrieve Emma from her safety seat.

"You get the diaper bag," Vince told her. "I want to carry Emma in. Okay?"

"Sure. I'd be happy for you to."

With the baby cradled safely in the crook of his arm, the three of them started toward the front entrance of the house. But before they reached the small porch, Noelle came hurrying down the steps to greet them. Evan followed behind her at a slower pace.

"Hello, you two! I'm so glad you finally got here!" the woman called to them.

The tall brunette immediately reached for Geena's hand. "I'm Noelle," she introduced herself. "And you're Geena, no doubt. I've been looking forward to this for days."

Geena smiled warmly at Evan's pretty wife. "This is so nice of you to have us for dinner. I hope we're not putting you out."

"Oh, not at all! We don't have company that often, do we honey?"

"Just Granddad Bart," Evan answered with a grin. "He's the only one who makes a nuisance of himself around here. He's crazy about Noelle and Joanna. I'm just an afterthought."

Laughing, Noelle, moved away from Geena and over to Vince and the pink bundle in his arms. "Okay, it's plenty warm enough out here to give us a peek," she said while pulling the blanket back from Emma's face.

"Aw, what a sweetheart," Evan crooned as he peered over his wife's shoulder at Emma. "And look at you, Vince. You look like you've had some experience at this daddy thing."

Vince darted a droll look at his partner while Noelle continued to exclaim over Emma.

"She's a doll!" Noelle looked hopefully at her husband. "Oh, honey, I know you want our next one to be a boy, but just look at her. She's precious!"

Laughing, Evan smacked a kiss on his wife's cheek. "Boy or girl, whatever we get will be precious. Now, don't you think we'd better get our guests into the house? Before the food gets cold?"

"Oh! Oh, yes. Let's go in. Everything is ready and waiting."

As the four adults walked onto the porch, Geena asked, "Where is your little girl, Joanna?"

Evan and Noelle exchanged glances before Noelle said, "Talulah, our nanny, agreed to stay over while we—had dinner. In case I needed her to help keep Joanna corralled. They're back in the den."

"Talulah? I thought your nanny's name was Helen," Vince said as the group moved through the door and into a small living area.

"Helen had to quit," Evan explained. "She needed hip replacement surgery. Grandmother Alice was acquainted with Talulah and recommended her. She's a young Paiute woman who lives on the outskirts of Virginia City."

"And frankly, she's wonderful," Noelle spoke up. "I don't know what I'd do without her."

"Honey, why don't you take Geena on to the dining room?" Evan suggested to his wife. "I'll take Vince and Emma to the den."

Noelle shot her husband a furtive smile. "Great idea,"

she agreed, then looped her arm through Geena's. "Come on, Geena. Don't worry about Emma. Evan's an old hand with babies. And we've set up Joanna's bassinet for Emma to use while you're here."

With Noelle tugging on her arm, Geena had no choice but to follow the woman out of the room and down a short hallway.

"That's so thoughtful of you. But maybe I should bring Emma with me," Geena suggested. "If she starts crying I might not hear her. I can hold her and eat at the same time."

"Of course you can. But don't worry. The men will see after her."

Puzzled, Geena looked at Evan's wife. "But aren't the men going to eat with us?"

Noelle suddenly began to laugh. The reaction only confused Geena even more.

"Not exactly," Noelle said with a wide grin, then drew her through an arched doorway and into a dining room filled with women.

Geena stopped in her tracks and stared in wonder at the group seated at a long table, beautifully decorated with bowls of pink roses and white peonies. In the center was a tiered pink cake edged with tiny white rosebuds. A few feet away was another smaller table piled high with wrapped gifts.

The moment the women spotted Noelle and Geena, their chattering stopped and they all began to smile.

"Finally," an attractive redhead spoke up. "Let's get this party started!"

"Oh!" Geena looked to Noelle for an explanation. "Are you celebrating someone's birthday?"

"This isn't a birthday party, Geena," Noelle explained. "This is a baby shower for you and Emma."

Completely dumbfounded, Geena glanced back at the

group of women. It was then she noticed Marcella's familiar face.

"I'm sorry, Geena," Noelle explained as she continued to lead her deeper into the room. "I had Vince tell you a little fib about coming out here to have dinner. I wanted this to be a big surprise."

Overcome with emotions, Geena's eyes brimmed with tears as she glanced up at Evan's wife. "I don't know what to say," she said in a small voice. "I'm totally stunned."

Noelle's smile was a picture of kindness and understanding. "You don't have to say anything. We just want you to enjoy yourself. Come on and I'll introduce you to everybody, and then we'll eat and you can open your gifts. I better warn you, though. I didn't fix a big dinner like Vince told you," she added with a laugh. "But there's plenty for all of us to munch on."

More than two hours later, after the food was eaten, the gifts opened and the guests departed, Noelle and Geena relaxed on a long, comfortable couch in the den. Little dark-haired Joanna had finally succumbed to all the excitement and was curled asleep in the cushion of a big armchair. Lying on the couch between the two women, Emma was wide-awake, squirming and waving her tiny fists through the air.

Noelle looked lovingly down at the baby. "I think everyone, except Marcella, was annoyed with me when I told them you weren't going to pass Emma around the group. I'm sorry, but she's still too young to be exposed to that many strangers. No matter how much they all wanted to hold her."

"I'm glad you took it upon yourself to tell them. I certainly wasn't going to," Geena said regrettably. "Not after everyone gave me such nice gifts and took time out of their schedules to come tonight. I feel bad about disappointing them."

Noelle batted a dismissive hand through the air. "Don't worry about it. They all got to see Emma from a healthy distance. And we had a great time. I'm still stuffed with cake." She rubbed her tummy and grinned. "Not a good way to start a pregnancy. After tonight I'm leaving rich desserts off my plate."

Surprised, Geena looked over at her. "You're pregnant? Congratulations!"

"Thanks. I'm only a few weeks along. But we're already very excited."

No doubt, Geena thought. Being an only child and losing her father at a young age had filled her with the hope that someday she'd have a big family of her own. In the first few years of their marriage, she'd often joked with Vince about wanting a dozen kids, or at the very least, a half dozen. In truth, she would've been over the moon to be pregnant with a first child, much less a second. But between her college studies and his job, they'd decided a child would have to wait.

After a while everything that had once been important to her had been put on the waiting list. Until she eventually began to feel like her whole marriage had been put on hold.

Pushing those sad thoughts aside, Geena said, "I'm sure the both of you are thrilled. It surprises me, though, that some of your friends or relatives didn't mention your pregnancy tonight. Especially with the party being a baby shower."

Noelle laughed softly, and Geena decided it wasn't just the brunette's physical appearance that made her such a lovely woman, but rather the glow of happiness that radiated from within.

"That's because no one knows about it yet. Except Evan.

I don't even think he's told Vince yet. Unless he lets it slip while they're down at the barn looking at the new colt."

The two men had left the house more than thirty minutes ago, and although Geena was growing a little tired from the long evening, she was glad he was enjoying this relaxing time away from work with his friend.

"I imagine those two have plenty to talk about."

Noelle nodded. "You know, Vince became a detective two years before Evan. And I'm so thankful they paired my husband with your—uh—"

"Ex," Geena finished Noelle's awkward pause.

"Well, okay, ex," she complied. "Although you two don't exactly seem like a divorced couple. I certainly couldn't picture my ex-husband doing the things Vince has for you since you arrived in Carson City."

Geena blushed. "I didn't realize you'd been married before."

"Unfortunately, I picked a real stinker the first time. But meeting Evan and building this ranch into a home with him makes all that seem insignificant now. I would've thought Vince had told you that much about me."

Vince didn't tell her much at all, she thought glumly. "No. When he's at home, he doesn't say much."

"Well, I'm certainly glad they wrapped up the Rinehart case this afternoon and nothing else happened to interfere with this evening."

"Rinehart case," Geena repeated blankly. "Was that something special?"

Clearly surprised, Noelle opened her mouth to say something, then quickly decided against it. "A prize stallion worth a quarter million dollars went missing on a ranch not far from here. Of course Evan and Vince would work just as diligently on a case that involved fifty dollars. But the suspicion that the rancher's daughter might be implicated really bothered Evan. With four brothers and a sister, he kept imagining how crushed his own father would be if one of his children betrayed him that way." With a wry smile, she shrugged. "Most of the time he tries to keep his emotions out of a case. But this one—well, he's happy it's over."

Noelle's revelation hit Geena hard, and suddenly layers of fog parted before her eyes and she was seeing things for the very first time. And it was not a pretty sight.

"Vince did mention something about a missing horse to me, but he didn't attach a name to the case. He doesn't discuss his work with me that much. Because I—while we were married, I discouraged him—I told him I didn't want to hear any of it." She shook her head miserably. "I thought if he didn't talk about it, he wouldn't love it so much. He wouldn't love it more than me. I made so many mistakes back then, Noelle. And now—I can't go back and erase them or undo them."

Noelle reached over and gently touched her shoulder. "Geena, don't misunderstand. Evan and I are very happy, but that doesn't mean everything is perfect for us. Sometimes it's very hard for me to deal with his schedule. When he's off chasing suspects while I'm trying to doctor sick cattle, tend to my daughter and rebuild downed fence all at the same time, I want to scream. And he's missed plenty of special occasions. Like the Christmas he was at the hospital, standing at Vince's bedside praying for his partner to live instead of with me and his family."

Praying for Vince to live. Before, Geena had never really dwelled on the dangers of his job. She'd been too selfishly concerned about not getting to spend enough time with her husband instead of thinking about the danger he had to face each time he slipped on his badge and walked out the door.

"But that was only right," Noelle went on. "Because Vince is family, too. And no matter how neglected I feel at times, I get over it the minute Evan walks through the door. I take one look at his tired face and I'm reminded of how very much I love him."

Reaching over, Geena tried to comfort herself by holding Emma's tiny foot. "I was eighteen when we got married," she explained. "At that time I wasn't grown-up enough to realize that making Vince my whole life wasn't healthy. But none of that matters now. It's not like the two of us are trying to get back together."

Noelle smiled gently. "Of course you're not."

Much later, as Vince drove the three of them back to his house, he slanted another glance at Geena. He'd expected her to still be excited over the surprise party and all the nice baby gifts she'd received. Instead, she'd hardly spoken more than ten words in the last fifteen miles.

"Geena, did something happen at the party?" he asked.

She frowned at him. "Happen? What do you mean? We ate finger sandwiches and chips and had cake and punch for dessert. I opened all sorts of lovely gifts. In fact, I got so many things for Emma I won't have to buy anything except diapers for a long time. And I met a group of lovely ladies. Evan's sister, Sassy, was there and so was his sister-in-law Lilly, and another sister-in-law, Ava. Actually, she's a nurse, too, and is well acquainted with Marcella. One of the women had beautiful red hair—her name was Jessi and she works as a waitress. She and Noelle appeared to be the best of friends. I really liked her, too."

"Yeah, Jessi's worked at the Grubstake Café for a long time." He took his eyes off the dark highway long enough to glance at her. "So you had a good time?"

"It was wonderful. I'm still overwhelmed that total strangers wanted to give to me and Emma."

"So none of them said anything to hurt your feelings?"

The frown on her face deepened. "Why, no. What makes you ask such a thing?"

Shrugging, he wondered why he should concern himself. It wasn't his problem if Geena was slipping into one of her depressed moods. Yet he didn't like to think of her being unhappy for any reason.

"Well, you've been rather quiet since we started for home," he reasoned.

She sighed. "It's been a long evening. And meeting everyone—it's given me a lot to think about."

He didn't say anything to that, and as the truck crested over another hill, the lights of town appeared in the far distance. Like a fool, he realized he didn't want these quiet moments cocooned with her in the truck cab to end. The thought caused him to ease his foot on the accelerator.

"While you and Evan were down at the barn, Noelle mentioned the case with the stallion. She said you two wrapped it up today, but she didn't finish telling me whether the daughter was involved. Was she?"

The Rinehart case was the last thing he'd expected Geena to bring up, and the fact that she did caused a strange feeling to pass through him.

"You really want to know?" he asked.

She squared around in her seat so that she was facing him. "Yes, I do."

"Liv Rinehart was involved. But she's agreed to testify against her boyfriend. So I think she'll get off lightly for her part in the caper."

"Noelle said Evan was bothered about Mr. Rinehart learning his daughter had betrayed him. It would be heartbreaking to discover your own child stole from you," she said thoughtfully. "Now that I'm a mother I can appreciate that even more."

"Well, old man Rinehart isn't about to forsake Liv. I talked with him this afternoon, while Liv was being booked into jail. He seemed to understand that love sometimes causes people to do crazy things."

"Yes, very crazy," she agreed. "Especially when you think you're in love, but you're really not."

Was she talking about Liv Rinehart and her misplaced affection, or her own love life? Deciding it would be best not to have her explain that remark, he let it slide.

After a moment, she asked, "What about the stallion?"

"A pair of deputies have already recovered him and took him home," he told her. "He was hidden at an old hunting cabin back in the mountains. Skip, Liv's boyfriend, had intentions of keeping him there until things quieted down, then taking the horse to Mexico to sell him. The drug cartel would've paid top dollar for such a stallion."

She said, "I didn't realize you worked on rural cases. I thought you only worked in the city. Mostly on violent crimes like assault or murder or rape."

He shook his head. "I don't work for the city police, Geena. I'm with the sheriff's department. We cover the whole county, and we do work violent crimes. But thankfully those don't occur around here as frequently as theft and assault."

Vince could feel her gaze sliding over the side of his face. It made him want to pull over to the shoulder and haul her into his arms.

"So you're not facing danger every day? Like confronting a crazy person with a gun or knife, or some other kind of weapon?"

Vince frowned. "Why are you asking me about this?

While we were married, you never worried about me being injured on the job."

She sighed. "No. That's one thing I didn't dwell on. I think—well, I always pictured you as invincible. You were always so big and strong and confident. It was impossible for me to imagine anyone hurting you. When I learned you'd been critically wounded, I realized how foolish my thinking had been—about a lot of things."

Things? Like his job, their marriage or the choice she'd made to blot out her misery with alcohol? No. He wasn't going to pelt her with those sorts of questions. It was too late. Far too late to wish and wonder how things could have been.

"Well, anybody can die, Geena. Even me."

Close to an hour later, Geena was sitting in the bedroom, nursing and rocking Emma, when Vince walked up behind her left shoulder.

Her first instinct was to cover her exposed breast with the corner of Emma's blanket, but then she realized how ridiculous that would appear. Vince had seen her breasts before, along with the rest of her body. There was no point in hiding from him now.

"I've carried in all the gifts and stacked them in the living room," he said. "There's more things there than I first thought."

"Thank you," she told him. "I'll go through it all tomorrow and only unpack the things I need most. The rest I'll put in an out-of-the-way place until I'm ready to move."

He stepped to the side of the chair and gazed down at them. Geena felt very exposed. In more ways than one.

"And when will that be?" he asked.

A chill rushed over her. "Hopefully, one day next week. I still have a few things to take care of. The main one being a car and some furniture for the house. Thankfully, the place is small, so I won't need much."

Since Emma had quit nursing and was sound asleep, Geena rose from the rocker and carried her over to the bassinet positioned near the head of the bed. She'd settled the baby and was in the process of pulling her dress up over her breast when she suddenly felt Vince's hands on her bare shoulders.

The touch of his warm fingers caused her whole body to pulse with heat, and she closed her eyes as she fought to ignore the pleasure.

"Geena, like I told you the other night. There's no need for you to hurry about moving."

She squeezed her eyes even tighter and tried to swallow away the aching lump in her throat. "There's plenty of need. I explained all of that the other night," she said hoarsely.

His fingers slid forward until they were resting on her collarbone. Every cell in her body was aching for his hand to move downward until it was cupping her breast, until his thumb was passing over the moist nipple.

"I've been doing some thinking since then, Geena."

Her heart thumping heavily, she twisted around and lifted her gaze to his. "About what?"

"Us. This."

She grimaced. "Meaning the fact that we want to get our hands on each other."

"You make it sound like a crime," he muttered.

His warm brown eyes were focused on her lips, and Geena instinctively passed the tip of her tongue over the dry skin.

"It is a crime when two people hurt each other."

He cupped a hand against her cheek, and Geena's insides began to melt like a bowl of sugar sitting out in a rainstorm.

"It doesn't make sense," he said gently. "When I look at you I get the past all mixed up with the present. All I see is the beautiful wife I used to have in my arms and my bed. When I touch you, I forget all about the tears, and the fights, and you looking at me through a haze of alcohol, as though you didn't care whether I ever came home."

His words made her ill. Sick with a regret so deep she could feel it all the way to her soul. And yet in so many ways just hearing his honesty was cathartic.

Resting her palms on the middle of his chest, she said, "I cared, Vince. I still do. But you were right the other night when you said sex wouldn't fix our problems."

"Running away won't fix them, either."

She shook her head while her arms ached to slip around his waist, her mouth longed to plant itself over his. "I'm not running away. I'm moving across town."

Bending his head, he rested his forehead against hers, and the nearness shattered her common sense. Before she could stop herself, she was pressing the front of her body to his and splaying her hands against his broad back.

"Geena," he whispered. "I don't understand myself. Or you. Or any of these damned feelings I've been having. I don't know why—but I've been asking myself if it might be possible for us to fix things between us."

Tears oozed from her eyes. "It's not possible, Vince."

Easing his head back, his gaze delved deeply into hers. "Why? Because of my job?"

Sighing, she twisted her head so that she couldn't see the accusing shadows in his eyes. "Not in the way you're thinking."

His thumb and forefinger caught her chin and forced her face back around to his.

"What does that mean?"

"It means that tonight I finally understand how much your job means to you. I realize how wrong it would be if I asked you to be something other than what you are—an important part of the justice system."

He looked at her for long moments, as though he was seeing her for the very first time. "You have changed, Geena. More than I ever thought."

Groaning with frustration, she pulled away from him and moved to the end of the bed, where she wrapped her fingers tightly around one of the tall foot posts. "Vince, after you left me and Reno behind, it didn't take long for me to wake up. I had no choice but to pull myself and the remnants of my life back together. The process didn't happen overnight, and along the way I finally began to see that we were wrong for each other. We still are."

He walked over to her. "A few weeks ago, before your accident, I would've agreed with you. But now—I'm beginning to think I took the easy way out. I shouldn't have ever divorced you, Geena. I should've fought to make things right between us."

Regret sent a crushing pain to the middle of her chest. To hide it, she turned her back to him and covered her face with both hands. After drawing in several long breaths, she said, "I should have handled a lot of things differently, too. But that's in the past and done with. I have Emma's happiness to consider now, Vince. I want what's best for my daughter."

"Don't you think it would be best for her to have a father?"

Fear such as she'd never experienced before froze her completely motionless. Except for her mind. It jumped into survival mode and began running desperately away from him and the future he was suggesting.

"Yes, Emma deserves to have a father," she said in a hoarse whisper. "One that will be there for her whenever she needs him. Not one who's off trying to solve a crime at any given time of the day or night."

"Yeah, you're right," he said gruffly. "I'm just an unfeeling badge and gun. Emma deserves more than I could give her."

Tears were blinding her when she finally managed to turn around and look at him, but by then it didn't matter. Vince had already walked out.

And taken the deepest part of her with him.

Chapter Ten

A week later, Vince had just finished testifying at an armed robbery trial and was standing on the steps of the courthouse waiting for Evan to pick him up when he suddenly spotted his partner strolling up the sidewalk toward him.

"That didn't take long," he said. "How did it go?"

"Pretty cut-and-dried. I don't know why a defense lawyer would waste his time on a habitual criminal like him. As far as that goes, why do we waste our time putting guys like him behind bars when the penal system will just give them a tap on the wrist and release them back into society?"

Evan frowned. "What the hell is wrong with you? If we didn't do our job, this place would be lawless. Like back in the mid-1800s, when men killed each other over mining claims and saloon gals."

Vince snorted. "Men are still killing each other over saloon gals. Guess the gold and silver mines have become less important than female companionship."

The two men descended the steps and headed down the sidewalk to their parked vehicle. While they walked, Evan said with a chuckle, "I'd take Noelle over the richest mine in the world any day."

"That's because she's priceless," Vince reasoned. "You're one lucky guy, Evan. And you're smart enough to know it."

The two men climbed into the SUV and buckled up before Evan replied.

"Luck has nothing to do with it, partner. Hell, you know how I met Noelle."

Evan started the vehicle and merged into the street traffic. Over in the passenger seat, Vince stared moodily out the window. "I'd hate to admit that a little sage grouse flew up and caused my horse to buck me off. You, a cowboy, raised on the biggest ranch in Nevada."

Evan laughed in spite of Vince's dour mood. "I got bucked off all right, and knocked clean out. But the important part of that fiasco was that I woke up with an angel looking down at me. And that's my point, ole buddy. God moves us around to put us in the right place at the right time to meet the right person. Did you ever think that's why Geena wrecked her car that night on the outskirts of town?"

Glowering at his partner, Vince said, "If Geena's accident was some sort of divine intervention, then it didn't work. Geena's moving into a place of her own today."

Evan brow lifted with speculation. "Today? Why didn't you say something? We both worked the robbery case. I would have testified in your place and you could've taken off work to help Geena. What with the baby and everything, I'm sure she needs every hand she can get."

Sure, she needed help. Just not his, Vince thought glumly. That night after they'd gotten home from the shower, she'd made it damned clear how she felt about him. Oh, Lord, it still made him cringe to think about how close he'd come to telling her he still loved her.

You might as well have said the words, Vince. You more or less told her you wanted to try marriage with her again. Can't you get it through your head she doesn't want a second round with you? Why would she? She's already had two men dump her. You think she wants to take a chance on being deserted a third time? Dream on.

Shaking off the bitter voice in his head, he said, "Marcella and a friend of hers are helping Geena. She doesn't have that much stuff to move, anyway. Everything she'd brought from her place in Oregon was wiped out in the car fire."

"Oh, I thought it was mostly clothing she'd been carrying in the car. You mean she didn't have her household goods and personal things shipped ahead of her?"

As Vince stared out at the dry, barren landscape, he realized he felt just as empty as the desert hills. "No. I think she sold most of it to help fund the move."

"That's too bad. You'd never know it by talking with her. She's certainly not crying or whining poor pitiful me."

"I offered to help her replace some of what she needs, but she doesn't want my financial help," Vince conceded.

Evan slanted a skeptical glance in Vince's direction.

"I always got the impression from you that Geena was the clingy, fragile sort. She doesn't appear that way to me."

Vince grunted. "People change, Evan. And I'm ready to change subjects, okay? So where are we going anyway?"

For a moment Vince got the impression that Evan didn't want to drop their conversation about Geena. But thankfully, after a long pregnant pause, he moved on.

"We're headed to the Sagebrush Lounge. Out on 50—near the Storey County line. Someone managed to charm the guard dog and tear down the back door to a storeroom. Carried off thousands of dollars of beer and liquor. Took the dog, too. Guess they wanted a Rottweiler to go with a good cocktail."

"I hope he bites the bastards."

The men fell silent after that, and miles passed until town became a speck in the rearview mirror. In front of them, there was nothing but a few wild burros grazing on clumps of dried grass along the edge of the asphalt and a highway sign that read Silver City 5 Miles.

Finally, Evan said, "You know, buddy, it won't hurt anything to admit that you wanted Geena and the baby to stay with you."

Vince wiped a weary hand over his face. He'd always been able to function on very little sleep. In fact, both he and Evan had pushed through their shifts with only an hour or two of rest. But this past week, he'd lain awake counting the hours and minutes until Geena and little Emma would be leaving.

"Okay, I'm an idiot. I can admit that and a whole lot more," Vince mumbled miserably. "I didn't want the two of them to leave. I even made the mistake of asking Geena to stay. She wouldn't have it. I suppose once you divorce a woman she pretty much writes you off her list."

"You've been apart for years, Vince. You can't expect her to just jump into your arms and start loving you again. Where you're concerned, I figure she has a lot of concerns."

But she had jumped into his arms, Vince thought. She'd practically invited him to make love to her. If she'd been fully recuperated from going through childbirth, they probably would have ended up in bed together.

Sex won't fix our problems.

He never should have said such a thing to her. Maybe

sex wasn't the entire solution, Vince reasoned with himself, but at least it would be a start, a connection to build on.

"Concerns about me? Hell, I have all kinds of reasons to be concerned about her!" Vince exclaimed. "Don't I?"

Evan shook his head. "From what I can see, Geena is a stable, responsible woman. Like you said a few minutes ago, people change. Obviously she's changed for the better. When do you think you will?"

Vince glared at him. "What is that supposed to mean?"

"It means there are times you're as stiff as a dead fish. And just about as cold."

In a voice dripping with sarcasm, Vince said, "Thanks, buddy. You're really helping me out here."

"I'm damned well trying to," Evan barked back. "I'm not that acquainted with Geena, but I am familiar with the opposite sex. Deep down a woman just wants to know her man loves her. That's basically all she wants. Your love. Get it?"

Vince bristled. "Yeah, I get it. I'm a failure in communication."

Evan suddenly steered the SUV off the highway, and Vince looked around to see they'd arrived at the bar and grill. The rambling wood-framed structure sat on a large dirt parking lot. Near one end of the building, a dusty red truck sat in the shade of a lone pine tree.

Vince jammed a notebook and pen in his shirt pocket and reached to unsnap his seat belt.

Behind the steering wheel, Evan appeared to be more concerned with Vince's misery than the bar's losses. He cut the engine, then stabbed Vince with a pointed look.

"Vince, I've seen you break a suspect with just a handful of words. Surely you can find the right ones to say to Geena."

"Geena isn't a suspect," Vince muttered. "She's my ex-wife."

Evan grinned. "See, you're already making progress. You've figured out the difference."

Biting back a curse word, Vince yanked open the vehicle door. "Come on, let's get to work before I decide to gag you."

A week and a half later, Geena was finally beginning to feel as though she was getting her life back in order. At least, the parts she could control.

She now had a dependable car to drive and a phone to keep her connected. The furniture she'd purchased had been delivered and her little house was beginning to look more like a home. Yesterday, she'd met the principal of the school where she'd be starting her teaching job in a few days. The woman had been friendly and outgoing and as she'd toured Geena around the building, she'd begun to feel excited about getting back to work. Especially since Annie had agreed to become Emma's nanny.

Yes, things were finally coming together, she thought as she sat on the front porch, holding her sleeping daughter in her arms. She was far removed from the lost woman who'd stared at the walls of a hospital room and strained to remember her own name. And yet she couldn't deny that, in spite of all her blessings, she felt like something was missing.

Not something, Geena. Someone. Vince is missing. And no matter how hard you try, you'll never be completely whole without him.

Sighing at the little voice going off in her head, Geena looked across the quiet residential street to where a man was mowing a small patch of lawn in front of a brick house. Nearby in the driveway, a boy, somewhere around six years of age, dressed in nothing but a pair of shorts and sandals, was trying his best to dribble a basketball.

The last time he chased the ball down the driveway, the child happened to notice Geena and immediately waved at her.

As soon as Geena smiled and waved back at him, the dark-haired boy carefully glanced up and down the street for traffic, then raced across to her driveway.

"Hi," he called as he bounded up the steps. "What's your name?"

"My name is Geena," she told him, while thinking what a little charmer he was with his toothy grin and freckled nose. "What's yours?"

"Randal Ray Morgan. Everybody calls me Randy, though." He drew closer, his gaze riveted to Emma. "Is that your baby?"

"Yes. Her name is Emma."

"I'm six. How old is she?"

"She's about a month old."

The boy's brown eyes widened. "Gosh! She ain't even one yet?"

Geena stifled a laugh. "Not until next summer."

He shoved at a hank of hair poking his right eyebrow. "I don't have a sister. I wish I did. I'd push her around in my red wagon. Where is Emma's daddy?"

Geena told herself not to let the boy's innocent question get to her. "He's not here right now."

"When will he be here?"

When, indeed, Geena asked herself. So far she couldn't imagine any man being in her and Emma's lives, except for Vince. And that just wasn't going to happen.

"I don't know for sure. Maybe—"

"Randy! Get over here where you belong!"

The booming male voice had the boy glancing anxiously across the street. "That's my daddy calling," he explained in a rush. "I'd better go. He gets mad if I leave the yard. Can I come see Emma again sometime?"

Geena smiled. "Of course you may. Just make sure you get permission first."

"I will! 'Bye, Geena!" He raced off the porch and back to his own yard.

Her heart heavy, Geena watched him follow his father until the two disappeared around the side of the house.

By the time Emma got to be Randy's age, would she have a dad to love and protect her, to praise her when she was good and scold her when she was bad?

Her gaze dropped to Emma just as her daughter was opening her bright blue eyes. Smiling tenderly, Geena bent her head closer so the baby could focus on her mother's face.

"So you woke up and decided to look around," Geena spoke softly. "Aw, and you just missed seeing the cute little neighbor who came to visit. He had a really nice smile, too. Just like…"

Just like your daddy's.

The remainder of her words were spoken silently as she realized the direction her thoughts had taken. Brad's image hadn't been anywhere in her mind. No, she'd been picturing Vince as Emma's daddy. Something she'd been doing ever since he'd stood next to her in the delivery room and cradled her newborn child as if she'd been his own.

Dear God, what was wrong with her? she wondered. It had been so easy for her to put Brad completely out of her mind. So easy to forget the few short weeks she'd been married to him. Why couldn't she do the same with Vince?

Because you didn't love Brad. You told yourself you cared about him. You believed he could fill the missing gap in your life. You had the rosy idea you could start over and

*build the family you always wanted with him. You over-
looked the real fact that Vince has never left your heart.*

Emma squirmed and let out an annoyed cry that closely
described the turmoil going on in Geena's head.

Lifting the baby to her shoulder, she patted her back and
spoke to her in a low, gentle tone. "I know, little darlin'.
Vince would be a good daddy for you. He even offered himself up for the position. But I was so scared. Too scared to
ever think the three of us could be a family."

She was still soothing the baby and thinking about the
night of the shower, when he'd come to her bedroom...
when a familiar dark truck pulled up in her short driveway. By the time the driver's door opened, she realized
with a start that the man stepping out of the cab was Vince.

He was dressed in a pair of worn blue jeans and cowboy boots. A faded black T-shirt was stretched taut against
his broad chest and lean waist, while a pair of aviator sunglasses shielded his eyes from the late-evening sun. In spite
of the casual clothing, he looked incredibly handsome, and
as she watched him slowly climb the steps to the porch,
her heart began to race with foolish excitement.

"Hello, Vince."

A faint smile touched his face. "Hello, Geena."

"I'd say drag up a chair and have a seat," she told him,
"but I only have this one."

"That's all right. I need to stand anyway."

Feeling like all the oxygen had been sucked from her
lungs, she tried to breathe without sounding like she'd
just run a mile. "I never expected to see you in this part
of town."

He leaned a shoulder against one of the carved posts
supporting the roof of the porch and swept a mindful
glance at the connecting neighbors. "I should have called

before showing up like this. But I didn't want to give you the chance to come up with some excuse not to see me."

Geena was glad she had Emma to hang on to. Otherwise her hands would be shaking badly. Since she'd moved out of Vince's place, he'd called her twice. Just to check on her and Emma, he'd said. And during both of those calls, he'd never hinted that he wanted to see them. Why was he here now? To make sure she hadn't slipped back to drinking?

Stop it, Geena! Vince might not trust you to be an understanding wife. But he can see you're not about to revert back to the broken woman he used to be married to.

"Why would I do that? We're friends, aren't we?"

He pulled off his glasses and hooked the earpiece on one of his belt loops. Then looking directly at her, he asked, "Is that what we are?"

Why did she suddenly feel like bursting into tears? There wasn't any reason for her to have such a ridiculous reaction to this man.

"That's better than being enemies."

His lips took on a wry twist. "Yes, much better. So how's Emma? She looks like she's grown a foot since I've seen her."

The tight coil in her stomach loosened enough for her to rise to her feet and cross the short space between them.

"Here. Why don't you hold her and see for yourself?"

She handed the baby over to him, and her heart winced with bittersweet pain as she watched him cradle the baby in the crook of his arm and smooth the hem of her dress over her diaper.

"Wow, she looks like she can really see me," he said as he bent his face toward Emma's. "Her eyes look bright and focused."

"She's nearly five weeks old now. She's starting to see things close up to her."

He smiled down at the baby. "She's so pretty now. Just imagine how beautiful she's going to be when she's all grown up."

Geena laughed softly. "I don't want to think of her grown up just yet. That will happen all too soon."

"So are you going to ask me in?" he asked. "I've not seen your place yet."

"Sure. I'll fix us some coffee or something."

He followed her into the house, and after fastening the storm door behind them, Geena gestured to the couch. "You can lay Emma there while I show you around. There's no danger of her rolling off—yet, that is."

"If you don't mind, I'd rather carry her with me."

Not wanting to read too much into his desire to keep holding the baby, she smiled at him. "I don't mind. She likes it when you walk with her. Come on, I'll show you how I fixed her little nursery."

A few minutes later, after she'd shown him through the small house, he sat holding Emma at the kitchen table while Geena prepared a fresh pot of coffee.

"You have everything looking neat and livable," Vince told her. "Have you had any visitors yet? Other than me?"

"Marcella has stopped by a couple of times after her shift at the hospital. And Noelle came by yesterday. She was in town getting a load of feed for the ranch."

She turned away from the cabinet counter to see his expression had gone solemn.

"I guess you know she and Evan are going to have another baby."

Geena nodded. "She told me the night of the shower."

"You didn't mention it to me."

She shook her head. "No. I figured Evan should be the one to give you the news. You two are very close."

And we're not? Even though he didn't ask the question, Geena could feel it hanging in the air between them.

Relieved to see the coffee had finished dripping, she quickly busied herself with filling two cups and carrying them and a plate of cookies over to the table.

"You probably should take Emma now," he said. "I don't want to take the chance of dripping hot coffee on her."

"I have her little infant seat right over here," she told him.

She fetched the brightly colored chair from a corner of the room and set it in a safe spot in the middle of the table. Emma fussed when she lifted her from Vince's arms, but the baby quieted as soon as Geena got her settled in the comfy seat.

"You must've gotten work wrapped up early today," Geena remarked as she sank into a chair angled to Vince's left elbow.

"The past week has been rather light in the way of crimes. At least, most of them haven't needed detectives on the scene. What about you? School should be starting soon."

She stirred powdered creamer into her coffee. "I start work next week. Tomorrow I'm going pick up a few things and finish getting my classroom ready. Not that there's much I need to add to it. The school has already stocked it with all sorts of art supplies."

"You think you're going to like it there?"

She nodded while wondering why they had to be so nice and polite to each other. Why did she have to sit here and behave as though he was nothing more than an old acquaintance instead of the man she wanted to kiss and hold and beg to let her back into his life?

Because you're a coward, Geena. It's safer to sit here

and pretend than to hand your heart over to a man who's already divorced you once.

"So far, I do. The staff all seem very friendly. And my room is really pretty. It has lots of windows that will give the students great natural lighting. And the view is a park across the street."

He smiled. "I thought teachers didn't want rooms with windows. Don't kids get distracted easily?"

"I teach art, Vince," she said with a laugh. "If I can't keep their focus on a subject that enjoyable, I'm in trouble."

He reached for a cookie. "You'll probably meet some nice men who work there. Maybe a big tough football coach with an eye for a blonde," he said.

Geena's short laugh was wrapped in disbelief. "Do you honestly think I'm going to be looking for a man? After all I've gone through?"

The cookie didn't quite reach his mouth as he slanted her a pointed look. "You told me you'd like to have a father for Emma," he reminded.

Her gaze instinctively drifted over to her daughter's cherub face. Right now it was impossible to imagine any man fathering Emma—except Vince. And that was a scary, impossible thought.

"Well, yes, I did," she admitted. "But that doesn't mean I'm going on an immediate search for one!"

He downed the cookie in two bites. "I'm glad."

"Why do you say that?"

His gaze caught hers, and Geena's heart thumped erratically.

"I don't want you to be hurt again, Geena."

He was concerned about her being hurt? All this time she'd believed he was thinking about his own feelings, not hers.

Completely shaken by the idea, she left the table and

walked over to where a paned window exposed a view of the tiny backyard. As she stared at the single piñon and the bare spots scattered among the scraggly grass, she swallowed hard and forced herself to speak.

"That's hard to believe, Vince. You were never worried about hurting me when you handed me a set of divorce papers."

In a matter of seconds he was standing behind her, and she closed her eyes as his fingers stroked the waves of hair lying against her back.

"Geena, I didn't come over here to rehash the past."

His husky voice vibrated through her. And suddenly images of the two of them making love, of his rough, masculine whispers telling her how much he wanted her, was enough to make her stomach clench with longing.

"Why did you come? A phone call would have been enough to check on my and Emma's well-being."

"I know how to use the phone. I wanted to see you in person. And—ask you for a date."

The last part of his words caused her to spin around and stare up at him. "A date! If this is some sort of joke, Vince, it's in bad taste!"

His hands closed over her shoulders, and as their eyes locked, Geena was certain her breathing had stopped completely.

"It probably does sound like a joke to you. I never was— well, after we married I guess I forgot about taking you somewhere nice," he said ruefully. "But I'm thinking about it now, Geena. And I'm asking if you'd like to go on a date—like people do when they want to spend special time together."

Special time together. How ironic he would use those words, she thought. That's all she'd ever wanted from the man. That and his love.

Her heart was suddenly beating so hard and fast she could hear the drumming noise in her ears. "I don't understand this—you. Why would you want to bother? We've already agreed that we're not right for each other."

"Have we?" His fingers lifted to her cheek. "Maybe we weren't right for each other all those years ago. But that was then and this is now. Things have changed. Shouldn't we see how things go before we walk completely away from each other?"

Although she tried to fight it, she couldn't stop a tiny ray of hope from creeping its way to her heart. "A moment ago you said you didn't want me to be hurt again. Well, I don't want to hurt you, either."

A smiled tugged at the corners of his mouth. "Then all you have to do is agree to go out with me—Saturday. As far as I remember, I never came through with my promise to take you to Lake Tahoe."

Surprise parted her lips. "You remember that?"

"That and a whole lot more," he said softly.

If she didn't step away from him, she was going to lose all self-control, fling her arms around him and beg him to make love to her. So she forced herself to step back until she was far enough away to draw in a fresh breath of sanity.

Licking her lips, she said, "I'm not sure I'd be smart to accept your invitation. But I will."

He smiled, and she made a silent groan. Vince didn't have to try to charm her. Just being in his presence enchanted her. That's why she was living here instead of his nice big house. Just so she could hang on to her common sense.

"Good. I'll pick you up about ten Saturday morning. Is that okay with you?"

She glanced over at her daughter. "Yes, but what about Emma? I realize I'm going to have to leave her with Annie when school starts Monday. But I—I'm just not ready to part with her any more than I have to."

"I wanted you to bring Emma anyway. We'll stay away from the crowds so she won't get exposed to anything," he assured her, then added with a sly grin, "She'll make a precious little chaperone."

As if a baby could stop her from making an utter fool of herself around him, she thought while stifling a helpless groan.

"I'll be ready," she told him.

He walked over to the table and smoothed a fingertip over Emma's gold hair, then pecked a swift kiss on Geena's cheek.

"I have to be going," he said huskily. "I'll see you Saturday."

He started out of the kitchen, and Geena followed him to the front door. "What if something comes up with your work? You will let me know?"

As he stepped onto the porch, he glanced over his shoulder at her. "That's not going to happen."

She wondered how he could be so certain of that, but kept the question to herself. Fighting over his work had ruined their marriage years ago. She didn't want the issue to keep shadowing every minute they spent together.

"All right," she said in the most casual voice she could muster. "I'll see you Saturday."

He gave her a little wave, then walked down the steps and out to his truck. As Geena watched him go, she didn't know whether to laugh or cry or make a beeline to the doctor who'd treated her for amnesia.

She must be having a relapse, she thought. Because her heart seemed to be forgetting all the aches Vince had put it through. All she could remember was how good it had been to love him.

Chapter Eleven

Saturday morning dawned very warm with a crystal-blue sky. Vince sighed a breath of sheer relief as he backed out of his drive and headed across town to Geena's place. He didn't know what he would've done if the sheriff's department had called this morning to say he was needed at a crime scene. He'd flatly promised Geena that nothing would happen to interfere with their date.

That had been a damned risky thing to do. Truth was, he had no way of predicting when he was going to be called to duty. Evan had been assuring him that if anything should come up today, he'd take care of it without Vince's assistance.

Vince was grateful for his partner's help. But this was only one day out of the year. What would happen if he and Geena actually tried to make a go of their relationship again? As soon as the demands of his work started to interfere with their time together, he feared the fighting and the turmoil between them would start all over again.

Stop it, Vince. It's too late to start having second thoughts now. These past weeks without Geena and Emma in the house have been the loneliest you've ever experienced in your life. You want to start a new beginning with your ex-wife. You want to make it work this time. So start believing it will. Otherwise, you'll never make Geena believe in you or a future together.

By the time Vince pulled to a stop in front of Geena's house, the pep talk going on in his head had lifted his spirits. All he wanted to think about now was enjoying this day with her and the baby.

Minutes later, as Vince drove the three of them out of the city, he could hardly keep his attention on the weekend traffic or his gaze off Geena. The blue-and-white dress she was wearing had tiny straps on the shoulders and a hem that stopped a few inches above her knees. The exposure of all that creamy skin was playing havoc with his senses. Not to mention the smile on her cherry-colored lips.

"You look very beautiful this morning," he couldn't help saying. "No one would ever guess you had a baby a few weeks ago."

"Thanks. I've lost most of the baby weight. But I still have a few pounds to go." She settled a hand on her practically flat stomach. "It's not easy for a girl who loves dessert."

"It's not easy for a guy who loves pizza, either."

She smiled with understanding. "You used to jog all the time. Have you given that up?"

"Not completely. I jog in the park on occasion. But when I have to choose between getting five hours of sleep and jogging, I take the sleep. If my mind isn't sharp, I'm in trouble." He braked the truck to a stop at the last traffic light before hitting the highway to Lake Tahoe. "Will you have to get up early when school starts Monday?"

She let out a light laugh, and Vince wondered how he'd gone all these years without hearing that special sound. When Geena genuinely laughed, it was like tinkling bells, ringing the joys of life. But during the last part of their marriage, her laughter had faded. He couldn't let that happen this time.

"That won't be a problem," she said. "Emma has a habit of wanting her breakfast around five o'clock. That should give me plenty of time to get her and myself ready to leave the house by seven."

He slanted her a questioning glance. "What are you going to do about her—uh—milk? I doubt this Annie of yours is a wet nurse."

Laughing heartily, she said, "At her age, I doubt it, too. But as for the milk, I'll pump what I can. If that's not enough, I'll supplement it with formula."

From Vince's angle to the rearview mirror, he could see Emma in her safety seat. For the moment, she was awake, with her arms thrown wide and her eyes bright. Geena had dressed the baby in a pair of tiny jeans and a long-sleeved T-shirt to give her more protection while being outdoors. A pink cap with a white bow covered her fuzzy golden hair, and matching pink shoes were tied on her tiny feet.

Just looking at the baby filled him with fierce, protective pride. He couldn't imagine any man stepping in to be Emma's father. Vince was her father. He'd felt that way from the very moment she'd been born.

"Emma definitely seems to be thriving now," he said.

"We both had our checkups yesterday. The doctor said Emma is right on schedule in all aspects of her development. You can't imagine how happy and relieved that makes me. All during my pregnancy I prayed that she would be normal and healthy. I guess that's something all mothers do."

"That's great news. And what about you?"

She smiled at him. "Fit as a fiddle. Well, maybe after a few workouts at the gym," she added with a little laugh.

Judging from her appearance, Vince didn't think she needed the gym. She just needed his arms around her.

With the eastern shoreline of Lake Tahoe being a few short miles away from Carson City, they were soon driving north through forests of enormous pines and evergreens. Glimpses of blue water sparkled through the branches, while in some spots open beaches could be seen.

Enthralled by the sights, Geena leaned forward in her seat and peered out the windshield. "Oh, my! This is incredible, Vince! It's so beautiful! Can we go down by the water? I'd love to see it up close."

Happy to oblige, Vince said, "Sure. I'll find a good place for us to explore."

Moments later, he parked the truck and they walked down to a cleared camping area equipped with picnic tables and barbecue grills. While Vince held Emma in her carrier, Geena explored the water lapping along the shoreline.

With a wide smile lighting her face, she called to him. "Come sit with me! This is perfect!"

He walked to where she'd taken a seat on a huge bleached white log a few feet from the water's edge. Easing onto a spot next to her, Vince placed the carrier between their feet and positioned it so the baby could look up at them.

"Mmm, now that is a lovely sight," he said, gazing out at the wide expanse of blue water.

"It's so much prettier in person than in pictures. I can't believe I lived in Nevada all those years and never visited this place before."

He watched her shake back the waves of golden hair being tossed about by the warm southwesterly breeze. "Well, some people just don't take advantage of the local scenery."

She bent forward and picked up a pebble from the sandy ground. "My dad used to promise to bring me and my mother down here. I always wanted to see it with all the snow and skiers." She sighed. "But he was always working, trying to keep the bills paid and food on the table. And then he died. Most of my dreams went with him."

"Yes, I remember you saying that," he said gently. "You were very close to him. I'm sure you've been wishing he could see Emma."

A sad smile touched her lips. "Every day," she agreed.

"What about your mother? Maybe if you contacted her now you might find she's changed for the better."

She grimaced. "Yes, that would be great. But she hasn't changed, Vince. I sent her my phone number and address not long after Brad and I split. I suppose being pregnant must have brought out my maternal instinct. Anyway, I wanted her to know about the coming baby. I never got any response. But that's not surprising. She probably doesn't want her latest man to know she's old enough to be a grandmother."

As soon as Geena's beloved father had died, her mother had started neglecting her. And things hadn't improved much for her after she and Vince had married, he thought ruefully. Not that he'd purposely neglected her, but he'd thrown himself into his job and expected her to find something besides her husband to occupy her time.

"I'm sorry I never brought you down here to Tahoe like I'd promised," he told her.

She shrugged. "I don't expect you come here often."

He shook his head. "No. I've only been here once before, and that was on an assault case that occurred just north of Glenbrook, so it was out of Douglas County jurisdiction."

She tossed the pebble into the water. "I thought you might have brought dates over here before. Maybe for dinner. Or boating."

His chuckle prompted her to frown at him.

"Is that funny or something?"

"Geena, the number of dates I've had since we've divorced I could count on one hand. And those consisted of casual outings in Carson City."

Her frown turned to one of disbelief. "Why? I mean, why haven't you dated more? You're a young, handsome guy. Don't tell me you can't find a woman willing to go out with you."

He leaned forward and touched a fingertip to Emma's dimpled cheek. The baby was loving being outdoors. Just as Vince was loving spending this time with her and Geena.

"Because it didn't take me long to realize I was wasting my time. I realized I'd never recapture what I had with you."

She shifted around on the log so that she was facing him, and her somber expression made him wish their conversation had never taken this direction. He didn't want her to be sad. She'd already had enough sadness in her life.

"I think you really mean that."

He frowned. "Of course I mean it."

Sighing, she gazed back to the water being gently ruffled by the wind. "We really messed each other up, didn't we? I didn't date much, either. And even after I met Brad— well, deep down I recognized it wasn't real love with him. But I was lonely and he was saying all the right things. I was stupid. I let myself be stupid. Because I wanted a family."

The need to connect with her was so great, he reached for her hand and folded his fingers around hers.

"Let's not think about such things now," he told her. "This day is supposed to be enjoyable. What would you like to do next? I can drive around the north or south rim and find a restaurant where we can have a nice lunch."

She glanced up at the sunny sky, then back to the water lapping onto the shore. "I was thinking how nice it would be to have a picnic. I should have filled a basket. We could've eaten right here."

Surprised by her suggestion, he asked, "You'd like that better than a restaurant?"

Her eyes were suddenly shining. "Oh, yes. We can eat in a restaurant anytime. I don't often have a chance to enjoy the outdoors like this."

"All right. That's what we'll do."

He'd hardly gotten the words out when Emma's face turned into red wrinkles and she began to cry.

"I don't think she likes our idea," Vince commented.

Laughing, Geena reached for her daughter. "Let's go back to the truck. I think she needs a dry diaper and a bit of brunch."

After Emma was tended to and sleeping contentedly, Vince drove north until they reached an old-fashioned trading post where groceries were sold. The place was busy with tourists and locals, forcing him to park at the far end of the building in the shade of a ponderosa pine.

Handing Geena a credit card, he said, "Here. You shop for our picnic lunch. Get whatever you'd like. I'll stay here with Emma."

She laughed. "I might go crazy with this," she warned. "I'm hungry."

"Good," he said. "That means you'll get more than rabbit food for our lunch."

While Geena disappeared into the old building built of huge chinked logs, Vince pulled out his cell phone and dared to check his messages.

Thankfully, the only text of any significance was from Evan, and it was short and sweet. It simply read, Everything cool.

Relieved, he put away the phone and glanced over his shoulder at sleeping Emma.

Everything cool. That's exactly the way he wanted it to be with him and Geena. Now and for the rest of their lives.

The sun was getting low in the sky by the time the three of them returned to Geena's house. After Vince helped her bring in the baby and the rest of her things, he stood awkwardly in the middle of the living room while she put Emma in her crib.

When she reappeared from the bedroom, he was still standing where she'd left him.

"What are you doing still standing?" she questioned. "Don't you want to sit down? I'll make us some coffee. There's still plenty of cake left over from our picnic."

"I'm still standing because I wasn't sure if you'd want me to keep hanging around. We've spent most of the day together. I thought you'd probably had enough of my company. And most likely you have things to do."

A gentle smile touched the corners of her lips and though he didn't tell his feet to move, he felt himself walking toward her.

"I like your company. Why don't you come to the kitchen and talk to me while I make the coffee."

Talk? He wanted to do so much more than talk. All afternoon, while seeing the sights and eating their picnic, she'd been near him. The feminine fragrance of her skin and hair, the sweet tempting curve of her lips and the sparkle in her eyes had been tugging on his senses until it had turned into a real struggle to keep his hands off her.

"Okay," he agreed. "I'll stay for a little while longer. But you don't have to make coffee just for me."

She swiped her palms down the sides of her hips as her gaze skittered over his face. "I could drink a cup. Besides, I need to put away the leftover food."

"I'll help you," he offered.

She turned and started out of the room. Vince drew in a deep breath and followed her.

What was happening to her? To them? The questions continued to roll through Geena's head as she spooned coffee grounds into a filter. This day with Vince had transported her into some sort of fairyland. She was beginning to believe he cared about her. Cared about her more than anything—even more than his job. One little picnic at the lake shouldn't have that much influence on her common sense.

No, this went beyond the picnic, she mentally argued. She was changing. He was changing. She could feel it happening. And it had nothing to do with the sexual tension that was arcing between them like lightning between two storm clouds.

"I've put the macaroni salad and the fruit in the refrigerator," he said. "You want to leave the cake out on the table?"

He walked up behind her and a masculine mix of cologne, wind and sunshine drifted to her nostrils. The scent, along with his breath rushing against the back of her neck, tilted her senses.

"I can't eat any more of it. But you might."

"I'm not hungry. Not for food."

His provocative remark had her slowly turning to face

him, and as her gaze locked with his, her heart slowed to a heavy thud. Desire was clouding his brown eyes. The same sort of desire that was gripping her body, her senses.

"Vince—"

"I want to make love to you, Geena." He slipped his arms around her waist, and she felt the oxygen rush from her lungs.

"Is that the reason for the date today?" she asked impishly. "To seduce me?"

He rested his forehead against hers. "No. You don't honestly believe that, do you?"

The hard bands of his arms were sending waves of heat crashing from her face all the way down to her feet, while the close proximity of his lips made her half-crazed with the need to kiss him.

"No. We both know that all you have to do to seduce me is walk into the room."

"Today was—I wanted both of us to get a glimpse of how it could be together—that's what today was about," he said. "And now, I don't want it to end."

Letting her body speak for her, she slipped her arms around him and drew herself closer to the hard warmth of his body. "We won't let it," she whispered.

Suddenly his hands were framing her face and tilting her lips up to his. When his mouth finally made contact with hers, something sweet and fiery swept through her, very nearly wilting her bones.

At first touch, the kiss was a tender exploration. But after a few short moments it deepened into a hungry foray that pushed its way deep into her senses until everything turned into a hazy mantle wrapping itself around her.

His hands slipped into her hair, then quickly slid down her shoulders and onto her hips. As he pulled her tight against him, Geena could already feel the bulge of his desire straining against the fly of his jeans.

She wanted to touch him there. She wanted to touch him everywhere.

Tearing her mouth from his, she grabbed his arm. "Come on," she whispered hoarsely. "Let's go to the bedroom."

"Emma is in there."

Geena shook her head as she urged him out of the kitchen. "I put her in the big crib—in the nursery."

With her hand wrapped around his, she led him to the bedroom, but before they reached the side of the double bed, Vince paused to pull her back into the tight circle of his arms.

Pressing his lips to the corner of hers, he whispered, "Geena, before we take another step. I want you to be sure about this. If you have any doubts—"

"Doubts about making love to you? No. How could I doubt something that's gone over and over in my mind for the past six years?"

He tilted his head back, and the wondrous light she spotted in his brown eyes jolted her. Because it looked very much like love.

"Oh, baby, my sweet Geena. You can't know how I've dreamed of this—longed for this."

With a hungry groan, he found her mouth, and for the next few moments he kissed her so deeply and thoroughly Geena feared she was going to melt right there in his arms. Breathing was nearly impossible, and her legs were threatening to buckle.

Finally, he began to walk her backward until they both fell onto the side of the bed. Somehow their mouths managed to remain connected through the fall, and as Vince continued to kiss her, his hands went on a wild journey over her arms and shoulders, then down her back and onto her buttocks.

Eventually, his fingers reached the hem of her sundress and he shoved the material up toward her waist. As he ran his palm over her bare thigh, Geena took the liberty of yanking the tails of his shirt from his jeans and moving her hands beneath the loosened material.

His skin was hot and smooth, begging her to widen the range of her exploration. Touching him, kissing him was like coming home, and yet something about the pleasures also felt new and exciting, as though they'd never made love before.

She pushed her hands farther beneath his shirt and then she felt it. A hard, jagged line of scar tissue running along the bottom of his right rib cage. The discovery caused her to pause, and he pulled his mouth away and looked into her eyes.

"You don't have to stop," he whispered. "It doesn't hurt."

"It hurts me to know a bullet ripped into you. That your flesh was torn apart. Let me see."

Not waiting on his response, she took it upon herself to unbutton his shirt and push it away from his chest. Bending her head, she pressed her lips to the rigid white line, then continued to slide her lips along the mended skin until the mattress prevented her from going farther.

His groan was a mixture of pleasure and pain as he snared a handful of hair and tried to tug her head away from his abdomen, but she didn't give in to the pressure. Instead, she pushed him onto his back and continued on an upward path until her lips fastened over a male nipple.

As her tongue laved the tiny brown bud, his hands reached to undo the zipper at the back of her dress. When the straps fell over her shoulders, she sat up and allowed the bodice to fall away from her bare breasts.

His gaze narrowed on the pale orbs and puckered pink nipples. "You were always so beautiful, Geena. Even more beautiful now that you've had Emma."

Reaching out, he gently wrapped a hand around one plump breast. Geena bent over him and plastered a long, hungry kiss on his lips.

Her lungs bursting for air, she was finally forced to break the contact, but Vince didn't let the interruption stop him. He immediately went to work removing her dress, panties and slip before finally moving on to the sandals on her feet. By then every cell in Geena's body was throbbing with anticipation. She'd never wanted any man this much. She'd never wanted him this much and she refused to keep her hands off him, even as he quickly shed his own clothing.

When he finally laid her back on the bed and stretched out beside her, Geena was trembling with need, and she pulled herself close to him and buried her face in the corner of his neck. "Oh, Vince, why has it taken us so long to get here, to this?"

His arms tightened around her as he brought his lips next to her ear. "I can't answer that. But it doesn't matter, my sweet. We're not going to regret what was lost. From this moment on we're going to concentrate on the future and making each other happy."

"Happy. Oh, yes, Vince. I want to make you very happy—and all mine."

"All yours. I like the sound of that."

Groaning, he tilted her head so that he could gain access to her lips. Once he started kissing her, the need to say anything more was lost to the passion quickly rising between them.

His hands were everywhere. Skimming over her breasts and belly, the curve of her hips and down the length of her thighs. Eventually, the kiss ended and his lips decided to take a meandering trip down the side of her neck, across her collarbone and down to one breast. When his tongue finally made a slow circle around the nipple, she wanted to shout with pleasure. She wanted to capture his head with her hands and hold him to her so that the magical pleasure of his mouth could never leave her.

After a few moments, Geena was certain she'd turned into a pulsing flame and Vince was the fuel splashing over her senses and pushing the fires inside her to an unbearable heat.

By the time he pulled back and questioned her about birth control, she was in such a fog of smoky desire, she hardly registered what he was asking.

"Birth control? No," she finally managed to answer. "The breast-feeding acts like a birth control. But it doesn't remove a slight chance of pregnancy."

He let out a long breath. "I'd better take care of the slight chance."

She didn't completely understand what he meant until he left the bed and dug his wallet from the pocket of his jeans. When he turned his back to her and she heard the faint sound of ripping paper, she realized he was dressing himself in a condom.

The added protection was the smart thing to do. Yet Geena wished it wasn't needed. She wanted to feel every part of Vince, feel his flesh sliding against hers.

But having another baby so soon would be risky, she silently reasoned with herself. Not only to her health, but also to this tenuous bond they were forging between them.

When Vince turned back to her, she opened her arms in a welcoming gesture and he moved over her, his head reeling with anticipated pleasure.

Making love to Geena. Yes. He'd wanted this for so long. Years, in fact. Yet it hadn't been until today, until he'd saw her laughing face lit up with sunshine and felt the trust in her hand as it wrapped around his, that he'd known it would finally happen. Now that it was, he was finding it a constant battle to contain his desire.

With his hands planted on either side of her head, he lowered his mouth to hers. As he began to kiss her once again, her legs opened and a moan sounded deep in her throat. Her invitation was obvious, and yet he hesitated. Because he realized that once his body connected with hers the ecstasy would end far sooner than he wanted and needed.

But when her hands grabbed his buttocks and pulled him forward, he had no option but to give her what she wanted.

"Oh, Geena, darling, tell me if I hurt you," he whispered, his voice rough with desire.

"I'm hurting now," she said with a breathless groan. "Because I want you so much. All of you."

Gripped with desire, he aligned his hips with hers and ever so slowly entered her warm body. The intimate connection caused his senses to splinter and scatter off into space like pieces of useless fluff.

Left without the ability to think or reason, all he could do was react to the racking desire pushing him forward. The moist heat of her body made him forget his plan to go slow, and even if he had remembered, he couldn't have stuck to it.

As soon as her hips arched toward his, he instinctively drove himself deeper, until there was no space left between them. Then he paused, as the need to see her face became nearly as great as the raging fire in his loins. And as his gaze swept over her tangled gold hair and dark kissed lips, he wondered how he'd gone on existing without this, her.

"Vince. Vince. This is—so perfect! So right! Make love to me. Never stop. Never stop!"

The urgency of her words snapped his momentary paralysis and he began to move inside her. Gently at first, then faster as their need for each other began to climb to impossible heights.

Quickly, the room began to fade around him to leave nothing but her soft, warm body writhing beneath his, begging him to take away the aching desire. Her hands were touching him everywhere, gliding over his sweat-slick skin. Her lips tasting, supping, traveling down his neck and onto the ridge of his shoulder.

The pleasures she was giving him were more than his body could handle at one time. And though he wanted to keep taking, wanted to keep giving, he was rapidly losing all control.

Delving his hands beneath her back, he pulled her upper body forward until her breasts were pressed against his chest and her mouth was captured beneath his.

Instantly, their ride grew even more frantic and wild. Until somewhere in the distance, Vince could hear her soft moans and recognized her body was tightening like a coil preparing for sudden release.

Her response was all it took to push him into a mindless place where there was nothing but burning hot stars shooting in all directions and dark, velvety skies brushing over his skin, sending shivers of delight vibrating through to his very soul.

The magnitude of the quakes overwhelmed him, blinded him with feelings so fierce he couldn't stop a guttural cry from escaping from his throat.

By the time the pieces of his shattered mind settled

into place, he realized they'd both fallen back to the mattress. Geena was lying on her side, facing him. She was still drawing in long, deep breaths, and a sheen of sweat glistened on her face. The sight of her dreamy, half-closed eyes and swollen red lips caused his throat to tighten, his chest to swell.

Smiling weakly, she rested her palm against his cheek. "You're frowning," she said. "Are you okay?"

Groaning, he gathered her close against him and buried his face in the side of her tumbled hair. "No. I'm not okay," he murmured huskily. "I'm hurting. My heart is about to burst with love for you."

For a moment she went so still he thought she'd stopped breathing. But then she tilted her head back and looked at him in stunned fascination.

"Love? After everything we've been through?"

Closing his eyes, Vince tucked her head in the crook of his shoulder, then gathered her in the tight circle of his arms.

"In spite of everything we've been through," he whispered roughly.

And now that he could admit his love to himself, and to her, he had to decide what he was going to do about it. Or was she going to tell him it was too late to make the three of them a family?

Chapter Twelve

Cocooned in Vince's arms, Geena pressed her cheek to his damp chest. The sound of his heart beating fast and hard echoed the pace of her own racing pulse.

During their marriage she'd made love to this man an endless number of times, but never had it felt so perfect. Never had she felt so completely happy.

After a moment, he asked, "You don't have anything to say?"

"I have a thousand things to say." She soothed her palm over his rock-hard belly. "But right now I'm lying here in your arms trying to decide the best way to tell you."

He brought his thumb and forefinger beneath her chin and tilted her face up to his. "Tell me what?"

Smiling tiredly, she raised up on one elbow and cupped a hand alongside his face. "How much I love you. How much I never stopped loving you."

With a hand at the back of her head, he drew her mouth

down to his, and as he gently kissed her, Geena felt certain her heart was going to dissolve into a handful of useless goo.

"Oh, darling," he murmured. "Why did it take us this long to come to our senses?"

Sighing, she eased down next to him and pillowed her head on his shoulder. "Because we were both so hurt. And neither of us wanted that to happen again. But I'm not afraid anymore, Vince. From now on, I'll never be afraid of loving you—making a family with you."

His fingers gently stroked her hair. "You sound awfully certain of that."

"Mmm. I guess my turnaround seems sudden to you. But actually, it didn't just happen. I've been thinking about this—us—for days now."

"Actually, I thought—well, I wanted today to be a beginning for us," he said. "I wanted both of us to have a chance to be together just for the sake of it. I wanted the chance to make a subtle pitch for the merits of us getting back together. I didn't imagine it was going to wind up like this."

She chuckled. "Really? You sounded pretty confident a few minutes ago in the kitchen."

"I was just putting on my best cool act."

Lifting her head, she gave him a tender smile. "You don't have to be cool with me, Vince. Or brave or funny. Or anything except you."

He grinned, and the idea that she could actually make him happy lifted her spirits as high as the sky.

"I'll try to remember that."

Sighing, she returned her head to his shoulder. "There is one thing that scares me, though," she admitted.

There was a long, pregnant pause before he finally asked, "What is that?"

"It scares me to think about what would've happened if I hadn't made the choice to move to Carson City. What if I hadn't wrecked my car or had amnesia? We would've never seen each other or been given this second chance. And that's a very scary thought to me."

His hand made soothing circles on her back. "Evan says God puts us in certain places at certain times for a reason. He believes divine intervention caused you and me to get back together."

"How did Evan know we were getting back together?" she asked impishly.

He chuckled. "Evan believes he's smarter than everybody else. To hear him tell it, he can figure things out before they happen. I'll tell you another thing about my partner. He didn't always like you."

"Oh. He's only known me for a short time."

"When we first became partners and I talked to him about you and our divorce, I think he got the impression that you were a bad wife. It was totally my fault he formed that opinion. I should've explained there was more going on than your drinking."

A few days ago, it would have bothered her for Vince to bring up the subject of her drinking, but now she was surprised to find that she welcomed it. "Well, I wasn't exactly a good wife."

"I wasn't exactly a good husband, either," he reasoned.

"We were too young to know the right things to do to make our marriage work," she told him.

He shifted the both of them so that she was lying flat against the bed and his somber gaze was searching hers. "You're right about that, Geena. But the other night when I talked about being Emma's father—you remember how that went."

She nodded with regret. "I'm sorry, Vince. Everything

you were saying scared me so badly I had to say something to knock you off track. That night—I just didn't think I was ready to be a lawman's wife again."

"Nothing has changed since then, Geena. I'm still a lawman."

"Yes, something has changed," she pointed out. "I have. Your work was never our problem, Vince. It was my problem. These past days without you have made me see that even though you're not with someone physically, you still continue to love them."

He stroked her hair. "I never know when I might be called from the dinner table or our bed. And I never have any idea how long I might have to be gone."

"That's not news to me, Vince. I understand it won't always be easy to deal with your absence."

"It will be hard, Geena. Even harder than when we lived in Reno and I was only a deputy. I see the things Noelle has to deal with. I don't want to ask that much of you. But I've come to the conclusion that I'm selfish and I love you. I want us to be together. As much as we can, for as long as we can."

She drew his face down to hers and kissed him with all the love that was in her.

"Mmm. You think we have a bit more time before Emma wakes?" he murmured against her lips.

Chuckling softly, she slipped her arms around his neck and pulled him down to her. "She'll probably be asleep for another hour."

"Perfect."

Rolling onto his back, he pulled her on top of him. Geena grabbed his shoulders and was bending her head to kiss him once again when the faint sound of a cell phone interrupted the moment.

Looking around, she tried to locate the origin of the

sound, then quickly realized it was coming from a pocket on Vince's jeans.

"It's your phone, Vince."

Groaning, he rested a forearm across his eyes. "I'm not going to answer it."

She scrambled to a sitting position on the side of the bed. "You are going to answer it! You might be needed."

Ignoring the ringing phone, he sat up and stared at her in disbelief. "I thought *you* needed me."

She bit back a groan of frustration. "I do. But there could be an emergency somewhere. It's your job to take care of it."

"There are other detectives on the force besides me."

She couldn't believe he was talking this way, but then maybe she could. For a few minutes this afternoon, they'd found paradise together. He didn't want to leave that place any more than she did. But that didn't mean they could shut the world away. They had to learn to live in it—together.

Climbing from the bed, she fished the phone from his jeans and tossed it on the mattress next to him. "Think about it, Vince. That night I was brought to the hospital after my accident, I was lost and alone. And very scared. I was told a detective was coming to help me. What if you'd shouldered that job to someone else?"

With a look of utter resignation, he reached for the phone. "Sometimes you make too much sense."

She cast him a loving smile. "You answer your call. I'll be in the nursery checking on Emma."

After a quick trip to the bathroom, Geena pulled on a blue satin robe and walked across the tiny hallway to the nursery.

Emma was still sound asleep, so Geena turned away from the crib and started out of the nursery, only to meet

Vince walking through the door. He was fully dressed, his expression grim.

"Sorry, Geena. I've got to go—Evan's already at the scene. There's been a shooting at a downtown bar. Two victims. One is in surgery. The other didn't make it."

She drew in a deep breath and let it out. "Of course you must go. I'll walk you to the door."

She watched with a mixture of love and fierce pride as he took a moment to press a kiss to Emma's cheek. She couldn't understand why it had taken her this long to understand that Vince's job was very special. Not many men could deal with the rigors and stress, the danger and most of all the sacrifice it took to serve and protect the public. Yes, she was very proud. And the next time they were together, she would make sure she told him exactly how much.

At the front door, he paused long enough to place a swift kiss on her lips. "This isn't the way I wanted our day to end," he said, his voice filled with disappointment.

Smiling gently, she shook her head. "There will be other days, Vince."

"Yeah, other days," he muttered, then opened the door and stepped onto the porch. "I'll call you later."

She blew him a kiss. "Be safe, darling."

He trotted out to his truck, and Geena watched him drive away before she finally shut the door.

No. This wasn't the way she would've chosen for this day to end. But as far as she was concerned, it was a beautiful start to the rest of their lives.

A week and a half later, Geena walked into the Green Lizard Bar and Grill for the first time and peered around the old establishment. Through the dim lighting, she took in the planked wooden floors and long polished bar with red padded stools. Mariachi music was playing faintly in the background, while the smell of Mexican food permeated the air.

She didn't see Marcella sitting at the long bar, so her friend must have found a table. But where?

"You don't have to wait to be seated, miss. Just sit wherever you'd like."

Geena glanced around at a young waiter standing a few steps to her right. A tray of drinks was balanced on one hand and stack of menus was jammed beneath his opposite arm.

"I'm looking for a friend," Geena told him. "A pretty redhead. Do you happen to know where she's sitting?"

"Sure. Follow me. I was headed in that direction."

After they worked their way through a maze of round wooden tables filled with customers, the room made a jog to the left and opened up to another dining area that was slightly less crowded than the outer room.

The waiter inclined his head to a table in the far corner, next to a window. "Is that her?"

"Yes, thanks," Geena said as she spotted the nurse.

"Can I get you anything to drink?" the waiter inquired.

"Coffee with cream would be great," she told him.

When Geena reached the table, Marcella rose to her feet and gave her a brief hug.

"I'm so happy you agreed to meet me for a drink," she said with a cheery smile. "Especially now that your teaching job has started and your time is limited."

"Well, it's not like you sit around eating grapes and watching television all day," Geena countered. "You work long shifts at the hospital and care for two boys. You got me beat."

Chuckling softly, Marcella reached for a tall glass of

soda. "So we're both superwomen. I'm sure you'd rather be picking up Emma now instead of meeting with me."

"I told Annie I'd be a little late this evening. She didn't seem to mind." Resting her forearms on the edge of the table, Geena looked at the nurse. "Okay, what are we doing here? We could've had coffee or something at my place."

Marcella wrinkled her nose. "Because I felt like you needed to be out and away from the house."

Confused by her friend's remark, Geena shook her head. "Marcella, I've been working for a week and a half now. I'm out of the house every day."

"You're simply too practical, Geena. I love coming here to the Green Lizard. I wanted you to enjoy it, too."

Geena was finding it impossible to enjoy much of anything. Not with Vince occupying her thoughts every waking minute of the day. After their beautiful day together touring the lake, she'd believed the past was truly behind them and their future together had started. When he'd driven off that evening, she'd been certain she would hear from him the next day. Now here it was ten days later without a call or visit or even a simple text. Her heart was breaking and she was wondering if she'd been worse than a fool for believing he'd actually wanted a future with her.

"Okay. I'll do my best to smile," Geena told her.

Her eyes squinting with concern, Marcella studied her. "Last night when we talked on the phone I could hear trouble in your voice. Is it Emma? Are you sure she's okay?"

"Perfect. Growing like a weed. She even smiled at me this morning. I realize she's still too young to give me a real smile, but nevertheless it was so sweet."

Marcella looked visibly relieved. "All right, if it's not Emma, then it must be your job. It's not what you hoped it would be. Or someone on the staff is already giving you a hard time."

"I'm loving my new job. Everyone at school has been great. And my students seem eager to learn, at least for now. A few of them are talkative, but that's only natural."

Marcella was about to make a reply when the waiter suddenly appeared with Geena's coffee.

"Would you ladies like something to eat?" he asked.

"No, thanks," Geena quickly answered.

"Yes, we would," Marcella told him. "Bring us some of those nasty good nachos. You know, the ones with everything piled on and all the calories taken out. My friend and I will share a plate."

"Nice choice. I'll bring them out in just a few minutes."

As soon as the waiter moved away, Geena rolled her eyes. "Marcella, I don't have time to eat! Besides, I'm not hungry. In fact, as soon as I down this coffee, I need to go."

"You're not going anywhere until you tell me what's going on with you. I can see that you haven't been eating enough. You look thin. Do you still have plenty of milk for Emma?"

With a smile of resignation, Geena shook her head. "Yes, I have more than enough milk for Emma. You never quit being a nurse, do you?"

Marcella smiled back at her. "Not totally."

Sighing, Geena picked up her coffee and took a sip. "I can't hide anything from you. So I might as well admit it—these past few days I've been miserable and confused. And I don't know what to do."

Concerned, Marcella leaned forward. "About what? Don't tell me that creep who signed away his rights to Emma is making noises about being a father now! If he is, don't worry for one second. I know a great lawyer. He handled Peter's adoption for me. He's married to Sassy Calhoun, in fact."

A faint smile touched Geena's lips. "Seems like everyone you know is connected to the Calhouns."

"They're a prominent family. They have connections to lots of folks around town, including that hunky ex of yours."

Geena sipped her coffee again, then returned the cup to its saucer. "Well, you needn't worry about Brad reappearing in my life. He's out of the picture forever." She looked hopelessly at Marcella, then shrugged. "I think I made a mistake—about Vince. Or maybe he made a mistake with me. I—don't understand what's happened. I—" She broke off, embarrassed that she was close to shedding tears.

Reaching across the table, Marcella patted the top of her hand. "Maybe you'd better start from the beginning. Has something happened between you two?"

Geena swallowed at the painful lump in her throat. "It has and it hasn't. I've been a fool in all kinds of ways!"

She went on to tell Marcella about her date with Vince and the wonderful day they'd spent together touring the lake. She left out the fact that their day had ended with them having sex. But Geena figured her friend could read between the lines without Geena having to spill the details.

"So when he left to go join Evan at the scene of the homicide, he promised to call," Geena explained. "Everything seemed okay. I mean, he wasn't too happy about being called away, but he appeared to be happy with me. The next day I expected to hear from him. But that never happened. After a couple more days went by without him contacting me, I called him."

Frowning, Marcella replied, "Don't tell me. It went to his voice mail and he's never returned your calls."

Geena stared at her friend. "You say that like—like you think he was using me. And now he's thrown me away! Again! Is that what you're thinking?"

"No! I might not be the greatest judge of character, but I'd bet my whole bank account that Vince Parcell is not a user."

"Then why won't he call? Or better yet, he knows where I live, why hasn't he come to see me? I realize his job keeps him tied up, but not to the point where he can't use the phone!"

"He's tied up, all right. But not in the way you're thinking," Marcella told her. "He's running scared. He jumped in with both feet and now they've turned cold."

For the past ten days Geena had gone over and over everything that had happened that day. Especially, the love-making. And in spite of the silent treatment he'd been giving her these past few days, she still had to believe he'd touched her with love. She had to trust that everything he'd said to her had come from his heart.

"So what am I supposed to do? And don't tell me to forget him! I've spent the past six years trying to do that and it didn't work, except for when I had amnesia."

"Tell me this, Geena. Do you want a life with Vince?"

Geena didn't have to think about her friend's question. "More than anything. We made mistakes the first time around. But I'm not afraid to try again. Because I love him. I'll always love him."

Marcella gave her a meaningful smile. "You don't need me, or a counselor, or anyone else to tell you what to do. You need to go to him. Right now. Tonight. And make it clear that you're not about to let him drop you again."

Geena thoughtfully chewed on her bottom lip. "That option has been going through my mind. But what if he refuses to see me, or he won't listen?"

"You'll figure that out when the time comes."

Coming to a sudden decision, Geena jumped to her feet

and gathered up her handbag. "You're right. I'm not some meek little 'fraidy cat. See you later."

She turned away from the table just as the waiter was arriving with the plate of nachos.

"Aren't you going to eat with your friend?" he asked.

"Sorry, not this time," she told him, then gestured back to Marcella. "And she'll pay for my coffee."

At the same time Geena was leaving the Green Lizard, Vince and Evan were returning to Carson City after a trip to the Sagebrush Lounge. For once their job had been an enjoyable one. Being able to reunite the owner with his beloved Rottweiler had made the trip more than worthwhile.

"Did you see the look on that guy's face when we jumped the dog out of the vehicle?" Evan asked. "It was priceless. You'd have thought we were returning his kid."

"I'm just glad we were able to track down the dog. And the booze. Even though half of it was already gone."

Evan shrugged as he negotiated the SUV over the narrow two-lane highway. "At least we got the thieves behind bars. And the owner's insurance should pay off on the missing beer and whiskey. So all is well with that case. Now on to the next one." He shook his head. "Right now I'm so tired I don't remember what's stacked on our desks."

"Yeah, on to the next case," Vince mumbled. He was scrunched down in the seat, his eyes half-closed against the ball of sun slipping behind the mountain peaks of Sierra Nevada. "I don't want to remember what's on my desk."

The police scanner on the dash rarely went for a minute without the dispatcher relaying some sort of message. More often than not, the calls were for the need of a deputy. When a request for a detective came over the speaker, Evan and Vince went on instant alert.

But tonight, Vince was finding it very nearly impossible

to listen to the radio or his partner's voice. For the past ten days he'd been so confused and torn, he'd been walking around in a damned daze. Every cell in his body was aching to be with Geena again. He wanted to see her smile, hear her voice, feel her loving arms wrapped around him. But his common sense continued to tell him to stay away.

"Hey, that address isn't far from where Geena lives," Evan spoke up. "I heard the dispatcher calling for Cooper and Graves to head to the scene. But maybe we should go by there."

Trying to shake away the miserable fog in his head, Vince glanced over at his partner. "What are you saying?"

Evan frowned. "I swear I think your hearing is going, Vince. I've had to repeat myself to you all day."

"Forget my hearing! What about Cooper and Graves?" he asked of the pair of deputies, who also worked in tandem with Evan and Vince.

"They've been called to investigate a stabbing. The address isn't far from Geena's place. I realize you haven't been talking with her. But I thought you might want to drive by. Just to make sure she's okay."

Feeling as though he'd just had a bucket of ice water thrown in his face, Vince sat straight up.

I was told a detective was coming to help me. What if you'd shouldered that job to someone else?

Geena's words had been haunting him for days now. Mostly because he knew she was right. People in need depended on him, or someone like him, to show up, to put things right, to help them make sense of a tragedy.

"I do—want to drive by."

"If I was a gambling man, I'd bet you'd like to stop and see her. And Emma."

"I don't want to talk about it," Vince barked at him. "So keep your mouth shut."

Evan let out a taunting chuckle. "And what if I don't? What are you going to do about it? I'm driving. You can't bust me in the mouth or we'd both end up in the bottom of that ravine over there with the lizards and the snakes."

Vince heaved out a heavy breath. "Sometimes I'd like to knock your head off."

"Not any more than I'd like to kick you in the ass!"

"Evan, you don't understand. I ruined Geena's life once. I can't do it again."

"What makes you think you'd ruin it?"

"As if you have to ask! You already know what happened. We had a great day together. I thought—well, I'd never seen Geena happier. For a while that day I could see a real future for us. Everything was perfect. And then I was called away."

"If that came as a surprise, then you were in la-la land. And in my opinion, you should've been thrilled you had that much time without interruption. Instead, you had a meltdown."

"Meltdown, hell," Vince muttered. "It jerked the blinders off my eyes."

Evan muttered a few choice curse words. "You're so blinded now I'm going to have to start leading you around! If you were really seeing things, you'd see that no one has a perfect life. And furthermore, Geena doesn't expect things to be perfect!"

Tossing his sunglasses onto the dash, Vince scrubbed his face with both hand. "Geena isn't Noelle," he muttered.

"That's right. She's the woman *you* love. Maybe it's time you started giving her a little credit for changing her life for the better. For being a single mother. For being a teacher. Most of all, for giving you a second chance."

Shadows were beginning to stretch across the desert floor while the lights of the city had begun to twinkle in the gloaming. As Vince looked out at the rugged land-scape, he wondered if Evan might be right. Had he been blinded to reality all this time?

Since that late afternoon when he'd left Geena's house, all he'd been able to think about was the way she'd looked at him when she'd said goodbye, the kiss she'd thrown him and the love glowing in her smile.

She'd not complained once about him being called to duty. No, instead of whining, she'd reminded him of the good he was doing. Yet strangely, her understanding and encouragement had made it even harder for him to walk away.

"All I want is for her to be happy," Vince said.

Evan darted a pointed glance at him. "Then give her the chance to be. Give yourself that chance."

Chapter Thirteen

Across town, Geena had just finished feeding Emma and was gathering things to put in her diaper bag when she heard a knock on the door.

Darn it, if that was Marcella she was going to choke her, Geena thought. As much as she loved the woman, she didn't have time for another visit. She was almost ready to leave for Vince's place, and she wasn't about to bother calling him first. He might not be home, but that wasn't going to deter her. She knew where he stored the extra key to the house. She'd let herself in and wait for the man. If he didn't want to talk with her, that was just too bad. Because as far as she was concerned, he had a lot of explaining to do!

Biting back an impatient groan, she walked out to the living room and peered through the small window on the door.

Vince!

Her hands trembling, she hurriedly fumbled with the

knob, yet once she pulled the door wide all she could do was stand there and stare like an idiot.

"Geena, may I come in?"

Silently, she pushed the door wider. After he walked past her and into the house, she glanced quizzically toward the driveway. Except for her little sedan, there was no sight of a vehicle.

"How did you get here?" she finally managed to ask.

"Evan dropped me off."

After securing the door behind her, she turned and was instantly whammed by the sight of his handsome face. Her crippled heart began to beat with foolish hope. "You two just happened to be in the neighborhood, so you thought you'd drop by for a quick hello?" she asked, not bothering to hide the sarcasm in her voice.

His jaw rigid, he said, "There'd been an incident a block over from here. A stabbing. I wanted to make sure you and Emma were safe."

She felt awful. "I'm sorry. I heard the sirens earlier. But I didn't go outside to look. I assumed it was a fire truck headed on down the street. What happened? Do you know yet?"

He shook his head, and Geena noticed the dark growth of beard on his face was longer than usual and his brown eyes were bloodshot. His weary appearance cut straight to her heart.

"Evan and I aren't working the case. But from what we've picked up on the radio it was domestic."

Her legs went weak, and she quickly stepped past him to take a seat on the couch. "That's awful. Since I moved here, this neighborhood has been nice and quiet."

He took a seat beside her and the trembling inside Geena grew to the point she thought her teeth were going to chatter.

"Domestic violence happens in every type of neighborhood."

"I'm sorry for sounding so petty a minute ago," she apologized, then drawing in a bracing breath, she lifted her chin to a proud angle. "But frankly, I'm a little more than angry with you, Vince. In fact, when you knocked on the door I was getting ready to drive to your place. I'm tired of you avoiding my calls—avoiding me! Furthermore, if you're not here to tell me you love me, then get the hell out!"

Before she could guess his intentions, he was wrapping his arms tightly around her and burying his face in the crook of her neck. "Oh, Geena, Geena, of course I love you! I've never stopped loving you. Ever!"

Stunned, she pushed herself far enough away to look into his eyes. "I don't understand, Vince. Why—"

"I've been a blinded fool, my darling. That's why I haven't called or come to see you. After our day at the lake and I had to return to duty, I felt sick and helpless. I kept thinking how better off you'd be without me. How much happier you'd be living with a regular guy with a nine-to-five job. I couldn't let the pain and unhappiness start all over again. So I thought I could give you up—again. But I can't."

Staggered by the emotion in his voice, she could barely speak around the raw lump in her throat. "Can't you see, Vince? I don't want a regular guy. I want you. A few minutes with you means more to me than a lifetime with someone I don't love."

His brown eyes suddenly began to glow with understanding, and then he was covering her lips with his, kissing her with more hunger and love than she ever thought possible.

When he finally pulled back to give them both a chance

to breathe, she asked impishly, "Does this mean your visit this evening was more than just a check on my safety?"

Chuckling, he pulled her onto his lap, then stood with her cradled in his arms. "I'm going to show you exactly what my visit is about."

Much, much later, in her shadowy bedroom, Geena and Vince lay in the middle of the bed, cuddled beneath a light blanket.

"Vince?"

"Hmm?"

"What really made you decide to come to me tonight? Other than trouble in the neighborhood."

"Every day that's gone by since we were last together has been pure hell," he admitted. "And nothing was getting better. Earlier this evening, Evan and I were driving back to town from the east county line. He was giving me a hard time, trying to make me see reason about you—and us. And I came to the conclusion that he was right. I had to try to make things right between us. That's when we heard about the stabbing. We both realized it wasn't your address, but it was close enough to scare me. I forced him to break the speed limit laws to get me here. What about you? Why did you suddenly decide tonight that you were going to go to my place and confront me?"

She laughed softly as she remembered the smug look on Marcella's face when Geena had jumped up from their table in the Green Lizard.

"Let's just say I had a well-meaning nudge from a friend."

"Marcella?"

Another chuckle slipped past her lips. "That's right. The woman is a hopeless romantic. It's a crying shame she's single."

"Hmm. Maybe you can do something to change her situation," he suggested.

Rising up on one elbow she looked at him. "Oh, no. If you're thinking about fixing her up with a blind date, forget it. She'd never go for that."

"That's not what I had in mind. I was thinking you could make sure she catches your wedding bouquet. That is how the adage goes, isn't it? The one who catches the bouquet will be the next one married?"

"Wedding! You mean you want us to have a real one?"

This time it was Vince who laughed. "I hardly want a fake one. Not after the hell we've gone through to get back together."

"A wedding," she repeated dreamily. "We had one all those years ago in Reno, but this one would be special. Like a new beginning."

"My thoughts exactly," Vince murmured. "A new beginning with a love that will last for a lifetime."

She was planting a kiss on his lips when Emma let out a loud fuss from the nursery. Geena quickly sat up and reached for her robe draped on the footboard of the bed.

"Would you mind fetching Emma from her crib?" she asked. "I have something I want to get from the kitchen."

Grinning, he flung back the blanket and retrieved his jeans from the floor. "Sure. It's time I started my daddy duties."

Moments later, Geena returned to the nursery to find Vince making a valiant effort to change Emma's diaper.

She stood to one side, her heart overflowing with love as she watched him tenderly dress the baby, then lift her into his arms.

"Not the neatest of jobs. But I don't think the diaper will fall off," he said as he shifted the tiny girl to a comfortable position against his chest.

"I can assure you that Emma thinks it's perfect," she told him, then pulled a large artist's pad from behind her back and thrust it in front of him. "This is what I wanted you to see. It's not perfect and I still have a bit to do on the shading, but it's almost finished."

She'd never seen such a look of astonishment on his face as he looked at the pencil drawing she'd been working on for the past several days.

"When did you do this? How—"

"Did I remember your father's face and the uniform he was wearing?" she finished the question for him.

He nodded, and she gave him a wan smile. "While I was staying at your house, before the amnesia went away, I used to stare at his photo—the one you have in the living room. I was sure I had a connection to him. Turns out I did."

Vince shook his head with amazement. "This is incredible, Geena. Every detail is perfect. I realize you're an art teacher, but I never thought you could do anything like this! And my father—"

His gaze met hers, and Geena's heart squeezed with a mixture of love and regret as she noticed the mist coating his brown eyes. They'd lost so much in the past, she thought, but now they had a future to make up for it.

"You understand how much he meant to me," he continued in a soft, wondrous voice. "How much he still lives inside me."

"I didn't realize it, Vince. Not during our first marriage. But I do now. That's why I wanted to surprise you with this gift of his image. To show you that your decision to become a lawman will never come between us again."

"I love you, Geena." Bending forward he kissed her slowly, thoroughly until Emma began to squirm in his arms.

Stepping back, Geena laughed softly. "See, it just goes

to show you that sometimes having the sense knocked out of your head is a good thing."

He curled his free arm around her back and tugged her close to his side. "A good thing is you and me and Emma. A family together. Finally."

Yes, Geena thought happily, a family together—for always. That was all she'd ever wanted.

Epilogue

Eight months later, on a cool Easter day, Vince and Geena peered down at the newborn infant lying in a wooden cradle. He was swaddled in a blue blanket, and a matching sock cap covered a thatch of thick, dark hair.

"Aw, how precious!" Geena crooned. "And all that hair!"

"I hate to say it," Vince joked, "but he looks like you, Evan. Same big mouth and horse nose."

"Vince!" Geena scolded. "This little boy is beautiful and you know it!"

Laughing, Vince raised up from the cradle and slapped an affectionate hand on Evan's shoulder. "Just kidding, partner. He's a handsome guy. Have you decided on a name yet?"

Evan looked over at Noelle, who was standing a few steps behind Geena. "She's named him Barton, after Granddad. Barton James Calhoun."

"He'll be little Bart until he grows up," Noelle said proudly.

"I'll bet the old man is as pleased as punch about that," Vince remarked. "Having his new great-grandson named after him."

Evan chuckled knowingly. "He and Noelle have a special bond."

"That's right," Noelle teased her husband. "I think I fell in love with Bart before I did you."

"Ha. The old codger always could charm the women," Evan said.

"Well, all the family has gathered at the Silver Horn today for an Easter celebration," Noelle explained, "except for us. I didn't want to expose little Bart to that big a crowd. He's only a week old."

"The family understands, honey," Evan told her. "Granddad Bart was disappointed that we weren't going to be there, but he'll get over it."

"So you declined a big celebration on the Horn and settled for a quiet little Easter with us," Vince joked. "Evan, your life is going to the dogs."

The four adults were still laughing when Joanna came running into the room, followed by Talulah, with ten-month-old Emma clutched in her arms.

"Eggs, Daddy! It's time to hunt eggs!" Joanna shouted with happy excitement.

Evan made a big show of consulting his watch. "I believe you're right, darlin'. I'll bet the Easter Bunny has already come and gone. Let's go see."

Everyone except Talulah and little Bart made their way outside to a large backyard fenced with cedar railing. For the next several minutes, colorful plastic eggs were discovered behind legs of lawn furniture, potted plants and anything large enough to partially hide the bunny's treasures.

When Vince offered Emma a large pink egg, she clutched it with both hands, then squealing with delight, drew it straight to her mouth. But thankfully, the object was too big for the toddler to do more than drool on it.

Laughing, Vince said, "I think she wants a real one to eat."

Smiling, Geena said, "She thinks everything is to bite. God help us when she gets a mouth full of teeth."

Vince adjusted his daughter's frilly bonnet, then glanced at Geena. If possible his wife had grown more beautiful to him since they married some eight months ago. Maybe that was because he was finally seeing her as a woman who loved him in spite of his flaws, his job and the mistakes of the past.

As Evan had succinctly reminded him, life was never perfect, and there'd been times it had been difficult juggling their jobs and the needs of the baby. But their love for each other had never wavered. And Vince never worried that it would.

If six years apart and a bout of amnesia couldn't tear the bond between them, then nothing would.

Geena's arm slipped around the back of his waist. "What is that sly smile on your face about?" she asked impishly.

"I was just thinking how special it is to be spending this beautiful day with our friends."

With a sigh of contentment, her gaze turned to the rolling bald hills that were just starting to turn green with spring grass.

"Yes, Easter signifies new life," she said softly. "That's why I waited until today to tell you that we're going to have a baby."

It took a moment for the significance of her words to sink in on him. When they finally did, he snatched hold of her shoulder and thrust her out in front of him.

His expression incredulous, he sputtered, "A baby! Are you positive?"

Her eyes misty, she looked at him and nodded. "That shopping trip I took yesterday afternoon was actually a visit to the walk-in clinic to see if my suspicion was correct. The doctor says we should look for him or her by mid-October. Are you happy?"

"Happy? Oh, my darling, I couldn't be more ecstatic! But what about you? Emma is still so young and your job is—"

Smiling, she placed a finger against his lips. "I can hardly wait for the challenge. Maybe after we have four or five kids, I'll be ready to slow down. But not now. We're going to have that big family, my love. The one we always dreamed of having."

"Yes, a big family," he agreed, then bent to place a loving kiss on her lips.

As he lifted his head, he noticed the tiny silver cross resting in the hollow of her throat. Touching the symbol with his forefinger, he murmured in awesome wonder, "I gave you this Easter gift so long ago. Now this Easter you're giving me a baby. Miracles really do happen."

Clasping her hand around his, she squeezed his fingers. "Come on, let's go share the good news with our friends."

* * * * *

Don't miss Marcella's story,
the next installment of
USA TODAY *bestselling author Stella Bagwell's*
MEN OF THE WEST *series!*
Coming in December 2016
from Mills & Boon Cherish.

This **was it.**

The challenge that was going to tell him who he really was. What his values really were and whether he was made of the right stuff to rule a country in the best interests of the many thousands of people who would be trusting him to do the right thing.

He'd convinced himself that resisting the attraction he felt towards Mika was that test, so why—in this moment after those words had been uttered, when it felt as if time was holding its breath—did it feel so utterly *wrong*?

As if he didn't really have a choice at all?

Again, he was reminded of when she had taken his hand, up there on the top of that cliff. Of when her trembling had finally ceased and he'd known she was trusting him.

He'd felt taller, then. Powerful in a way that had had nothing to do with him as a prince but everything to do with who he was as a man. Nothing would have persuaded him to break that trust.

And right now Mika was trusting him with so much more than her hand. She was asking him to take hold of her whole body, and by doing so he would still be leading her to safety— wouldn't he?

THE FORBIDDEN PRINCE

BY
ALISON ROBERTS

First Published in Great Britain 2016
By Mills & Boon, an imprint of HarperCollins*Publishers*
1 London Bridge Street, London, SE1 9GF

© 2016 Alison Roberts

ISBN: 978-0-263-92010-9

23-0816

Our policy is to use papers that are natural, renewable and recyclable products and made from wood grown in sustainable forests. The logging and manufacturing processes conform to the legal environmental regulations of the country of origin.

Printed and bound in Spain
by CPI, Barcelona

Alison Roberts is a New Zealander, currently lucky enough to live near a beautiful beach in Auckland. She is also lucky enough to write for both the Mills & Boon Cherish and Medical Romance lines. A primary school-teacher in a former life, she is also a qualified paramedic. She loves to travel and dance, drink champagne and spend time with her daughter and her friends.

For Becky
With all my love

CHAPTER ONE

So this was what freedom felt like.

Raoul de Poitier sucked in a deep breath as he paused to get his first proper glimpse of the view he'd climbed about two thousand steps to find.

He had the whole world at his feet.

Well…he had what looked like a large part of the Amalfi coast of the Mediterranean down there, anyway. Far, far below he could pick out the tiny blue patch that was the swimming pool on the roof of the hotel Tramonto d'Oro where he'd stayed last night. Beside that was the tiled dome and spire of the ancient church against the terracotta tiles and white houses of the small coastal town of Praiano.

Beyond the village, the waters of the Mediterranean stretched as far as the horizon, a breathtakingly sapphire blue as the sunlight gentled its way to dusk. Somewhere out there was his homeland—the European principality of *Les Iles Dauphins*.

Another deep breath was released in what felt like a sigh, and with it came a pang of…what… homesickness? Guilt, perhaps?

His grandfather was ill. His heart was failing and it

was time for him to step down from ruling his land. To hand the responsibility to the next-in-line to the throne.

His grandmother would be anxious. Not only about her beloved husband but about the grandson she'd raised as her own child after the tragic death of his parents.

'I don't understand, Raoul. A holiday...yes. Time to prepare yourself for what is to come. For your marriage... But alone? Incognito? That's not who you are.'

'Maybe that's what I need to find out, Mamé. And this is the last chance I will ever get.'

No. The pang wasn't guilt. He needed this time to centre himself for what was to come. To be sure that he had what it took to put aside his own desires if that was what was required to protect and nurture a whole nation, albeit a tiny one. He was thirty-two years old but he hadn't been really tested yet. Oh, there'd been formal duties that had got in the way of private pleasures, and he had always had to curb any desire to push the boundaries of behaviour that might be frowned on by others. But, within that reasonably relaxed circumference, he'd been able to achieve the career that had been top of his chosen list—as a helicopter pilot in his country's first-rate rescue service. And he'd had his share of a seemingly infinite supply of beautiful women.

All that was about to change, however. The boundaries would shrink to contain him in a very tight space. Almost every minute of every day would be accounted for.

He had always known it would happen. He just wasn't sure how ready he was to accept it. Somehow, he needed to find that out. To test himself, by himself, which was why this had to be in a place where he knew no one and no one knew who he was.

Was it homesickness, perhaps? Because he was feeling a new and rather extraordinary sensation of being alone? No. He'd dealt with homesickness many years ago when he'd been sent to the best schools that Europe had to offer and, while the love of his family and homeland would always draw him back and enfold him, he loved to travel.

It was relief, that was what it was. He had won this time. A reprieve from thinking about the overwhelming responsibility of being in charge of a nation, along with the daunting prospect of a marriage that had been arranged when he'd been no more than a child. A union that would bond two similar principalities together and strengthen them both.

Raoul turned away from the view of the sea. Les Iles Dauphins was out of sight and he was going to try and put it out of mind for just a little while.

He was free. All he had was in his backpack and he could choose any direction at all, the time he would take to get there and how long he would stay when he did. As of yesterday, nobody knew where he was and he was confident that nobody would recognise him. His hair grew fast and he'd deliberately missed his last cut. His beard was coming along well, too. With his dark sunglasses, he could pass for any European tourist. Italian, French… Spanish, even.

He could feel the corners of his mouth curve. If he'd had a guitar case on his back instead of his backpack, he would probably have looked like a flashback to the sixties. He was completely alone for what felt like the first time in his entire life. No family, no friends and, most importantly, no bodyguards or lurking paparazzi. He had won the freedom simply to be himself.

He just needed to find out who that was, exactly, because he had a feeling there were layers to his personality that had been buried for ever. Even his earliest memories involved a performance of some kind. Of behaving in a way that would never have been expected of others.

How many five-year-olds could take part in a national ceremony to mourn both parents and not cry until they were finally alone in their own beds and presumed to be sound asleep? Who had childhood friends chosen for them and, even then, had to be careful of what was said? What young adult knew how much had been sacrificed by a generation that had already raised a child and shouldn't have had to start all over again? The burden of a debt that could never properly be repaid had never been intended but it was there all the same.

He had never been drunk enough to do anything inappropriate or create a scandal by dating indiscreet women. He had excelled in his university studies and military training and, until he'd taken this leave, had shone in his role as a helicopter pilot for a service that provided both military transport and emergency rescue services.

Sometimes, it felt like his life had been recorded by photographs that had been staged for public consumption and approval. A picture-perfect life of a happy prince. And the next album would have all the pomp and ceremony of his coronation, then his wedding and then the births of the next generation of the de Poitier royal family.

The happiness was not an illusion. Raoul loved his life and knew how incredibly fortunate he was but his curiosity of the unknown had teased him with increasing frequency of late. Was there something solid that formed the essence of who he was as a person? Something that would have been there if he hadn't been born a prince?

He had four weeks to try and find some kind of answer to what seemed an impossible question and the only plan he had come up with was to see if he could find a challenge that would be testing enough to make him dig deep. He had set out with no more than the bare essentials of survival in a backpack—a phone, a fake ID, limited funds and a change of clothes. This demanding climb up a mountain to the track that led from Praiano to Positano was just the first step on a very private journey.

Or maybe it wasn't quite that private.

Frowning, Raoul stared at the narrow, winding track ahead of him. He could hear voices. One voice, anyway.

Faint.

Female.

'Aiuti... Per favore aiutatemi...'

The vertigo had come from nowhere.

Utterly unexpected and totally debilitating.

Tamika Gordon was clinging to the side of a cliff and she didn't dare open her eyes. If she did, the nausea would come back, the world would start spinning again and there would be nothing to stop her falling into that terrifyingly sheer drop onto rocks hundreds of feet below. But keeping her eyes shut didn't wipe out the knowledge that the unprotected edge to this track was no more than the length of her arm away.

The panic that led her to cry for help was almost as terrifying as the yawning chasm below.

Mika didn't do panic. She'd been told more than once that she was 'as hard as nails' and she was proud of it. It was a badge of honour, won by surviving. Of course she was tough. Who wouldn't be when they'd been dragged up through a succession of disastrous foster homes and then had ended up on the streets as a teenager? She'd fought for everything she had achieved in her twenty-nine years on earth so far and she'd been confident she could cope with whatever life chose to throw at her.

But this...this was totally out of her control. She'd fought it for as long as possible with sheer willpower but the symptoms were physical rather than mental and they had increased in ferocity until she'd reached a point of complete helplessness—reduced to a shivering blob of humanity clinging to a couple of tufts of coarse mountain grass. It was beyond humiliating. She'd be angry about it as soon as she got out of this and the terror had a chance to wear off. *If* she ever got out of this...

She hadn't seen anyone else on this supposedly popular walking route so far. Maybe that was her own fault. She'd chosen to set off from Praiano much later in the day than most people because she knew the light would be so much better for taking photographs. And maybe she'd spent too much time down at the monastery halfway up the steps, taking photographs with her precious new camera and scribbling notes in her pristine journal.

How long would it be before it got dark?

'*Help…*' She tried English this time instead of Italian. 'Can anyone hear me?'

Her voice wavered and tears stung as they gathered behind her eyelids. This recognition of a despair she hadn't felt since she'd been too young to protect herself had to be the worst moment of her adult life.

'I'm coming… Hold on…'

She wasn't alone. There was hope to be found now. A glowing light in the darkness of that despair. It was a male voice she'd heard, the words short, as if he was out of breath, and in the space after those words Mika could hear the sound of shoes crunching on the sparse gravel of the track.

He was *running*?

When there were only a few feet between the steep wall of the cliff above and that appalling drop into nothingness below?

The speed of the footsteps slowed and then stopped.

'What is it?' A deep voice with a faint accent that she couldn't place. 'Are you hurt?'

Mika shook her head, her eyes still tightly closed. The overwhelming relief at not being alone any more made speech impossible for several breaths.

'Vertigo,' she managed finally, hating how pathetic her voice sounded. 'I… I can't move…'

'You're safe,' the man said. 'I'll keep you safe.'

Dear Lord…had anybody *ever* said that to her? Being so helpless had made her feel like a small child again, so it was too easy to imagine how it would feel to have somebody say those words to that frightened little girl. To feel fear and desolation start to drain away as if a plug had been pulled. To have an insight into how different her life might have been if somebody had said that to her, back then, and meant it. If somebody had been there to protect her. To love her…

How humiliating was it to have her outward breath sound like a child's sob? She'd learned long ago that weakness was something to be hidden very deeply.

'It's okay,' the man said. 'You're going to be fine. How long have you been stuck?'

'I…don't know.' It felt like for ever.

'Are you thirsty? I have water.'

She heard a shuffling sound and then a zip opening. She was thirsty but to accept a water bottle would mean opening her eyes, and what if the spinning started again? Sobbing in front of a stranger was bad enough. Imagine if she threw up?

'It's okay. I don't need a drink.'

There was a moment's silence. 'What's your name?'

'Mika.'

'It's a pleasure to meet you, Mika.'

This time her breath came out as a huff of something closer to laughter than tears. Her rescuer had very nice manners. He sounded as though they'd just been introduced at a cocktail party.

'I'm Ra…um… Rafe.'

She had only been speaking to him for a minute or two, and she didn't even have any idea what he looked like, but the hesitation seemed out of character. Did he not want her to know his real name? Was it possible that she was about to step from the frying pan into the fire and put her faith in an axe murderer? Or a…a rapist?

It might have been five years ago but the fear was always too close to the surface. If he hadn't chosen that precise moment to touch her, she could have dealt with it. It wasn't like the vertigo; she could persuade herself to think rationally and conquer it.

But he touched her arm and moving away from that touch was too instinctive to avoid. Mika let go of her tufts of grass with every intention of trying to run but her legs were still shaking and she lost her footing. Desperately trying to stop the skid, she reached for the grass again, but it slid through her fingers. Her foot made contact with something solid and she pushed against it but that, too, slid out of touch. She landed on her hands and knees, aware of a sound like rocks falling that provided a background to the soft but vehement curse that came from her rescuer.

And then silence.

Cautiously, Mika sat back on her heels as she tried to process what had just happened.

'Are you all right?'

'Yes. I'm sorry. I... I slipped.'

'Hmm...'

She could feel him watching her. 'Did I...um...kick you?'

'No. You kicked my backpack. It went over the cliff.'

Mika's eyes opened smartly. '*What?* Oh, no... I'm *so* sorry...'

'Better the pack than you.'

It seemed extraordinary but he was smiling at her. A smile that made the corners of his eyes crinkle. Dark eyes. Dark, shaggy hair and a dark jaw that had gone well past designer stubble but wasn't quite a beard. And he was big. Even crouching he seemed to tower over her.

Weird that the fear that had prompted this unfortunate development was ebbing away instead of increasing. Maybe it was those eyes. This man might be in a position of power over her right now but he wasn't any kind of predator. He looked…nice. Kind?

You're safe. I'll keep you safe.

'Did it have anything important in it? Like your wallet?' A churning in her stomach reminded her not to try looking over the edge of the cliff.

'There's no point worrying about that right now. The light's going to fade before long, Mika. I need to get you off this track.'

Mika nodded. She scrambled to her feet, her own light pack still secure on her back. If she didn't look into the chasm, maybe she would be okay. She looked towards the solid side of the cliff, reaching out her hand to touch it as well.

'I'm trying to decide which way would be best. You've come a long way onto the open part of the track already. It's probably better to keep going towards Positano rather than go down all those steps when it's getting darker.'

Mika swallowed hard and then nodded again. 'That's where I'm living at the moment. In Positano.'

'The track is quite narrow. Do you want me to walk ahead of you or behind?'

'Ahead, I think… I can watch your feet. If I don't look at the drop, maybe the dizziness won't come back.'

It worked…for a little while…but, try as she might, Mika became more and more aware of the emptiness on the left side in her peripheral vision. Using her free hand to provide a kind of blinker also helped for a while but it wasn't enough. Her stomach began to fold itself into spasms of distress and her brain began a slow, sickening spin. She tried to focus on the boots in front of her: smart, expensive-looking leather hiking boots. Thick socks were rolled down above them and then there were bare legs, muscles under olive skin outlined with every step.

'How's it going?'

Mika dropped the hand she was using as a shield to look up as Raoul turned his head when she didn't respond immediately. She tried to smile but changing the focus of her vision seemed to have made the spinning sensation worse.

'Here… It might help to hold my hand.'

It was there, right in front of her, palm downwards and fingers outstretched in invitation.

And it was huge.

Not the hand, although it had long, artistic-looking fingers. No. It was the idea of voluntarily putting her own into it that was so huge. Five years was a very long time not to have allowed the touch of a man's skin against her own.

But the need to survive was an overwhelmingly strong motivation. Strong enough to break a protective barrier that was inappropriate in this moment. She put her hand in his and felt his fingers curl around hers. She could feel the strength of the arm attached to that hand. The solidity of the body attached to the arm. The confidence of each step that was being taken.

He was half a pace ahead of her, because there was no room to walk side by side, but the hand was all that mattered.

He was holding her.

And he would keep her safe.

* * *

She was a fighter, this Mika.

And there was something wild about her.

She was certainly unlike any woman he'd ever met before. For a start, she was out here all by herself, which advertised independence and courage, but she was tiny. Her head barely reached his shoulder, which probably made her look younger than she really was— an intriguing contrast to those big, dark eyes that made you think she'd seen far more than her age should have allowed for. She had spiky dark hair, which should have seemed unattractive to someone who'd always favoured long, blonde tresses, but he had to admit that it suited Mika. So did the clothes that looked more suitable for a walk on a beach than a mountain hike—denim shorts that were frayed at the bottom and a loose white singlet, the hem of which didn't quite meet the waistband of the shorts.

The shoes weren't exactly suitable either, being well-worn-looking trainers, and it looked as though her feet were bare inside them, but the surprise of that choice had been well and truly surpassed when Raoul had noticed her tattoo. The inked design looked tribal—like a series of peaked waves encircling her upper arm just below armpit level. No. Maybe even that observation had been trumped by spotting the tiny charm on the simple silver chain around her neck.

A dolphin…

The symbol of his homeland. What would she think if she knew that she was wearing something that gave her an instant connection to everything he held most dear in his life?

But it had been that instinctive flinch from a touch

that had been intended as no more than reassurance that had really given him the sense of wildness about her. It wasn't just the physical appearance that said she made her own choices or the fact that she was alone in a potentially dangerous place. It was that wariness of the touch, the hesitation in accepting contact from another human, that had been revealed by her body language when he'd offered to take her hand.

The trembling he'd felt when she'd finally accepted the offer.

Or perhaps it was the way she'd been doggedly following him even though it was clearly an enormous struggle. She'd been as white as a sheet when he'd turned to check on how she was doing. He could see that she was pushing herself beyond her limits but he could also see the determination that she wasn't going to let it defeat her. Anger, almost, that she'd been beaten into submission. Like a wild creature that had been trapped?

Another hundred metres along this goat track of a path—past a rustic wooden sign with Praiano written on one side and Nocelle on the other—and Raoul could feel that the trembling in her hand had ebbed. The holding had all been on his part to begin with but now he could feel a return pressure from that small hand he was holding and it made him feel…good.

Protective. She hadn't wanted him to touch her but she'd allowed it when she'd reached the end of her endurance.

She was trusting him and he wasn't going to break that trust. He would look after this wild creature of a woman until he was absolutely sure she was okay.

'Don't worry,' he told her. 'It'll wear off as soon as you don't have that drop beside you.'

'I know.' It sounded like she was speaking through gritted teeth.

'It's nothing to be ashamed of,' he added. 'Vertigo is like altitude sickness. It makes no difference how fit or strong you are. These things just happen.'

A tiny huff of sound suggested that Mika didn't let things just happen to *her* and Raoul felt a flash of empathy. Imagine if it had happened to him. If he'd set out to discover the qualities in himself that would allow him to face his future with confidence and he'd been left helpless and totally dependent on the kindness of a stranger…

Oddly, he felt almost envious of Mika. Maybe it took something that dramatic to strip away every layer that life had cloaked you with. To face that kind of fear would certainly reveal any strengths or weaknesses. Maybe the kind of challenge he needed was something like Mika had just faced—something that you would never choose voluntarily.

But you couldn't create one. Like the vertigo he'd told her about, it either happened or it didn't.

He *was* facing an unexpected development, however—a small thing, compared to Mika's challenge, but how on earth was he going to cope with losing that backpack? The clothing and toiletries didn't matter but he'd lost his wallet, passport and phone. It would be easy enough to place a call from a public telephone to request help but, even if his grandmother said nothing, he would hear the subtext of 'I told you so'. Going incognito to be a nobody in the real world was not something a prince should do. It wasn't who he was.

Failure wasn't an option. He just needed to come up with a new plan. Maybe he'd find inspiration by the time this walk was over.

The sigh he blocked after a few minutes of nothing remotely inspirational occurring seemed to transfer itself to Mika, as she pulled her hand from his.

'I'm okay now.'

He'd been so lost in his thoughts that Raoul hadn't noticed how the track had changed. They weren't on a cliff edge any more. The path had widened and there were trees on either side.

A glance at Mika and the change he saw in her appearance was startling. She was still pale but the tension in her face and the panic in her eyes had gone. And, if that hadn't made her look different enough, her mouthed curved into a grin that he could only describe as cheeky.

'Stupid, huh?'

It was impossible not to grin back.

'Not at all. Like I said, it can happen to anybody.'

'It's like a switch has been flicked off. Now that I can't see the cliff, I'm fine.' She ducked her head and when she looked up again there was something soft in her eyes. Something that made Raoul feel a flush of warmth like the tingle you got when you held cold hands out to a fire.

'Thank you *so* much. I… I think you might have saved my life.'

'It was my pleasure.' The words were quiet but he meant every one of them. Oddly, he needed to clear his throat after he'd uttered them. 'Let's hope there are no more open parts to the track.'

'I don't think there are. We should get to the village

of Nocelle soon and then it's just a whole lot more steps down into Positano.' Mika raised her eyebrows. 'I wonder if the police station will still be open.'

'Excuse me?'

'So you can report the loss of your backpack. In case someone finds it.'

'I think that's highly unlikely. It didn't look like the kind of cliff anyone would be climbing for fun.'

'I can't believe I did that. I feel awful.'

'It doesn't matter. Really...'

For a few moments they walked in silence. Dusk was really gathering now, and it was darker amongst the trees, so coming across a small herd of goats startled them both. The goats were even more startled and leapt off the track to scramble up through the forest, the sound of their bleating and bells astonishingly loud in the evening stillness.

'Sorry, goats,' Mika called, but she was laughing. She even had some colour in her cheeks when she turned towards Raoul. 'I *love* Italy,' she told him. 'I might live here for ever.'

'Oh? You're not Italian, then?'

'Huh? We've been talking English since we met. What makes you think I'm Italian?'

'When I first heard you call for help, you spoke in Italian. And you've got a funny accent when you speak English.'

'I do *not*.' Mika sounded offended. 'I can get by in Italian pretty well but English is my first language.'

'So you are from England?'

'No. I'm half-Maori, half-Scottish.'

'You don't *sound* Scottish.'

'I'm not. I'm a Kiwi.'

Raoul shook his head. She was talking in riddles. Her smile suggested she was taking pity on him.

'I come from New Zealand. Little country? At the bottom of the world?'

'Oh...of course. I know it. I've seen the *Lord of the Rings* movies. It's very beautiful.'

'It is. What about you, Rafe?'

'What about me?' He was suddenly wary.

'Rafe isn't your *real* name, is it?'

The wariness kicked up a notch. 'What makes you say that?'

'You sounded like you were going to say something else when you introduced yourself, that's all. Do you have a weird name or something?' That cheeky grin flashed again. 'Is Rafe short for Raphael?'

Relief that he hadn't been unexpectedly recognised made him chuckle. 'Um...something like that.'

'Rafe it is, then. Are *you* Italian?'

'No.'

'How come you speak English with a funny accent, then?'

He had to laugh again. 'I'm European. I speak several languages. My accent is never perfect.'

'It's actually pretty good.' The concession felt like high praise. 'Are you here on holiday?'

'Yes. You?'

'No, I'm working. I'm doing my OE.'

'Oh-ee?' The word was unfamiliar.

'Overseas Experience. It's a rite of passage for young New Zealanders.'

'Oh...and is it something you have to do alone?'

'Not necessarily.'

'But *you* are doing it alone?'

'Yep.' Her tone suggested she wouldn't welcome any further questions about her personal life. 'Oh, look—civilisation.'

Sure enough, they had reached the outskirts of the mountain village. There was no real reason to stay with Mika any longer. She had completely recovered and she was safe. But Raoul was enjoying her company now and he had to admit he was curious. Mika was a world away from her homeland and she was alone.

Why?

They walked in silence for a while as they entered the village of Nocelle. Raoul's eye was caught by big terracotta pots with red geraniums beneath a wooden sign hanging from a wrought-iron bar advertising this to be the Santa Croce *ristorante* and bar. Extending an invitation was automatic.

'Can I buy you a coffee or something to eat? I don't know about you, but I'm starving after that hike. We could get a bus down to Positano if it's too dark to use the steps later.'

The invitation had been impulsive—a polite thing for a gentleman to do. It was only after he'd voiced it that Raoul realised how much he actually wanted Mika to agree.

He wanted to offer her food, not just because he was reluctant to give up her company—he wanted to look after her for a little while longer. To recapture that heart-warming sensation of winning the trust of somebody who needed his help although they would have preferred not to accept it.

It was just to make absolutely sure she was okay, of course. Nothing more. Hooking up with any young woman on this trip was an absolute no-no and, besides, he'd never be physically attracted to somebody like Mika. She was a tomboy, possibly the complete opposite to any woman he'd ever invited into his life or his bed—those picture-perfect blondes that knew how to pose for an unexpected photograph. Maybe that explained the fascination.

She was looking almost as wary as she had when he'd offered his hand to help her along the track and suddenly—to his horror—Raoul realised it might be better if she declined the invitation. He could feel the smile on his face freeze as he discreetly tried to pat the pocket on his shorts. He might have enough loose change to cover a bus fare for them both but it was highly unlikely that he could pay for a meal.

He was still smiling but Mika seemed to be reading his mind. A furrow appeared on her forehead.

'Your wallet *was* in your backpack, wasn't it? You don't have any money, do you?'

'Ah…'

'What about your passport? And do you even have a place to stay?'

'Um…' The echo of the 'I told you so' vibe that he would very much prefer to avoid made him straighten his spine. 'I'll find somewhere.'

He found himself nodding. A short, decisive movement. Maybe this unfortunate occurrence was actually a blessing in disguise. Exactly the kind of challenge he needed to find out what he was made of. Whether he could cope with a bit of genuine adversity.

'Do you have any friends around here?'

The nod morphed into a subtle shake, more of a head tilt, as the question unexpectedly captured Raoul on a deeper level. He'd never lacked for people desperate to be his friends but experience had taught him that it was all too often due to his position in life rather than any genuine personal connection. He was probably as wary of making friends as Mika was about letting someone offer her assistance. Of letting someone touch her. It was impossible to know, in fact, whether he had any real friends at all because he'd never been in this position before.

Being ordinary.

Meeting someone who was judging him on who he *really* was—as a man and not as a prince.

'Doesn't matter. You've got one now.' Mika's face lit up with that impish grin but it faded quickly to a much more serious expression. 'You saved my life, mate.' There was still a gleam in her eyes that didn't match her sombre expression. 'I'm afraid I can't subscribe to the Chinese tradition of becoming your slave for life to repay the debt but…' Her face scrunched into lines that suggested serious thought. 'But I can buy you dinner.' The grin flashed again. 'I might even splash out on a cold beer.'

Raoul couldn't take his eyes off Mika. Witnessing the confidence that was returning now that her frightening experience was over was like seeing a butterfly emerge from its chrysalis. The way her expressions changed so quickly, and the lilt of her voice with that unusual accent was enchanting, but perhaps the most extraordinary thing was the effect that smile had on him.

He wanted to see it again. To make her laugh, even…

And she'd declared herself to be his friend. Without having the faintest idea who he really was.

Oddly, that made him feel humble. It gave him a bit of lump in his throat, if he were honest.

'Come on, Raphael.' The pocket rocket that was his newest friend was already heading down the cobbled street towards the arched entrance to the restaurant. 'We'll eat and then we'll figure out what you're going to do. If you're starving, it's impossible to think about anything but food, don't you think?'

'Mmm…' But the lopsided grin—almost a wink—that had accompanied her use of what she thought was his real name made Raoul smile inwardly.

It was a rare experience indeed for him to be teased. He had no siblings, and apparently it hadn't been the done thing for others to tease a prince, even in childhood.

He liked it, he decided.

He liked Mika, too.

CHAPTER TWO

IT WAS ONE of the things that Mika loved about Italian villages—that she could rock up to a place like this, in shorts and a singlet top, probably looking as weary and in need of a shower as she felt, and still be welcomed with a smile and gestures that suggested they had been waiting for her arrival.

The change when Raoul entered the restaurant behind her was subtle but unmistakable. Instead of a welcome guest, Mika suddenly felt like a…*a princess*?

'This way, sir, please; this is the best seat in the house. And you're lucky. You get to catch the last of this magnificent sunset.'

The whole wall of the restaurant was glass and the building seemed to be perched on the side of the mountain. It was the same view they'd had from the top of the Footpath of the Gods, only now the Mediterranean was on fire with red and gold light, and the islands way up the coast were dark, mysterious humps. It was a similar drop over a cliff right beside them, too, with no more than a low, railed fence outside the window and a roof or two of houses well below on the steep slope.

The slight quirk of Rafe's eyebrow along with the expression in those dark eyes was remarkably eloquent.

He wanted to know if she was okay to be sitting, over-looking the drop. He would be more than happy to forgo the view if she wasn't and he would request a change without embarrassing her by referring to her recent disability in public.

It made Mika feel even more like a princess.

No. It made her feel the same way that taking hold of his hand on the track had made her feel.

Protected.

Safe.

She had to clear her throat to get rid of an odd lumpy sensation before she spoke.

'This is gorgeous,' she said. 'Perfect.'

The white linen tablecloth was more of a worry than the view, in fact. Along with the silver cutlery, and the way their host flicked open a huge napkin and let it drape over her bare legs told Mika that this was nothing like the café she currently worked in. Was it going to be horrendously expensive? She remembered those nice boots Rafe was wearing. How well he spoke English when his accent advertised that it wasn't his first language. How the *maître d'* had instantly recognised somebody that deserved respect. Mika suspected that Rafe had come from a far more privileged background than hers. He was probably quite used to eating in restaurants that had linen tablecloths and silver cutlery.

Thank goodness she'd been paid yesterday.

'I will bring you the menu,' the *maître d'* said, reaching out to light the candle on their table. 'For drinks, also? We have a wide selection of the finest wines.'

It was Mika's turn to raise an eyebrow in Rafe's direction. At least, that was what she intended to do, but as soon as her gaze met his she completely forgot and found herself smiling instead. Was he as amused by this as she was? Here they were, looking like scruffy tourists, and they were being offered a selection of the finest wines.

'A glass of your house red, perhaps,' Rafe said.

'I'll have a beer, please,' Mika added. 'A really cold lager.'

With a nod, their waiter turned away. Mika glanced back at Rafe and this time her eyebrows did rise. He looked as though he was assessing something important. Something to do with herself? His face looked quite serious as he turned his head.

'Excuse me,' he called. 'I've changed my mind. Can you bring me a beer, too, please?'

It was a bit silly to feel so pleased about a simple change of drinks but it was as if Rafe was sealing their friendship in some way. Telling her that he liked her choice and was prepared to follow it.

She liked him, she decided. It was a bit disconcerting that merely his presence could alter an atmosphere in a room, as if he had an aura of some invisible power, but she didn't feel threatened by him in any way. Quite the opposite—and that was probably as disconcerting as how ridiculously good-looking that glow from the sunset through the window was making him seem.

Nobody was *that* perfect.

To cover the tumble of thoughts she had no intention of exploring, Mika opened her bag to take out her camera.

'I've got to get a photo of this sunset,' she told Rafe. 'How stunning is that?'

'It's amazing,' he agreed. 'I bet we could see as far as Capri in the day time.'

Mika wished she'd read more of the instruction booklet for her camera last night. She had to hope the settings were appropriate for the level of contrast out there.

'Nice camera,' Rafe said when she'd finished snapping.

'I know.' Mika sighed happily. 'It's a Nikon D4. Sixteen-point-two megapixels. It's my new baby,' she added quietly. 'I've been waiting a long time for this.' The first step to a new career. A new life.

'You're keen on photography?'

'Mmm.' Mika was scrolling through the photos she'd just taken. The dream of becoming a travel writer and supplying great photos to accompany her stories was too new and private to share. 'Look…' She tilted the screen of the camera towards Rafe. 'These are the ones I took of the monastery on the way up the mountain.'

He leaned forward and reached out to hold the other side of the camera as she kept scrolling.

'These are great. I just stopped long enough to look at the view but you've captured so much more. That close-up of the stonework in the arch… And that hand-painted sign: *Convento San Domenico*,' he read aloud. '*Sentiero Degli Dei*.'

'Ah…you've walked our famous path.' The waiter delivered tall, frosty glasses filled with amber liquid. '*Sentiero Degli Dei*—Footpath of the Gods. It is beautiful, isn't it?'

'An experience I will remember for ever,' Mika answered truthfully.

Was the touch of Rafe's foot against hers under the table accidental? No. Judging by the gleam of mirth in his eyes, he was sharing a private understanding that the experience was not what the waiter might be assuming. It had been the lightest of touches…how come she could feel it all the way up her leg? Into an almost forgotten spot deep in her belly, even.

Mika put her camera down to pick up the menu that had come with the drinks. 'At least I got some good photos before it hit me. And I have my notes.'

'You took notes? What kind of notes?'

Oh, help… Mika had spotted the prices beside some of the dishes, like the *pesce del giorno*. Had they sent out their own boat to select the best fish the Mediterranean had to offer?

'Um, oh, interesting things. Like, there's a bit of confusion over whether that's a monastery or a convent. The church, *Santa Maria a Castro*, was there first. It was donated to the Dominican Friars in 1599 and they were the ones who built the convent. And…um…' She turned a page in the menu, distracted by the rumbling in her stomach. 'What are you going to have to eat?'

'Do you like pizza?'

'Of course.' Mika bit her lip. Did he really want to eat street food when there was so much more on offer? Or was he choosing the least expensive option because she had revealed too much when she'd said she'd waited a long time to get her flash camera? Had he guessed that she'd had to put so much effort into saving up for it? She could feel herself prickling defensively. She didn't need looking after financially. She didn't need looking after at all, in fact. Today had been an anomaly and it wasn't going to happen again.

'It goes with beer,' Rafe said smoothly. 'And they're usually so big I don't think I could eat one on my own.' He shrugged. 'I just thought that maybe we could share. How about this one? It's got wild mushrooms, asparagus, caramelised onion and *scamorza*. Do you know what *scamorza* is?'

'It's a cheese. Similar to mozzarella.'

'Sounds delicious.'

It did. And suddenly it was what Mika wanted to eat more than anything else on the menu. That the shared meal would be so affordable was merely a bonus.

Were they being watched by the staff? That might explain why—despite other tables being occupied—Rafe only had to glance up to have the waiter coming to take their order. But Mika couldn't help the feeling that this man was used to having control of his life. That he was one of that golden breed of people for whom things happened easily.

He had a problem now, though, didn't he?

He'd lost everything, she reminded herself.

And it was *her* fault.

Raoul could feel himself relaxing.

There'd been a moment when he'd thought the game was up because the *maître d'* had recognised him when he'd followed Mika into this small restaurant, but it seemed that it had simply been deference to his being Mika's male companion—an outdated assumption that he was in charge?

Whatever. It wasn't lost on Raoul that being in Mika's company, with people assuming they were a couple, was actually a layer of going incognito that he could never achieve on his own. Not that he would ever use someone like that, but it was an unexpected bonus. Like her company. Not only was she so easy to talk to, but every new snippet he was learning about her was adding to an impression that he was with a rather extraordinary person.

He didn't even have to say anything to communicate with her. Just a glance from those dark eyes, that seemed too big for the small face that framed them, had been enough to answer his concern that she might not want to sit beside a window that looked out over the kind of drop that had triggered her vertigo. The deliberate nudge of her foot had rewarded him with another glance and that one had cemented a bond. They were the only people in the world who knew about Mika's unfortunate experience up on that mountain track and it was going to stay that way. As far as anyone else was concerned, the journey would be memorable for ever because of the extraordinary view or the accomplishment of a not inconsiderable physical challenge.

How often did you find somebody that you could communicate with like that?

He'd seen it—between people like his grandparents, for instance—but they'd been together for decades and adored each other.

He and Mika were complete strangers.

Although, that strangeness was wearing off with every passing minute as he got to know more about her.

He'd glimpsed a dream by the way she handled that camera and a note in her voice when she'd told him that owning it had been a long time coming. Was she planning a new career as a photographer, perhaps? He already knew how determined she was by the way she'd handled her desperation at being in the clutches of vertigo, so he was quite confident that she would find a way to achieve any dreams she had.

Weirdly, it made him feel proud of her...

He'd also seen her pride. He'd deliberately searched for the least expensive item on the menu because it was obvious that Mika didn't have unlimited funds. He'd picked up on that, when she'd said she had waited a long time to own that precious camera, as easily as he'd been able to absorb communication from a glance. And he'd seen the way she'd reacted. It had reminded him of that curious little creature he'd come across for the first time when he'd been at his English boarding school— a hedgehog that curled itself into a ball to protect itself so that all you could see were prickles.

But Mika had relaxed again now. And she could *eat*... There was real pleasure to be found in the company of a female who actually tackled food like a boy. There was no picking at a low-calorie salad for Mika. She was attacking her big slices of pizza with so much enthusiasm, she had a big streak of tomato sauce on one cheek.

This was so different from anything he'd ever experienced. The only note of familiarity was the offer of the best table the restaurant had to offer—and another table would have been found, of course, for the discreet security personnel who were never far away. Photographers would have been shut outside for the moment but his female companion would have excused herself possibly more than once, to make sure she was ready for them later, to touch up her make-up and check that there were no stains on the figure-hugging evening gown she was wearing.

Imagining any of those elegant women he'd dined

with in the past with food on her face made it virtually impossible to hide a smile. Raoul also had to resist the urge to reach out and wipe it clean with his napkin. Or maybe just his thumb. He could imagine how the prickles would appear again if he did, though. He already knew Mika quite well enough to know that she would not appreciate being treated like a child.

'It's good, isn't it?'

'*So* good.' Mika eyed the remaining slices of the pizza but reached for her beer first. She frowned at Raoul when she put her glass down. 'What's funny?'

The smile had escaped. 'You've got a moustache.'

'Oh…' With the back of her hand, Mika erased the foam above her lip. The gesture captured the streak of tomato sauce as well. 'Better?'

'Mmm.' But Raoul was still smiling. He'd never sat a table with a woman who would use her hand rather than a napkin and it was quite possible he'd never enjoyed a meal quite this much, either.

'Tell me more about this OE you're on… Do you have an itinerary?'

'Not really. I find a place and a job and work until I've saved enough to go somewhere else. I'll be here for a while longer after investing in that camera, but it's a good job and I love it here, so that's okay.'

'What's your job?'

'I'm in hospo.'

Raoul blinked. Maybe his English wasn't as good as he'd thought. It took only as long as that blink for Mika to realise his lack of comprehension and rescue him.

'Hospitality. I'm a waitress in a café down in Positano.'

'And that's a good job?'

'It is when you're travelling. It's easy to get work and nobody's too bothered about permits or anything. You can get paid in cash, too. It's what most people do on their OE. Part of the rite of passage, even. Everybody should work in hospo at least once.'

'Why?'

'Because it changes the way you see the world. You get to see the best and worst of people in ways you wouldn't believe. And it changes how you see people who work in the kind of jobs that usually make them invisible—you know what I mean?'

Raoul nodded slowly but his interest had been piqued. How many people were there in his world that quietly came and went, making life easier for himself and his family? Advisors and bodyguards. Cooks and cleaners. He'd never served anyone so he had no idea what life would look like from that kind of perspective. He was ashamed to realise he hadn't even given it much thought.

Until now...

So that kind of job could change the way you saw the world... Was that what *he* needed to do?

There was only one slice of pizza left.

'You have it,' Raoul said.

'No, it's all yours. You're a boy. You need to eat more.'

'How about we go halves?'

Mika's face lit up. 'Okay.' She tore the big triangle into two pieces and then eyed them up.

'That one is bigger,' Raoul pointed out. 'You have it.'

Mika hesitated for a moment then she picked up the larger piece and took a big bite out of it before putting it down again.

Raoul snorted with laughter. 'Okay, now they're the same. I choose this one.' He picked up the piece that now had a semicircle of tooth marks where the point of the triangle had been, his hand grazing hers as it passed. Or maybe it hadn't actually touched her skin—it just felt like it had—because she didn't move hers further away. His gaze met Mika's over the slice as he bit into it…and there it was again…

That feeling of a connection he'd never felt before.

Was this what having a real friend was like?

Oddly, it was as exciting as that first flutter of physical attraction could be.

Mika washed down the last of her pizza with the last swallow of her beer. She sighed with contentment and then leaned back in her chair.

'Right, mister. What are we going to do with you?'

The expression on her face was a mix of concern and a determination to fix things. She was fiddling with the charm on her necklace in a way that suggested it was an automatic accompaniment to a process of deep thought.

The irony wasn't lost on Raoul.

'Why do you wear a dolphin charm?'

Mika's fingers stilled. She was staring at him with those huge eyes and Raoul felt that he'd stepped over a boundary of some kind. He'd asked a question that had personal significance and, right now, she was weighing up whether or not to trust him with an honest response.

'It's a symbol,' she finally said softly. 'Of being wild and free. And…and happy.'

The wistful note in her voice went straight to Raoul's heart and struck a very unexpected chord.

Mika was searching for happiness, as everybody

did, but she was already almost as wild and free as one of the beautiful creatures his homeland had been named for. She didn't have to step into a life that was pretty much set in stone—a life that meant personal happiness was unimportant compared to the greater good. If happiness was there, as it had been for most of his life, it was a bonus.

Raoul envied her. Okay, there was a twinge of sympathy that she hadn't yet found her ultimate happiness, but she was free to create it. To go anywhere and do anything that might help her reach her goal.

As if she knew she might have revealed too much, Mika lifted her hand away from the charm and pushed her fingers through her already spiky hair.

'What are you going to do?' she asked bluntly. 'I can't go home and leave you out on the streets. Not when it's my fault you're in this predicament.'

'What would you do, if you were me?'

She probably didn't notice that her fingers strayed back to the dolphin charm. 'I guess I'd find somewhere to stay and then I'd find a job. If you can get one like mine, you get at least one meal a day thrown in as well. It all helps.'

Raoul nodded. Something was falling into place in his head. Impressions and ideas that had been accumulating over the course of this dinner. He'd set out on this private journey to learn about himself but what if he was approaching his quest from the wrong angle? What if he actually needed to learn about *other* people? The invisible kind, like those in service? Or the individuals amongst a mass like the people he would very soon be ruling?

He could get himself out of his predicament with a simple phone call.

Or, he could embrace his situation by deciding that fate had provided an opportunity that would have been unthinkable even a few hours ago. He could see if he had the personal fortitude to face being homeless. Penniless and without even the prospect of a job. How many of his own people had faced a challenge like this at some time in their lives?

He'd been silent for so long that Mika was chewing her lip and frowning, as if she was trying to solve the problem of world peace rather than his own immediate future.

'Have you ever worked in hospo?'

He shook his head. 'Never.'

'Oh…it's just that our café is really busy with the start of the high season. I reckon you could get a job there too.'

'I could try.'

'You wouldn't cope if you've never done it before. With no experience, probably the only job you'd get would be washing dishes.' Her eyes widened. 'The dishie we've got was talking about moving on yesterday. I'll bet Marco hasn't found a replacement yet.'

Washing dishes. Had he *ever* had to wash dishes? Meals away from his residential apartment at university had always been in restaurants, like meals away from the mess during his time with the military. As for the palace…he hadn't even been near the kitchens since he'd been a small child in search of an extra treat.

Dishwashing was possibly one of the most ordinary jobs there was out here in the real world. And wasn't 'ordinary' exactly what he'd set out to be in this time away from his real world?

'I... I wouldn't mind washing dishes.'

Mika's nod was solemn. It was her turn to be silent for a while now. At last she spoke, and he could see by the way her throat moved as she swallowed first that she was making a huge effort.

'I owe you one, Rafe...for today. There's a couch in my room that you can sleep on tonight...as long as...'

She wouldn't meet his gaze. There was something important that she didn't want to say. Something about her body language reminded him of the hedge-hog again. She was poised to curl into a ball to protect herself. With a flash, he realised what it could be and the thought was horrific. Had she been hurt by a man? Did that explain the way she'd reacted when he'd touched her? How hesitant she'd been to take his hand even when she'd been desperate?

'Mika...' He waited until she looked up and, yes, he could see uncertainty. It wasn't fear, exactly, because there was a fierceness that told him she was well prac-tised in defending herself. But she was clearly offering him something that was well out of her comfort zone.

He resisted the urge to touch her hand. Eye contact was more than enough, and even that he kept as gentle as he could. 'We're friends now, yes?'

Mika nodded but she wasn't quite meeting his gaze.

'You're safe with me. I give you my word.'

She looked straight at him, then, and for a heart-beat, and then another, she held his gaze, as if she was searching for confirmation that his word was trust-worthy.

That she found what she was looking for was revealed by no more than a softening of her face but Raoul could feel the gift of her trust as if it was solid enough to hold in his hands.

His vow was equally silent.

He would not drop that gift and break it.

CHAPTER THREE

WHO KNEW THAT military training would end up being so useful in the daily life of an ordinary person?

It meant that Raoul de Poitier was conditioned well enough that yesterday's strenuous exercise had been no more than a good workout. It also meant that he'd been able to sleep on a lumpy old couch that was actually a lot more comfortable than sleeping on the ground.

He'd tapped into a bit of initiative in making the best use of available resources, too. Mika had a laptop computer and he'd borrowed it for long enough to send an email to his grandmother to let her know he was safe but not to expect to hear from him for a little while.

Mika had been busy with her technology for a while after that, downloading photographs she had taken that day, her busy tapping suggesting she was adding notes to the images. Her frequent glances away from the screen told him that she wasn't entirely comfortable having him share this small space; the idea to turn the couch around so that the back of it faced into the small room came to him in a flash of inspiration. The effect of the change had been to create the illusion of a wall and, once he was lying down—with his legs bent and his knees propped on the wall—he couldn't see Mika in the single bed that was only a few feet away. Any tension ebbed as it became apparent that the arrangement would give her more privacy as she worked and then slept.

The bathroom facilities were shared with all the other occupants of the rooms on that floor of the old boarding house. That had been more of a shock than Raoul had expected after a lifetime of a sparkling clean, private *en suite* bathroom always having been available but, on the plus side, there was no queue at this early hour of the morning.

Mika wasn't due to start her shift in the café until eight a.m. but it opened at six a.m. and she was taking him in to meet the owner, Marco, in the hope that there might be some work available for a new dishwasher. She'd used the bathroom first and came out in her uniform of a short black skirt and a fitted short-sleeved black shirt. It was an outfit designed to cloak a member of the army of invisible people and, when Mika tied on a pretty white apron with a frill around its edge, he realised the uniform was probably also intended to make her look demure.

The shirt certainly covered the tattoo on her arm but Raoul doubted that anything would make Mika look demure—not with that aura of feistiness, combined with the impression of intelligence that one glance at her face was enough to discern.

'It's a horrible job,' she warned Raoul. 'A dishie has to be a food-hand as well and help with the food prep to start the day, with jobs like chopping onions and making sauce, and then he has to keep up with all the dishes as soon as service starts, and that's not easy.'

'I'm sure I could get up to speed.' How hard could it

be to do such menial work? This was the twenty-first century. Even a small establishment would have commercial dishwashing machines, surely?

Mika turned a corner as they headed downhill towards the beach. They walked past a series of shops still shuttered and sleeping in the soft light of a new day.

'Dishies get yelled at by the chefs if they get behind,' Mika continued. 'The waitresses hate finding they've suddenly run out of cutlery or something and the *barista* will have a tantrum if he runs out of coffee cups.'

'Who's in charge?'

Mika looked up to grin at him. 'Marco *thinks* he is but everybody has to keep the head chef happy. A dishie is right at the bottom of the pecking order, though. He has to keep *everybody* happy.'

Raoul wondered where the waitresses fitted into the pecking order. He would do his best to keep Mika happy if he got this job.

It was a surprise to realise how much he *wanted* to get this job. It wasn't simply the opportunity of gaining a different perspective on life—the idea of it was beginning to tap into a yearning that went way back.

Didn't every kid dream of being invisible at some time? And maybe that fantasy had more meaning to those who grew up under a very public spotlight. He would be visible to the people he worked with here, of course, but it felt like he would be stepping into an alternative reality. Nobody who knew him would expect to see him in this kind of work and that would be enough to make him blend into the background, even if they took notice of the people who spent their lives in service of some kind.

'Here it is.' Mika began to cross the cobbled street to a shop front that had canvas awnings over the footpath. The name of the café was printed on the dark terracotta canvas in big, white, cursive letters—*Pane Quotidiano*—the 'Daily Bread'.

A short, middle-aged man with a long, white apron tied around an ample waist was lifting wrought-iron chairs from a stack to position around small tables. '*Buongiorno*, Marco.'

'*Buongiorno,* Mika. Why are you so early?'

'I've brought a friend—Rafe. He needs a job. Is Pierre still here?'

Marco threw his hands in the air and his huff of breath was exasperated. 'He walked out yesterday, would you believe? Demanded his money and that was that.' Raoul was receiving a shrewd glance. 'You got any experience?'

'I learn fast,' Raoul replied in Italian—the language Mika was speaking with impressive fluency. 'Try me.'

Marco had his hands on his hips now as he assessed Raoul.

'He speaks English,' Mika put in.

'And French,' Raoul added. And Dauphinesque, but that was hardly likely to be useful to the majority of tourists this café served, and he had no intention of giving anybody such a clue to his nationality.

'Makes no difference.' Marco shrugged. 'All he needs to know is how to follow orders and work hard.'

'Try me,' Raoul said again. He should probably have added 'please' but, curiously, it rankled that he was being assessed and possibly found wanting. Not something he was used to, that was for sure.

'One day,' Marco said grudgingly. 'You do a good job, I will hire you. Mess up and you won't get paid for today.'

A glance at Mika gave him another one of those lightning-fast, telepathic messages. This was a good deal and, if he wanted the job, he'd better grab the opportunity.

Marco was clearly confident he had an extra set of hands for the day, at least.

'Finish putting these chairs out,' he told Raoul. 'And then come back into the kitchen. Mika? Seeing as you're here so early, make me a coffee.'

'One macchiato coming right up.' Mika didn't seem bothered by the crisp order. She was looking delighted, in fact, by the way this job interview had panned out. She gave Raoul a quick thumbs-up sign as she disappeared into the café behind her boss.

His boss, too, if he could prove himself today. Raoul lifted a couple of the heavy chairs and carried them to the table on the far side of the outdoor area. As he went back for more, he caught sight of himself in the windows that hadn't yet been folded back to open up the café to catch the breeze and what he saw made him catch his breath and look again.

He'd had to comb his hair with his fingers this morning so it was more tousled than he'd ever seen before. He'd rinsed out his only set of clothes and hung them over the tiny line outside the window of Mika's room, so they were clean enough, but so wrinkled it looked as if he'd slept in them for a week. He'd noticed that the stubble on his jaw had felt a lot smoother yesterday but now he could see that it was beginning to look like a proper beard.

Nobody was going to recognise him. He barely recognised himself.

He wasn't a prince here. Nobody had even asked him for a surname. He was just an ordinary guy called Rafe. And Rafe was on the way to finding his first paid employment.

Maybe he was delighted as well.

The trickle of breakfast customers had grown into a steady stream of holiday makers who preferred a relaxed brunch. Mika's section today covered all the street tables so she had the added hazard of stepping around dogs lying by their owners' chairs as she delivered plates of hot food or trays laden with coffee orders. Tables were being taken as soon as people stood up to leave so they had to be wiped down fast, and a new carafe of chilled water along with glasses provided.

She was almost too busy to wonder how Rafe was coping out the back but he entered her thoughts every time she cleared a table, being careful to scrape the plates and put all the cutlery on the top. Carrying the piles to the kitchen, she found herself scanning shelves to see where they were running low on supplies.

'We're going to need more water glasses soon. And don't forget the lemon slices and sprigs of mint in the carafes.'

'Okay.' Rafe had a huge apron on and a dish brush in his hand. He started to push a pile of plates further towards the sinks so that Mika had room to put hers down.

'Careful…' Without thinking, Mika caught his hand.

'Margaret's left cutlery between the plates. That whole pile could topple and smash on the floor.' She could feel the heat of his skin beneath her fingers. Had it been soaking in hot water for too long to feel as if it was burning her? Hastily, she pulled her hand away and scooped up the knives and forks on her top plate to put them into the big, sudsy bucket on the floor. Pierre, the last dish-washer, had trained her not to drop them too fast and splash his legs.

'Thanks.' Rafe cast an eye over his shoulder and lowered his voice. 'I don't want to annoy him again. He had to show me how to run the dishwasher twice.'

Mika smiled. 'Gianni's bark is worse than his bite. He's a pretty good chef.'

'*Service…* Table eight.'

'Oh, that's me…' Mika turned swiftly, uncomfortably aware that she'd been distracted. 'Behind,' she called in warning on her way to the pass, as one of the other waitresses backed through the swing door with another tray of dirty dishes. Would she have room to dump them on the bench? Rafe was going to have to work faster if he wanted to get this job. He might not even get a break, at the rate he was going.

There were plenty of water glasses on the shelf the next time she settled new customers and every carafe was decorated with mint and lemon. This was good. Rafe hadn't been exaggerating when he'd promised Marco that he was a fast learner. Mika delivered another tray of coffees to the table where her boss was sitting—as usual—with a couple of his mates, right on the footpath, so he could greet anyone else he knew and keep an eye on how the whole café was functioning. If things got really crazy, he would pitch in to help, or sometimes he would just wander around to check that everybody was enjoying their time in Positano's best café. He had the best job, which was fair enough, given that he was the owner of the establishment.

Poor Rafe had the worst job but he seemed to be managing. Mika stopped worrying about him as the day sped on. It wasn't her problem if he didn't like the work or didn't get offered a paid job, was it? She'd repaid her debt by giving him dinner and a place to stay last night. Finding him work was just a bonus.

Except...

She liked him. And she liked having him around. Instead of grumpy Pierre, whom she had to be careful not to splash, she could look forward to a smile every time she carried dirty dishes out the back.

It was growing on her, that smile.

The other waitresses must be getting smiled at too, she decided. There was a faint undercurrent of something different amongst her colleagues today. They seemed to be putting more effort into being charming with the customers. Was it her imagination or was Margaret, the English girl who was here to improve her Italian, making more frequent trips to the kitchen than usual? She'd spotted Bianca reapplying her lipstick more than once and Alain, the gay barista, had even gone to collect clean coffee cups himself instead of calling for one of the waitresses to do it.

No surprises there. Hospitality workers were usually young, travelling and eager for any fun that came their way. Rafe was new.

And gorgeous...

It was his eyes even more than that smile. The warmth in them. And that wicked gleam of humour.

Would she ever forget the way he'd looked at her over that slice of pizza that she'd already taken the huge bite out of? It had been a silly joke but he'd bought right into it and for a heartbeat, as she'd been caught in his gaze, she'd felt like she'd known him for ever.

Like he was her best friend. Or the brother she'd never had.

'Sorry?' Mika had to scrabble to retrieve her pad from the pocket of her apron. She pulled her pencil from behind her ear. 'Was that one seafood risotto?'

'Two.' The customer glared at her. 'And the linguine with lobster. And side salads. And we need some more water.'

'No problem. Coming right up.'

Mika stepped over a sleeping poodle, dodged a small child and turned sideways to give Margaret room to carry a tray past her.

'Thanks, hon.'

Margaret had a nice smile, too. And long blonde hair. And legs that went on for ever under that short skirt.

Mika ducked into the kitchen to put the order for table six under the rail above the grill. She glanced sideways to see Rafe scraping plates into the rubbish bucket. He had promised that she was safe with him and he certainly hadn't done anything to undermine that promise last night. They were friends. He hadn't given her so much as a glance that might have suggested any kind of attraction and that was exactly what she'd wanted.

So what if he was tempted to hook up with Margaret? Or Bianca? Or even Alain for that matter? It was none of her business and she wasn't bothered.

With a sigh, Mika collected another carafe of water and headed back to table six.

It wasn't completely true, was it?

She *was* bothered.

It was that smile that was doing it. Other people smiled at her and it could make her feel good but there was something about Rafe's smile that made her feel much better than good. It felt like her body was waking up after a long, long sleep and that every cell was tingling in the bright light of a brand new day. She was over-sensitive to the slightest touch, like the way his hand had barely brushed hers in taking that piece of pizza last night. Or the heat of his hand when she'd laid her fingers over the back of it to stop him unbalancing that pile of crockery.

The tingling bordered on being painful. And it was confusing. She didn't *want* to feel this way but there it was. Like that horrible vertigo, it had just appeared from nowhere.

And, now that it was here, she didn't really want it to go away, either. It was making her feel so…alive…

Forty euros.

Raoul stared at the notes in his hand. For more than ten hours of back-breakingly hard work, it was a pittance but, having had no more than enough for a bus fare in his pockets at the start of the day, it looked like a small fortune.

It was a clever ploy of Marco's to give him cash at the end of his day's trial as well as offering him as many shifts as he wanted to take in the café. If he hadn't had actual money in his hand right now, it would be very tempting not to show up tomorrow.

Military training hadn't set him up very well for this particular challenge. His hands felt waterlogged and swollen and he had tiny cuts from not handling the cutlery well enough that would probably sting later. His back ached from so many hours standing and, even though he'd wolfed down a meal when he'd finally been given a break, he was starving again already.

'You did it.' Mika was waiting for him outside the café and her expression made him think of a proud mother collecting her child from their first day at school. 'Go you.'

Suddenly Raoul felt proud of himself, too. 'It was a close call. When I forgot to warn Gianna that I was behind him and he dropped a whole pizza, I thought I was going to get fired on the spot.'

Mika shrugged. 'Worse things happen. Pierre had a huge stack of dishes crash onto the floor and smash when he started.'

'Did he have to pay for them?'

She shook her head. 'If Marco had expected that, he would have lost his worker as well as the dishes. People working in hospo don't usually have that kind of money and employers can't afford to chase them.'

'Why not?'

'It's easy employment. Casual. If we get paid in cash, we don't have to worry about paying tax, and employers can get away with paying less than minimum rates. It works for everyone.'

Raoul was frowning as he walked alongside Mika. Taxes were essential because they paid for things like hospitals and schools but he could understand why having part of an already low wage removed would add insult to injury. What was the minimum acceptable rate to pay people in his own country? And how much tax were they expected to pay?

He should know things like this.

'What's wrong?'

'Nothing…why did you ask?'

'You sighed. It sounded like you had the weight of the whole world on your shoulders.'

'Oh…' He'd have to be a bit careful what he thought about while he was with Mika. 'I'm a bit tired, I guess. It's been quite a long day.'

'I know how to fix that.'

'Oh?' The sound was wary. Considering that Mika had been racing around working just as hard as he had been for the same length of time, she looked remarkably chirpy. Raoul hoped she wasn't going to suggest an evening in a nightclub when he knew that all he would want to do later would be to sleep.

And he might need to find a place to sleep. Mika had only offered him a night on her couch.

'Do your feet hurt? Is your back sore? Have you got a bit of a headache?'

'Ah…yes, yes and yes.'

Raoul was beginning to wonder how long he might have the fortitude to keep it up, in fact. He'd never spent such a concentrated length of time doing such menial tasks. How horrified would his grandmother be if she knew? How astonished would his people be if they found out? In public opinion, it would be beneath his station in life—the work of servants.

But what made *him* so special, other than an accident of birth? Equality was a core value of the constitution of his land. Other people did this kind of work and some did it for their entire working lives. And Mika had worked just as hard today, hadn't she?

She was nodding, as if agreeing with his unspoken thoughts. 'Me too. And I know the cure.'

'Wine?' Raoul suggested hopefully. 'Sleep?'

Mika laughed. 'A swim. It's what I usually do when I have time after work. I collect my bathing suit and jump on a bus to Praiano and go down to my favourite beach. Want to come with me?'

'I don't have a bathing suit.'

'You could just wear your shorts. It would save washing them later.' Mika's head turned, scanning the tourist shops they were passing that were still open. 'You should get another tee shirt, though. Let's have a look.'

Raoul had to stop as well but he shook his head. 'I can't afford a tee shirt. It's my turn to buy dinner tonight and…and I need to find somewhere to stay. I'll need money for that, too.'

'But you've got somewhere to stay.' Mika seemed to have gone very still, her hand touching the rack of tee shirts on the footpath. 'If you don't mind the couch.'

Raoul blinked. 'You want me to stay?'

'I know it's not ideal but it's only for sleeping, and you're only here for a few weeks. I'm either at work or out exploring for the rest of the time. I'm happy to share if you are.'

She was making it sound as if it was fine if he liked the idea but she wouldn't be at all bothered if he decided otherwise. Her attention seemed to be on the shirts as she began to ruffle through them. Her tone and body language didn't quite fit with the flash of something he'd seen in her eyes, though. It wasn't any kind of come-on—she'd made it quite clear she wasn't interested in anything more than friendship—but there was something that made him think she would like him to agree to the plan a lot more than she was letting on.

Was Mika *lonely*…?

Part of him was more than a bit horrified by the idea of continuing to live in one room and share a bathroom with who knew how many other people, but was it because he was spoiled and soft or was it more to do with always having to be over-vigilant as to what others might think? When you lived in the public eye you had to behave perfectly at all times because you never knew if you were under observation by a journalist or the paparazzi. For as long as he could remember, he'd never been able to be impulsive and just do what he happened to feel like doing. Or even let how he was feeling show on his face sometimes.

But now he could. Nobody was watching. If his reluctance stemmed from the fact he was spoiled, it would do him good to toughen up. And if it was because of what others might think, well, there were no rules he had to follow other than his personal morality right now. What would happen if he really let his guard down?

'Maybe one more night? We can talk about it again tomorrow. Right now, I love your idea of a swim.'

Mika nodded. 'Stay here. Buy a tee shirt and maybe some shorts to swim in. Look, this might help…' She put her hand in her pocket and when it came out she was holding a small handful of gold-rimmed silver coins. 'I always put all my tips in the communal jar but…' Her shrug made light of any residual guilt. 'I thought we might have something to celebrate tonight.'

'No way.' Raoul put his hand over Mika's to close her fingers firmly around the coins. Such a small hand. He liked the way his could enclose it completely. 'You earned that. You keep it.' His voice was stern. 'You've got to stop paying for things for me, okay? I'm beginning to feel like a gigolo.'

Mika was smiling as she pulled her hand free and put the coins back in her pocket, but she avoided meeting his gaze, and Raoul gave himself a mental shake. Gigolos were rewarded for services that he had no intention of offering, and that would be the last thing Mika wanted anyway.

'I'll be back in ten minutes.' Mika was already walking away from him and it felt like a rebuke. Perhaps even a subtle reference to sex was dodgy territory that he needed to steer well clear of. 'Happy shopping.'

A gigolo?

With those looks and that charm, there would probably be any number of rich older woman who would be happy to have Rafe at their beck and call. While Mika knew that the comment had been no more than a joke, it had sexual connotations that had put her well out of her comfort zone.

Had she turned into some kind of prude in the last few years?

Or was it because it was Rafe who had said it and that was tapping into feelings she wasn't sure how to deal with yet?

And why had she been so quick to renew the offer of having him sleep on her couch? Did she want that painful prickle of awareness to get worse? Was she trying to test herself in some way?

Maybe she was but it wasn't something she wanted to think about because, if she did, she'd find somewhere to hide. She could find the concierge of this boarding house, perhaps, and see if there was an empty room that Rafe could rent.

Tomorrow would be soon enough for that. Right now, she needed to hurry, to change out of her uniform and put her bikini on under her favourite shorts and singlet top. She swapped her soft, black tennis shoes for lightweight sandals and draped her towel over her arm. With her camera hanging from her shoulder, she was ready to go and find Rafe.

She'd made this trip for a swim after work many times already but how much better was it to have company?

Company that was now wearing a huge white tee shirt with *I heart Positano* emblazoned on the front. Rafe didn't look the least bit embarrassed to be wearing it.

'It was on the sale rack,' he told her. 'An absolute bargain.'

'Mmm…' Mika's lips twitched. 'Fair enough. I heart Positano, too. Oh…there's our bus down the road. We'll have to run.'

The bus was crowded and they had to stand but the journey was short enough for it not to matter. Mika led him down the cobbled alleyways in the heart of Praiano and many steps that led down to a beach that had no sand. There were rows of sun loungers to hire, like on every European beach, but they were on a huge, flagged terrace, and further back there were tables and chairs spilling out from a beachside café. Rock music was also spilling out and the place was crowded with young people.

Mika made a beeline for a couple of empty loungers and she put her camera on one and covered it with her towel. Then she kicked off her sandals and peeled her singlet top off. Taking her shorts off in front of Rafe gave her an odd feeling, as though something had thumped her painlessly in her belly. A sideways glance showed that he wasn't taking any notice, however. He was too busy pulling off his new tee shirt. The sight of all that bare skin created ripples from the thumping sensation that felt like small electric shocks. It sent Mika swiftly to the edge of the terrace where she could dive straight into the deep, cool water.

The sea had always been her ultimate comfort zone. It was her place of choice to unwind and to think clearly, and it was definitely the best place to burn off angst of any kind, whether it was emotional, physical or—like now—possibly a combination of both.

She knew Rafe had dived in right behind her but Mika wasn't here to float around or play, like most of the other young couples in the water. She set out for the pontoon that was moored a hundred metres or so offshore. And when she became aware that Rafe was keeping pace, she doubled her efforts. This was a race she knew she could win.

'Where did you learn to swim like that?'

The words were hard to get out because Raoul was unexpectedly out-of-breath by the time he heaved himself up onto the pontoon. Mika was already sitting on the edge, her feet just touching the water.

'My mother always said I had dolphin blood.' Mika

didn't seem at all out of breath. 'I grew up by the sea and apparently I could swim even before I could walk properly.'

Raoul smiled, liking that idea. Yes…there was something about Mika that reminded him of the creatures his homeland was named for. Confident and a little bit cheeky. Graceful… He'd seen Mika moving around the café today, twisting and turning her body to ease through small spaces or avoid obstacles. Friendly but still wild. Yes, you could touch them sometimes, but it was an honour to be allowed to do so.

They were both sitting on the edge of the pontoon, facing the shore, where they could see the crowd in the popular bar growing. They could still hear the music from here and it was a quieter number—a folk song that was wistful enough almost to create a sensation of yearning…

A need to feel less alone by connecting with another human being…

'I don't remember my mother very well,' Raoul said quietly. 'She died, along with my father, in a plane crash when I was only five.'

People were always shocked that he'd been orphaned so early but the glance Mika gave him had no pity in it.

'I wish I'd never known mine very well,' she said. 'Maybe it wouldn't have hurt so much when she abandoned me.'

Raoul was definitely shocked. '*Abandoned* you? How?'

'She took me into the city for the day. Put me in the play area of a big department store and just never came back.'

'How old were you?'

'I was five, too. I'd just started school.'

Wow… To have lost a parent at such a vulnerable age was something that he'd never found he had in common with anyone. Ever. Even now, he could remember how lost he'd felt. How empty his world had suddenly become.

Had Mika had loving grandparents to fill such an appalling void? A small army of kind nannies, tutors and so many others, like cooks and gardeners, who would go out of their way every day to make a small, orphaned prince feel special?

'What happened? Who looked after you?'

'The police were called. I got put in the hands of the social welfare people and they found a foster home.'

'Did the police find your mother?'

'Oh…eventually. She turned up dead about ten years later. Drug overdose. Maybe she thought she was doing me a favour by shutting me out of her life.'

'What about your father?'

'Don't have one. My mother never told me anything about him other than that he was Scottish. A backpacker she'd met in a bar somewhere. I have no way of tracing him. No idea of where I came from, really.'

'I'm sorry…'

'Don't be. It has a good side. I'm as free as a bird. Or a dolphin, maybe. I can't imagine living away from the sea. I had to do that in a couple of foster homes and I hated the cities.'

Raoul was silent for a long moment. He could trace his family back to the twelfth century when their islands had become a principality. He knew every drop of his bloodline and almost every square mile of the place that was where he came from and where he would always belong.

How lost would someone feel not to have that kind of foundation? Did he really envy the freedom she'd had in comparison to how precisely his own life was mapped out?

Was that what Mika was looking for—a place where she felt she belonged? A life that offered the safety of a real home? How much heartache had been covered by that casual reference to 'a couple of foster homes'? How often had she been passed from home to home? Abandoned again and again?

The sun was low now and Mika's nut-brown skin seemed to have taken on a golden glow as Raoul's silent questions led him to turn his head towards her. Her bikini was white—small scraps of fabric that left very little to the imagination.

It wasn't his imagination that was his undoing, though.

Mika had her hands shading her eyes from the glare of the setting sun so she didn't see him looking at her. She might be tiny, Raoul decided, but she was most definitely perfectly formed. And *real*... It would probably never occur to Mika to make her breasts larger or wear killer heels to make herself look taller and sexier. He couldn't imagine her plastering her face with make-up, either. She didn't need it, with those amazing eyes of hers.

She was...gorgeous.

He'd come to the conclusion that Mika was an extraordinary person within a short time of knowing her and learning about her rough start in life somehow didn't surprise him.

What did surprise him—and not in a good way—
was the strength of the attraction he was feeling towards her right now. Had either of them really been
aware of how close to each other they were sitting?
He would only have to relax his arm a little for their
shoulders to touch. He could feel the warmth of her
skin just thinking about it.

His hands tightened on the edge of the pontoon as
he realised how much he *wanted* to touch Mika. He
pressed his lips together to try and stifle the urge to
kiss her.

Given the uncanny way they could communicate
with no more than a glance, it was unfortunate that
Mika chose that moment to lower her hands and turn
her head.

For too long, she held his gaze. Too long, because
Raoul knew that she was aware of him physically, too.
That the attraction might well be mutual.

It couldn't happen. Not when, in a matter of a few
short weeks, he had to step back into his real life and
prepare to marry the woman he'd been promised to for
almost as long as he could remember. The engagement
was about to become official, which had to put an end
to any sexual adventures, and surely he'd had enough
over the years, anyway?

He'd never known anybody like Mika, though, had
he?

Maybe being homeless and poor wasn't going to be
the ultimate challenge that would tell him whether he
could be the ruler his people deserved. Perhaps *this*
was going to be the biggest test. Could he put aside
his personal desires in order to do what he knew was
the right thing to do?

It would be shameful if he couldn't.

The tumble of his thoughts took no longer than the shared glance. It was Mika who broke the eye contact, and she did it so abruptly, Raoul was left wondering if he'd imagined what he thought he'd seen. Or had she been shocked by what *she'd* seen?

'Hot chips,' she said.

'What?' The randomness of the words cleared his mind with a jolt.

'Bernie—the guy who runs the bar on the beach. He's English and I think he was in a band that did quite well back in the seventies. He makes the best hot chips I've ever tasted. Everyone comes here for his fish and chips, and I've just realised that I'm absolutely *starving.*' Her grin held all the cheek he was coming to expect from Mika. 'I seem to remember you saying something about it being your turn to buy dinner?'

'I did. And it is.'

'Race you back, then…'

It was a huge relief to sink into the chill of the seawater. As good as a cold shower, in fact.

He could do this, Raoul decided. He could enjoy the company of the first genuine friend he'd ever made without ruining that friendship with sex. That way, Mika wouldn't end up being hurt, and it could be possible that the friendship might never be completely lost. Sure, Mika would get a shock when she found out who he really was, but by then maybe she would know him well enough to understand and forgive the deception.

This feeling of connection to another person was too special to lose.

Raoul had a distinct feeling that he might never experience it again.

CHAPTER FOUR

HAD SHE IMAGINED it?

That buzz of physical awareness she'd seen in Rafe's eyes when they'd been sitting side by side on the pontoon, in the glow of a sunset, the other night…

Maybe it had just been a product of a combination of things. The gorgeous sunset, how relaxed a swim in the sea could make you feel after a long, hard day at work, and the fact that they were both as close to naked as public decency allowed. If—for a moment in time—Rafe had fancied her, he had done nothing to confirm any interest since.

And Mika would have noticed the slightest indication because she'd been so nervous about it. Emotionally, she'd run as hard and fast as she could when she thought she'd seen it. She'd tried to wash away the confused jumble of feelings by swimming hard enough to beat Rafe back to the shore, and had kept the conversation deliberately impersonal as they'd eaten the fish and chips that Rafe had declared the best he'd ever tasted after she'd snapped a few photos of the fading sunset and their surroundings. One of Rafe, too, that he hadn't even seen her taking.

He'd been standing watching that sunset—one hand

shading his eyes, the other holding the damp towel he had insisted she used first. His hair had been still wet and drops were landing on his shoulders to trickle onto that bare chest. There'd been something poignant in the way he was staring out to sea and even through the lens of her camera the beauty of this man had been enough to give Mika that curious sensation in her belly again— the thump and the electric tingles of physical attraction.

The action had been instinctive. Something had told her that there could well be a time she'd want to re- member this day and this man who'd stirred these feel- ings she thought she'd lost for ever. It was an action that had taken only a split second and was as private as the reasons she had taken it.

It had been only a momentary blip in the impersonal atmosphere that Mika had been determined to foster as a safety buffer zone, and the tactic had worked so well that it had cemented what seemed to have become a pattern. They did their long shifts at the café, went for a swim after work, ate a meal that they took turns paying for and, by the time they got home after dark, they were both so tired that sleep was essential before another early rise.

Had the tactic worked *too* well?

A couple of days later, Mika realised that her ner- vousness had evaporated. That she had to conclude that she *had* imagined any desire on Rafe's part.

And, if she was really honest, there was a part of her that was…what?…disappointed?

Frustrated, even?

If things had been different—if *she* was different— that moment on the pontoon could have played out in a very different way.

She would have seen that look in Rafe's eyes and fallen into it instead of running away. They would have held that eye contact as they'd slowly closed the distance between them and then…then she would have felt Rafe's lips against her own…

The way she had so many times in those unguarded moments of the last few nights when she'd been slipping into sleep and could hear the sound of Rafe's breathing only a few feet away. The intensity of her body's reaction to the fantasy kiss had been enough to make her think that she'd never wanted anything as much as she wanted Rafe to kiss her.

But it wasn't going to happen, was it? Oh, he still seemed to be enjoying her company. He still smiled just as readily. But there was something different about the way he looked at her. Or *didn't* look at her. Yes, that was it. There was a wariness that hadn't been there before. That connection that she felt when her gaze met his was missing…because he never held her gaze long enough for it to kick in.

Because he was avoiding it?

Had he seen her fear?

Mika's thoughts seemed to be a series of questions that were becoming increasingly unsettling.

Would she react the same way if she had another chance?

Did she *want* another chance?

Part of her seemed to. Otherwise, she wouldn't have had a quiet word with Marco yesterday to ask if Rafe could have the same day off as she had this week. She wouldn't have told him about her plan to explore the valley of the ancient mills in Amalfi and slipped in that casual invitation for him to join her if he had nothing else he wanted to do with his day off.

They wouldn't be here now, standing in the central square of Amalfi beside the cathedral stairs, gazing at the narrow, cobbled streets and trying to decide which one would take them uphill to where they would find the entrance to the valley.

A woman walking a small dog glanced at Rafe and paused. Smiling, she asked if they needed any help.

'Please,' Rafe answered. 'We're looking for the way to the Valley of the Mills.'

'Ah…the *Valle dei Mulini*… Go up the main street here, which leads into *Via Pietro Capuano*…'

Mika was listening to the directions but she was also watching the body language in front of her. Did Rafe know the effect he had on women? Of course he did, she decided. How could he not know?

He could have anyone he chose, couldn't he?

Was it no more than a fantasy that he might choose *her*?

The answer to that was simple. Of course it was. He saw her as a friend, nothing more. And maybe this was the best thing that could have happened for her—the reason why fate had made him appear in her life. She could play with the possibility of something physical developing in her mind, and perhaps that was the step she needed to take so that she would be ready when someone came into her life that she was attracted to— someone who wanted to be with *her*.

Someone other than Rafe…

'Did you get all that?' The woman and her dog were walking away. Rafe's glance was unreadable.

'Yep. Let's go.' Oddly, the excitement of this adventure had faded a little for Mika.

'We go past the paper museum. You want to go there, don't you?'

'Mmm…' Mika was slightly ahead of Rafe now. 'It won't be open yet, though. I'll go on the way back. You don't have to do the museum, though, if they're not your thing.'

They walked in silence until they'd passed the museum and reached a set of steps going uphill. Rafe went ahead of Mika as they climbed the steps and, by the time they'd walked on for a few more minutes, the silence had become awkward.

'Can we stop for a second? I'd like to take a photo of that lemon grove.'

Rafe stopped. He turned and, for the first time in days, Mika found her gaze properly caught.

'Would you rather be doing this by yourself?'

'What? No…of course not.'

'But you want to go to the museum by yourself?'

'No… I…' Mika retrieved the snatch of conversation from her memory. She'd been feeling out of sorts when she'd thrown that comment in. Aware that the next man in her life was not going to be Rafe… 'It's just that some people don't like museums, you know? I don't want to bore you.'

He was still holding her gaze.

'You would never bore me, Mika.'

Oh, help…that connection was still there, wasn't it?

And that look. She could fall into that, if she let herself.

Maybe she couldn't *help* herself falling…

'Same.' Mika felt her heart skip a beat. 'You're…

good company, Rafe.' She had to break the eye contact because she felt suddenly, inexplicably, shy. She pulled her camera out of its case. 'It's…um…really nice to have a friend to do things like this with.'

'But you'd do it on your own if I wasn't here, wouldn't you?'

'I'd have to.' Mika focused on the terraced rows of lemon trees, the fruit glowing goldlike giant gems against the glossy, green foliage. 'But it's better when you have company. Makes it feel… I don't know… more real?'

'Mmm…' Rafe's nod was thoughtful. 'I get that. They say a problem shared is halved. Maybe a pleasure shared is doubled.'

She kept the camera in her hand as they carried on. There was so much pleasure to be found in this walk. They entered the valley into woodlands where the bird calls were the only sound to break the cool silence and the forest floor was a wash of pink from wild cyclamens. The ruins of the ancient paper mills were tall, mossy, concrete structures with haphazard holes where windows had once been, perched beside the river as it tumbled over huge boulders. The drama of one of the waterfalls they passed was enough to make them pause and sit beneath one of the massive old trees for a few minutes.

So much pleasure…and it was definitely doubled by having Rafe's company. More than doubled…

Mika could have simply sat here and soaked it in but she needed more than photographs to record the journey. She pulled her notebook from the pack Rafe had been carrying for her.

'What are you writing?'

'I'm adding to the research I did online. Putting the things I notice in as well. Like how gorgeous that carpet of flowers was under the trees. I won't have room to include every photo I take.'

'Include in what?'

'My article.'

'You're a *writer*? You never told me that.'

'That's because I'm not. Yet...' That very uncharacteristic shyness resurfaced. Mika didn't tell people her dreams. Was that because she didn't have anyone in her life that she wanted to share them with?

'I want to be a travel writer,' she said quietly. 'I'd like to earn my living by doing things like this all the time, instead of working in cafés.'

Rafe looked impressed. But then he frowned. 'You want to spend your whole life travelling? Never settling down anywhere?'

'Oh, I'll settle somewhere. I just don't know where yet. I know it will be near the sea because of my dolphin blood.' Mika smiled, hoping to make light of revealing something so personal. 'And I think it will be somewhere warm, because that way you can spend more time in the sea, but there's a lot of places in the world that fill those requirements—especially round here.' She closed her notebook and slipped it back into the pack. 'I'm killing two birds with one stone, here. When I find the place I want to be for ever, I think I'll know who I really am.'

Did everyone wonder who they really were at some point in their lives, or was this another extraordinary bond that Raoul had just found with Mika?

He wanted to tell her everything at that point. Who

he was and why he was here. He could share his problems and maybe they would be halved.

Except they wouldn't be, would they? Okay, he
could imagine that Mika would understand the need
to reveal the strongest, most basic, layers of his personality so that he would know he had a foundation
that would serve him well for the rest of his life—because wasn't she doing pretty much the same thing?
She was searching for a layer he didn't need but one
that was even more fundamental—a place where she
felt she belonged.

But, if he did tell her the truth, she would realise he
didn't belong here, in her world, like this. She might
feel that the dream she had shared with him was insignificant in comparison to his future and she might
show her prickles again—the way she had, inexplicably, in suggesting that she could go to the paper museum by herself.

And, if the prickles came out, the pleasure of this
day would be dimmed and it was too good to spoil.
The serenity of the dappled light in this forest had the
echoes of a long and proud history in the ruins of the
ancient mills but the bubbling river was timeless. A
link to the future and a reminder that nothing stayed
the same. Life moved on and changed...

He could accept that with a new sense of peacefulness in this moment and it felt really good.

Being with Mika felt really good, too. Maybe it
wasn't just their surroundings that made him feel
so much closer to embracing his future. There was
strength to be found simply in her company and in the
way she faced life and made the most of every moment.

The sensation of feeling so close to another person's

soul—as if his own could reach out and take the hand of hers—was a new thing for Raoul. As if he needed to see if it was real, he turned his head, to find Mika looking up at him. Her eyes were very serious but her mouth had the hint of a curve to it, as if she knew how deep his thoughts had been and that he was happy with where they'd taken him.

The need to connect on more than this weird, telepathic level was so strong Raoul could feel his head drifting. Tipping in slow motion until lowering it a little would be all that was needed to kiss Mika.

Did she know how overpowering the pull was? She didn't break the lock of his gaze and he could see a reflection of his own wonderment at how close it was possible to feel to someone else. And then her lips parted and he saw the very tip of her tongue touch her lower lip.

The shaft of desire was painful.

If ever there was a moment to test himself to see whether he could resist this overwhelming temptation, this was it.

Surely a kiss couldn't be such a big deal?

But it wouldn't stop there, would it?

If he wanted it *this* much, even a touch could be dangerous. What if it ignited something so powerful, he lost control of his best intentions? Exposed a weakness that could make him doubt himself even more?

He had to find out if he had the strength it would take to resist this. Closing his eyes helped because it was a shutter against how it made him feel to be holding Mika's gaze.

Forcing himself to move helped even more because he could get to his feet and walk away to put some

distance between them. But the effort was draining
and a good part of the peace he'd found ebbed as well.
When they got home, he decided, he would have to
find the concierge and ask about the availability of
another room to rent. How could he sleep so close to
her without having to fight that particular battle again
and again? How many times could he fight it and not
weaken to the point of giving in?

He knew Mika was following him but it was some
time before he could break the silence.

'How many articles have you done already?'

'A few. I haven't tried to get any published yet,
though. I need a really special one to send to the good
magazines.'

'Maybe this will be the one?'

'Maybe…' Mika still had her camera out as they
finally left the valley behind and came into the small
village of Pontone. She stopped to take photographs of
the wide, stone archway they walked through that had
antique kitchen utensils and old woven baskets hanging
from the walls. They found a picturesque café and sat,
sheltered from the sun by big umbrellas, amidst bar-
rels of bright flowers with tumblers of chilled home-
made lemonade in front of them as they waited for the
lunch they ordered.

'I love this,' Mika said, a while later.

'The salad? Me, too.' They had ordered *insalata
caprese,* a salad of sliced mozzarella cheese layered
with slices of the delicious bright red tomatoes grown
locally, drizzled with olive oil and sprinkled with tiny
basil leaves. It had come with crusty, just-baked bread
and it had to be the most perfect lunch ever.

Mika laughed. 'It's my favourite lunch, but no, I

mean all of this. This part of Italy. It's the closest I've come to feeling that it's my place.'

'Where else have you been?'

'I went to Scotland first, seeing as it's apparently where half my genetic history came from.'

'Ah, yes…you said your father was Scottish.'

'Mmm…'

There was a hint of something sad in her eyes. Something lost. Raoul couldn't remember his father very well, but he knew exactly who he was and what he looked like, and he could remember how important he'd been in his life. Knowing where your place was in the world was inextricably linked with family, wasn't it?

But Mika didn't have family. She was roaming the world in search of a link to something but, clearly, she hadn't found it in the birth place of the father she'd never known.

'You didn't like Scotland?'

Raoul loved the way her face scrunched up to reveal the impression she'd been left with.

'I loved the oldness. And the accent. I even loved the bagpipes but I didn't love the weather. It was too cold and the sea was so wild. I decided you'd have to be a bit mad to swim there so it wasn't ever going to be *my* place.'

'Maybe you need people to make it feel right. When you find your special person, you'll make a family and then the place will be yours. And theirs…for ever.'

Mika shook her head and her voice was quiet. Cold, almost. 'I'm never going to get married.'

'Why not?' The thought of Mika growing old alone was shocking.

But she simply shook her head again—a warning

that the subject was off-limits. 'It's just not going to happen. I've learned that I'm better off on my own.'

How had that lesson been learned? Raoul wondered, in the slightly awkward silence that followed. He wished he hadn't said anything, now, because they'd lost that easy flow of conversation. Could he fix it?

'What about New Zealand?' he asked. 'Doesn't that feel like your place?'

'I love New Zealand, don't get me wrong, but… there's something about the oldness of Europe that calls me.' Mika seemed as relieved as he was to forget that forlorn blip in the conversation and start again. She grinned, as if embarrassed by being fanciful. 'Maybe I lived here in a previous life.'

Maybe she had. Maybe Raoul had, too, and that could explain why he felt like he'd known her for ever. Why they had this extraordinary connection.

'There's still so much of the coastlines to explore, too. It's exciting…' Mika's face lit up. 'I want to go to the south of France. And Spain. And the Greek islands. And Sardinia and Corsica and…' Her hands were tracing a map of the Mediterranean in the air.

'And…' Raoul only just stopped himself adding *Les Iles Dauphins* to her list.

Mika's eyes widened as she waited for him to finish what he'd been about to say.

'And…you will,' he managed. 'You could be anything at all you really wanted to be, Mika, and…and you're going to be the best travel writer. Your passion will make the pages glow and everyone who reads your articles will want to go to those places. To be where you've been.'

He would want that.

She was smiling at him. A soft smile that had nothing of the characteristic cheekiness he had come to expect. This was the smile of someone basking in unexpected encouragement. Of having their dreams become a little more real because someone else believed in them too.

He would want more than to read her articles, Raoul realised. He would want to go to those places *with* Mika, not after her. And he could make it happen, so easily. He could choose almost any place in the world and the means of getting there would be sorted instantly. A helicopter, a luxury yacht, a private jet... There would be comfortable accommodation waiting at the other end, too, and Mika could have all the time she wanted to do the thing she loved doing, without the prospect of having to get back to a mundane job.

But would she want that?

And wouldn't it change how she saw a new place? Earning a day off, as they'd had to, to make this trip possible, made it so much more valuable. Exploring somewhere by having to use public transport and eating at inexpensive restaurants made everything so different.

Maybe Raoul wouldn't want to go back to having the best of everything so easily available. If he had the choice, perhaps he would choose to go to those places with Mika in the same way they'd set off today. On foot, with no more than a bit of spare change to rely on.

This longing for more days like today had nothing to do with the desire to touch Mika physically, although he could still feel that simmering in the glow of her smile. This was about what it was like simply to be in her company. To contribute to Mika's strength to achieve any dream she held…and to feel like he had someone walking alongside him as he achieved his.

Was this what real friendship was about?

…Love?

Was he falling in *love* with Mika?

No. That couldn't be allowed to happen.

They could be friends. Very good friends. But that was all.

Some people were lucky enough to marry their best friends but he wasn't going to be one of them. His future was mapped out and he couldn't imagine Francesca being his best friend.

He barely knew her. Oh, they'd spent time together—usually at formal occasions—and he knew how beautiful she was, and that she was intelligent and easy to talk to. He could fancy her, even—in the way that any man could fancy a gorgeous woman—but would he ever feel like this about Francesca? That helping her get everything she wanted out of life could be as important as his own ambitions?

He had to hope so.

Maybe Mika had been sent into his life to teach him about what was really important in relationships.

Raoul would never forget this moment.

Or that particular smile…

'What time does the paper museum close?'

Mika blinked as if she had to drag her thoughts away from something that had nothing to do with the article she was planning to write. 'I'm not sure… I imagine we've got plenty of time.'

'Shall we head off now? Just to be sure?'

'Okay…'

Mika hadn't moved a muscle but something in her

tone told Raoul that she was much further away from him than she had been a moment ago, when she'd been smiling at him.

It was an odd thing, this connection he could feel between them. Like the sun emerging from the screen of thick clouds, there were moments when it scorched him; then it would vanish again and the whole world felt so much cooler.

What created the clouds? Was it because he was getting hot enough to feel uncomfortable, so that he pulled them in for protection, perhaps?

Or did Mika feel the heat, too; and was she using them to hide behind?

Whatever was causing those clouds, they were a good thing, because it made this friendship manageable and it needed to be manageable because Raoul was nowhere near ready to risk losing it.

He thoroughly enjoyed the time they spent in the *Museo della Carta* that was housed in a wonderful thirteenth-century mill. Raoul was no stranger to museums and was, in fact, the patron of the largest in his own country; he had toured it many times, usually in the company of a large group local dignitaries and important contributors. He had to look fascinated even if he wasn't and remember to turn a little whenever he shook someone's hand or stopped to admire a new exhibit, so that the best photographs could be taken.

This was a new experience because, for once, he was less important than the exhibits and he found that he was watching Mika as much as the treasures on display, and that made him see things differently and in far more detail. He stared up at the huge wooden mallets that were powered by a hydraulic wheel that could beat rags of cotton, linen and hemp into a pulp.

He stood beside the ancient vat with its murky water that housed the pulp and watched Mika crouch to take a close-up shot of the majolica tiles that lined the vat. Pale blue tiles, with red flowers and delicate green swirls for leaves. Would he even have noticed them if he'd been here alone?

'I'm going to write this up tonight,' Mika announced, as they waited for the bus to take them back to Positano. 'And I'll finish the one about the Footpath of the Gods.'

'I'll get out of your way,' Raoul told her. 'I'm going to find the concierge and see if there's another room available. That way, you'll get plenty of time to write without interruptions.'

The bus was approaching the stop but Mika didn't seem to notice. Her gaze had caught his and those clouds had evaporated again as instantly and mysteriously as they had on every other occasion.

This time, the heat felt different. It wasn't the burn of desire. It felt more like the kind of heat that came with the prickle of shame.

Mika knew exactly why he was going to find the concierge. He wasn't finding his own place to sleep in order to give her more space, he was doing it because he needed to get away from her. And she felt…rejected?

The bus seemed to bring the cloud cover back as it jerked to a halt beside them and Mika turned away to climb on board.

Maybe it would be the last time he got to experience the heat of that connection.

That would be a good thing, wouldn't it? It would

make it so much easier to step back into his own world and his own life when the time came and that wouldn't be very far away. A whole week of his month of freedom had vanished already.

But, if it *was* a good thing, why did it feel as if he'd just broken something rather precious?

CHAPTER FIVE

It HAD BEEN one of *those* days.

Right from that first customer who'd put his hand in the air and clicked his fingers loudly enough to make Mika freeze as she hurried back to the pass to collect more plates for the table.

'I ordered my eggs to be poached, not fried.' He didn't look at Mika as he spoke. 'Take them back.'

'I'm so sorry, sir.' Mika picked up the plate. 'There's been a mistake. I'll get you a fresh plate.'

'Make it snappy. And I'll have another coffee while I'm waiting. On the house—it's the least you can do for messing up my order.'

'Of course.' Mika looked over her shoulder, thinking that Alain had probably heard the loud voice. His subtle nod told her that he had and his smile offered sympathy at her dealing with a rude customer.

The customer wasn't the only person Mika had to deal with. She knew she hadn't written the order down incorrectly but the person who'd made the mistake wasn't likely to admit it. Not this morning, that was for sure, when they were being run off their feet.

Sure enough, Gianni was furious.

'How could you get something so basic wrong?' he

shouted. 'You think I have time to be cooking another full English breakfast when I've got orders coming out of my ears?' His spatula splattered oil on the dockets lining the rail above the grill.

He'd picked the wrong morning to have a go at Mika. It had already started badly when she'd opened her eyes to remember that she was alone in her room. That Rafe had chosen to be a lot further away from her. Had that been her fault? Had she said or done something to put him off her? She hadn't been able to think of anything. Quite the opposite, really, when she'd gone over and over everything they'd said during yesterday's outing.

Okay, she'd upset him by being offhand about whether she wanted his company to visit the museum, but they'd got past that, hadn't they? More than past it. She could swear that he'd almost kissed her when they'd been sitting under that tree by the waterfall. And the way he'd looked at her when he'd told her that he was so sure she would succeed in her dream of becoming a travel writer. As if he believed in her completely.

As if it was important to *him* that she did achieve her dream.

But having him use that dream as an excuse to find somewhere else to sleep felt like she was being punished for something that she didn't feel was her fault, and now it was about to happen again so this pushed a button harder than it might have otherwise.

'Have a look at the docket,' she told Gianni. 'I didn't write the order down wrong. You *read* it wrong.'

'Don't tell me how to do my job!' Gianni yelled. 'You want to come in here and start cooking? *Do* you?' He'd stepped away from the grill and by the time he fired his last, aggressive question he was right in her face.

Mika stiffened. She knew that Gianni wouldn't hurt her but there were huge buttons being pushed now and it took everything she had to control her reaction. Behind her, she could sense that Rafe had stopped loading the dishwasher. He was staring, probably horrified, at the altercation. The second chef hadn't blinked and he was now busy trying to rescue the food that Gianni had left unattended on the grill. Margaret took plates off the pass and vanished swiftly. Gianni's temper tantrums were nothing new and it was best for everybody not directly involved to carry on with their own jobs. There was no point in escalating things further so Mika tried to push past Gianni's arm to put the offending plate back on the pass. Hopefully he would calm down and do what had to be done to satisfy the customer.

But standing up to him had been a mistake. Gianni grabbed the plate before it got to the bench. Maybe it slipped out of his hands, or maybe he threw it. It didn't matter because the effect was the same. The sound of smashing crockery caused a sudden silence in the busy café and, from the corner of her eye, Mika could see Marco glaring from his table on the footpath.

Rafe was right beside her now and she could feel him bristling. Was he ready to defend her? She shot a warning glance in his direction and followed it up with a firm shake of her head. It would only make things a lot worse if Rafe said or did anything. This was between herself and Gianni. The more people that got involved, the worse the whole day would become for everybody.

'What's your problem?' Gianni shouted at Rafe.

'Can't find the broom? Can't do *your* job, either?' He threw his hands in the air. 'Why do I have to work with such *stupid* people? Nobody can do the jobs they're being paid for.' He turned back to the grill in disgust, narrowly missing a collision with his junior chef who was putting new plates on the pass.

'Service,' he said. 'Table four.'

Mika's table. He'd managed to add a replacement plate with poached eggs to the remaining orders going to table four. Mika let out a breath she hadn't realised she'd been holding. If Alain had already delivered the free coffee as well, this small crisis might be over.

Even the mess. Rafe might have a face like thunder but he had a broom and pan in his hand and was sweeping up the broken crockery and food as she collected the plates, balancing one on her arm so that her hands were free to hold the other two.

In the end, it was no more than a commonplace disruption to smooth service but it had set the tone for the day. All of Mika's least favourite tasks had appeared, one after the other. Having to return an incorrect order was the biggest but others were equally irritating. Like the group of middle-aged women who treated her like their personal servant for the duration of their visit, requesting fussy changes to every dish they ordered, more ice for their water and replacement cutlery for all when one of them noticed a smudge on the handle of a knife.

Then there were the unsupervised toddlers who'd been allowed to smear smashed avocado all over the table, laminated menus and the wooden spokes of two chairs and up-end the sugar dispenser so that the crystals crunched underfoot. Mika knew that cleaning this particular table in time for the next group of customers was going to be a mission that would have her running behind for a considerable length of time.

And now, when the end of her shift was finally in sight, she had a table of young men who were getting progressively more obnoxious with every order of drinks she delivered to their table.

Their attempts to grab her legs was something she was adept at avoiding but the verbal innuendoes were harder to shake off.

'Whatcha doing after work, cutie? We could show you a good time.'

Her smile was tight. 'Are you ready to order?'

'I know what *I'd* like to order…' One of the men licked his lips suggestively as he leered at Mika, his gaze raking her body from head to toe.

She gritted her teeth, her smile long gone. 'I can come back in a minute, if you need more time to decide?'

'Just bring us pizza. And more beer.'

'Yeah…*lotsa* beer.'

The sooner this group left, the better. By then it would be time for Mika's shift to end and she could escape and go for a swim, and maybe she could wash away the unpleasantness of this entire day.

But would she be walking home alone? Back to the silent room she now had all to herself again? Would Rafe decide she might need the space to go swimming by herself, too?

The hollow feeling inside her chest was the worst thing about this bad day.

She was missing him.

If she was honest, she'd started missing him at the

bus stop in Amalfi yesterday when he'd dropped that bombshell about finding the concierge and arranging a room for himself. She hadn't ended up doing any of the writing she'd planned to do. Instead, she'd relived every moment of their day together. Tried to second-guess every glance or remembered tone of voice. Tried—and failed—to understand how she could be so drawn to someone who didn't feel the same way.

It was Rafe who had needed the space—that much was clear.

She'd hardly seen him at work today, either, except for the incident of Gianni's outburst, when she'd made it clear she wouldn't welcome his involvement. Had that been why he'd seemed so preoccupied every time she'd been near the pass? Why he'd kept his back to her, intent on loading or unloading the dishwasher whenever she was depositing a pile of crockery? Why he'd been outside, in the alley for his break at a completely different time from her own? Had she offended him again, the way she had when she'd tried to push him away just a little bit by suggesting he didn't have to go to the museum with her?

When she thought about that, she realised it had been a forlorn effort to protect herself because she knew how much she was going to miss him when he disappeared from her life as suddenly as he'd entered it.

But all she'd achieved was to find herself missing him already, when he was still here. How stupid was that?

It had confirmed something, though. She needed to protect herself. If it felt this bad with him still here, how much worse was it going to be when he was gone for ever?

At least she hadn't fallen in love with him because Mika instinctively knew that that would make the missing unbearable. Not that she had any real evidence to base it on because she'd never been in love. Not the kind of love she'd seen other people experience, anyway. Mika was confident that that would never happen to her because life had taught her both to rely only on herself and to avoid anything that made her more vulnerable than she already was.

Falling in love with someone was to make yourself ultimately vulnerable, wasn't it?

She'd told Rafe that she would never marry and have a family of her own and she believed that. How could she chase a dream of something like that when she had no idea what shape it really was? She wasn't looking for her *person*. A home that she could call her own was the closest she was going to get to finding her place in the world.

This was a physical reawakening, that was all. An attraction that might have been enough to break down a very big barrier, if Rafe had been interested.

The messages she'd received on that score were mixed, to say the least, and Mika didn't like feeling confused.

Feeling rejected was even more of a downer.

She delivered pizzas to the table of young men and followed that up with another order of their drinks, avoiding their wandering hands and letting their crude comments become no more than the background buzz of a busy café. As soon as they'd gone, she could wipe down their table and she'd be finished for the day.

Would Rafe be due to finish then, too?

Maybe she should give him some more of that space

and not even check to see if his shift was going to finish close enough to hers for it to be only friendly for one of them to wait so they could walk home together.

He knew she'd be going for the usual swim. If he chose not to join her then at least she'd know for sure that whatever had been gathering between them was not going to go any further. She could start pulling herself together, then. She'd been fine before Rafe had come into her life. It was ridiculous to be afraid of how lonely she might be when he left.

The anger had been building all day.

How did someone like Gianni think he had the right to put people down like that? Mika wasn't stupid. Neither was Raoul, but the bad-tempered chef had left them both feeling at fault for a situation and its consequences that Raoul was quite sure had been the result of the chef's lack of attention to detail. Part of him had wanted to put everybody in their place. To reveal his identity and use the power he could summon with a click of his fingers that could potentially change the lives of these people. To get the chef fired. Provide Mika with enough money to let her achieve her dreams without having to put up with any of this kind of abuse.

And the way she'd put up with Gianni's tantrum hadn't been the only thing he'd noticed today.

She'd told him that you got to see the worst of people in a job like this and she hadn't been wrong. Raoul could see out into the café when he collected pans from the chefs or replaced water carafes and glasses on their shelves. He'd seen people clicking their fingers to get Mika's attention. A group trying to sit down at a table she was trying to clean had glared at her as if it was her fault there was sugar or salt that had to be swept up before the table could be wiped clean. And he'd seen a low-life make a grab for her legs as she'd leaned over the table to deliver tall glasses of beer.

It wasn't right that someone like Mika had to put up with being treated like this because she needed a job to live and she just happened to be so far down the pecking order.

Because she was vulnerable.

He hadn't been allowed to stand up for her this morning as she'd faced Gianni's wrath and he'd thought he understood why, even if he didn't agree with it. Hospitality workers were easy to replace and Marco probably wouldn't have thought twice about firing them both if he'd faced the prospect of losing a good chef who'd be far harder to replace. He couldn't do anything about the way people treated her in the café, either, but it fed the anger. Maybe he was angry with himself, too, that he'd quashed the notion of revealing who he was because it would mean the end of this time of being so successfully incognito.

He'd seen that look in her eyes yesterday. That smile, when he'd offered her encouragement to believe in herself and her dreams. Had it been so special because it hadn't happened to her very often in her life? Was she more used to being treated as if she didn't matter? As if it was obvious she'd had to put up with whatever people felt like dishing out so many times in her life it didn't matter if they couldn't be bothered considering how she might feel?

She *did* matter, dammit. Raoul had wanted to help and her gestures had told him she didn't need his help. That she could look after herself, just the way she always had—except for that time when he'd first met her, when she'd been in the grip of something totally beyond her control.

She'd needed him then but he knew how hard it had been for her to accept his help.

To take his hand…

But this was her world and she knew what she was doing. Raoul had never been in a position of having to put up with being treated as being stupid or worthless. He didn't have to be in it now. He could walk out of here whenever he wanted to and step back into a life of privilege. A life where people looked up to him as being important even if he wasn't doing anything to earn that respect. It was the opposite end of the spectrum and it was an eye-opener, for sure.

Maybe he'd learned enough. He'd walked a few miles now, in the shoes of the invisible people, and it would change his perspective on many things. It would make him a better ruler. A better man. It wasn't that he hadn't always had a strong sense of what was right or wrong, but this experience of life as an ordinary person was sharpening his perception of the shades of grey within those boundaries.

It was wrong enough to anger him that Mika had to put up with people treating her so badly, even if she was tough enough to deal with it. When Raoul had caught a glimpse of the table of young idiots who were out to have a good time with whatever feminine company came within reach, it had been the last straw. He hadn't forgotten his impressions of Mika as a wild creature. Or the horrific thought that some man had hurt her in the past. She deserved protection even if she didn't think she needed it. She deserved to know that how she felt mattered.

That *she* mattered.

Raoul had had to fight the urge to march out of the kitchens and warn them to keep their hands and their crass comments to themselves. Or else…

Or else what?

Choosing to reveal his identity and throwing his power around would have been one thing. What if he got into a fight and maybe ended up getting arrested, being forced to admit who he was, and creating a scandal that would embarrass his entire nation? And what about his beloved grandparents? They'd sacrificed retirement to raise him and wait for him to be ready to take up his destiny and maybe doing that had contributed to his grandfather's failing health. How sad would it be to have the final days of their position as ruling monarchs marred by something so unfortunate?

He couldn't do that. Any more than he could act on the attraction towards Mika that was getting steadily more difficult to contain.

It would be easier to leave now.

Safer.

But would it also be cowardly? He'd already been tested in ways he had never imagined he'd be faced with in his quest to uncover his core strengths. If he left now, might he be running away from the opportunity to face an even more intense challenge?

Perhaps it was frustration more than anger that was making his gut churn today.

Frustration that his offer of help had been dismissed.

That he couldn't let Mika know how important she had become to him.

Most of all, that he wasn't being honest with her.

She'd revealed things to him that he knew she'd never told anybody else. Her search for a place where she felt she belonged—the idea that she would know who she was when she found a place to call home. Her dream of using her talents in photography and writing to make a new—better—life for herself.

But she knew nothing of him on such an intimate level.

What she thought she knew was no more than a pretence.

A lie...

He would tell her, Raoul decided as he finally hung up his apron for the day. He would tell her how he felt about her and why they could be no more than friends. He could offer her a new life, perhaps. Surely there would be a way to find her work within the vibrant tourism industry of his own country? Above all, he could thank her for giving him a perspective on life he would never forget, and they could talk about how best he could use his remaining time before he was due to report back and take up the reins of his future.

When was Mika due to finish her shift? The last glimpse into the café had shown her wiping down a very messy table after the rowdy group of young, male tourists had finally moved on.

But now Raoul couldn't see her anywhere. Margaret was looking after that section and Bianca had come in for the late shift.

'You looking for Mika?' Bianca handed an order form to Gianni. 'She just left a couple of minutes ago.'

Without him?

Raoul headed for the alley behind the café. The hope

of having an honest conversation with Mika was fading rapidly but he'd created this new distance himself, hadn't he? He'd put up new barriers—literal barriers—in the form of the four walls of his new, private room in the boarding house.

Mika had felt rejected and she was running away. He couldn't blame her but, if he left things this way between them, it would haunt him for ever.

He needed to find her.

Had she taken the main street as her route home, detoured past the beach or marina to give herself a longer walk, or had she chosen the narrow back alleys that offered far more solitude?

The alleys, he decided. Because that would be the route he would take if he wanted a space away from other people after a bad day and knew it was the fastest route to get to the best part of the day—that swim...

He turned another corner, skirted a bank of rubbish containers and passed the open back door of a restaurant kitchen where he could hear a chef yelling at his kitchen crew. They were shouting back and the noise level should have been enough to cover up a much fainter cry but the sound caught something in Raoul's chest.

His heart...

He knew that sound even though it was so muffled. He recognised that note of distress and it felt like a knife in his own chest.

The place it was coming from wasn't an alley, it was more like a hole in a wall—a bricked space that was a tiny courtyard with rear entrance doors to shops that were already closed and locked for the day.

And, right in the corner of the shaded space, was Mika.

Surrounded by the young men she'd been serving in the café. One of them was holding her from behind as she struggled, his hand over her mouth. Another was trying to put his hand up her skirt as she kicked out at him.

The impression of Mika's face was only in the periphery of Raoul's line of sight as he launched himself into the space but he didn't need a clear look to be painfully aware of what he would see.

He'd seen it before. The terror of a wild creature who had been trapped—unable to save herself from the dreadful situation she had found herself in through no fault of her own.

And this was worse than the vertigo that had left her stranded on a cliff side. This was unthinkably horrific.

The frustration and anger that had been building all day gave Raoul the strength to tackle four men without giving the odds a moment's thought. He had an advantage because they were so fixed on their evil intent that they hadn't seen him coming.

With a roar of pure rage that he didn't recognise as coming from his throat, Raoul grabbed the one who was lifting Mika's skirt by the scruff of his neck and hefted him into the air, before throwing him to one side. In almost the same motion, he swung his arm and let his fist connect to the jaw of one of the leering bystanders.

A blow to the side of his own head blurred his vision and seemed to intensify the sounds around him. The swearing of the thwarted attackers still on their feet and trying to defend themselves. Groaning from the one still on the ground where Raoul had thrown him. A scream from Mika as the man restraining her shoved her aside viciously. More raised voices as other people came running. From the corner of his eye, Raoul could see white aprons that suggested it was the staff from the nearby restaurant who had been alerted to the trouble and he caught the impression of them being pushed, and falling as the young men decided to make a run for it, but he didn't turn his head as he leapt forward with his arms outstretched to catch Mika before she fell and hit her head on the cobbled ground.

He had only held her hand before this moment and he remembered the trembling within the gentle circle of his fingers.

This time he was holding her entire body as tightly as he'd ever held anybody and he could feel the shuddering of someone who'd been pushed past the brink of fear.

Oh, God…had he been too late?

'Did they…? Are you…?' He couldn't bring himself to say the words, and Mika clearly couldn't say anything, but she knew what he was asking and she was shaking her head forcefully. Letting him know that he had been in time to stop the attack.

Just…

The restaurant staff were picking themselves up. More people were gathering in the narrow street. The chef was shouting for someone to call the police and a waitress stepped closer.

'Is she all right? Can I help?'

Mika was shaking her head again, curling closer within the fold of Raoul's arms. He heard her stuttered words and bent his head.

'Home…' she whispered. 'Please…take me home…'

She was so small, it took no effort to scoop her

off her feet and into his arms. She wrapped her arms around his neck and clung like a child.

Raoul pushed politely through the worried onlookers.

'She's okay,' he told them. 'I'll look after her.'

'Who is she?' someone asked. 'The police will want to talk to her.'

'She's my friend,' Raoul told them. He straightened his back, instinctively calling on the kind of presence that he might have had if he'd been arriving at a royal function. He was in control and he expected it to be respected. 'She's safe.'

The crowd parted. In silence, they made space for him to carry Mika onto the open street and carry on up the hill.

He could have put her down then but he didn't want to.

This time, he wasn't going to let her go.

Even when he got to the boarding house and into her room he still didn't let her go. He sat down on the couch he'd slept on for those first nights and he cradled her in his arms and let her cry until the shuddering finally ebbed and he could feel her fear receding.

How ironic was it that Mika could feel so safe with a man's arms around her? When her worst nightmares of men touching her again had come so terrifyingly close actually to happening?

But this was Rafe.

And this felt like the safest place she had ever been in her entire life.

More than that.

Would she ever feel safe again if he wasn't in her life?

Missing him wasn't something that she could protect herself from and it wasn't something that was ever going to get easier. Given her lifestyle, it should be something she had become very used to, but when Rafe left it was going to feel like he was taking a big part of her with him.

Even if she hadn't fallen in love with him.

As calmness won over the shaking and she could breathe without triggering a sob, Mika felt something like a wry smile gathering strength somewhere deep inside.

Who was she kidding?

She might have been in denial about the process of falling but she already loved this man. That physical reawakening had come in the wake of finding someone who had touched her soul.

Someone she could trust.

Her breath came out in a sigh this time instead of a sob. She could find words finally.

'You did it again.'

His arms tightened around her. 'I wanted to kill them. Are you sure they didn't hurt you?'

Mika swallowed hard. 'They would have. If you hadn't found them.' She tilted her head. 'How did you find them? I knew as they dragged me in there that nobody would be able to see from the street.'

'I heard you. Just the faintest sound but I knew it was you. I think my heart heard you rather than my ears.'

Mika could feel tears prickle behind her eyes again but these were very different tears from those in the aftermath of fear.

She would remember those words for the rest of

her life. They had to be the most romantic words she had ever heard.

Had Rafe just told her that *he* loved *her*?

It felt like he had.

One of those tears escaped and she could feel it rolling slowly down until it caught on the side of her nose. Rafe had seen it, too. He used the pad of his thumb to brush it away.

'It wasn't the first time something like this has happened to you, was it?'

Mika blinked, shocked. 'How did you know that?'

Silly question... Somewhere along the line, they'd had one of those lightning-fast, totally private conversations. Like the one where he'd asked if she would be okay sitting beside the view of that drop to the sea and had told her that he would change the arrangements if that would help.

He'd seen her fear even though she thought she'd kept it so well hidden. Had it been that moment she'd pulled away and headed for neutral ground after she'd seen the attraction in his eyes when they'd been sitting on the pontoon?

No. Maybe it had been there right from the start. When he'd touched her and she'd panicked and kicked his backpack over the side of the cliff.

It didn't matter. He knew. And, while it made her heart rate skip and speed up, it didn't make her feel any less safe that he knew.

'This was worse,' she whispered. 'There were more of them...and they were strangers.'

She felt the sudden increase in tension in Rafe's body.

'You *knew* him? Last time?'

Mika swallowed, closing her eyes against the shock she could see in his eyes. 'He was my boyfriend. But I didn't know how angry he could get. That he would think nothing of hurting me…that he would come after me when I tried to get away and force me to…to…'

Rafe's arms tightened around her and Mika could feel his cheek pressed to the top of her head. Then she felt his head turn and she could feel his lips on her hair. A slow, tender press that felt like a deliberate kiss of comfort.

For the longest time, they were silent. Mika knew she didn't have to go into the horrible details. That she didn't have to uncover those dreadful memories and make them fresh again.

It was Rafe who broke the silence.

'I think you're wrong,' he said softly. 'I think what happened to you before was worse than what happened today.'

Mika nodded slowly. 'Because you saved me…'

'No. Because you were betrayed by someone you thought you could trust. Someone that was supposed to care about you and keep you safe.' His breath came out in a sigh. 'I'm so sorry that happened to you, Mika. I'm not surprised you don't trust men.'

Her eyes snapped open. It was important that she could see Rafe. That he could see her.

'I trust *you*,' she said quietly.

'I care about you,' Rafe said. 'You're safe.'

It seemed like the most natural thing in the world that he would kiss her again to seal the truth of those words. It was a gentle kiss but it stirred up everything that had been woken and waiting in Mika's body.

The fear and bad memories were becoming a distant memory. *This* was what mattered. This moment.

This man that she *could* trust.

Her heart was beating wildly as she shifted in his arms. There was one way, she realised, that she could put not only today's horror but the memories that had kept her trapped for so long behind her for ever.

One thing that could restore her faith that there were good men in the world and, amongst them, one that she could trust with not only her heart but her body. If she was brave enough...

'Rafe?'

The subtle quirk of those dark eyebrows was enough to tell her he wanted to hear her question.

'Would you do something for me? Please? Something that will really make me feel safe?'

His eyes darkened. 'Of course. What is it?'

Mika licked suddenly dry lips. The words were so hard to get out that they emerged in no more than the ghost of a whisper.

'Make love to me...'

CHAPTER SIX

FOUR TINY WORDS.

How could they be enough to make it feel as if the bottom of Raoul's world had simply vanished?

As if he was falling and there was nothing he could find to catch hold of and save himself.

He'd started slipping without even realising it was happening. Touching his lips to Mika's head. That gentle kiss on her lips. He'd stepped over a boundary and now he had the choice of which direction his next step was going to take him. He'd been right in thinking that kissing this woman was always going to be more than a small thing. That it would unleash a desire unlike any he'd ever experienced before. Physical control was still possible, of course. He wasn't an animal—like those brutes who'd captured Mika this afternoon. He could stop, if that was the right choice.

This was it.

The challenge that was going to tell him who he really was. What his values really were and whether he was made of the right stuff to rule a country in the best interests of the many thousands of people who would be trusting him to do the right thing.

He'd convinced himself that resisting the attraction he felt towards Mika was that test so why, in this moment after those words had been uttered, and it felt like time was holding its breath, did it really so utterly *wrong*?

As if he didn't really have a choice at all?

Again, he was reminded of when she had taken his hand, up there on the top of that cliff. Of when her trembling had finally ceased and he'd known she was trusting him.

He'd felt taller, then. Powerful in a way that had nothing to do with him being a prince but everything to do with who he was as a man. Nothing would have persuaded him to break that trust.

And, right now, Mika was trusting him with so much more than her hand. She was asking him to take hold of her whole body and, by doing so, he would still be leading her to safety, wouldn't he?

To a place where she could believe it was safe to trust a man. To let him touch her.

Was it so far-fetched to imagine that she was trusting him with her entire future?

Raoul was aware of the part of his brain that was reminding him of the challenge he'd set himself—to put aside his own desires in order to do the right thing—but what *was* the right thing in this case?

It was astonishing how fast a brain could work. How thoughts could coalesce into a split second of time.

If he refused Mika's whispered plea, would she ever have the courage to ask again?

This moment had come in the wake of Mika being forced to face her worst nightmare and now being in a space where she felt safe. With someone she trusted as the closest friend she had available.

It was a no-brainer to hope that this particular combination of circumstances would never happen again. He would never want Mika to be attacked or even threatened ever again.

And if he was really honest with himself—and wasn't the point of this journey he was taking to be exactly that?—the thought of Mika being this close to any other man felt wrong and he knew there was a part of him that would always be envious of that man.

He could feel the whole shape of the small, lithe body he had cradled in his arms. He could still feel the incredible softness of her lips against his own. Mika had no idea how much she was asking of him but Raoul had a very good idea of how huge this gift he could give *her* was.

It was something that nobody else could ever give her, because this moment would never happen again, and she would remember it for the rest of her life. A life that might very well be happier because of this gift.

The choice had already been made, Raoul realised, as he slowly dipped his head to touch Mika's lips again with his own, knowing that this time it was going to be with passion, not an intention to comfort.

He'd been right in that there really wasn't a choice to be made at all. This had nothing to do with whether he was fighting or submitting to his own desires.

This was the right thing to do.

For Mika.

Because he loved her...

Nothing else existed the moment Rafe's lips touched hers and it was nothing like the gentle comfort of that first kiss.

Mika could fall into the overwhelming spiral of feelings that were so much more than a blinding physical need. This was an expression of love, and the combination of what both her body and her heart were experiencing was more than Mika could ever have believed was possible.

Rafe was so gentle with her that Mika knew he would stop in an instant if she gave any indication that she was afraid, or that she'd changed her mind, but neither of those things was going to happen.

She'd been waiting her whole life for this—she just hadn't known it was possible.

This was why people took the risk of being ultimately vulnerable, wasn't it? Because sex could never be like this if you weren't in love with your partner.

Surely nobody else had ever felt quite like this, though? She already had that weird kind of telepathic communication with Rafe that meant an entire conversation could happen in a glance. Maybe it was a natural extension of that connection that meant that every touch said so much as well.

Which was why she could feel his initial hesitation—the edge of gentleness that was still there enough to suggest Rafe needed reassurance as much as she did that this was a safe thing to be doing. It was Mika who slipped her hands under Rafe's tee shirt, to feel his skin beneath her hands and encourage him to take it off. She started to unbutton her own shirt but Rafe caught her hands, catching her gaze at the same moment.

And it was then that everything seemed to come together. The attraction that had been sizzling between them for so long, the desire unleashed by those first kisses and what was being said in that glance.

That this was about so much more than sex…

Mika was aware of the moment when everything else ceased to exist for Rafe, as it had done for her , and she tipped her head back with a sigh as she felt him take over the unbuttoning of her shirt and then the touch of his lips on the swell of her breast. They could both let go now and see just how close to paradise this was going to take them.

And surely it was as close as anybody could ever get in this life?

Mika had no idea when her tears had begun or when they had stopped; she could only feel them cooling her cheeks as they dried as she lay, still within the circle of Rafe's arms, waiting for the moment when she could catch her breath again enough to speak.

And, when she could, there was only one thing to say.

'Thank you,' she whispered.

'Oh…' Rafe still had his eyes closed, and the sound was no more than a soft groan, but Mika could see the way Rafe's lips were curling into a smile. And then he opened his eyes to look straight into hers. 'Believe me, it was my pleasure.'

The smile made everything perfect. It brought Rafe the friend back into the body of Rafe the amazing lover.

It made this real.

Mika hung onto his gaze. There were more words aching to escape. Words she had never said to anyone. Ever.

Oddly, they were harder to get out than the extraordinary request she'd made that had led to this.

But she couldn't *not* say them. Even though they made something else scarily real.

How vulnerable she had just become.

'I...' It was that smile that made this possible. The smile that seemed to underline the warmth and humour in those gorgeous, dark eyes. 'I love you, Rafe.'

Something she couldn't begin to define flared in his eyes but then the lids came down to shutter them and Rafe pulled her more closely against his body. For the longest moment, he simply held her, and Mika could feel the steady thump of his heart against her cheek.

The silence continued for so long that Mika forgot she was waiting for him to say anything. The rhythm of his heart and the warmth of his skin, in the blissful aftermath of their love-making, were lulling her towards what promised to be a deep and dreamless sleep. Or maybe not dreamless.

When Mika woke, it was completely dark and Rafe was sound asleep in the narrow bed beside her, his arm still cradling her head against his chest.

She could hear the words. A low rumble that still seemed to reverberate in every cell of her body.

I love you, too...

Had she heard those words with her ears or her heart?

Maybe it didn't matter. Mika pressed her lips gently against the soft skin at the base of Rafe's neck and then, with a sigh, let herself slip back into sleep.

Life could change in the blink of an eye.

Or over the space of one night.

The world felt different when Raoul woke in the morning. All his senses seemed to be heightened. He could smell the coffee Mika was brewing, having boiled the electric kettle on the only power point her room provided, and he felt more awake long before he tasted it. He could hear the trickle of the water as she poured it into the coffee jug and the tiny sound—a faint hum of pleasure—that Mika made as she glanced up to see that he was awake and acknowledged his company with a smile.

It was the most beautiful smile he'd ever seen. Mika was beautiful. Her skin seemed to glow this morning and he could actually *feel* the touch of her glance against his own eyes. Through his whole body, in fact.

Was *this* how being in love made you feel?

He'd waited until he was sure Mika was asleep in his arms last night before he'd echoed the words she'd said to him.

I love you, too...

They were dangerous words to say aloud because they carried a promise that he knew he would not be able to keep.

Last night had been a gift for Mika.

It hadn't occurred to him how much of a gift he was also receiving but, there it was, sitting inside his chest. Something huge, warm and comforting.

He knew exactly who he was.

A man who could feel this kind of love. Who could protect and nurture. Who could follow his instincts about whether something was the right thing to do, even though there were loud arguments against it, and trust those same instincts that were telling him it would be worth it, despite any inevitable consequences.

He was a man he could be proud of being.

And there was something even bigger that had brought him to this space.

Mika loved him.

She had no idea who he was or where he came from. She barely knew anything about him, but she loved what he was in this moment of time, and that had nothing to do with his elite position in life or his wealth. It was based entirely on who he was as a man.

A man worthy of being loved.

Would she still feel the same way when she found out the truth?

She had to know the truth. Was he really a man worthy of being loved if he was being dishonest?

On the other hand, wasn't he being more honest than he'd ever been in his life before? He had nothing to hide behind. Mika was seeing him as simply the person he was inside, without any of the trappings that were inescapable if you were a member of a royal family.

By a quirk of fate, he had escaped them completely, albeit temporarily.

With a huge effort, Raoul slammed a mental lid on that can of worms. He knew it was wrong—just as much as he'd known that giving Mika the gift of feeling safe to be touched had been right—and he was not impressed with himself for doing it, but he couldn't go down that track just yet.

He would break Mika's trust if he did and that would erase any of the magic that had happened last night.

It would be easy to persuade himself that this continued deception was to protect Mika but he knew he needed it for himself as well. This discovery was too important. This was what he'd set out on this journey to discover—who he was at the very core of his being—and he'd only just found it, this very instant.

He needed time. To hold this precious gift up to the

light and look at it from every angle he could find. To revel in the beauty of its simplicity and its strength.

To make sure it was real…

'Hey, sleepyhead…' Mika's voice was a smile in itself. 'You'll need to hurry up if you want to have coffee and a shower before we go to work.'

Work.

Washing dishes. The most mundane of employment but even this felt completely different today.

Knowing that, at any moment, he might catch a glimpse of Mika coming to the pass to collect plates, or that she could arrive beside his sink to deposit dirty dishes and share a glance and a smile, made even the worst jobs of the day worthwhile. With his senses so heightened, he could actually hear her voice at times amongst the cacophony of customers chatting, dishes clattering and even the chefs arguing. And whenever they were close enough for their gazes to meet, and one of those silent, lightning fast conversations to happen, he could feel a swell of what he could only identify as joy.

This was…happiness, that's what it was.

And, okay, it couldn't last—not in this form, anyway—but Raoul needed to hang onto every moment of it that he could because…

Because it felt perfect.

As though nothing else at all mattered.

Nothing else mattered.

There was nothing that could happen that day that could dent the astonishing joy that encased Mika like a private force field. Rude customers and crying babies, even the small dog that bared its teeth and snarled whenever she approached that table, did nothing to spoil her day. It made no difference that there were only snatched moments here and there when she actually saw Rafe or could share a glance or a smile. He could have been a thousand miles away and it would have still felt as if he was right by her side.

It was just as well she was so good at her job because every task was being accomplished on an automatic level. Most of her head was filled with thoughts of Rafe. Thoughts that were more like sensations, really, that she could feel right down to the tips of her toes. A memory of his smile. The sound of his voice. The touch of his fingers or lips on her skin...

So this was what it was like to be in love.

It was extraordinary.

Crazy.

She barely knew him but that didn't seem to matter. In a way, it was exciting, because there was so much still to find out. She had taken the first steps on a journey she had never expected to take, but the unknown wasn't daunting, because she wasn't on this journey alone.

Okay...maybe it *was* daunting. There was a rollercoaster of emotions that came with such heightened awareness and, as the day wore on, the dips caught Mika when she was least expecting them. There were aspects of this that were quite possibly terrifying.

What if this wasn't real?

What if Rafe didn't feel the same way?

What if his holiday came to an end and he simply said goodbye and she never saw him again?

An answer to the disturbing whispers came as their

shifts ended and Mika found Rafe waiting for her outside the back door of the café.

'Time for a swim?'

'Oh…yes. I can't wait.'

'Neither can I.' Rafe held out his hand. 'Let's go.'

Maybe it was the way he took her hand, as if it was the most natural thing in the world to do. Or maybe it was his smile or the expression in his eyes. Whatever it was, it made Mika's fear evaporate.

If Rafe vanished from her life without a backward glance, she would have *this* for ever.

The knowledge that it was possible to feel like this.

As if life was perfect and only this moment mattered. That was what she needed to hold onto. This moment.

The future would happen, and it wasn't something she could control in the same way she had been controlling her life, because she had, for the first time in so long, chosen to open herself to being vulnerable. To allow someone else to hold the gift of her heart and her happiness.

CHAPTER SEVEN

THERE WAS NO race out to the pontoon today.

It was tempting to stay close to the rock wall, in fact, with the music from the bar right above them— to simply float in the deliciously cool water and play like other young couples always did here—but it felt too public. As if what they had discovered with each other was too new and special to be on display just yet. It only took a shared glance for that suggestion and agreement to be made and Mika had no idea whether it had been her idea or Rafe's. Not that it mattered.

They swam side by side this time, and their hands touched the side of the pontoon at the same moment. Their bodies bumped together as they sank into being upright, and Mika let go of the pontoon to wrap her arms around Rafe's neck and her legs around his waist as she lifted her face for the first kiss since last night.

For an instant, she was aware of a tiny hesitation on Rafe's part and the dip in that emotional rollercoaster was so fierce it felt like she was leaving her stomach behind as she fell. But then his lips softened on hers and she felt his legs move to keep them both afloat as he let go of the pontoon to wrap his arms around her. It was only a matter of time before the water washed over the top of their heads and they had to surface to breathe, but who knew that kissing under water could be so amazing?

The sea was Mika's ultimate comfort zone. To be in that space, with the added magic that being in love seemed to bestow on everything, made that fraction of time something that she knew she would remember for ever. This would be the moment that she could return to if she ever lost sight of how perfect life could be. This total embrace of the cool water that made the heat of Rafe's skin against hers so intense. How safe it made her feel to be within the circle of his arms. The blinding heat of passion that licked her whole body from just the touch of his lips and tongue.

It lasted for ever, but it was over in a moment, and ended with a tangle of limbs, some frantic kicking to get back to the surface and a lot of laughter as they both hauled themselves up to sit on the solid planks of the pontoon. Again, by tacit consent, they sat quietly to watch the sunset with Mika's head against Rafe's shoulder and his arm draped loosely over hers, his fingers covering her tattoo.

The sunset was as gorgeous as ever but Mika closed her eyes after a minute or two because she wanted to bask in this feeling of such astonishing closeness. It was hard to pinpoint where her body ended and Rafe's started—as if they were two parts of one being. How had she not known that she had been missing another part of herself? That she had never felt complete?

It was the movement of Rafe's fingers on her arm that finally distracted her. Purposeful movement of just a single finger that was tracing the peaks and troughs of the inked design.

'It's the sea, isn't it?'

'Yes. It's a Maori design. The sea—and the land—have a huge spiritual significance in Maori culture.'

'I get that. I come from a country of islands, too. The sea is everything.'

Mika's breath caught. Rafe never talked about where he came from. Or anything else about his past. The only thing she really knew was that he'd been left without parents early in his life—as she had. This was the start, then, of finding out about this man she had fallen in love with.

'What islands? Where are they?'

'Out there…' Rafe tilted his chin towards the expanse of the Mediterranean, now gilded rose-pink by the rays of the sun. He was silent for a long moment and then his words were so quiet Mika barely heard them. 'They're named after the creatures they're famous for. *Les Iles Dauphins*.'

'No *way*…' Mika sat up straight so that she could turn her head to stare at Rafe. His arm fell away from her shoulder and the connection between their bodies was broken.

He stared back at her, an oddly wary expression in his eyes, and weirdly Mika felt a chill run down her spine. She swallowed hard.

'How did I not know that a place like that existed?' Her fingers had gone to the charm around her neck. 'Why didn't you tell me before?'

That wariness was still there but it was softened as Rafe offered an apologetic smile. 'I guess it didn't seem important. I'm here. And you're here. Maybe I'm just living in the moment.'

Which was exactly what Mika had decided she

needed to do. But questions were bubbling to the surface now and she couldn't hold them back.

'How far away are your islands? Do you live there now? How many dolphins are there?'

The curiosity in Mika's eyes was enchanting as her questions tumbled out like those of an excited child.

The moment of dread, when he had been sure she knew about his homeland and had suddenly made the connection and knew who he was, was evaporating.

He had taken the first step towards being really honest with her and it felt good. If he was gentle in the way he carried on, perhaps they could get to a place that would make their inevitable parting less painful.

He took a deep breath as he smiled back at her. 'They're not so far away but they're isolated enough to stay under the radar of the more usual tourist haunts. They're known as a tax haven. There's a thriving industry building luxury yachts. And the waters are a dolphin sanctuary. And, yes, I do live there now but I was away for quite a long time to go to school and university.'

'What did you study at university?'

'Oh…history. Politics. Environmental things…'

Mika's breath came out in a huff. 'Good grief… are you going to be a politician when you grow up?' She shook her head. 'I don't even know how *old* you are, Rafe.'

'I'm thirty-two.'

'Do you have a job?'

It was time to back off. 'I'm kind of between jobs right now. I wanted to try something different.' He'd had no idea, had he, of just how different that something was going to turn out to be?

Mika was grinning now. 'How's that working out for you, then?'

'I'm loving it.'

'But you're not going to be washing dishes when you go home, are you?'

'No.'

'What will you be doing?'

'Too many things, I expect.' He could feel the weight of those duties pressing in on him. The politics. The pomp and ceremony. The lack of personal space and choices. The sense of duty that would be ever-present…

The clock was ticking loudly now. This time was precious. He would never have anything like it, ever again.

Mika frowned. 'Are you a politician already?'

Raoul laughed. 'No…why?'

'Because you're so good at not giving a straight answer to a question.'

It really was time to distract Mika and there was a sure-fire way to do exactly that. By kissing her.

Or maybe he had wanted to distract himself. To remind himself of this extraordinary connection to another person that he had discovered and what it was teaching him about himself. That he wanted to buy a little more time simply to experience this.

Lost in the sheer pleasure of Mika's response, it was a surprise to find how brightly the lights of the bar on shore were shining. It told them how late it was getting but Raoul stole one more kiss. And then he held Mika's face between his hands.

'I don't want to think about my next job right now,' he said softly. 'Can't we just have this time? Just for us?'

Despite the fading light, he saw the shadow that clouded Mika's eyes. But he also saw determination and a smile that made light of any misgivings she might have.

'Okay. But will you answer one more question? Honestly?'

Raoul's heart skipped a beat. 'I would never lie to you, Mika.'

But he had already, hadn't he?

No. He just hadn't told her everything. But what if her next question was the one that ruined this moment? He wasn't ready for that. Not yet.

These memories would have to last him for ever. Surely one more night with Mika wasn't too much to ask for?

That curiosity was still lighting up her face and it was encased in a warmth that made him feel like he could tell her anything and she would accept it. Would forgive him, even. It was a risk but, in that moment, he felt safe enough to take it.

'One question,' he managed. 'Go for it.'

But Mika's face scrunched into thoughtful lines. 'Can I have one question tomorrow, too?'

He had to laugh. 'That's your question?'

'Oh, no…' Mika was laughing too. 'That's not fair. It's not a real question.'

'Why not?'

'Because it's not about *you*…'

There was something shy in her eyes. She was asking to be allowed closer but not quite sure if that was something he wanted. Raoul felt a tiny pang, as if a hairline crack had just appeared in his heart.

'Okay. We won't count that question. And, yes, you can have another one tomorrow.'

'And one the day after that?'

Oh…how tempting was that? The idea of more days. And nights. Of more hours than he could count just to be with her like this…

Mika was nodding as though he'd already agreed to the plan. And she was smiling.

'In that case, I have my last question for today.'

'What is it?'

'Whose turn is it to buy dinner?'

The trouble with questions was that one was never enough.

One question could open a door but then you stepped through it and it seemed like you were in a corridor with more and more doors stretching ahead of you.

Even deciding on that one question was tricky. One minute Mika would know for sure what she was going to ask next, but then she would come up with the potential answer she might get and she would see all those new doors. And she wasn't at all sure she wanted to open them.

Like, if she asked whether he would be going home to his magical-sounding islands as soon as his holiday ended.

It didn't make any difference whether his answer would be positive or negative because there were other doors that might change her life completely if she walked through them.

Like the one that might open if she asked if he wanted her to go with him…

It was too soon to open a door like that. What if the answer was no? That would break the bubble they had found themselves in now and Mika couldn't bear to do that. She had never been this happy.

Rafe hadn't moved back to his own room. Last night, when they'd caught the bus back to Positano after the swim she would always remember for that underwater kiss, he'd stopped when they'd found a pharmacy that was still open. They'd both been a little embarrassed by the purchase of condoms but Mika had been secretly thrilled. The love-making wasn't about to stop.

The fact that she was so happy about that was unbelievable. Was it only a couple of weeks ago that she had been so sure she would never let another man that close to her again? Her life had changed and her future was looking completely different.

Better.

Okay, they'd taken a stupid risk last night, but the moment had been too intense to think about something as premeditated as contraception and the odds were fortunately low enough for both of them to ignore, apparently. Well, not entirely ignore, because they'd had one of those silent conversations that had taken all of a heartbeat the moment that Rafe had picked up the box in the pharmacy and his gaze had met hers.

Is it too late?

It was a safe time, I'm sure of it.

Are you sure? You'd tell me, wouldn't you? If…

Yes, of course I'd tell you. Stop worrying… I'm sure…

She *was* sure but continuing that risk was definitely unacceptable. Mika hadn't yet found the place she would be content to call home. Getting pregnant would bring her journey to a grinding halt. Worse than that, it might scare Rafe so much that he would vanish from her life—the way her own father had. She would probably have to retreat to a place where life was familiar enough not to present extra challenges and that place was half a world away from where she was now.

With Rafe.

She watched as he paid for his purchase. Seeing his profile reminded her of that photo she'd taken the first evening they'd gone swimming together. Shifting her gaze, she took note of the printing machine in the corner of the pharmacy. She could pop in here with her camera card on a break from work and nobody would notice. How good would it be to have a copy of that photo that she could hold in her hand? A small, private thing to treasure.

One day, she would confess and check that he didn't mind, but that was an insignificant question compared to so many others.

So many questions that piled up in a corner because it was too hard to put them in an order of priority and appropriate times to ask were few and far between. There was never a chance to ask a meaningful question while they were at work together and, lying in his arms at night, random conversation was the last thing that came to mind.

This place—in this particular part of the world, with Rafe—was too good for Mika to want to risk changing a thing. In the end, she actually forgot to ask a personal question that day in the precious time between work and bed.

And she decided not to the day after that. Rafe seemed happy to be taking a day at a time—just for them—so maybe she needed to do that, too.

And it was enough for a few days. More than enough. This was a healing time for Mika and every day she felt safer as a little bit more of her protective shell crumbled and fell away. There were no tears in the wake of love-making now. She was becoming more playful and often there was teasing and laughter that added something completely new. Rafe was not only the most amazing lover she had ever found but he was her best friend as well.

The sense of something so solid between them made those doors far less daunting. So much so that there came a point, when a personal question came out so casually, it felt as natural as taking hold of Rafe's hand whenever they walked somewhere, like to the beach or home from work.

'What did you do?' she asked. 'In your last job?'

'I was a helicopter pilot.'

Mika's jaw dropped. His answer had come so automatically she knew he wasn't kidding but it was the last thing she had expected him to say. As far-fetched as him being an astronaut, perhaps. Or a brain surgeon.

'A commercial pilot?'

'No. I was with the military. We ran a rescue service as well.'

'Did you save people?' Mika smiled as she shook her head. 'Silly question. Of course you did. You've saved me twice already—it's second nature for you, isn't it?'

'I wouldn't say that.'

'Will you go back to a job like that?'

'No.'

'Why not?'

'I have another job waiting for me. That's why I needed a break. I wasn't sure how ready for it I am.' He squeezed Mika's hand. 'Are we going for a swim today?'

'Are you trying to change the subject?'

The discomfort in his glance confirmed her suspicion and Mika felt a chill run down her spine. What was he hiding? She hated the sudden tension that seemed to increase the heat of the late-afternoon sun enveloping them.

Her mouth simply ran away with her next question.

'You're not *married*, are you?'

'No.' Her hand was jerked as Rafe stopped in his tracks.

'Have you been in jail recently?'

His breath came out in an incredulous huff. '*No.*' But he was smiling as he tugged her into his arms and silenced her with a kiss. 'Enough questions, already...'

Mika could feel both the need to ask anything and that odd chill of premonition evaporating in the wake of his kiss.

'Okay...but I get to ask another question tomorrow.'

'Maybe.'

'You can't say that. You agreed.'

'Not exactly. And, even if I did, there's a problem with that arrangement.'

'Which is?'

Rafe's smile widened into a grin. 'You can't count.'

They started walking again and a welcome puff of a sea breeze lessened the heat around them. Or maybe it was that the tension had been blown away.

Mika's lips quirked. 'How many times will you make love to me tonight, Rafe?'

'One.'

She glanced up to catch his gaze and they both laughed.

'So I'm not the only one who can't count, then...'

CHAPTER EIGHT

IT WAS RAFE'S idea to do something special on their
next day off.

The day was still early and deliciously cool but the
clear sky suggested that being close to the sea would be
the best way to enjoy the rest of it. Waiting for a beachside café to open for breakfast, they wandered past the
main beach in Positano where the deck chairs for hire
were already being set up in orderly rows, colour-coded
for the businesses that owned them, and they began to
explore the marinas where boats of all sizes and shapes
bobbed gently on their moorings.

It was Rafe who spotted the sign advertising a day
trip out to the island of Capri. The cost was an extrav-
agance in Mika's opinion but Rafe persisted as they
retraced their steps to find coffee.

'You want to see it, don't you? It would make a great
subject for one of your articles.'

'I would love to see it. I've been intrigued ever since
I saw the outline of those rocks in the distance.'

'The *Faraglioni*? The Three Spurs? They're very
distinctive. Did you know you can go right though the
gap in one of them?'

'No…really?'

'If we find the right boat, it'll be part of the trip.'

'It's too expensive.'

'It would be my treat. And you need a new subject. You've finished your articles on the Footpath of the Gods and the Valley of the Ancient Mills now, haven't you?'

Mika caught her bottom lip between her teeth. 'I emailed them last night.' She scrunched her nose. 'I can't believe I took your advice and sent them to *National Geographic* and *Lonely Planet*. They only take the best.'

'It's a good thing.' Rafe squeezed her hand to make her pause and then dipped his head to kiss her. 'Always start at the top. Why settle for less if you don't have to?'

'Mmm…' The sound was a sigh of happiness in the wake of that kiss. 'Okay…if you're sure. But you could buy a lot of new clothes with that kind of money. I'll bet you haven't replaced half of what you lost when I kicked your backpack over that cliff.'

'Ah, but I've learned how little you actually need to survive,' Rafe said quietly. 'And, more than that, how good life can be when you keep things simple.'

The look in his eyes told Mika that *she* was the reason life was so good for him right now and the bubble of joy that caught in her throat exploded to send ripples of pleasure right through her body.

'I'll have to go home to get my camera. And my notebook.'

'We've got an hour or so before the boat leaves. I'll go back and make sure we can get tickets while you fetch your camera. We'll still have time for a quick breakfast. Let's meet at the café beside the bus stop.'

Excitement was chasing joy now. 'Race you, then.'

Mika stood on tiptoes to press another kiss to Rafe's lips. 'I'll be back here first.'

She wasn't, because she took a little extra time to throw their sunhats and some sunscreen into her small backpack, but it didn't matter, because Rafe had ordered coffee and croissants and had the tickets in his hand that were a passport to a new adventure. Mika couldn't wait. She was first on the boat to ensure the best position to take photographs and already had her camera in her hands as more and more people climbed aboard. The powerful launch took them swiftly up the coast and Mika started taking a series of shots as the massive spurs of rock the island was so famous for came closer and closer.

The side of the boat was not going to be the best place to record the experience of going through the gap of the middle spur, so Mika edged her way through the group to get to the back. A young man, holding a remarkably similar camera to her own, made space for her beside the rail.

'Nice…' He tilted his head as he looked at her camera. 'It's a D4, isn't it?'

'Yes. What's yours?'

'A D5. It's the latest.' He sounded English. And very confident. 'The best.'

'Wow…'

'I need it for my job. I'm a pro.' He grinned at Mika. 'I'm James.'

'Nice to meet you. I'm Mika.'

The boat was slowing, coming closer to the arched hole. Mika readied her camera but took a sideways glance at her new companion. He was going to get very hot today in those tight, black jeans and tee shirt but he certainly looked professional. The huge lens he had on his camera at the moment made her think of paparazzi.

The passage through the gap was exciting, with the roll of the sea and the height of the ceiling of rock over-head making the walls feel closer than they probably were. Mika tilted her camera, trying to capture it all.

'You need a wide-angle lens.'

'It's on my list. I'm saving up.'

Mika lowered her camera as the boat picked up speed, turning her head to see where Rafe was in the crowded boat.

'Hang out with me for the day and you might earn enough for any lens your heart desires.'

'What?' She turned back swiftly. 'How?'

'There's a rumour that there are some big names coming to the island today for a spot of shopping.' He tapped the side of his nose. 'Can't say who, but they're the hottest ticket there is right now. Get a good shot, and you could sell it for serious cash.'

So he *was* paparazzi. Mika took a step back, shaking her head. 'Thanks for the offer, but I'm spending the day with my boyfriend.' Another glance showed her that Rafe was still in the spot she'd left to come to the back of the boat. And he was watching her. Or, rather, he was staring at James.

James was staring back. 'Lucky guy,' he said. 'My loss.'

'Who was that?' Rafe asked when Mika got back to his side.

She shrugged. 'He said his name was James and he's a professional photographer. Apparently there's a movie star or someone going to Capri today and he wants to get a shot he can sell.' She made a face to express her distaste. 'He said I could make big money if I hung out with him for the day.'

A glance over her shoulder revealed that she was still an object of interest for James. Or was it Rafe he was staring at? Impossible to tell now that he had sunglasses on, and he turned away as soon as Mika spotted him. Or, rather, he waited a heartbeat before he turned away. And he was smiling. Did he want her to know that he was still watching? That he was enjoying whatever game he thought he was playing?

'We picked the wrong day for this, I think.'

There was a note in Rafe's voice that Mika had never heard before. He sounded angry. Disgusted, even.

'Why?' Anxiety formed an unpleasant knot in her stomach. She didn't want this to be a 'wrong' day. She wanted a day like their walk through the valley of the ancient mills when that feeling of being connected to Rafe had become so incredibly strong. He'd fought the attraction, though, hadn't he? He had come so close to kissing her but had pulled away—so much so that he'd moved out of her room.

But now…everything had changed. If they were totally alone in a beautiful place, and returned to that kind of space where there was nothing else but that connection, would it grow even more? And, if it did, where would it take them? Could she ask the questions that would open the scariest doors of all?

Maybe she wouldn't need to ask them. Maybe he would tell her that he didn't want to stop sharing his life with her. Ever…

But, right now, he was scowling.

'Paparazzi are like wasps. When one gets attracted, you know there'll be dozens more. I hate them.'

Mika blinked. 'Hate' was such a strong word—as if he had personal experience of something extremely unpleasant. Or did he hate the principle of privacy being violated? That was more likely. Despite how little she still knew about him, Rafe was clearly a very private person.

And that was fine. Privacy was exactly what she was hoping they could find today.

'We won't hang around the shops,' she said. 'Look, I've got a brochure. There's a map. We could go walking and see something historic. Like this—the *Villa san Michele*. That looks amazing.'

Their boat wasn't the only one docking at Capri and the streets were already crowded. When they made their way to the funicular train to ride up the side of the cliff to the *piazetta*, they were urged on to squeeze in with dozens of other tourists.

Maybe Rafe was right, Mika thought, as she was jostled hard enough to cause momentary alarm. They *had* picked the wrong day for this. But then his arm went around her shoulders and his was the only body she was pressed against, and she felt safe again. They emerged into the square and the crowd thinned as they dispersed towards the cafés and shops. Mika breathed a sigh of relief and unfolded the brochure she was still holding in her hand.

'Let's find the road we need. Looks like the *Via Acquaviva* to start with and then the *Via Marina Grande*.'

'How long will it take to get to the villa?'

'It says about forty-five minutes.'

'It might be a good idea to buy some water and something to eat.' Rafe still sounded out of sorts, and he wasn't looking at Mika. He seemed to be scanning the crowds around them and wasn't happy with what he could see.

'Okay. My turn to pay this time.' Mika touched her shoulder to slip off the strap of her camera case and retrieve the euros she had tucked into a side pocket for easy access. 'Oh, my God...'

'What is it?' Rafe was looking at her now, his brow furrowed with concern. 'What's wrong?'

'My camera... It's *gone*...'

'You didn't put it in your backpack?'

'No. It was over my shoulder. I had it when I got on the train.'

When she'd been jostled hard enough almost to fall.

'You must have dropped it. We'll go back to the station and see if someone's handed it in.'

Mika's sinking heart told her that this was probably too much to hope for. The head shaking of the train officials was bad enough. Being given a lecture about being wary of pickpockets in tourist destinations was worse. She left her details with the officials and a woman assured her that she would pass the information to the police in case the camera turned up elsewhere.

The shine had been taken off the day and it seemed like they were both out of sorts now.

'I'm sorry,' Rafe said. 'Your camera can be replaced but you won't get photos today. You've saved your earlier pictures, haven't you?'

Mika nodded. They were all safely on her laptop. The most precious one of all—that she'd printed into a passport size the other day at the pharmacy—was tucked into the wallet she'd left at home for safekeeping.

And, yes, the camera could be replaced but how long would it take her to save up that kind of money again?

It was a setback, one that could very well ruin this
day, but Mika couldn't afford to let that happen—not
when she didn't know how many more days like this
she would have with Rafe. Where they could find the
right time and place that would make it natural to talk
about what the future might hold…

With a huge effort she pushed the negative effects
of her loss to one side.

'You know what?'

'What?'

'I've still got my notebook. I can come back and get
photos another time. Maybe one of my articles will sell
and that'll be enough to buy a new camera.'

Raoul could see the effort Mika was making. He knew
how hard it was for her and he loved her for that courage and determination in the face of adversity.

That camera was precious. She had worked so hard
for it and it represented her dream of a better future.

He would replace it for her. Not only the camera,
but he would get every type of lens available as accessories—a tripod too, perhaps, and a beautiful case to
carry everything in. He could have it gift-wrapped and
delivered as soon as he got home.

When he'd left Mika behind...?

He didn't want to think about that. Not today, when
it might be the last day they got to spend together like
this. While they were both still invisible as far as his
real world was concerned.

In the meantime, he needed to encourage her. To
make them both feel better. His own mood still left
a lot to be desired. The day had soured for him when

he'd seen the way that photographer had tried to hit on Mika. It hadn't been as simple as jealousy, though, had it? His instincts had been validated by knowing that James was a paparazzo. One of the army of watchers that had never been far away for his whole life—a symbol of why he'd never really known what he'd needed to know about himself because he'd always had to be what others expected him to be.

He could be who he really was today, though. Not being able to protect Mika from that theft rankled but he could fix that, in time. For now, perhaps all he could do was offer comfort.

'Someone might still hand it in. We could check in at the police station on our way back.'

A police station was the last place Raoul wanted to go, though. What if they wanted his ID and awkward questions led to him having to confess the truth?

Mika's gaze was steady. Given the way they could communicate, it was more than likely that she could sense his reluctance. Was that why she was shaking her head?

'They've got my details. It's pretty obvious the theft was deliberate so I doubt it'll be handed in anywhere.' She shrugged. 'It's rotten but I don't want it to spoil our day. Let's try and forget about it.'

Her smile was pure Mika, with that edge of feisty cheekiness, but there was a hint of apology in her eyes.

'Have you got enough money for some water and a sandwich or two? Mine was in the camera case.'

Raoul could only nod because he didn't trust himself to speak for a moment. It summed up so much, didn't it? How much he loved her zest for life and the courage she displayed in living it. How little she knew about him to think that paying for a simple meal might be stretching his resources. How much she loved him, that she didn't want their day to be spoiled.

Escaping the crowds of the *piazzetta* and the streets of boutique shops that were luxurious enough to attract the kind of customers that the paparazzi loved to follow was a huge relief but, for a long time, their walk was silent and a little sombre.

Maybe it was the magic of the quiet, residential streets with their pretty gardens and wafting scents of lemon trees and lavender. Or maybe the increasing peacefulness had something to do with the summery sounds and sights of bees busy in the flowers and butterflies drifting past. By the time they had reached their destination, it felt like they had left the unpleasantness of James, the theft and the crowds of tourists far behind. There were so few people at the villa right now that, for long stretches of time, they could wander in peace and admire the beautiful, old house and its breath-taking views.

Mika was enchanted by everything.

'I wish I'd known we were coming here. The brochure doesn't tell me nearly enough—just that it was built by a Swedish physician, Alex Munthe, who came to Capri in 1885.'

'You'll have plenty of time to do some research later.'

'Mmm... Oh I love this quote...' Mika's eyes were shining. 'He said, "My house must be open to the sun, to the wind and the voice of the sea, just like a Greek temple, and light, light, light everywhere". Isn't that just how it makes you feel?'

It was impossible not to smile back. Not to be drawn into the joy Mika was sharing.

'We've got it all today, haven't we? The sun and the wind. I can't hear the sea yet, though.'

'You can see it from almost every window. And, if you can see it, you can hear it. In here…' Mika touched Raoul's chest, laying her hand over his heart. 'It's a song. The most beautiful music ever…'

He put his hand over hers, dipping his head so that his forehead rested on her hair. He knew exactly what she meant and the connection between them had never felt so strong.

Maybe they'd both been born with dolphin blood in their veins…

He could smell the scent of the shampoo she used, something lemony and fresh. And, more than that, he could smell a scent that was unique to Mika. Something sweet but with a hint of spice. Something he knew he would never smell on anyone else.

Something he would never, ever forget.

They got lost wandering from room to room when they were finally ready to explore outside.

One room was the biggest yet.

'It's like a ballroom,' Mika breathed. Her gaze snagged his. 'Let's pretend…'

'Pretend what?'

'That this is our house. That there's a small orchestra just over there and they're playing music, just for us…' Her eyes shone. 'I'm wearing a dress…a really pretty, swirly dress… Dance with me, Rafe…'

She held up her arms like a child asking to be cuddled and there was no way he could refuse the request. And then he started moving. It was obvious Mika had never had the kind of formal dance instruction that he'd had but she was so easy to lead and so astonishingly light on her feet. Even without music, this was a dance he would remember. And maybe they did have music…that song that came from the voice of the sea…

It was Mika who stopped the dance. She pulled away, holding only his hand as she took one more look around them.

'Imagine *really* living somewhere like this,' she whispered. 'How unreal would that be?'

Raoul didn't have to imagine. Many elements of this wonderful old house were very similar to the palace he would soon be returning to, like the intricately tiled floors, Grecian columns and works of art that could grace any museum. His home had a ballroom much larger than this, with an area that could seat an entire orchestra. That the idea of living in such opulence was a fairy-tale for Mika drove home the realisation that he'd been avoiding for so long.

She didn't belong in any part of his world. Even wearing a pretty dress was the stuff of make-believe and that was only a tiny piece of the jigsaw that made up the lives of the people in that world.

The thought was unbearably sad. How could he leave her behind when he couldn't imagine not having her in his life now?

But how could he *not* leave her behind?

Raoul's love for his country and his grandparents was bone-deep. His destiny was already written and it included a marriage that would bring two small kingdoms together and make them both stronger, which would be of great benefit to the people he was about to take responsibility for. He couldn't walk away from any of that. He didn't want to walk away from it but...

But doing so was going to hurt them both.

He could cope. He had to. But to hurt Mika so much? He wasn't sure he *could* do that.

A few days or weeks were nothing in the timeframe of a lifetime. How could snatching this gift of something so perfect have become such a dilemma?

He'd felt his heart crack once before when she'd touched it in an unexpected way and it felt as though that crack was widening with every gasp of astonishment or pleasure that escaped Mika as they kept exploring.

Hand in hand, they walked along the paved pathway beneath vine-covered pergolas supported by columns with splashes of vibrant colour from the flowers in perfectly manicured gardens on either side.

Their path led them past a granite sphinx that Mika had to touch, and that was the moment that Raoul felt that crack in his heart start to bleed.

Such small, clever hands. Such a light, reverent touch—as if she was still dancing.

That made sense. She was dancing her way through her life like some kind of magical creature.

He knew what it was like to be touched by those hands. How it made him feel like he was the best man he could ever be. He'd learned so much about himself in the last few weeks and it was too bound up in how he felt about Mika for the fragments ever to be separated.

When he left Mika behind, was he also going to leave behind the part of himself she'd helped him discover?

They came to a circular viewing point with an un-interrupted panorama of the Bay of Naples.

'You can see for ever,' Mika said in awe. 'I bet you can see *Les Iles Dauphins* if you look hard enough.'

Raoul stood behind Mika because he could see perfectly well over the top of her head. She leaned back against him and he put his arms around her, his breath escaping in a long sigh.

He would certainly be leaving a part of himself with Mika. A large part of his heart. But he had to believe he wouldn't lose what she had taught him. He'd learned things that were ingrained in his soul now. Things about love. Things about life. They would serve him well in the future and he would be a king that his people would be proud of.

Gazing out to the sea and the islands he knew were out there gave Raoul a pang of homesickness and, in that instant, he knew he was finally ready.

It was time he stepped back into his life.

And that meant that any reprieve was over. It was time to tell Mika the truth.

He tried to find a way to begin as they walked back to meet their boat but the words turned themselves over and over in his head and, whenever he caught Mika's gaze, they became an incomprehensible jumble.

It would be better to do it when they got back to her room, he decided. That way he could at least slip away and give her privacy to deal with the shock. How awful would it be for both of them to have to face heartbreak in public?

And it was *so* public. The crowds seemed to have swelled so much it was difficult to navigate through them to get to the train and down to the marina. Whatever celebrities had come to Capri today had certainly caused a stir. There were paparazzi everywhere, and James wasn't the only one on their return trip to Positano. He was still snapping photos. Raoul pulled the brim of the baseball cap he had been using as a sunhat further down his forehead and pushed his dark glasses further up his nose. It was probably Mika that the sleaze was trying to get a picture of but it was making him extremely uncomfortable.

Was this the kind of guy that would step in to fill the gap in her life when he had gone?

The dilemma was doing his head in.

On the one side was his duty that he could never walk away from.

On the other was his love for Mika and the overwhelming desire to be the man he was when he was with her.

There had to be a way through this that wouldn't destroy them.

And maybe there was…

Crazy thoughts were coming out of the turmoil in his head and his heart. He wasn't married yet. He wasn't even formally engaged, although the whole world was expecting the announcement. Would Francesca still *want* to marry him if she knew that his heart was with someone else?

His grandparents adored each other. Wouldn't they be prepared to allow him the same happiness of being married to the one he loved?

He needed more time to think.

Positano seemed to be as popular as Capri for tourists today and, oddly, the *Pane Quotidiano* seemed to be the most popular café. From the end of the street, it looked as if there was a crowd of people queuing to get in.

'What's going on?' Mika sounded worried. 'Maybe we should see if Marco needs extra help. They'll never be coping with that kind of crowd.'

As they got closer, the hairs on the back of Raoul's neck started to rise. He could see the cameras and he knew exactly who all these people were. A glance over his shoulder and he could see James a step or two behind them, and that was when he knew the game was up.

It was too late to try and escape. Mika was holding his hand—obliviously leading him further and further into enemy territory. He could feel her grip tighten as she realised that something unusual was going on. It was normal enough to see Marco waving his arms in the air as he spoke, but for Gianni to be out on the street as well, holding a newspaper? Other staff were filling the doorway, too, watching what was going on—Alain, the barista, and probably all the waitresses working today.

They were easily close enough to hear Marco now.

'He's *not* here. And how many times do I have to tell you that you're barking up the wrong tree? Go away— you're scaring off my customers.'

And then he spotted Mika.

'She'll tell you. *She* knows… He's her boyfriend, for heaven's sake.'

They moved as a pack, shifting their attention, lifting their cameras. Raoul could feel Mika's whole body stiffen as she froze. He could see the fear in her eyes as she looked up at him.

'*Prince Raoul…*' a dozen or more voices shouted in the instant the flashes started exploding around them. 'Look *this* way…'

CHAPTER NINE

NONE OF THIS made any sense.

Blinded by the bright flashes going off right in her face, Mika clung to Rafe's hand. He was pulling her away but her legs wouldn't co-operate. The roaring sound around them was starting to coalesce into recognisable words but it still didn't make any sense.

'*Why?*'

'Crown Prince of *Les Iles Dauphins*...'

'Washing *dishes*...?'

'Who's the girl, Prince Raoul?'

'Does your fiancée know?'

That did it. Like having a bucket of icy water thrown over her head. The word settled into Mika's consciousness and ricocheted around, inside her skull, like a bullet.

Fiancée...fiancée...fiancée...

She ripped her hand from Rafe's grip.

Rafe? Oh, yeah...he'd stumbled over the name when he'd introduced himself, hadn't he? Up there on the Footpath of the Gods, when he'd rescued her. Some instinct had suggested that maybe he didn't want her to know his real name. Who he really was.

But...a *prince*...?

With a *fiancée...?*

She was free of his touch now. The pack of paparazzi was moving in from all sides but Mika was small.

And as hard as nails. It was easy to launch herself at a gap between two of these men, squeeze through and then start running. She didn't realise she was holding her breath until she'd almost reached the end of the street and had to stop, doubled over as her lungs screamed for some oxygen.

Turning her head, she could see that Rafe was coming after her—getting away from the crowd that had now attracted a police presence—but he'd been ambushed by someone further up the street. A slim figure wearing tight, black jeans and a tee shirt...

James?

Her world had turned upside down and Mika had to find safety. Her lungs burning, she started running again and didn't stop until she got to the boarding house and into her room, where she could slam the door behind her and push the bolt into its slot to lock it.

Now what?

Should she throw herself onto her bed and hide her face in her pillow?

The bed that she had been sharing with the man she loved so much...who wasn't the man she'd thought he was...

Should she sink onto the couch and put her face in her hands?

The couch that she'd offered to someone whom she had believed had lost everything and had no money and no place to sleep.

Oh…there was humiliation to be discovered amongst this shock.

If it was true…

But how *could* it be true?

Why would a prince pretend to be nobody? To take on an unskilled, underpaid, physically hard job and work amongst people like herself?

Why would he have chosen to *be* with someone like herself—in the most intimate way it was possible to be with someone?

Instead of choosing either the bed or the couch, Mika stayed exactly where she was, standing in the middle of her small, dingy room. She wrapped her arms tightly around herself and, instead of hiding her face, she stared at the blank wall.

His last job had been as a helicopter pilot.

She'd thought that was as unlikely as him being an astronaut or a brain surgeon.

A huff of something like laughter escaped her throat.

Why hadn't *'prince'* been at the top of that list?

And he hadn't really chosen to be with her, had he?

He'd been determined not to be. Now she could see that hesitation on his part, when she'd believed he had been about to kiss her for the first time in the valley of the mills, in a whole new light.

She'd forced him into it.

She'd *begged* him to make love to her.

Shame was a step down from humiliation. Who knew?

No wonder he hadn't wanted her to ask too many questions. He'd known all along that there was no possibility of any future for them. He'd wanted to have this time *just for them*…

Just for him, more likely. A final fling before he got married.

A bit of...*rough*?

The rattle of her door handle, swiftly followed by a sharp rap on the door, made Mika flinch.

The sound of Rafe's voice sent a spear of pain in its wake.

'Mika?' Her name was a command. 'Let me in. *Now...*'

Things had hit the fan in an astonishingly spectacular way.

The last way Raoul would have chosen.

It would have been bad enough that his identity had been revealed before he'd had the chance to tell Mika the truth but never in a million years could he have imagined how much worse it could actually be.

Clutched in his hand was a copy of the newspaper that James had shoved in his face when he'd stepped out in front of him.

The front page of a national evening paper that had the provocative headline *Prince in Hiding* and a huge photograph.

A photograph he had no idea had been taken and could have only been taken by one person.

Mika.

He remembered the moment. Standing there on the flagged terrace in front of Bernie's bar in Praiano, watching that glorious sunset. After that swim with Mika, sitting on the pontoon and feeling that first, heady realisation that he'd found someone with whom he had an extraordinary kind of connection. He was staring out to sea, with one hand shading his eyes and clearly deeply in thought. With no sunglasses on and his beard still in the early days of its growth, it was no wonder that someone had recognised him.

How much had James been paid for that picture?

How much of a percentage had he offered Mika?

He'd been so smug.

'Say thanks to your girlfriend for me. Here—have this as a memento...'

He'd shaken off the rest of the paparazzi but it wouldn't take them long to run them down. His cover was blown and Mika's life was about to turn into a circus.

But maybe she deserved it...

Raoul banged his fist on the door again.

He'd been betrayed. And he was angry.

'Open the door, Mika. You owe me an explanation.'

The door flew open a second later.

'I owe *you* an explanation?'

Raoul unravelled the newspaper and held it in front of her.

'*You* took this picture, didn't you?'

He'd never seen her look this shocked. Not even in those first few minutes of knowing her, when she'd been in fear of her life on the side of that cliff. Or when she'd been threatened by those men intent on rape.

'How did *that* happen? Oh, my God...it was on my camera...'

For a heartbeat, he believed her. He *wanted* to believe her. But he could see the smirk on James' face as he'd asked him to pass on his thanks. And he knew how well a lot of women could act. They could make men believe whatever they wanted them to believe—

especially when they had eyes like Mika. He'd believed everything she'd told him.

Had trusted her.

And she'd betrayed him. He caught hold of that anger again, like a shield.

'The camera that got so conveniently stolen.' Raoul pushed his way into the room, forcing Mika to back up, slamming the door closed behind him with his foot. 'It must have made a great cover, being jostled in that crowd on the train.'

'What on earth are you talking about?'

'You handed it over, didn't you? To your new friend. *James*. Did you decide that being a travel writer wasn't a fast enough way to get to fame and fortune? Did you realise you had a much quicker route right at your fingertips?'

'You think I was *responsible* for this?'

'He told you that you could make big money if you hung out with him for the day, didn't he?'

Raoul could imagine all too easily what had really been said in that conversation.

'You think a movie star is a big deal? Boy, have I got a story—and photo—that you'd kill for...'

'What is it?'

'Hang on. Let's talk money first...'

Mika was looking stunned rather than shocked now. They hadn't lost the ability to communicate in the space of a single, sharp glance.

She was as angry as he was now.

'Why the hell would I have done that? When I didn't have the slightest idea who you actually were?

'Didn't you? *Really?* Not even when I told you where I came from?'

Raoul remembered that chill he'd felt when he'd told her the name of his homeland—the fear that she might have guessed the truth.

Had she just been waiting for an opportune moment to use that knowledge to change her life?

That was what was so much worse than everything hitting the fan.

He'd been taken for a fool.

He'd believed that Mika was in love with him for who he was as a man and not as a prince.

'I don't believe this. *I'm* the one who should be angry here. *You're* the one who lied to me.' There was a flash of something stronger than anger in her eyes now. Something like despair. 'And you said you never would...'

'I didn't lie to you.' Anger was a great way to obliterate anything like misgivings. 'I just didn't tell you who I was. I didn't *have* to, did I?'

'I didn't give that photograph to James. Even if I *had* known who you were, I would never do something like that.'

'I saw the way you looked at each other.' He'd seen it when she was back by his side on the boat and she'd turned to look at James. 'I saw the way he smiled at you. It's obvious that the deal had been done. That the arrangements for a handover were in place.'

Mika gave an incredulous huff, stepping further away from him.

'And you didn't want to go to the police, did you? I wonder why that was?'

He'd thought it was because she'd sensed his own reluctance, but now the new explanation was too obvious to ignore.

'It's not the first time this has happened,' he snapped. 'Tell me, is it easy for girls to pretend they're in love in order to get what they really want?'

Mika's face looked as if it had been carved out of stone and her voice was chillingly quiet.

'Get out,' she said. 'Get out of my life, Rafe. Or should that be *Raoul*?'

The chill of her voice and the stare he was receiving cut through the anger just enough for something else to surface.

A wash of something that felt ridiculously like… fear.

This was it, wasn't it? The last time he would ever see this woman.

And it made no difference what she'd done. He would still be leaving his heart behind.

A part of himself that he might never find again.

He did have to go, however. He could hear noises on the street below. He had to get out—probably via the fire escape—and then get himself out of sight. Summon whatever assistance he needed to get back to where he belonged. There was far too much more fallout to come from this and he had to front up and deal with it as soon as possible.

He owed his grandparents that much.

He owed his people that much.

Raoul turned. With a flick of his hand he threw the newspaper onto Mika's bed. The bed he'd been sharing with her. A symbol of just how much trouble he'd heaped on himself and those he loved.

Mika spoke as he let himself out of the room and the words followed him like an icy draft as he headed for the fire escape at the back of the old building.

'It's happened to me before, too, you know. Men pretending to be in love with me in order to get what *they* want.'

The slam of the door behind him came a split second after her final words.

'Never again.'

CHAPTER TEN

NO COMMENT...

How often had Mika used those words in the last few days?

What a nightmare.

Rafe...no, *Raoul*...had been sucked out of her life in an instant and the void had been filled by a crowd of ugly strangers who had no respect for her privacy. They wanted photographs of, and interviews with, the girl who had been the constant companion of a prince who had been hiding from the world.

That dreadful first night—and the whole of the next day—Mika had been too terrified to leave the safety of her locked room. She had never felt so alone and so scared. So utterly devastated.

A broken heart should be the least of her worries. She had undoubtedly lost her job and she couldn't even try to find another one. Not in this town, anyway. Probably not anywhere in Europe. New Zealand would be the best place to hide, but how on earth could she get there? It was half a world away and travel was expensive. She'd spent all her savings on that camera and barely had enough to meet this week's rent.

The camera that Rafe thought she'd sold. Yes...he

would always be *Rafe* in her head. And her heart. The man she'd fallen in love with. Not a fairy-tale prince who couldn't exist in her world.

Did he really believe that she'd sold *him* as well?

That hurt so much that her precarious financial situation seemed to pale in comparison for long stretches of time. Time when, with the spotlight of despair, she could understand why he'd believed that. She could look back on that encounter with James from his point of view and see exactly how the shreds of evidence had come together in a way that made it look as if she'd betrayed him.

And she *had* taken that photograph. Secretly. Thinking that she might need a memento of a very special time in her life.

What a joke… There were a thousand images of Prince Raoul de Poitier on the internet. Pictures of him in his military dress uniform with a red jacket, a row of medals and a sword hanging by his side. Formal pictures that probably hung in gilded frames in his palace. There were less formal ones of him in his flight uniform at the controls of a helicopter and some with him in a suit, performing royal duties, like opening a new museum. And there were way too many of him in immaculate evening dress with a beautiful woman by his side.

Tall, blonde women in designer gowns who clung to his arm and looked up at him, smiling, as if they'd never been so much in love. Like his *fiancée*, Princess Francesca…

His *almost* fiancée, her heart whispered.

As if it made any difference, her mind answered. It

was a done deal. And this Francesca was precisely the sort of woman the world expected this prince to wed.

Besides, none of those pictures was of Rafe. The smoothly shaved man with impeccable hair was nothing like the tousled, bearded stranger she'd met on the Footpath of the Gods that day. And maybe that was something that would give her some comfort one day. None of those beautiful, polished women knew this prince the way she had.

Even if she had been nothing more than a holiday fling, he *had* loved her, she was sure of it.

Not that anyone else would ever know.

Mika had read the articles that had been splashed everywhere in the media frenzy. What a shock it had been to see her name in print. She had been a friend, apparently. A friend who'd reached out to him when he'd needed help, having lost his wallet and other possessions. A friend who'd helped him find employment and shown him what it was like to live in the kind of world a prince never really got to experience.

They must have excellent media consultants on those islands, Mika decided. The spin that this prince's heart was so much with his people that he'd actually wanted to experience the kind of hardship that many people dealt with in their lives had turned him from a spoilt royal looking for escapism into some kind of hero.

A prince of the people who would very soon become their beloved King.

And she was who she'd always been and always would be. An ordinary person. Someone who'd been a *friend*. Nothing more…

But she had been more. And, like the secret they

had shared during that first meal together—that what had made the day so memorable had been that crippling episode of vertigo—there was silent communication to be found in things that she read as well. The prince's personal history was revisited again and again. She saw pictures of the stoic little boy standing beside his grandparents when his parents were being laid to rest after the tragic plane crash that had claimed their lives, and it made her heart ache for him.

They both knew what it was like to grow up without their parents and Mika could actually feel what the glance between them would always have been like—if they'd stayed together—as they acknowledged that bond again and again. At Christmas time, perhaps. Or when they saw a young mother holding the hand of her small child. Maybe he had been luckier than her, in that he'd had loving grandparents to raise him, but how hard would it have been for a boy to grow up without his father as a role model and advisor?

It had been bad enough for her. She'd never met her father—had no idea what he even looked like—and it felt like a part of herself had always been missing. If he had known she existed, would he have come to find her? Looked after her? Given her a safe place to live and loved her, even?

Given her a place to call home?

Mika could understand why Rafe had had to leave as soon as his true identity had been revealed. She could understand how he had been convinced that she'd betrayed him.

What she couldn't understand was how he hadn't realised how wrong he was as soon as he'd had time to think about it. Time to remember exactly what things had been like when they'd been together.

How much she had trusted him.

Loved him…

They had been so, so much more than merely *friends*. And they had been, ever since the moment they'd met. Had she given him her heart, without even realising it, in the instant she'd taken his hand up there on that mountain track? Had he given her at least a part of his, in that same instant? Even when he'd known it was something forbidden?

They'd both denied the physical attraction, hadn't they? They'd been fighting it for very different reasons but the barrier had been huge for them both and it had taken something traumatic to push them past the point of no return.

And Rafe had wanted it to continue as much as she had. She'd joked about him being a politician because he didn't want to give her a straight answer to her questions. He had wanted that time *just for them*…

Because he'd known it had to end the moment she knew the truth.

That was what hurt the most. That he'd taken her heart and soul *knowing* that he was going to destroy her in the near future. How could you do that, if you really loved somebody?

Had he been trying to protect himself from further scandal by dismissing their relationship as no more than friendship?

There was a part of her that refused to suffocate under the weight of betrayal. The part that would always love Rafe. It had a tiny voice but it made itself heard occasionally during the cacophony of heartbreak. It told her that he *had* loved her. So much that he couldn't bring himself to hurt her by telling her the truth. And that dismissing that love in public was the only way he had now to try and protect her.

If that was the case, it was working. Slowly. The number of paparazzi was dwindling as the days passed and her best friend amongst the waitresses—Bianca—had come to knock on her door one evening.

'You can come back to work,' she told Mika.

'Really? Has the crowd gone?'

'There's a new crowd now. People who want to see where a prince was working. Business has never been so good.'

'Marco wouldn't have me back. I didn't even tell him I was taking time off.'

'He knows why. We barely got to serve anyone apart from the journalists for a few days, anyway. And I think Marco likes being so famous. He's still sitting at his table all day, every day, happy to have his photo taken and talk to everyone.'

'I don't want to have my photograph taken. I haven't even been for a swim for days because I'm too scared to go out there. I'm terrified someone's going to be outside my door whenever I go to the bathroom. They shout at me from the street but I'm not going to give any interviews, no matter how much money I get offered.'

'They're offering you money?'

'Huge money. If I told them that we'd been sleeping together, I could probably buy a house.' Mika's eyes filled with tears. 'But I wouldn't do that. I couldn't…'

'You really loved him, didn't you?' Bianca drew her into a hug. 'Oh, hon…'

Mika drew back from the embrace with a sigh. 'You do need money, though. What are you eating?'

'I had some cans of stuff. And coffee. I've almost run out, now, though.'

'So come back to work. Not front of house yet—that's the message I was told to give you.' Bianca's smile was wry. 'Marco probably doesn't want to share the spotlight. But he says you can have Rafe's old job, if you want. We're all having to take turns washing dishes at the moment and nobody's very happy about it.'

There really wasn't a choice to make. Mika was going to be in serious trouble if she didn't start earning a wage but how ironic would that be—to take Rafe's old job?

How much more miserable was it possible to become?

Quite a lot, it seemed.

Sneaking around to get in and back from the restaurant and avoid being seen was horrible. Not being able to go swimming was even worse. The job itself was unpleasant and backbreaking but Mika fronted up to do it day after day. It became automatic and gave her mind far too much time to wander.

To remember things that made her feel so stupid. Like sharing her dream of becoming something as important as a travel writer. Or suggesting to Rafe that they pretended they were living in the villa that was as close to a palace as she'd ever been inside. Things that made her so sad, too. Like the conviction that giving her heart to Rafe would be worth it even if he disappeared because she would always know how perfect life could be.

It didn't help at all now because Mika knew that her life could never, ever be that perfect again.

Her whole body ached.

Her heart was splintered. Nothing could ever put that many broken shards back together again.

Even her belly ached. So much that it made her feel sick sometimes. One day, Bianca brought in a load of plates that had congealed egg and bacon rinds on it and Mika took one look and had to flee to the toilet to throw up.

She was splashing cold water on her face when Bianca slipped into the tiny restroom and closed the door behind her.

She met Mika's gaze in the spotted mirror above the hand basin and her eyes were troubled.

'Are you in trouble, hon?'

'What do you mean?'

'Are you pregnant?'

'*No.*' The thought was so shocking, Mika had to grip the sides of the basin to persuade her legs to keep holding her up.

'Is it possible?'

Was it? Her mind flew back to that silent conversation in the pharmacy that night.

Is it too late?

It was a safe time, I'm sure of it.

But how long ago had that been?

Weeks…

Way *too* long…

'Oh, my God…'

The basin wasn't enough support any more. Mika's shoulder was already against the wall of the tiny room. She leaned against it as she let herself slide to the floor where she could curl up, hug her knees and hide her face by resting it on her arms.

She would have to ask Bianca to go to the pharmacy and buy a test kit for her to avoid attracting the attention of any lurking journalists but Mika already knew what the answer was going to be.

It would be better, in fact, if she went somewhere else to do it herself so that her friend wouldn't be involved. Somewhere a long way from here where nobody would recognise her as being the 'friend' of the prince. She couldn't afford to go back to New Zealand but there were a lot of big cities in Europe that she could hide in. A train ticket wouldn't be expensive and she could carry everything she owned in a backpack, couldn't she? If she sold her laptop, that would not only give her enough money, it would make the backpack lighter to carry.

The thought of being so totally alone was terrifying. The prospect of facing it came with a wave of dizziness that reminded her of the moment she had realised she was in so much trouble on that mountain track.

The day that Rafe had come into her life…

As impossible as it might have seemed, her heart broke a little more.

Had she really thought that working as a dish washer would be the most miserable extra change in her life now?

How wrong had she been?

CHAPTER ELEVEN

Prince Raoul de Poitier was standing in front of his bathroom mirror. A gilt-framed mirror that reflected just how completely the circumstances of his life had returned to normal. How different was this to the shared facilities of that boarding house, with the vastness of the private room, its generous showering and bathing facilities, countless soft, fluffy towels and a selection of skin products any pharmacy would be proud to display?

The aftershave he'd just splashed on his face still stung even though the beard was long gone. How long would it take for his skin to stop feeling oddly raw and exposed?

His heart still felt raw, too.

Unbelievably heavy.

And he didn't like the man he was staring at in the mirror.

His journey of self-discovery had been a disaster. He'd learned something that he wasn't sure he could live with.

That he was a man who could take someone's heart and then crush it for the greater good of others.

Had he really believed—in his heart—that Mika

had sold that picture and betrayed his identity? That she knew she'd fallen in love with a prince?

Of course she hadn't. She had fallen in love with the man she believed him to be. An ordinary bloke by the name of Rafe.

He'd let his mind overrule his heart in that instant. Allowed himself to feel betrayed and then angry because that was the easiest escape route as the reprieve of an ordinary life had exploded around him.

He'd left Mika believing that he'd simply used her.

That he hadn't really loved her.

And she deserved so much more than that.

But what could he do?

His duty.

As he had been doing ever since he'd been whisked back to *Les Iles Dauphins*, away from the media circus in Positano. The look of shock on the faces of his grandparents when he'd walked into the palace with his long hair and beard, wearing his shorts and the 'I heart Positano' tee shirt had told him just how far past acceptable boundaries he had wandered. The days that followed had been a matter of damage control and, thanks to a quick-thinking team of media experts and the unwavering support of his grandparents, what could have been a complete scandal had been turned around to make him some kind of hero.

A man of the people who, thanks to a courageous action, now knew exactly what it was like to be an ordinary person. He was someone who understood them and whom they could trust to rule them with compassion and wisdom.

But Raoul would never feel like a hero.

He had a million images of Mika imprinted on his

mind and in his heart, but the only one he could hold in his hand was the one taken in that dreadful moment they'd been spotted at *Pane Quotidiano*. She had been wearing that white singlet top that was his favourite, because it showed off her gorgeous brown skin and revealed the tattoo that was a symbol of the sea that meant so much to her.

Dolphin blood…

The voice of the sea…

The way he could dance with her with only the music in their hearts to follow…

The mosaic tiles of his bathroom floor were not unlike the surface they had danced on in that old villa.

The house that Mika had thought a palace.

That she'd wanted to pretend to be living in. With him…

Dear Lord…he'd never known how much it was possible to miss someone.

Or maybe he had and that was why this was so difficult. It took him back to being that scared five-year-old, standing so stoically during the final farewell to his parents.

Doing his duty, even then, because he knew what was expected of him by so many people.

And today, he was about to take his next step into doing what was expected of him. Francesca was due to arrive later. It was time to propose. To make the engagement official. His mother's ring was in a velvet case on his dressing table, waiting for him to slip it into his pocket. There would be a celebratory lunch and many, many photographs to go with the press release. There would also be the first of what would probably be many, many meetings to arrange their wedding—

a train of events that there would be no possibility of stopping once it had begun.

The sensation of a ticking clock had never been so strong. He had to do something before it was too late. Something that would, at least, give Mika the comfort of knowing that he cared.

That he was truly sorry.

One of his personal assistants had his suit ready for him when he left the bathroom suite that adjoined his bedroom.

'Their Royal Highnesses are taking breakfast in their suite,' he was informed. 'They would like you to join them.'

'Of course.' Raoul donned the crisp, white shirt and held out his wrists to have the cufflinks inserted. His favourite ones, which were gold, embossed with the image of a leaping dolphin.

His heart grew even heavier. It was like a very personal punishment that the symbol of his homeland was going to remind him of Mika every day for the rest of his life.

'Pierre?'

'Yes, sir?'

'I have a task for you this morning. I want you to source a camera. A Nikon D4—or something better if there's a new model available.'

'Certainly.'

Pierre was his most trusted assistant. Raoul would have described him almost as a friend, except that he now knew what real friendship felt like.

What true love felt like...

Pierre held out his jacket so that he could slip his

arms inside the silk lining. 'Are you becoming interested in taking up photography?'

'No. It's a gift. I want you to buy a range of lenses to go with it, too. And any other accessories that are recommended. And I want everything in a case. Gift-wrapped.'

'No problem. Would you like me to arrange delivery, as well?'

'Not yet. I need to think about that. It will need discretion.'

Pierre didn't bat an eyelash. 'Just let me know, then, Sir. I'm sure something can be arranged.'

The palace of *Les Iles Dauphins* was on a headland that gave it sweeping views of the Mediterranean and the suite of rooms that was his grandparents' private domain had a terrace with the best view of all because you could see the royal beach—a tiny, private bay that could only be reached via the stone staircase from the palace gardens.

On a beautiful morning like this, the only thing that could disturb the clear blue of the calm water was the way the bay's permanent residents greeted a new day. The joyful leaping of the small pod of dolphins that claimed this well-protected bay as their home base was such a pleasure to watch, it was no wonder that this was the preferred spot for Prince Henri II and his wife, Gisele, to take their breakfast.

There was something about the scene on the terrace that made Raoul pause for a moment before he joined them. His grandparents, as always, were sitting close together on both sides of a corner. At this particular moment, they weren't eating or admiring the view, they were looking at each other. Smiling.

The heavy lump that was Raoul's heart this morning twisted a little in his chest. He loved these people—his family—so much. And he loved that they still loved each other, after so many decades of being together. Remembering that they were both well into their eighties now was a poignant reminder that their time was limited, and as Raoul moved close enough to bestow his customary kiss on the soft skin of his grandmother's cheek he made a silent vow to make the rest of that time as perfect as possible.

They had given him so much.

'Good morning, Mamé… Papé.' The childish names for his grandparents had never been relinquished in private. 'It's a beautiful day, isn't it?'

'Help yourself, darling.' Gisele waved at the covered platters on the serving table behind them. 'I ordered your favourite cheese and mushroom omelette.'

'Can I get you something? More coffee?'

'Some orange juice for Henri, perhaps. He hasn't taken all his pills yet.'

His grandfather made a grumbling sound that suggested he didn't need to be nagged but he winked at Raoul.

'Big day for you, today,' he said. 'What time does the beautiful Francesca arrive?'

'Late this morning.'

'There's a formal luncheon,' Gisele added. 'And photographs this afternoon. It's in your diary, Henri.'

Raoul put the plate with its fluffy omelette and pretty roasted tomatoes in front of him at the table. He picked up his fork but then put it down again. He really wasn't hungry. He sipped his coffee, instead, and watched as his grandmother arranged the morning medication for his grandfather, handing over each pill and watching carefully as it was taken. It was impossible not to notice the tremor in his grandfather's hand and the way Gisele put each tablet into his palm with enough care that it wouldn't be dropped.

'Is there something wrong with the omelette, Raoul?'

'No, Mamé. It's perfect. I'm just not very hungry.'

'But you're losing weight. You haven't been like yourself ever since you got home. I'm worried about you, darling…'

His grandfather reached out to pat her hand. 'The thought of marriage makes any man a little nervous.' He smiled at Raoul. 'Don't worry, lad. It gets better.'

But Gisele looked anxious. 'It is a big step. And so close to your coronation. Is it too soon? We haven't finalised the date. Francesca's grandmother is one of my oldest friends and I'm sure we could arrange for it to be delayed…'

Raoul saw the glance his grandparents exchanged. A delay wasn't something they wanted and he could understand why. These two had been together since before Henri had become the ruling Prince of *Les Iles Dauphins*. He had always had the loving support of his wife by his side.

They wanted the same thing for him, didn't they?

That support was something that came naturally when you loved someone. Mika could have given him that. As he would have given her…

Would delaying his marriage change how he felt?

No. It would make things worse because he'd have

more time to imagine a very different future. With Mika as his princess. Sitting out here, one day in the future, having breakfast and watching dolphins play...

'What's the secret?' The question came unexpectedly. 'For a happy marriage?'

'Respect,' his grandfather said.

'Love,' His grandmother smiled.

'Were you both in love when you married?'

'In *love*?' His grandfather grunted. 'Stuff and nonsense.'

But Gisele's eyes twinkled. 'Oh, yes, we were. You couldn't keep your hands off me, Henri.'

A huff of surprised laughter escaped Raoul. 'Too much information, Mamé.' His laughter faded. 'You chose each other, though, didn't you?'

'What do you mean?'

'Your marriage wasn't arranged.'

'That's true,' Gisele murmured. 'I was his mother's secretary. It was all a bit of a scandal, really.'

'But everybody forgave you, didn't they? Because they knew how much in love you were?'

'Oh... Raoul...' Gisele's words were no more than a sigh.

A coffee cup rattled loudly as Henri tried to put it down on its saucer. 'Are you saying you don't want your marriage to go ahead?'

The coffee had spilled onto the tablecloth. His grandfather was suddenly looking older. Almost grey. Unwell...?

Raoul backed off from whatever he might have been about to say. 'Francesca is beautiful. She's already a princess. She's an ideal choice.'

'But not *your* choice.' His grandmother's faded blue

eyes looked suspiciously bright. 'You're not in love
with her…'

'In *love*.' Henri's words were dismissive. 'Stuff and
nonsense. It's no more than lust.' The old Prince was
rubbing his chest with one hand. He pushed back his
chair and got to his feet, leaning on the table as he
did so.

'Are you all right, Papé?' Raoul was alarmed. 'You
don't have a pain in your chest, do you?'

'I'm fine. I'll see you…*and* Francesca…at luncheon.'

Raoul caught his grandmother's gaze.

'I'll go,' she said quietly. 'I'll call the doctor.' She
paused to touch Raoul's head as she passed. 'It'll be
all right,' she added. 'Don't worry…'

That Gisele chose to join him in what was supposed
to have been a private meeting before lunch was more
than a surprise to Raoul. How was he supposed to propose with an audience?

'Is something wrong? Is it Grand-père?'

His grandmother took a seat beside Francesca, opposite him, on a matching small, overstuffed couch.

'He's resting,' she said. 'The doctor thinks it was
his angina. He needs to use his spray more often.' She
turned to smile at Francesca. 'How are you, my dear?
I've just been having such a lovely chat to your grandmother.'

'Oh?' Francesca's smile wavered.

Raoul frowned. This meeting had been going well.
He and Francesca had a lot in common and, while
things felt a little awkward still, they just needed more

time to get to know each other better. He liked her and she seemed to like him.

They hadn't got near discussing the really important business between them but it had been a good start.

'You've done so well in your studies,' Gisele continued. 'I didn't realise how close you were to graduating as a doctor.'

Francesca bit her lip. 'I've arranged to take leave from my studies. I'm hoping I can finish them one day and, while I know I could never practise as a physician, I hope I can become involved with the health systems in both our countries.'

'It's your passion, isn't it?'

Francesca looked down at her hands. She spoke quietly. 'I've been brought up to understand my position in life and my duty—to both my family and my country. I would never do anything to harm the people I love.'

She raised her head to look at Raoul and he could see a determination that reminded him so much of Mika that he had to smile back. He could respect that.

'But what about Carlos?'

Francesca turned her head with a gasp. 'Oh…my grandmother swore she would never say anything…'

Raoul blinked. 'Who's Carlos?'

Gisele patted Francesca's hand. 'Another passion, I think.'

Francesca's eyes filled with tears as she looked back at Raoul 'I'm sorry,' she whispered. 'I would never have said anything. And it's over now. It had to be…'

Raoul's smile was gentle. 'I understand. Believe me…'

'Of course he does,' Gisele said. 'Now, I'm going to leave you two to have a talk. Just bear one thing in mind. Anything is possible.' She was smiling as she got to her feet. 'Just look at what Raoul managed to do in his time away. And how well it was handled. Everybody understands true love.'

The silence in the room grew louder as he and Francesca sat there, both more than a little stunned.

'What did she mean?' Francesca asked finally.

'I think she knows more than I realised,' Raoul admitted. 'I... I met someone while I was away.'

'You're in love with her?'

Raoul swallowed. And then nodded. He cleared his throat. 'And you're in love with...with Carlos?'

The glow in her eyes was more than enough to confirm it.

'But you were going to go ahead and do your duty and marry *me*?'

It was Francesca's turn to nod.

He had been going to do the same thing but this changed everything, didn't it?

If there was one thing that Raoul had learned from his escape from his real life, it was that he was, at heart, a good man. Someone who could love, nurture and protect. A man who could trust his instincts about what was right and wrong.

And this was wrong. Was that the message his grandmother had been trying to leave him with? That it was possible to follow his instincts? That anything could be managed and forgiven in the name of true love?

'We both have a position in life that carries a huge responsibility,' he said slowly. 'A duty to do the best for all those that we are responsible for.'

'Yes.' Francesca's head was bowed. 'I'm only

twenty-five,' she whispered. 'But I feel like a parent. One with many thousands of children.'

'Have you flown anywhere recently?'

'What?' Her head jerked up. 'Of course... I flew here. What's that got to do with anything?'

'I don't mean on a private jet. I meant on an ordinary commercial flight.'

'Oh, yes. I've done that.'

'Did you watch the safety briefing?'

Francesca's eyes were wide and puzzled.

'They tell you what to do if an oxygen mask appears,' Raoul continued. 'They tell you that you should put your own on before you help others.' He took a deep breath. 'We have a duty to many people, Francesca, but we also have a duty to ourselves. To make sure that we are in the best position to do our best for others.'

'You mean...?' Her words died but he could see the birth of hope in her eyes.

'I mean that you should be with the person you love,' Raoul said softly. 'And so should I...'

The private helicopter with its royal insignia touched down in Positano late that afternoon. Carrying the heavy, beautifully wrapped parcel, Raoul and his bodyguards made their way as discreetly as possible to the *Pane Quotidiano*.

Marco was sitting at his usual table on the pavement. His jaw dropped when he saw the group approaching.

'I've come to see Mika,' Raoul told him. 'I...have something for her.'

'She's...ah...she's not here.'

Others had noticed his arrival. Bianca came outside.

'She's gone,' she told Raoul.

'Where?'

'I don't know.' Bianca shook her head. 'She just vanished. Days ago. I went to her room when she didn't show up one day but it's empty. She's gone…' She touched Raoul's arm. 'You have to find her,' she said quietly. 'It's important.'

CHAPTER TWELVE

IT WAS A fairy-tale palace.With tall stone walls and turrets and spires that were becoming a dramatic silhouette as the blinding sunshine of the day began to fade.

With her dark sunglasses, a big, floppy hat on her head and the backpack over her shoulders, Mika knew she passed as any ordinary tourist who'd come to these remote islands.

Someone who even advertised her love for the creatures this land was named for by wearing a tiny, silver replica around her neck.

She had walked up a big hill from the marina where her ferry had docked and she hadn't needed a map to find her destination. She might have sold her laptop but it had been easy to find an internet café, in the village where she'd been lying low for the last week or so. She'd done her research as thoroughly as she always did and the route to the de Poitier Palace was imprinted on her mind.

So was another email she had received. One that had given her confidence to face a new future. The *National Geographic* not only wanted to buy both her articles, they wanted more...

She could do this.

She could support not only herself but the baby she was going to bring into the world.

What she couldn't do was repeat the mistakes of the past.

Her baby was not going to grow up with no idea of who its father was. Not knowing a land where so many generations of his family had come from. He—or she—was never going to feel abandoned. Or unwanted.

This baby was going to be loved. And cared for and protected.

And that was what had finally given Mika the courage to make this journey.

Her father had never known she existed, so he'd never had the chance to fill even a tiny part of the gap that had been left in her life.

In a way, Mika was doing this for herself—to put right a past wrong. She was doing it for her baby, too, of course. And she was doing it for Rafe. He had the right to know that he was going to be a father. And, because she had no intention of hiding the truth from her child as it grew old enough to understand, the royal family deserved the courtesy of a warning.

It would cause a scandal one day, but maybe, with enough time to prepare for it, something could be arranged to protect the small, illegitimate prince or princess who was going to be born.

Mika had no idea how that might be done.

Now that she was here, she had no idea of what to do next. How did one go about asking to speak to a prince? She was just an ordinary tourist, standing here outside the palace, gazing through the enormous, wrought-iron gates. A rather wilted tourist. It had been such a hot day and a long walk up a decidedly steep hill.

The sound of an approaching helicopter made her look up. The sound grew louder and louder as the helicopter circled and came lower, finally disappearing on the other side of the palace where, presumably, there was a heliport.

Was Rafe at the controls?

Mika's heart skipped a beat and then sped up.

If she stood here long enough, would a guard of some kind come and ask her what she wanted? There had to be people watching. Security cameras at the very least.

And, if someone did come, would they simply laugh at her request or was it possible they could pass on a message of some kind?

It wasn't possible.

Raoul had barely caught a glimpse of the figure standing outside the palace gates as his helicopter had come in to land but he had known instantly who it was.

Had he seen her with his heart instead of his eyes?

He barely registered what the voice in his headphones was telling him.

'She hasn't used her passport.' His head of security had been busy on the flight home. 'Not at an airport, anyway. So she can't have gone back to New Zealand.'

'No.' Raoul closed his eyes as the aircraft touched down gently. He could still see the shape of that small figure standing there outside his home. 'I don't think she has. Don't worry about it any more, Phillipe. I can handle it now.'

Mika had come to find *him*…

Hope was filling the dark space he had entered after finding that she'd disappeared from the café in Positano.

He ducked his head to stride beneath the slowing rotors of the helicopter. He waved off his bodyguards as he avoided the nearest palace entrance. He knew there would be many eyes watching him as he ran through the gardens, only slowing as he finally reached the front of the palace, but he didn't care.

Would Mika still be there?

The turrets and spires weren't the only silhouette against the fading light. Indecision had kept Mika immobile but it seemed that her plan might be working. A guard was coming around the corner of the palace. Not someone in a military uniform that she might have expected but a tall man in a dark suit. He looked like a bodyguard. A member of some special forces, perhaps, who'd been dispatched to find out what she thought she was doing, standing here and staring for so long.

Except…there was something about the way this man was moving. And well before he got to her—when he'd only just reached a long, rectangular pond with its blaze of flowering water lilies and the fountain that was a whole pod of leaping dolphins—the massive gates in front of Mika magically began to swing open.

Inviting her in…

But she couldn't move.

Not until the figure got even closer. Until she could see the expression on Rafe's face. Until he'd taken off his sunglasses and she could see the expression in his eyes…

Even then, she couldn't move.

This was like nothing she could have prepared herself for.

Rafe didn't even know she was pregnant.

But he wanted *her*.

As much as she wanted *him*…

This was perfect.

If he'd had a magic wand to wave, this was the one place he would have chosen to bring Mika.

A place that could provide the things that she loved most in the world.

The sea.

And dolphins.

He'd done no more than take her hand as the palace gates swung shut behind them because he knew how many people were watching.

'Come with me,' was all he said.

There was no one here on the private royal beach. Oh, it was quite possible his grandmother could see them, but if she was watching she would be smiling.

Crying, perhaps. The way she had when she'd taken him aside after Francesca had gone earlier today.

'You reminded me this morning of what it was like,' she'd said. *'When Henri and I were so much in love. If this is where your heart is, Raoul, you have to follow it. You have my blessing. You'll have the blessing of your grandfather, too, when I explain. And your people…'*

Mika's backpack lay abandoned on the sand. He might have guessed she would be wearing that white bikini as her underwear. His own suit was discarded alongside the backpack. He had nothing more than his silk boxer shorts to swim in, but it didn't matter. The light was fading fast anyway and the rosy glow of the sunset made the shapes of the dolphins swimming around them dark and mysterious.

As dark as Mika's eyes as he finally pulled her into

his arms and kissed her. They way he'd been dreaming of kissing her every night they'd been apart.

'I was so afraid I wouldn't be able to find you,' he whispered, his lips still brushing hers. 'I thought I would be missing you every minute of every day for the rest of my life.'

'I'm here.' Mika was smiling against his lips. 'I had to come. There's something I have to tell you…'

That she forgave him for the accusation he'd made? That she still loved him?

A note in her voice told Raoul that it was time they talked properly. This time in the water had taken them back enough to re-establish their connection. To wash away the pain of their time apart. It wasn't the place really to talk, though.

He led her from the shallows onto the sun-warmed sand. The air around them was still warm, too, but he picked up the jacket of his suit and draped it around Mika's shoulders. And then he sat beside her and took her hand again.

'There's something I need to tell you, too.'

It felt like he was still out of his depth in the sea, looking into her eyes. As if he could drown…

'I love you, Mika. And I'm sorry.'

'For thinking I'd sold that picture? It doesn't matter.'

'I'm sorry for more than that.'

Mika ducked her head and nodded. 'I understand. I know you couldn't tell me who you were. It would have ruined everything, wouldn't it? We'd never have…' A soft sound escaped her lips. An incredulous sort of huff as she left her sentence unfinished. And then she looked up. 'You saved me, you know? Three times…'

'Three?'

'Up on the track. From those men. And…and from maybe spending the rest of my life too scared to ever trust someone. Of never finding someone to be with like that. Of never…becoming a mother…'

It took a long, long moment for the implication of those words to sink in.

When it did, it took another long moment for Raoul to find his voice.

'You're not…?'

Just a single nod and his world changed for ever.

'I'm sorry. I really did think it was a safe time. I must have got my dates mixed up…'

'And that's why you came here today? To tell me?'

Another nod. 'I want this baby to always feel wanted. Loved. Even if we could never be together, I want it to know who its father is.'

Like Mika never had. Raoul's heart felt so full it was in danger of bursting.

'He—or she—will always feel loved,' he said softly. The wonder of it was really sinking in now. He was going to be a *father*? 'Will always *be* loved,' he added. 'So will you…'

It was a long time before they could speak again but it made no difference because the touch of their lips and bodies would always be a conversation in itself.

How had he ever thought he could live without this woman in his life? By his side?

'This is going to cause trouble, isn't it?'

'No.' Raoul pressed another gentle kiss to Mika's lips. 'It will be a cause for great celebration. My grandmother is going to be so happy. She wants nothing more than to see me settled and happy. To be married and raising a family.'

'But…what about your fiancée?'

'We were never officially engaged. And Francesca will be just as happy as we are. She's going to be with the person *she* loves. We will maintain a friendship and work together to strengthen both our countries.'

'But…'

'But what?' Raoul swallowed a sudden fear. 'Are you worried that this isn't the place that you've been searching for? That you couldn't be happy living here?'

'I've only seen a tiny part but I already know this is the most beautiful place on earth.' Mika was smiling as she looked out at the small bay, as if she could still see the beautiful creatures who had shared their swim. She turned back to Raoul. 'And you know what?'

'What?'

'I've discovered something. A place isn't a *place*.' She touched Raoul's cheek softly. 'Or it is, but it doesn't actually matter *where* it is. That place only exists because it's beside a person. You told me that, but I wasn't really listening.' Her voice sounded like it was choked with tears. 'My place in the world is beside you, Rafe. Wherever you are, if I'm beside you, I'm *home*. But…'

Raoul was blinking back tears too. Because he couldn't have put it better himself.

'But…?'

Mika shook her head. 'I can't marry you.'

Maybe the air wasn't as warm as he'd thought. The sudden chill went right to Raoul's bones.

'Why not?'

'Are you kidding? Me? A…a *princess*? It's impossible.'

'You've forgotten something else I told you, haven't you?'

'What?'

'That you can be anything at all that you really want to be. It's one of the things I adore so much about you, my love. Your courage. And your determination. You could be a princess. *If* that's what you want.'

'If it means being with you for the rest of my life, why wouldn't I want it?'

'I was afraid you would never want to be part of my world. That's another thing I love about you. That wildness. Your freedom. Your…dolphin blood. There are constraints with being royal and it might be like putting you in a cage. A gilded cage, but the walls are still there.'

'You'd be inside those walls, too.' Mika's smile was so tender, Raoul could feel his breath catch. 'It's still the place I'd always want to be. But fairy-tales don't really happen. I don't have a fairy godmother out there to wave her wand, put me in a pretty dress and let me dance away with my prince…'

'Oh, but you have.' Any fears evaporated as Raoul kissed her again. 'You just haven't met my grandmother yet…'

EPILOGUE

HER ROYAL HIGHNESS, Princess Gisele, adjusted the folds of her dress as she settled onto the ornate, red velvet chair with its gilded arms and headrest.

Being in this prime position at the front of *Les Iles Dauphins'* historic cathedral meant that she could take in the full majesty of the wonderful old, stone building—the ornate archways and pillars, the glowing wood of the rows of pews and the statues of her country's most significant figures whose mortal remains had been laid to rest in the raised vaults. The stained-glass windows were renowned as well and right now the intricate panes of glass were glowing as they were touched by the day's fading sunshine.

It could be—and often had been—a sombre place to sit but not today.

Today there were garlands of snowy white flowers on every pew and around the base of every statue. There was joyful music thundering from the enormous pipes of the organ and the harmony of a choir to add to its tone. And there was a sea of colour wherever Gisele's gaze roamed. So many beautiful dresses in shades of pink, blue and mauve. So many wonderful hats on the women in the pews that gave way to tiaras and crowns towards the front of the congregation. Nobody had refused the invitation to attend this function so it was a 'who's who' of European royalty.

Only one seat was empty and that was the one right beside Gisele.

Henri's chair.

With a sigh, Gisele shifted her gaze once more and caught that of her beloved grandson. He looked every inch the Prince he was in his military uniform with its red sash and gold epaulettes. His medals shone and the silver scabbard of his sword had been polished to within an inch of its life.

Their gazes held for a long moment. This was such a happy occasion but there was sadness, too. Loved ones who couldn't be here had to be acknowledged.

The music was softer now, so it was possible to hear the faint roar coming from outside the cathedral walls. The sound of thousands of voices in a collective cheer. Gisele could imagine the scene as vividly as if she were standing out there on the top of that huge sweep of wide steps.

The ornate, gold dolphin coach that was only brought out on the most momentous of occasions— pulled by the immaculately groomed white horses of the royal stables—would have just come to a halt at the bottom of the steps.

Another man, in a uniform even more impressive than Raoul's, would alight from the open coach and would be holding out his hand to help the bride climb down.

How wonderful was it that Mika had asked Henri to be the man to escort her down the aisle today?

And what a blessing he was still well enough to do

this. He seemed to have taken on a whole new lease of life, in fact, with such joy to look forward to.

He hadn't really needed Gisele to remind him of what it had been like to be young and in love. Or of how much strength that love had given them both over the decades and how it had got them through some very difficult times.

Mika had won Henri's heart so quickly.

Had won everybody's hearts.

What could have been a dreadful scandal had miraculously become the love story of the century. Raoul was now firmly ensconced as 'the People's Prince' and he had clearly found a princess worthy of ruling by his side. Not only could everybody rejoice on the occasion of a royal wedding, they still had the coronation to look forward to and—even better—the anticipation of the birth of a new prince or princess in the near future. The first member of the next generation of the de Poitier family.

So much happiness.

Gisele had a lace-edged handkerchief clutched in her hand and she had a feeling she would need to use it very soon. She could feel tears of joy gathering as the music paused and then swelled into the triumphant opening bars of Wagner's *Bridal Chorus*. She rose to her feet, as did everybody else in the cathedral.

It was beginning.

The tears started as soon as she saw her beloved husband by the side of this exquisite young bride. They continued as her heart caught at the sight of all the children following the pair. It had been Mika's idea—to go to the orphanage and choose everyone who wanted to be a flower girl or a page boy. The girls wore long white dresses and had colourful garlands of flowers on their heads and the boys looked adorable in sailor suits.

Mika looked beyond adorable. She had approached this intimidating occasion with the same kind of good-humoured determination that she was applying to every aspect of royal life she'd been learning in the last few months. The design of her dress was simple and didn't accentuate her growing bump. Mika had asked for a 'swirly' dress that would look pretty when she danced with her new husband later and the dressmakers had been delighted to oblige. With an empire line, it fell in soft folds, the beaded bodice having a sweetheart neckline.

Gisele had offered a diamond necklace to match the tiara that was holding her veil in place but Mika had been right in choosing something else.

Her own necklace of that tiny, silver dolphin charm.

The priests leading the procession up the aisle reached their positions at the front of the cathedral now and there was nothing to obstruct the lines of vision as Raoul and Mika got closer to each other.

Henri left Mika by Raoul's side and came to sit beside Gisele. Would the television cameras pick up the way their hands touched and then held? It wasn't exactly protocol on a formal occasion but Gisele needed the touch. Her heart was so full it almost hurt.

Squeezing his fingers, she watched as Raoul lifted his bride's veil back and revealed her face. And then, for a heartbeat, and then another, the bride and groom seemed to be lost in each other's eyes.

And those smiles…

Gisele had to let go of Henri's hand, then. She needed her handkerchief too much.

So much joy was simply too contagious…

* * * * *

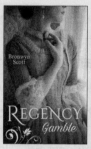

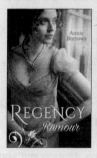

MILLS & BOON®

The Regency Collection – Part 2

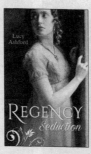

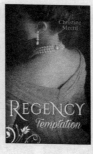

Join the London ton for a Regency
season in part 2 of our collection!

Order yours at **www.millsandboon.co.uk/regency2**